stepha

pre

a novel

Jane
and
Austen

Also by Stephanie Fowers

TWISTED TALES SERIES (young adult fantasy)
With a Kiss
At Midnight
As the Sun sets

HOPELESS ROMANTICS BOOKS (sweet romances)
Jane and Austen

ROMANTIC COMEDIES (LDS/ inspirational)
Prank wars
Meet Your Match
Rules of Engagement

stephanie fowers
presents
a novel

Jane
and
Austen

Triad Media and Entertainment
SLC, UT

ISBN: 1500233110

1. Fiction. 2. Romance. 3. Comedy. 4. Inspirational.

Published by Triad Media and Entertainment, Salt Lake City, UT
Triad.film.productions@gmail.com

LINE EDITOR: Shannon Cooley
CONTENT EDITORS:
Rachel Nunes
Cindy Baldwin
Amanda Sowards
April Rudd
Sandra Barton
Cindy Roland Anderson
Ian Anthony
Debbie Gessel

COVER DESIGNER: Jacqueline Fowers
COVER PHOTOGRAPHER: Kristi Linton
AUTHOR BIO PHOTOGRAPHER: Ashley Elliott
TYPESET: Stephanie Fowers

Dedication

To Debbie

She insisted that I write this book when I joked about the title.

We've had some fun times brainstorming together in our scanning cave, haven't we?

Chapter 1

"In vain I have struggled. It will not do. My feelings will not be repressed. You must allow me to tell you how ardently I admire and love you."

—Jane Austen, Pride and Prejudice

"Jane," Austen said, playing with the leather-braided bracelet on my wrist. He hadn't stopped touching it since the moment he had noticed that it was too loose. He leaned against the counter of the resort where we were both working during my summer internship. "Doesn't it ever fall off?"

I shrugged, loving the feel of his hands on my skin. I smiled. "It will if you keep touching it."

"I can't make any promises." He gave it another tug. Austen had turned flirtatious over the past month, but yesterday our relationship changed into something else completely. He had spent the whole day on Brightin Beach teaching me to surf. I'd tried to make our last hours together in San Diego count before he flew out, and now I had the sunburn to show for it.

"This is too big for you." He pulled the bracelet from my wrist and tied it on tighter with a little bow in the back. "There," he gave it a little pat, "now don't say I didn't do anything for you."

I admired the knot, not because Austen had actually done a good job, but because he'd cared enough to do it. It had been a magical summer—we'd shared our favorite cult classics, collected shells on the beach, laughed at each other's stupid jokes. And now it was almost over.

After finishing college, I had signed up to work for a summer internship at one of the most beloved vacation hideaways in San Diego. That was where I met Austen. His parents owned the bed-and-breakfast-turned-resort. It had been dubbed the "North Abbey," since it had been built on the same land as an 1800's monastery and still held some of the ruins from it. The place boasted lavish courtyards, a reception hall, cottage-style bungalows branching out from the main house, and a quaint grove of trees that led to an ocean of beaches complete with tiki shacks and an exciting nightlife. The resort was comfortable, beautiful, and expensive, but for me, the real draw to North Abbey was Austen. Now that he was leaving, I couldn't imagine spending another moment without him. He handed me the key to his room.

"Don't judge me," he said. His thick brows came together, adding comic distress to his already expressive face. "There's sand all over the carpet. Just make sure the maids look for lobsters before you check the next people in."

The electronic key lay between us, and, after waiting far too long, I slipped it out of his palm. Austen's impending departure turned my gut into an oozy puddle of sadness. I wasn't ready to say goodbye.

I knew his room wouldn't stay vacant for more than a few days. This was a place where romance happened, and Austen was heartily sick of it. His parents had put him to work here at a very early age. Now that he was twenty-five, he ran the business side of things. It was the same for all employees at North Abbey. No matter what our official job title was, we all did a little of everything—manning the checkout counter in the lobby, taking bags, wheeling guests on golf carts to their bungalows, fixing holes in the walls. No one was exempt.

Giving me his endearing smile, Austen flashed straight white teeth. His jawline trended towards thickness no matter how lanky he was, and I thought it was adorable—everything about him was adorable. Shoving his bags under his arms, he said, "I can't get out of here fast enough."

I dropped my eyes to a burnt mark on the polished counter and traced it with my finger. "I never understood why Boston was so much better than here."

"Are you kidding? It will be an amazing opportunity. I can finally put my schooling to good use." Austen knew that his parents' connections would open any door in Southern Cali. Unfortunately, he'd decided that financial consulting was a career best explored in Boston.

As if lost in thought, he rummaged through his messenger bag. "There was something I meant to give to you."

"Really?" My heart sped up. This was the moment that he would show me how much he cared about me—I wasn't a die-hard romantic for nothing. Every goodbye scene in my favorite books ended like this.

Austen laughed when he found a broken leash from his surfboard in his bag. He set it on the checkout counter. His flight schedule followed, until finally he pulled out some sunscreen and gave it to me. "It's a little too late to save you now . . . and it's raining, but next time, right?" His wink made jelly out of my knees before he barged through the lobby doors into the storm outside.

I rushed to the bay windows, watching the rain slide down the thick glass between us as he traveled down the long cobbled lane to wait for his taxi. It would be a long time until he came back to us. One year. That was how long his job would last in Boston, and if I wasn't hired on at North Abbey after my internship finished in two weeks, we might never see each other again.

The rain dripped down Austen's curly, honey-colored hair, turning it the color of molasses. Seeing him surrounded by North Abbey's old-world charm of finely-tended gardens, with its gothic pillars and vintage architecture, it was easy to imagine him from a different time. As effortlessly as flipping on the TV, my daydreams turned his dark jeans into nankeen breeches, his hoodie to a bottle-

3

green superfine jacket, and his earbuds to a snowy cravat. But just like the heroes from my dreams, Austen was every bit as make-believe if I couldn't tell him how I felt.

A giggle jerked me out of my reverie. My friend Ann-Marie had come into the lobby without me realizing. She stood at the counter, staring past me through the window—her eyes wide like a Gerber baby's. "Wow, got to give it to Austen; that guy is hot in the rain." She popped the rest of her breakfast into her mouth and talked through the sticky crumbs. "I can't believe he didn't come find me before he left. He just missed out on the best goodbye kiss of his life."

Ann-Marie wouldn't hesitate to go through with her threat. Today, she had blunt bangs and hair the color of burnt caramel. She wore a flashy red top and jeans a size too tight. Despite her tragic flaw of claiming every cute guy in existence, I was protective of her. The girl was fresh out of high school. She only had to blink her big, soulful, brown eyes to get anything she wanted from the male population, and I wouldn't hesitate to clobber the next guy who tried to take advantage of it.

"I always had a crush on Austen," she said. "I just couldn't get him alone long enough for the sparks to fly."

Somehow she had found the broken leash from Austen's surfboard and threw it into our "Unintended Gifts" basket near the register. The basket looked like any lost and found box with its discarded clothing, receipts, and ticket stubs. Ann-Marie kept all the memorabilia in it that she collected from cute guys who came through the resort. I had added a few things here and there—lost buttons, discarded pens, and numbers I was too scared to call. After a while it became a challenge to collect meaningless treasures and pretend they meant something more. When Austen had discovered it, he added a few things of his own: a broken shoelace from a dissatisfied customer and used tissues from some cranky old guy—he didn't really get it.

Ann-Marie added Austen's flight schedule to the box. My forehead knitted at that. "Look at those muscles on Austen's arms,"

4

she said, staring back out the window to where Austen waited for his taxi. "I'd love to feel those around me. Oh, the arms, too. I'd like to feel all of him—"

"Ann-Marie," I cut her off, only to imagine Austen's arms around me. My sunburn started to sting, and I shook away the thought. "The guests in the Allenham Lounge are asking for you."

The girl was a musical genius at nineteen. Not only did Ann-Marie provide live entertainment at the piano bar, but she was picky about whom she entertained. "Oh brother, don't they know I have things to do?" She giggled. "Like watching a hot man stand in the rain."

I tried not to stomp my foot. She was missing the best things about Austen. Sure, he was cute, but he was more than that. The guy was geeky, fun, and endearingly clueless. Before I could distract Ann-Marie from leering at my man, she shrieked and pointed.

Turning, I felt my stomach plummet. The taxi meandered up the long driveway. This was it—the moment Austen would break my heart. It couldn't end like this, not without a promise of something more to come. At the very least, he needed to remember me while he was away. I remembered my bracelet. He had played with it all day, as if he couldn't keep his hands off me.

I pushed past Ann-Marie and bolted through the double doors into the storm after him. The rain was better than any paintbrush. It splashed the world around us in dark colors—making the trees greener, the sky an azure only found in the tropics, the soil black as ebony. Waves crashed and lapped against the beach beyond the jungle of trees.

"Wait!"

Austen glanced back. His lips quirked into a broad grin when he saw me coming. He pulled a newspaper from under his arm and held it over my head. I peered up at him. Droplets of rain speckled his eyelashes. Ann-Marie was right about one thing—he looked really good wet. "Austen!" I cried. "I need your hand."

He looked confused a moment before giving it to me. Quickly, I untied his bow and wrapped the bracelet around his much bigger wrist. I gulped, my breath already coming out ragged. "Keep it—it fits you better than . . . than me."

Austen stared down at it, his thick lashes shielding his expression. The moment felt right in the rainstorm. Austen was even on his way to the airport. All chick flicks went this way before wrapping up into a really good, happy ending. Now all I needed was to chase after his taxi while declaring my undying love.

When Austen met my gaze again, his face was sober—full of meaning. "Jane, I've been thinking. I left the iron on in my room. Could you turn it off for me?"

I nodded wordlessly, trying to fit the words in my mouth that could reclaim the moment. I had to tell him that I loved him, that I couldn't live without him. I had to beg him not to leave. I tried the next best thing. "I'll miss you," I said.

"Sure, me too." His hazel eyes fastened to my face, and he drew me into a gentle hug. My scorched back blazed with pain, but I ignored it and hugged him until he let me go. Austen always gave the greatest hugs. He was tall, with shoulders broad enough to lay my head on. He drew back to give me a meaningful look. "Now who will I argue with?" He leaned in, his lips brushing my ear as he whispered, "By the way, Batman is still better than Superman."

I smirked. It was almost better than naming off ten things he liked about my smile. "Text me, Austen."

"When?"

"Well," I hedged. He had stumped me—almost like he didn't get the significance of keeping in touch. "You could tell me if you made it to Boston safely."

He laughed. "I'll let you know if the plane crashes."

"You know what I mean."

He stepped closer to the taxi, away from me. "I'll be fine."

I didn't know what else to say, except the obvious. "Yes, but I happen to actually *want* to keep in touch with you!"

"Sure, me too." It came out way too nonchalantly. "I'll see you around." He reached out and patted my sunburnt shoulder.

"Ow. Austen, my sunburn!" But that wasn't the real problem. Why couldn't he take any of this seriously? He didn't seem to care about our separation at all.

He pulled back, hardly looking contrite. "Sorry."

His flippant tone stung me. He could at least act upset that he was leaving me behind. "Are you saying that you don't want to text me? Is that it, Austen?"

He gave me an uncertain smile. "About what? That I made it safely?"

"About anything," my voice broke. I blinked back tears and swiveled away before he could see them.

"If you really want to text me, Jane, I'll text you back. I have unlimited texting, so it won't cost me anything."

Oh, real sentimental.

"Not that I'll have much time," he went on casually, like he wasn't ripping my heart from my chest. "I'll be busy with my new life. I plan on getting complete closure from this place."

And he'd have closure from me, too. Now the truth of my mistake hit me like a shock of ice running down my back. Austen didn't feel the same way for me.

His head tilted at me. "Why the sad face?" He went in for another hug and then stopped himself, eyeing my sunburn with misgiving. He gave me a comforting smile, instead. "Now that I'm gone, you'll have more time to go out with all those men in love with you. Redd is dying to take up where I left off on those surfing lessons."

"Redd?" Now he was talking about other guys for me? I recognized the teasing glint in Austen's eyes. Neither of us had been crazy about Redd, and Austen could always guess when I was keeping

7

my distance from a guy. He had always seemed so observant, so how had Austen missed my crush? He wouldn't, which meant I had been wrong about us the whole time—Austen didn't want a future with me at all.

I stepped back, slipping from the protection of the newspapers he had used to shield us from the weather. I wanted to cry, but instead waved behind me so Austen couldn't see my face. "I've got to go."

"Wait."

I looked up to see his hand lingering on the door of the taxi. "You can't really mean you want an itinerary of my whole trip?"

He was back to the texting thing again. It was like he was purposely being obtuse. I shook my head, hoping that the rain masked all evidence of my anguish. "No, I changed my mind. Angry birds is more your thing. I get it. Don't waste your time by texting." I left him then, tempted to snatch back my bracelet, but too proud to go back now or he'd see my tears. I ripped open the door to North Abbey to find a surprised Ann-Marie standing in the lobby.

She brought her hands to her heart. "Oh, that looked so romantic. I had no idea that you two had a thing."

I shook my head and wiped at my face, hoping she'd think the wetness came from the rain. "No, no, there's nothing going on between us."

"Oh." She looked doubtful for a moment. "So then you're okay if I go for him?"

I almost laughed in my hysteria. That would put Austen in yet another romance that he knew nothing about. "Sure," I said. "Go for it."

I went back to the checkout counter and sat heavily on the stool behind it. Who was I fooling? Austen was safe from Ann-Marie. *He was safe from me.* I groaned at the thought. Where did I go wrong? I squeezed out the rainwater from my auburn hair to save it from curling into a mass of ringlets around my head. I had thought that Austen found me attractive. I had a ready smile, a heart-shaped face. I countered my unhealthy chocolate habit by taking up jogging. I wasn't hideous—that left my personality, but it couldn't be *that* lacking, because Austen always liked talking to me. He laughed at all my jokes, tried to get me alone, couldn't stop touching me. I didn't get it.

According to all the signs, Austen should have at least swung me around in the rain, kissed me on the forehead, my nose, my lips. Or better yet, our hands would take too long to release and as he pulled away he was supposed to look back a couple of times as I walked away. He was looking back all right—his adorable face screwed up in confusion. The taxi honked and, a moment later, swallowed him inside.

My face burned with embarrassment and regret. I crossed my arms and tried to tune out the TV that Ann-Marie had turned on in the center of the room. Sweet music wafted from it. It was showing a sappy love story meant to swallow us up in an unbelievable tale where every dream came true.

And so the vicious cycle began again. For every romantic girl like me there was an unromantic guy . . . who clearly wasn't interested. I didn't know how I'd missed the signs this time around. I had dedicated all my free time to him—if we weren't together, I was thinking about him. And for what? While I wove dreams of our future together—dancing in the kitchen, children playing at our feet, growing old together—he was in the now.

His thoughts: *We are sitting on the couch together watching a movie. I think that kissing scene is coming up. Maybe I should make some more popcorn.*

My thoughts: *We are sitting on the couch together because he doesn't want to be anywhere else but with me and he's desperately thinking of a way to keep us together.*

There was certainly a disconnect. So who was in the wrong? Him or me? Before I could do any more uncomfortable soul searching, Taylor marched into the room. She was my supervisor and the brainchild behind North Abbey's fabulous weekend getaways, business parties, and week-long weddings. Money meant nothing to her and why should it? Taylor was born with a silver spoon in her mouth, a socialite from a prestigious family that lived somewhere in the east.

Taylor organized events for the sheer pleasure of hearing laughter and glasses tinkling as they crashed together in toasts. She was famous worldwide as one of the most prestigious event coordinators in the country, and landing a summer internship under her made me the most hated graduate of public relations from California State. Everyone was jealous; though, to be honest, I was a little intimidated by her. She was my mentor and idol, so it came as a surprise when Taylor and I had become such good friends over the summer.

"Jane!" she squawked, as if I were lost somewhere in the dimness of the room. She wore a no-nonsense pinstriped grey-and-black skirt with a button-up blouse. Her black hair was short and chic, her green eyes sharp. "Jane. Jane!" She halted under the glowing light of the front chandelier, and I noticed that her usual mask of professionalism had been stripped from her face. "There you are!" She ran to the desk, faster than I had ever seen her move. "He wants to meet me!" It came out a squeal.

She hopped up and down, wrinkling her fine Armani skirt in the process. I had never seen Taylor this way. On a normal girl, this behavior would be giddy, but on Taylor I knew it meant a national emergency. Immediately I drew myself up. "Who wants to meet you?"

Taylor shoved her phone at me, giving me a thumbnail view of a cute, blond guy—he was no Austen, of course. I scanned his bio.

This one looked like he was into bodybuilding and suits—kind of a weird combination. But as I read through his dating bio, I saw that he was British, and that made him triply attractive. *Chuck Bigley,* I read.

"We've been writing back and forth for a while now," Taylor said. "Then we chatted on the phone. And I've been Skyping him ever since. He's everything I want!" She skipped up in excitement.

"Wait," I said. "Why didn't you tell me any of this?"

She pursed her lips, adjusting the guarded look back to her face. "Nothing is ever sure with online dating. I didn't want to get your hopes up."

My hopes up—what about hers? Taylor clicked her long fingernails against the counter in an unsteady rhythm. "Bigley has passed every test—the family test, the social test, the career test, the IQ test."

I didn't even want to ask how she managed those. She gloried in online dating and being able to put her men through a rigorous interview process to avoid getting hurt. But if I read Taylor right—she was positively glowing, which put her heart more at risk than ever before.

"I'm so happy for you!" I came around the counter and squeezed her in a hug. For once, she accepted the affection. I was, after all, the one who had set up her dating profile on Em's Matchmakers. It had been under her orders and I'd done it during work hours, but our little Miss Taylor looked amazing on it.

She pulled away from my hug, only able to take so much, and met my eyes squarely. "I'm meeting him in Britain . . . in a week!"

I was jealous and excited and envious all at once. Maybe online dating was the way to go—no games, no lies, zero miscommunication.

Taylor's eyes rested on the worn key card on the table. "Wait. Did Austen leave already?"

I nodded, feeling the flush creep to my cheeks now that I was the one with my heart out in the open. Taylor had been trying to get me to admit my feelings to Austen for a while now. "We didn't exactly have a meaningful conversation," I said. "I don't really think that . . . uh . . . he's interested."

She rolled her eyes. "Jane, it's Austen. There's not a romantic bone in his body. If he were interested—*he* wouldn't even know."

Ann-Marie managed to tear herself away from the blaring TV to laugh uproariously. "Hey, I never realized it before, but Jane? Austen?

11

You know your names make Jane Austen together, right? That's hilarious!"

I jerked at the realization. *Hilarious or pathetic?*

My eyes were drawn to Ann-Marie's show—like an alcoholic turning back to drink. It was an episode of *Petticoats and Pretty People*—borrowing heavily from one of Jane Austen's better-known works, *Pride and Prejudice.* I groaned—not because I hated these movies, but because I loved them. I had watched every Jane Austen remake out there. It hit me hard that my doomed love interest and I were both named after her.

Taylor rolled her eyes. "Look away, Jane. Remember the last time you got caught up in *Petticoats?* You didn't come to work on time for a week. You'll never find a man like the ones in those movies anyway—not even the actors who play them are like that."

Besides her own Mr. Chuck Bigley, of course.

I made a noncommittal sound. Sure, the men in those shows seemed to read more into things than most men, but they weren't perfect either—they were just the right touch of mystery, challenge, and likeability. Then again, they were inspired by works written by a girl. Not that Jane Austen was delusional or a liar or doomed to never get what she wanted, but I realized that besides sharing a first name, Jane and I had a lot of things in common: our ideals.

Yes, there was a lack of romance in this world—but even if it was scarce, it was real. Ms. Austen and I were determined to find it. Love existed. We had to have that hope that it did. If not? Then what was life about anyway?

"I've got it!" Taylor turned to me with a smile. "You should go for my friend Redd. He's perfect for you. He'll be on leave for at least another month. That should be plenty of time to let the sparks fly."

I grimaced. Redd again? First Austen teased me about taking up surfing lessons with him, and now Taylor thought we'd make a good match. Redd was Taylor's best friend from high school. He was stationed in the naval base in San Diego, and we saw him practically every night. Even Austen had noticed that Redd was a little off, and I agreed. Just because my heart had been broken didn't mean I'd try to force love where it wasn't.

I never had before.

Everyone accused me of being picky because of that, and maybe they were right. I wasn't much of a dater, but that was because I didn't want to waste my time on the wrong man. It wasn't that I didn't love men or understand them. With five older brothers, I knew how they worked. In fact, I wanted that same good relationship with a boyfriend that I had with my own family—the easy laughs and smiles, the quick banter and endless fun. I had that with Austen, and even if our relationship hadn't worked out, I wouldn't give up on finding someone that I could share that connection with. Sure, it made for lonely evenings, but I had waited twenty-four years to find someone, and I'd happily wait twenty-four years longer. I wasn't desperate. I was a romantic, an emotional adventurer; I'd have my dreams, just not with *my* Austen.

My Austen. Ugh. How long would it be before I stopped thinking of him that way?

My phone vibrated in my pocket and I brought my eyes to the ceiling, knowing exactly who it was. I read the words on my cell phone screen.

AUSTEN: WHAT WAS THAT ABOUT?

ME: DON'T TEXT ON A PLANE, AUSTEN. YOU'LL CRASH IT.

hapter 2

"An engaged woman is always more agreeable than a disengaged. She is satisfied with herself. Her cares are over, and she feels that she may exert all her powers of pleasing without suspicion. All is safe with a lady engaged; no harm can be done."

—Jane Austen, Mansfield Park

Leaning against the checkout counter, the man gave me an abrupt nod, though his piercing blue eyes lingered too long on me. He was strangely attractive, and there was something about his manner. Familiar yet distant. He gave me back the keycard to his room, stopping briefly to shove the sleeves of his jacket to his elbows. In a moment, I knew why he was so fascinating: he acted like the stereotypical hero in a Jane Austen movie with his stuffy air and prim manners.

After taking one look at him, I could see a whole backstory of forbidden love and tragic past. I imagined that instead of pushing up his sleeves, he snapped on pristine white kid gloves to attend the theater. His eyes roamed imperiously over me as if I were a maidservant standing outside the cloak room. In a way, I guess I was. I slipped his keycard into an envelope, smiling at where my thoughts led me.

He leaned over the counter and, in a whisper, said, "Why are you smiling? Life's not that good."

I blinked a few times before it registered. Those words didn't belong to a gentleman. It would be much better if he had said, "Your smile warms me more than a kiss."

To which, I would cast my eyes downward. "Oh la, sir," my imaginary self would say, whipping her silken fan around. "Remember the differences of our social standing. 'Tisn't proper for you to speak to me in such a familiar manner."

"No, it would *not* be proper for me to steal that kiss."

My eyes would snap up to his.

He'd lean closer, his mouth irresistibly near. "But," he'd amend as only a true gentleman should, "I will have to satisfy myself with the memory of your smile."

I couldn't help it. My lips curved up at the pretty little scene. The customer stepped back, and I realized belatedly that our conversation had only taken place in the furthest stage of my mind. And now I stood there grinning at him like an idiot.

The guy's black greatcoat with at least three capes melted back to his everyday work jacket as he became the tired businessman on the last leg of his trip. Blushing, I wished him a good day, and he gathered his bags while I gave myself a mental shake. These daydreams were getting worse. What used to be an innocent pastime to find romance in everything had become a mission to find the ideal man. The problem was that no man was as charming or as romantic as my imagination led me to believe.

Taylor's big grey cat meowed plaintively up at me. Mister was hungry again. I left to fetch him some cat food, absentmindedly patting down his wild mane of grey fur. Ever since I had accepted the position as assistant event coordinator, Taylor had left North Abbey so often that part-ownership of her cat fell to me. It had been eight months since Taylor first left to meet the man of her dreams in London. After an intense courtship, Em's Matchmaker had claimed Taylor as their latest online-dating success story when she announced her engagement to a Mr. Chuck Bigley. My friend was riding off in the sunset with the man of her dreams and claiming her British citizenship there. London would be her new permanent residence.

That meant if I wanted Taylor's job as the event coordinator of North Abbey, it was mine. I just wasn't sure if I'd survive Taylor's wedding to accept the honor. She took Bridezilla to a new level. The big day was less than a week away, and as her replacement-in-training, all the planning of it fell to me.

"He did it! He did it." Taylor burst into the room. Gone was the bristling woman afraid to act irrationally. Love made her crazy, and after her trip to Britain, she'd only become worse.

"Who?" I asked. "Did what?"

She shoved another updated guest list at me. "It's a PR's dream. Consider it my parting gift to North Abbey." I grabbed the list she danced around my face while she screamed out in excitement. "Chuck convinced his best friend to take time out of his music tour and come to my wedding! Will Dancey is coming! Can you believe it?"

I could and it made me want to throw up. I didn't want to take care of a rock star along with Taylor's wedding. The rooms in the main building were already full. All nine bungalows built on the outskirts of the resort were taken by the wedding party besides the one closed for renovations.

"But—but, Taylor," I said. "Where will he stay?"

She smiled brightly. "Don't worry. I'll move out to the Wood House."

That was the lodge in the back and hardly fit for a bride. It was falling apart and partially hidden in the grove behind the bungalows. It would've been torn down by now except for sheer sentimental value.

I shook my head. "No, no, Taylor, you have to keep the Bennet room. It's where you belong. Your family would freak out if they knew you were in the Wood House."

Taylor thought a moment, then snapped her fingers. "I know. We'll give him the Eliot Room."

16

That room was named after T. S. Eliot when he had come to visit the mysterious Emily Hale. And it also happened to be taken. "Your parents are getting that room," I said.

"What?" her voice turned shrill. "But they'll want the Randall House. They always get that bungalow—it's big so they won't have to see each other that much while they're here. They're very particular."

"It's in the middle of renovations." I ran my hands through the tangled curls in my hair, trying to think as I tried to tame the massive mane. "We'll have to do some major rearranging as it is to fit in Dancey."

"Yes, yes, and we'll also have to up security now for him, too." Taylor tapped her fingers across the counter. "We have to keep the paparazzi out . . . within reason. We could allow the papers a few stolen snapshots maybe . . . with North Abbey as Dancey's backdrop to his first visit to the United States. He'll be flying the red eye tonight and he'll be here in the morning! Jane, his stay must be as comfortable as we can make it. Maybe we should find him a personal assistant during his stay here. That could be you!"

"But . . ."

"Taylor," a deeper voice interrupted her scheming—it had a lilting British accent and was utterly charming. I turned to Chuck Bigley—he had slipped in without either of us noticing. Taylor's fiancé wore one of his fitted grey suits, his blond hair slicked back. Everything about him screamed British. "I believe that honor falls to DeBurgy," he said, "Dancey's *actual* personal assistant."

Taylor grimaced. "He's more of a publicity manager. Anyway, I don't like DeBurgy. He has no idea how to treat people. Dancey should just leave him home. Besides, there's no room for him here. Jane can take care of your best friend."

Chuck Bigley's arms found the waist of his future wife, and he squeezed her, looking deeply into her eyes. I'm pretty sure Taylor melted at his tenderness—I did. "Jane's hands might already be full planning our wedding," he said.

17

"But Jane is well trained." Taylor flashed a rare smile at me. "I made sure of that. What price did Highbury Bakery quote for the new modifications on the wedding cake, Jane?"

I flipped through my notes. "At least a few thousand more," I answered, "but I managed to get them to agree to an even thousand."

She didn't flinch. "You see—she's fully capable. Oh, we'll need to change the time for the rehearsal to Wednesday. Dancey's going to L.A. Thursday night on business; it was how he convinced his agent to let him take the time off." She patted Bigley's arm. "Anything to get Chuck's best man standing next to him."

Bigley laughed.

Thursday was out. That meant I had to book the church on Delaford Street for Wednesday, change the wedding rehearsal dinner to that night, and juggle around the bridal shower so I could get the best man to the bachelor party, too. It was lucky we owned most of the venues where these would take place and the guests attending were planning on staying for the whole week. The notebook where I kept all of Taylor's wedding revisions was beginning to resemble a complicated chemistry calculation. She meant to outdo every party that she had ever planned. I felt like I was coordinating for the royal wedding.

The lovebirds started babbling to each other in the strange love talk that I associated with newlyweds. I cleared my throat to interrupt them. "Kingham Florists are out of calla lilies, Taylor. We cleaned them out. Harriet's too. I had to order the rest from Carlsbad. Yates said they'll ship them overnight as soon as they get them in—that means we'll barely get them in time if we change the rehearsal dinner to Wednesday, and it'll cost us extra."

Taylor took a break from making googly eyes at Bigley and twisted around to give her permission. "Put the lilies in a cooler once we have them. I want them dripping from the ceilings of Pemburkley Hall, not wilting."

"There will be no wilting," I said, making a check in my notebook.

Bigley touched her arm. "Are there any poppies in your flower assortment?"

Taylor's almond-shaped eyes slanted at him. "What? No!"

"But they're your favorite flower," he said with a laugh. "I want you to have everything you want for your wedding."

Taylor wrinkled her pert, little nose. "I had too much of poppies in Britain. No, I never want to see another one again. I want this wedding to go without a hitch, Jane. Which of my guests will be arriving today?"

I clenched the list but didn't look as I recited: "Your maid of honor and both of your bridesmaids. Bigley's brother. Oh, I forgot to tell you. The minister and his wife came this morning. Ed and Elly McFarey. Ann-Marie checked them into the Dashwood Room."

Taylor laughed giddily at that. The minister's wife was Taylor's adored cousin. If I could believe everything Taylor said about her, meeting the couple would be a treat.

"What about my mother?" Bigley asked.

Taylor tensed at the reminder. Bigley's mother was tricky. His parents' separation wasn't amicable; it became even less so after his father remarried a much younger woman who looked like a younger model of his first wife. "She'll be in the Price room," Taylor said. "It'll be nice and far from Netherfield House where we'll put your father, Chuck."

"Right." I jabbed my pencil in the air. "And most of the guests will be arriving tomorrow. Um, if you could give me Dancey's flight information, I can arrange his escort here."

"Leave that to me," Bigley said. "I'll be at the airport, waving my arms in circles."

"Just don't leave him stranded, honey," Taylor warned, "or he'll write another sad song and make another million."

19

Bigley broke into a big, contagious grin. "I don't have a problem with that as long as he shares the profits with me."

Taylor rolled her eyes. "He wouldn't have so many songs go platinum if he wasn't so depressed and brooding all the time. It certainly does nothing for his love life." She sounded bitter about it. Her trips to Britain must've given her a front row seat to Dancey's private life that the majority of the female population would love to know.

Bigley brushed her forehead with a kiss. "Fame and riches are rather hard on the poor man, I think. I'd rather have you than all the money in the world." His mouth found hers, and I had to turn away or risk potential embarrassment. They were my proof that true love existed, though that didn't mean I wanted to spy on it. I was happy for them . . . and just a little resentful.

Truth be told, if the rock star shared Bigley's beautiful British accent, then I was in very real danger of losing my heart for the second time this year. But I seriously doubted that the most sought-after bachelor with the most sought-after voice would ever have a chance to talk to me during all the festivities we had planned.

A rustle near my elbow made me jump, and I found Ann-Marie shuffling through the knickknacks in the drawer behind me. Her hair was now a glorious red that resembled no natural hair color that I was aware of. She found a pair of scissors and slammed the drawer shut, leaning against the counter, her eyes devouring Taylor and Bigley's romance like it was a chocolate cream puff with strawberry filling. "Is *the* Will Dancey coming to North Abbey?" she asked. "He's so hot I could burn my mouth on him."

I tried to shush her, but too late. Taylor stiffened when she overheard. She peeled from her husband-to-be's fingers and smoothed back her hair, her sharp eyes never leaving Ann-Marie.

"Great." I clapped my hands together to ease the sudden tension. "How about I have Freddy take a look at the Lucas Lodge, then?

Taylor? We could air it out. It can't stink as bad as those last guests said. We could put Dancey in there and—"

"Certainly not," Taylor snapped. I hid a smirk. My ludicrous suggestion had distracted her anger from Ann-Marie. "I blame the Kellynch Hotel for that smell. Don't think we won't hold them responsible for it."

The overflowing sewage was another point of contention we had with the neighboring hotel. I couldn't help but use the feud to my advantage. "We could book a room for Dancey in the Kellynch."

Taylor cut me off with a wag of her finger. "He will stay here. I know you'll handle everything beautifully without my interference." She stopped a moment, her brow wrinkled in thought. "On second thought, I believe you should put Dancey in the Wood House."

Freddy would have to take a blow torch to that place to make it presentable, but at least that meant I wouldn't have to kick myself out of my own room and sleep with Taylor's cat on the sofa. "Sure," I said. "We'll make sure that Dancey feels right at home."

"As soon as I have him in my arms," Ann-Marie said with a little squeal.

Taylor gasped and pulled next to me to whisper in my ear. "Keep *her* away from him." Giving me a penetrating look that meant business, she led her dear Chuck Bigley from the lobby. He went willingly, his muscular arm capturing her around her tiny waist as though he was fully capable of handling such a spitfire.

Ann-Marie made a sigh that sounded like she had poured her whole heart into it. "Yes, Jane, she's right. Please, keep him far, far away from me. I don't ever want to meet the man behind the name. Not really." She dropped her arms to her sides and traveled despondently across the room where she collapsed onto the soft leather sofa that rested near the big screen TV. The scissors that had dangled from her hand toppled to the floor.

"Dancey is one of those people you only want to dream about," she said into the cushions. "Meeting him would only make him real.

And no one wants a real guy, especially one like him—he'd just reject us normal people, and then we'd never be able to enjoy his music again."

"Hey, it's not that bad." I went back to my seat behind the counter, studying my to-do list. "These guys have to marry someone, and why not a down-to-earth girl? I mean look at Elizabeth and Darcy in *Pride and Prejudice*."

". . . who aren't real." Ann-Marie lifted her face from the pillows.

"No, but . . ." I crammed my brain for a real couple. "Well, let's just say that there are a lot of real people who get married." I smirked before I cracked a joke, "Maybe more than fictional people."

Ann-Marie's smile grew. "Yeah. I mean, people are only people. You strip them of their skin and they're all just skeletons inside."

My own smile froze. Too late I realized that while I'd thought I was philosophizing, I had actually encouraged Ann-Marie to go after the rock star. "But we should really give Dancey his space," I said. "I bet the last thing he wants is to be bombarded by fans. He just needs to be treated like a normal guy."

"I plan on it." She rose from the couch with a determined air. Throwing her glorious hair behind her shoulder, she cracked her knuckles and retreated from the room with a flounce. A complicated concert went off in the Allenham Lounge in the short amount of time it took Ann-Marie to find her piano bench.

I groaned when I recognized the remake of "Fur Elise." It was her theme music dedicated to the times when she was deeply and passionately in love.

This would not go well. I knew how she treated normal guys. Will Dancey had no idea what he was in for.

Chapter 3

"I am worn out with civility."

—Jane Austen, Mansfield Park

A woman pulled up to North Abbey in a BMW convertible. She wore huge sunglasses, one of those fancy, oversized floppy hats, perfect make-up, and a sundress that showed off her every curve—or lack of them. She'd make heroin-addicts everywhere jealous.

She lifted one of her rail-like arms and pressed down on the horn. My eagerness to check in Taylor's wedding guest evaporated like a magician's rabbit as I searched around for anyone to help me. All of the golf carts were taken. The maids were off making the rooms presentable. Freddy Tiney was on a run for more detergent. The job was up to me. I hurried outside, hoping I didn't look like I had to run.

"Welcome to North Abbey, ma'am," I said as I approached.

She took her hand off the horn and pulled her shades down so that she could peer at me over the rims. "Mrs. Bertram-Rush, if you please." She wriggled her ring finger so that I couldn't miss the sparkling diamond weighing it down. "I'm the maid of honor."

Though technically her married state made her the matron of honor, I nodded. "Yes." I fought the urge to curtsy—or laugh. All of Taylor's bridesmaids were her friends from a tightknit community in Massachusetts. They had attended private schools together, roomed in college, and their parents belonged to the same clubs. Looking at Mrs. Bertram-Rush, I guessed Taylor's friends were like bad habits—hard to quit.

"Taylor has told me so much about you," I said.

"Has she?" She snapped her shades back up, turning away to stare off into the distance, dismissing me. Her pink-and-white polka-dot luggage next to her lap yipped, and I realized that it held a living teddy bear. At least, the tiny puppy looked like a stuffed animal, except for the black eyes that blinked up at me from a white, furry face.

This woman was really Taylor's best friend? She could pass as a desperate housewife from Orange County. In my mind's eye Bertie's sun hat transformed into a chip straw hat with a riot of flowers and ribbons dangling from the brim. I didn't have to imagine anything different in regards to her face. It was already gaunt and drawn like a Jane Austen villainess—though three times more orange.

"My baggage is in the trunk," she informed me, popping the trunk.

I stifled a sigh. The informality of the North Abbey had turned their event coordinator into a bellhop.

Mrs. Bertram-Rush dangled her car keys from her car window for me. "You will also show me my room, I take it?"

I abandoned the trunk for the time being and took the keys from her. "A cart to drive you to your accommodations will be here shortly. If you will just wait in the lobby."

The thin woman gaped at me like no one had ever asked her to wait for anything. I smiled blandly back at her as if I had no idea that she was so annoyed. She pursed her lips, stepping delicately out of her car as another guest pulled up—in a minivan this time. The window rolled down and a breathless face popped out. "Is this the right place?"

The sign for the resort framed her head behind her.

"Are you looking for North Abbey?" I asked.

The woman nodded. Her straight, auburn hair came out in greasy strings from a tight ponytail that looked as though she had slept on it for hours. "I'm Taylor's . . ." She turned mid-speech and coughed into her hand, a great wheezing, hacking sound that made me think she had just crawled from her deathbed to get here. Mrs. Bertram-Rush scrambled to keep back from the invisible germs, her heels clacking against the ground.

"I'm Taylor's bridesmaid," the woman said as soon as she had breath to speak. "Mary Musswood." She wiped her hand off on her shirt and poked it through her car window for a handshake.

Thinking fondly of the hand sanitizer in the lobby, I shook it. "Glad you could make it, Mary. If you could pull over to the side there, we'll take care of your bags and park your car for you."

She coughed again and did as told—parking only three feet over the yellow line. The coughing fits bursting from her minivan told me that was the best we were going to get. It was apparent that this socialite had fallen on hard times. She staggered out of her vehicle and slammed the door hard behind her, putting her hand over her heart as if she had startled herself.

I took her keys, wondering what was taking Freddy so long. He was making me look like a one-woman operation here. Mary Musswood wiped at her reddened nose with an oversized tissue. She seemed a frail lady, which she only emphasized by wearing clothes a size too big. She turned to squint at Taylor's maid of honor. "Wait, don't I know you? You've lost so much weight. Bertie?"

"Mrs. Bertram-Rush," the woman said in a voice that could freeze fire. If possible, "Bertie" was more distant with Mary than with me, which was an amazing feat.

Mary drew forward, gushing. "Wow, Bertie! It's been so long. I see you on the front of all of those sleazy gossip magazines. I can't believe you're not at one of those drunken Hollywood parties right now. Didn't you date that rapper for a while? What was his name? Chris Slum-Diesel or something? Well, who cares? He was beautiful. Why did he break up with you?"

Bertie gaped until she seemed to snap. "I broke up with *him*."

"Yes, yes, of course." Mary stared at Bertie for an uncomfortable moment. "Of course."

25

With their keys in hand, I gestured for Taylor's friends to follow me. Bertie strode ahead of Mary, looking annoyed. She finally swiveled to Mary and informed her, "I'm married now." She flashed her oversized diamond ring once again. "My husband makes every man I'd ever been with look like a used car salesman."

Mary appeared suitably impressed. We stepped into the lounge just as a grey ball of fur slipped past our feet. "A cat?" Mary's hands dug through her purse until she found a package of tissues. She snapped three out with practiced hands and rubbed them across her nose. "Keep it back. I'm allergic."

"That's Taylor's cat," I said. "Mister stays in the lobby, so your room will be fine, Mary. We'll be sure to keep him far from you."

Bertie sniffed in disdain—I wasn't sure if it was directed at her friend's loyalty to a cat or to Mary's health misfortunes or even at me. Maybe all of us at once? Her little dog whimpered, and she absentmindedly kneaded its knobby head.

Mary set her purse on the counter, digging through an array of pill bottles, muttering the whole time. "I'm also prone to dusts and mold. This is an old place, I take it."

"Yes." I pulled behind the counter. "This Queen Ann Victorian has been a resort since the sixties. It was first turned into a bed and breakfast in the twenties. Before then it was a family estate, built in 1887."

Mary yelped in distress. "You must have all sorts of allergens here." She took out her nasal spray and began to apply in earnest. Bertie drew out a long sigh. I tried to reassure Mary that she was staying in one of the bungalows built outside the property, which was newer than the main building, but she downed a handful of pills just as Ann-Marie came hurtling into the room in her usual heedless fashion.

I pretended I wasn't desperate to see her. "Ann-Marie, would you please take these ladies to their bungalows? They're in the Southerton and the Uppercross. I'll have their luggage sent after them."

"Yes, of course." Ann-Marie's eyes drew to the four pill bottles Mary stuffed back into her purse. Mary then collided into Bertie's arm on her way to the door, making Bertie's purse yip in response.

Mary backpedaled in horror. "Oh dear. That houses a dog? He looks just like a little bear, but he's the size of a rat. A little rat-bear!"

"*She* is a micro-teacup Maltese," Bertie corrected in chilly tones. "My mother's favorite. Do you know how much these little rat-bears cost?"

Mary's manner immediately changed and she became more fawning. "I bet that little rat-bear is worth more than my four sons combined. Why, just the cost to the vet alone." She wiped at her drooping eyes as if she was having an allergic reaction, but so far no tears had come. "Of course you've already shot the little guy up with all sorts of vaccines to keep back all the diseases that he carries."

Bertie's glare dripped icicles. "My baby is tired," she addressed Ann-Marie. "Could you please show me where I'm staying before I sprout roots and grow leaves in here?"

"Yes, of course." Ann-Marie exchanged a stricken look with me and led the way from the lobby.

"So brave of you to take on the puppy," Mary said to Bertie, following her out. "Does it shed? I wish I had the money to throw away on such odd things." I listened to Mary's voice fade as she persevered in the face of Bertie's silent treatment. "That's why Taylor is paying for my stay here. My husband said, 'go,' I deserved the break. My boys are a handful. Dirty, too. They do nothing for my health."

I let out a breath as soon as they were out of earshot. Two bridesmaids down, only one more to go. I wasn't eager to see Bella Thorne's entrance, because so far I couldn't see how Taylor associated with any of her friends. They made her look . . . well . . . normal.

Maybe that was the point.

Chapter 4

"Can he love her? Can the soul really be satisfied with such polite affections? To love is to burn - to be on fire, like Juliet or Guinevere or Eloise . . ."

—Jane Austen, Sense and Sensibility

I wrestled the baggage onto the cart. Bertie had brought enough for a month instead of her allotted week here. Silently, I prayed that didn't mean she planned on extending her stay. I scooted the cart to Mary's minivan, and after pushing past four sticky car seats, I found her one worn bag. It was wrapped in plastic. I didn't want to know why as I hauled it next to Bertie's matching designer luggage and shoved the cart back into the lobby.

There was no sign of Freddy inside. Knowing my luck, I'd have the whole job done the moment our missing bellhop got here. And knowing Freddy, he probably planned it that way. The door from the back opened, and a tall man pushed his way inside, covering the old-fashioned doorframe with a broad shoulder. "Freddy!" I called. "I need your help over here!"

"You're still here?"

That didn't sound like Freddy. The man cleared the door, and the dull glow of the chandelier showed me that the shoulder belonged to Austen. I almost fell over at the sight of him. He carried a bike over his shoulder and was a sight for sore eyes—the same classically good looks, brown unruly hair, and crooked smile as before—but when I looked at him now, no romantic image sprang to mind, which was strange because I managed to procure one for everyone nowadays.

Maybe it was because he still wore his biking clothes. He set the bike down and leaned against it. "Wow, I didn't expect you to still be here, Jane. I thought for sure you'd find somewhere better to work."

Austen had caught me completely off guard. I had planned this moment for so long—I was going to be defiantly gorgeous, carefree and witty, and completely on top of the situation. It wasn't supposed to be like this. I was all sweaty and scruffy from my workout with the luggage—and he thought that my job was a joke. Even if it was, he didn't have to point it out. And where did he get off teasing me like we were still best friends, anyway?

I turned from him. "You survived the plane crash, I see."

"What plane crash?"

He didn't even remember our last conversation. Typical. What was he doing here, anyway? No one had said anything about Austen returning, and now he acted as if no time had passed between us. It had been eight months! He hadn't even come home for Christmas. I tried to match his relaxed tone. "Taylor's somewhere around here," I said. "You're looking for her, right?"

"Not really. I'm just looking for anyone who will talk to me."

"Then you'd better wait for Taylor."

"Good. Wait. Why?" I heard the laughter behind his words, laced with confusion. It frustrated me. Hadn't he spent at least half as much time as I had stewing about our failed relationship? Judging by the sound of his voice, he didn't know that there was anything between us to lose. Dredging up the past would only get me more riled up and possibly prove that I was overreacting. I wasn't about to reveal to him that I had wasted months grieving over a misunderstanding.

I decided to play it cool, and so I gave him a forced smile. "I just don't want to hear how much you loved Boston more than us."

"Well, it definitely wasn't as exciting as I thought it would be. Give me a second; I have to change into some real clothes." He left his bike against the wall and disappeared into the restroom. I stared after him. So that was my big dramatic reunion with my long-lost love?

29

Long-lost *nothing!* How anticlimactic. I realized that I had gone stiff, and I uncurled my fists so that they lay more naturally against my sides.

The luggage was still waiting. I squared my shoulders just as another car pulled up outside. This one I recognized as Taylor's. Her fiancé was driving, and he stole the freight parking space. Only Taylor could get away with that and not get towed. After a couple of loud slams from their car doors, Chuck Bigley got out and helped his sweetheart to the front door of the lobby. The two talked excitedly outside, which predictably ended with another deep kiss before they peeled open the glass doors.

"The train on my dress isn't that long!" Taylor complained once she was inside.

"Well, they're twins," her fiancé said. "Try to explain to one girl that only her sister will have the honor of carrying your train."

"Then I'll have to get a longer train," Taylor said. "Jane! What do you think? Would it look strange if I had two flower girls with how short the train is on my dress?"

"Not at all," I lied.

Taylor nodded. "I'll get a longer train; that's all there is to it."

Bigley winked at me. "Good thing we have Jane, the miracle worker here. She'll arrange the whole romantic setting with just a twitch of her pen."

"Uh . . ." I found my worn notebook on the counter and sat down heavily on the stool. My legs were still shaky from my Austen encounter. He was only one room away, and it took everything in me to concentrate on Taylor. I glanced up at her. "You'd like me to contact the dressmakers at Elton's then?"

Taylor smiled—apparently it went without saying, so I wrote down yet another errand for myself. Before I could tell Taylor about Austen's big arrival, she was pelting me with questions. "Have Bigley's grandparents come in from England yet?"

"Honey," Bigley interrupted. "I told you that they are not coming in until tomorrow."

"Dear, you did not tell me that."

"Yes sweetheart, I did."

Now they were fighting with terms of endearment. I was glad that I had listened to Bigley about his grandparents, or I'd be the one freaking out right now. The Rosings House where they were staying was not ready for guests yet, and I still had to find Freddy so that he could transform the Wood House into something fit for a human, let alone Dancey.

The door to the restroom opened and Austen came out, having changed from his biking gear to jeans and a T-shirt. It gave him a lean look and emphasized his height, making him look too good for words, which only served to irritate me.

Taylor jumped when she saw him. "Austen!"

Bigley hesitated for a moment, sizing Austen up—to anyone else but me, Austen just looked like a friendly dork, and Bigley's face cleared of jealousy. "I don't believe I've had the pleasure." He came forward with his big hand extended. Austen took it, and they exchanged a firm handshake before stepping back to a more comfortable distance.

"Austen, this is Chuck Bigley, my fiancé," Taylor said. "Austen's a big financial consultant out in Boston, but he's taking a break for a month to help us out here. Aren't you, Austen?"

I couldn't believe it. She already knew about this? No one had bothered to tell me. I was so chopped liver around here, it wasn't even funny.

Austen shook his head. "It's more like I'm doing my parents a favor. I'll be going through their books to write up a financial plan while I'm here . . ." My gaze flew to him. I knew that tone of voice. Austen was lying. "I already put my things in the Wood House," he said. "I hope that's okay?"

No, it was not. Where would I put Dancey? Before I could say anything, Taylor interrupted with a rush of words. "I'm so glad that you're here. Your mother said that you were coming to help us."

"Well, yeah," Austen said.

"You had better, because we are drowning. Drowning!"

"Dear." Chuck caught Taylor's face in his hands. "We'll be just fine. Jane has it all under control."

"What about my brunch tomorrow? We ran out of olives. The lettuce is limp! Austen, please, we need you!" Taylor escaped her fiancé to grasp Austen's arm. He grimaced while she dragged him aside, using a half-whisper that we all could hear, "I know you have a lot on your plate right now, but if you could be Jane's assistant, just until after the wedding, then I'd dearly appreciate it. Your mother would, too."

"I don't need his help," I said at the same time Austen said, "She doesn't need my help."

I felt my eyes widen to betray me. "You don't want to work with me?"

"Are you kidding?" Austen had the look of a man caught in the middle of two firing squads. "It's not about that. You are more than capable of taking care of this, Jane. Besides, you just said you didn't need my help." He attempted a smile and turned to Taylor, talking fast. "I barely have time to look through the books. It's a lengthy process, and I'd say it would be in everyone's best interests to give me a little space."

"You made it! I didn't believe you." Ann-Marie attacked Austen with a hug from behind. We all stiffened for him; and what did she mean by not believing him? Had they been talking and yet he couldn't find any time to text me? "Oh!" She stuffed her nose into the middle of his back and inhaled him deeply. "You changed your cologne." She took another sniff. "I like it too much. You should *not* wear that ever again."

Austen laughed, a little uncomfortably. "Why?"

32

"You don't want to know."

"Message received." He inched away from her, patting her head. She grinned back at him and touched the stubble he had grown on his face.

"Ann-Marie!" Taylor said, snatching her back. "Don't you have something more important to do? Like entertaining guests in the lounge?"

Ann-Marie nodded. She didn't take her eyes off of Austen. "I had a dream about you last night."

"Ann-Marie!" Taylor's words came out strangled. "This is not the time. We are in a situation here. I am *trying* to convince Austen to work with us again. We have an event to plan!"

"Honey." Bigley took on his soothing voice and found her hand. He looked deeply into his fiancée's eyes. "Your wedding will be beautiful. It will be talked about for years to come. Prince William and Kate have nothing on you."

That coaxed a reluctant smile from her. "That's sweet, Chuck, but I don't care about that . . . I just want my mom and dad to know that their little girl is *happy*." Her voice broke.

"They will." He smoothed down her hair. "Everything will be perfect—you'll see. The train on your dress, the olives in the salad, the fresh flowers that drip from the ceiling; it will be everything you've dreamed about since you were a little girl." His words left Ann-Marie smiling and Austen frowning. I was utterly confused. I had never seen Taylor act this way before. If she kept at this, we'd all have to check into a mental hospital by the end of the week.

"Sure," Austen muttered. "Chuck and Taylor—that will look great on the napkins."

I elbowed him. Hard. He grunted. Luckily Taylor didn't overhear the comparison of their names to a shoe brand. "I'm not being too overbearing, am I?" she asked her husband-to-be.

Bigley kissed her in response. "Everything you do is perfect. Now, leave the worrying to the ones you paid to worry about it, honey. You need some rest." Taylor allowed him to lead her out of the room. The door swung shut behind them, leaving us in uneasy silence.

Ann-Marie sighed. "They are so in love."

"Something's wrong with Taylor," Austen said.

I refused to look at him. "Taylor's just stressed out. She'll be her old self when things settle down."

"No. She's not happy. Didn't you see her? This wedding's not going to happen."

I wasn't sure if he was joking again, but it wasn't funny. I swung around to face him. "What do you know, Austen? This is the first time you've ever seen Taylor together with Bigley. They are *very* happy!"

"Yeah? Then why is she making herself crazy over nothing? Have you heard of anyone who actually wants their wedding to be an *event*?"

"Um," I raised my hand, "event coordinator here. Yeah, plenty of people do."

"No." He set his backpack by the counter and hooked his leg around a stool before sitting down. "No one remembers their own wedding. Nobody . . . and if they do, they're not really in love."

"Oh, wow." Ann-Marie gazed up at Austen like he had just recited poetry. "That was beautiful. I hope you're not a mind reader. Are you?"

I tried to will Austen not to answer that, but it was like he couldn't help it. An unsure smile danced at the corner of his lips. "Why do you ask, Ann-Marie?"

"Because I don't want you reading my thoughts right now."

"Why?" he prodded. "What are you thinking?"

He asked. He asked!

"Oh, you don't want to know," she said. "It involves you and me and bubbles and—"

I cut her off, "Ann-Marie, I really think you need to go back to the lounge and play us some 'welcome home' music right now."

She let out a giggle and scurried away, making eyes at Austen until the door slammed behind her. I realized that left me alone with the man that I didn't want to have a conversation with. He watched me over the counter. I took a deep breath. "Taylor and Bigley are in love," I said. "And they're happy. They are so in love and happy that they make everyone around them sick."

He broke into a smile. "Hey," he said in a soft voice. "I didn't mean to give you a hard time. I missed you. Did you miss me?" His eyes were on mine and he gave me that pleading look that had always worked on me before. But I knew exactly what this was now. Spending time together didn't mean love—it meant Austen was bored and wanted to hang out with someone fun. Well, I refused to drop everything just to entertain him.

"Austen." I leaned over the counter so that he could see the serious look on my face. "You didn't miss me or you would've called. Were your fingers too big and fat to fit the numbers on the screen?"

He smirked, not even looking guilty after I'd called him out. "I told you I'd text back. Besides, I'm not good at the long distance thing."

Interpretation: I wasn't worth the effort.

"Yeah?" I asked. "Well, I'm not good at the short-distance thing." It came out before I could really think what it sounded like and he reacted by giving a short bark of laughter. I pointed at him before he could tease me about it. "With you!" I corrected. "Only with you." I knew he was lying about the whole accounting thing; I had heard it in his voice. I pulled closer to him. "Why did you really come back here, Austen?"

He hesitated before answering, "How could I miss the big *event?*"

And now he was back to insulting my job again. As if he sensed my annoyance, Austen reached out and took my hand. With a start, I saw that he was still wearing the bracelet I had given him before he left—it hurt that he thought more about my gift than he did about me.

"You need a break," he said. "I can already see Taylor running you ragged. We should go to the beach today. I haven't gotten a sunburn in way too long."

I jerked away from him, more violently than I intended, but he just didn't get that I didn't want to grow attached. "I just heard you tell Taylor that you were much too busy with the books to help us out. I'm not dumb. I get it. You think my job is a joke."

"What? Are you kidding me? I did *not* say that."

"You didn't? Okay, let's see. The first thing out of your mouth when you saw me was, 'Wow, Jane, I can't believe that your job sucks so much.'"

"No, I didn't."

"Not in so many words—it sounded like you were asking me why I would still want to be here. And now you think you can just be charming and I'll blow off the opportunity of a lifetime—even if you think Taylor's wedding is a train wreck—so that I can have the privilege of entertaining you at the beach?"

"So you think I'm charming?"

I fumed. "Yes! Too much! Should I pay you for this honor of taking you out, or maybe we can work out some kind of trade? Let me give you my life savings. Oh, wait, I don't have one because my job's worthless!"

"Jane, are you really mad at me, or are you doing that thing you do when you're stressed out and you take it out on me? You know I'm here for you if you need to let out a little aggression." He thought this was a joke. I let out a deep, shuddering breath and he threw his hands up in a defeated gesture. "Okay," he said. "Fine. I'm sorry if I hurt your feelings . . ."

"Oh, you can't," I interrupted in a calmer voice, "because I don't have them now." He looked surprised, and I quickly amended my words. "For you. For you!" And then I flushed, because that sounded even worse. I knew the telltale redness had crept up my neck and nestled into my ears, because Austen stared at me in fascination. I hadn't meant to let him know how I'd felt. I was like one of those idiots who gave everything away to the bad guy in the first five seconds of an interrogation.

Austen's brows furrowed. I didn't dare move, but if he did, I'd be out the door faster than he could get to me and try to smooth things over between us. I couldn't face him after what I'd just admitted. Except here we were, face to face, and I couldn't breathe. I listened to the jingling bells of the door behind me.

"Hello? Uh, hello, do you work here? Who gets my car keys?"

I swallowed and turned. A beautiful girl at the doorway gave us an uncertain smile. A dimple deeper than the Grand Canyon appeared at her right cheek. "I'm one of Taylor's bridesmaids. I have reservations. Bella Thorne."

The girl walked in and I was immediately sorry when I got her full glory. Bella Thorne was the youngest in Taylor's group of friends, and I felt like an evil stepsister staring down Cinderella. She had long blond hair that hit the middle of her back. Freckles decorated a sun-kissed face. Her jeans and wrap shirt might as well have been a paper sack, because she'd outshine anything she wore.

Freddy, our errant bellhop and valet, careened into the driveway on his golf cart. His red porter jacket mirrored a captain's in the British army, and the way he held himself made me think he never lost a battle. His dark hair was messy but purposely so, and his normally brooding looks were more pronounced than ever. He had barely parked before he was out of the vehicle and hurrying for the front door. Since he was never that eager to report to duty, I had a feeling he had seen the girl on her way in and was *desperate* to be of service.

"Jane," he greeted me. He normally wasn't so pleasant. Without sparing me another glance, which *was* completely normal, Freddy swept his dark hair from his arrogant eyes. "I've got this," he told me under his breath. My suspicions were immediately confirmed when he swept an elegant bow to the beautiful bridesmaid and plucked her luggage from her hands only to drop it at my feet. "I'll take you to your room," he said.

Bella dimpled again, looking pleased at the effect she had over our handsome baggage handler. Freddy was already ushering Bella onto his golf cart before I came to another realization. He had left me with all the luggage again. Even worse, I was afraid to look back at Austen and see just how little my accidental declaration of love meant to him after he had seen the perfect girl. I took a deep breath and dragged Bella's luggage to the pile in the middle of the room.

"Hey, Jane," Austen said.

I turned cool eyes on him, hoping I looked like the heartless jade I wanted to be. "Are you offering to help me with the luggage?" I asked.

"No."

Of course he wasn't. If he cared about me at all, he'd stumble all over himself to make sure that my dainty hands never felt any kind of strain. I knew the true-love drill. I was fooling myself that I meant anything to him. I managed to get the smaller bags under each arm and the larger bags in my hands. I backed my way to the door that led out to the hallway—which unfortunately made it so that I was facing Austen again.

He looked as though he wanted to say something, but then when he saw my struggle, he started to laugh again. "If you need help, just ask."

"Oh, you mean I have to beg?" I hit the door with my back and realized that it wasn't going anywhere unless I possessed a third hand to turn the knob.

He sighed and circled the front desk to get to me. "I've got it."

He cornered me against the door and tried to wrestle Mary's plastic-covered bag from my hand. "No," I said. "You lost out on the opportunity to be a gentleman. Now it's my turn . . ."

"To be a gentleman?"

"At least my mother raised one."

"Give me the bags." He sounded stern this time.

No, I was a strong, independent woman, and I didn't need a man who didn't need me. "Austen, if you really want to help, you can . . . guard the front desk. Help me out by taking keys."

"You mean be your assistant?"

"If it isn't too lowly? Being the slave of a slave?"

I dropped the bags and my fingers fumbled behind me until they found the doorknob. Though he guffawed, he also looked torn. He had just told Taylor that he had more important things to do than to help me, except I happened to know that he wanted to steal me off to the beach instead. I tottered through the door into the hallway, hoping it didn't look like the handles from the luggage were digging holes into my hands. Austen retreated to the counter, taking one last backwards glance at me and shaking his head in frustration. I planned to leave him there all day if I could swing it.

Dragging the bags through the hallway to the backdoor, I readjusted them in my hands. There was no golf cart in sight and I'd have to take them through two courtyards to get them to Mary's and Bertie's bungalows. After the first two steps, I ran into an archway. I grunted and scrambled past it only to knock my shoulder against the rough stucco wall of the Rosing's house. I blindly felt my way through the first courtyard, running into anything hard I could find so that by the time I reached the first bungalow, I was aching and out of breath. I dropped the luggage onto the steps, hearing Mary's complaints inside the Uppercross. Her door was open in the back and she was shouting over to Bertie whether the former runway model liked it or not.

"It is freezing in my place." Mary gave a loud sniff. "My nose is cold. Feel it."

"I'd rather not," was Bertie's clipped reply.

I stretched out my fingers to get some feeling back in them and hauled up the luggage again, staggering over the shared patio of the two bungalows.

"Oh, there you are." Bertie stepped from her door, the bright sunlight outside making her silhouette look like a paper doll turned sidewise. Mary also came out, wiping at her nose with a wilted tissue—her nose wasn't dripping at all. I dropped Mary's plastic-covered bag off first in her living room. She eagerly ripped off the plastic from it, searching through the contents until she found a thermometer. "I'm sure I have a temperature. My brain is burning up!"

Mary was making a war zone out of the Uppercross Bungalow by taking out a ton of plastic bags from her suitcase and throwing them around the room. "I can't afford waterproof luggage," she said. "I'm sure Taylor's husband will give her such things after they're married. He's rich. I won't mind taking a cruise with them if they paid for it," her voice came in huffs through her exertions as she spread the plastic bags over her bed and searched around the mattress perimeter with shaking hands. "You don't have bedbugs, do you? Horrible bloodsucking things—I saw a documentary. It would just be my luck to get them."

I edged past her to Bertie's place in the Southerton Bungalow and dropped the designer luggage onto the plush carpet. Bertie didn't spare them a glance. She crossed her arms like the crossbones on a pirate flag. "My cutie needs some exercise. Please take her, J."

J?

Before I knew it, the scrawny, white teddy bear was in my hands, and Bertie had slammed her door behind me. The puppy was smaller than my hand and wore a red-and-white-striped onesie. What was I going to do with the little rat-bear? She licked my arm with a tiny pink tongue, and my heart melted. I could always add her to the collection of stuffed animals in Mister's kitty box.

I cradled the puppy against my neck and kissed her grape of a head while I skirted around the palm trees and fountains in the courtyard. Unhindered by bags, I made faster time on my way back. Reaching the back door to the lobby in the main building, I spied Austen still at his post at the checkout counter. He had resorted to taking out his laptop and working irritably on his bookkeeping. No wickedness in his smile, no concerned looks; and when I entered the room, he showed no undue interest in me at all.

I refused to feel bad. Nothing had been ruined between us because nothing existed there, except for the fact that we liked to get on each other's nerves. That meant that I was ahead of the game today.

I handed him the puppy and went back to the last of the luggage.

"Jane!" he said. "A teddy bear? Really?"

"She needs to take a potty break." I picked up the bags that belonged to Gorgeous or Beauty or whatever her name happened to mean and threw the one with a strap over my shoulder.

"I can't believe it!"

Ann-Marie's voice made me jump. I had been so distracted with Austen that I hadn't noticed that she had come back to torment him. She had taken her usual spot on the sofa near the TV. "Do you know who John Willoughby is?" She whipped around to pierce us both with a look.

I wasn't sure who she was talking to, but Austen got rid of the suspense and shook his head. "No idea."

"Well, he's dead! He got shot ten times. They think it's a murder-suicide and he was trying to break up with his girlfriend. She shot him over and over and then killed herself."

"Hmm, and *that* is why I stay clear of relationships." Austen peered over the dog's head at the books of accounts. "But you never know. Maybe he shot himself ten times and then killed her."

Ann-Marie stumbled to her feet and dashed over to the desk. "How could he do that? That's impossible."

"Stranger things have happened."

"What sort of world do you live in?" Ann-Marie was practically shouting at him now. "He couldn't even do that!"

41

I felt my lips twitch up, but then forced them back down. Austen's completely inappropriate jokes weren't funny. Ann-Marie caught sight of the wriggling animal in Austen's hands. "Puppy!"

She quickly divested him of the wriggling creature and gave it more loving than it could possibly want. "You cute little thing. Is this yours, Austen? Hot man with puppy—that only makes you ten times hotter, you know. I always wanted a puppy."

"Look." I held my hands up to stop the volley of words. "Whoever takes the puppy, just make sure that she flushes after she uses the facilities outside. Then you can return her to the witch in the Southerton Bungalow for processing."

Austen laughed. "What are the witch's plans for the little doggy? The glue factory or a witch's brew?"

"I . . . I . . ." He was already joking with me. I wasn't sure what I thought about that. "I think the lady just wants to weigh down her purse with it," I said.

"Too bad," Austen said. "Poopsy would make a perfect little hot doggy."

"Oh no!" Ann-Marie snuggled the puppy closer. "Don't you listen to those horrid people. You stay with me and I'll keep you safe." The puppy licked her nose. She took the little rat-bear outside, continuing to talk as if the puppy might answer her back. The TV blared behind Ann-Marie, forgotten. A headline ran across the news station, reporting that a certain Will Dancey had taken a break from his music tour and was rumored to be heading to California.

That's when I remembered that he had nowhere to stay.

I turned off the TV and whirled to face Austen. "You can't stay in the Wood House. There's another guest staying there."

"The Wood House?" he asked. "You realize there are rats staying there too, and spiders and sand? Not to mention me. Sorry, it's taken."

"Now, wait a second. Freddy was going to clean it up to make it suitable for guests."

He laughed at that. "Isn't there a crummy little loft upstairs? The last time I saw it, no one was paying full price for that."

And it was also mine. "Not funny, Austen."

"I guess neither of us wants to give up our rooms for a guest. Look, Jane, there's a nice hotel next door. It's not a sin to put it to use. Put the extra guest in the Kellynch." He flipped lazily through his books at the counter like I was the most boring thing on earth.

And he had *not* solved my little dilemma. Taylor would kill me if I put Dancey in the Kellynch, but no argument would stir Austen. And since his parents owned the place, I didn't really have a say. My fingers landed on Bella's luggage. There was nothing more to do but to retreat with it through the narrow hall. I trudged out the back, occasionally muttering a complaint or two every time I slammed my fingers against the wall. Courtship was dead, true gentlemen were deader—well, once I was through with Austen. Okay, the luggage was my fault, but at least I was stronger for it. Already I was getting a great arm workout.

It wasn't too hard to find Bella out by the Norland Courtyard. Her giggles led the way there. The deep timbre of Freddy's voice answered her soft flirtations. "You're not afraid of bad boys, are you?" he asked her.

"Is that what you think you are?"

"I'll let you decide. Give me your phone."

I grimaced, knowing he was typing his number into her fancy iPhone. Little fountains spurted water all around them to create an enchanting scene. Despite the romantic gesture, Freddy was a player. He'd leave her heart in a pile of splinters on the ground after he was through with her—he'd done it to so many girls that I'd lost count.

I sidestepped a potted palm and dropped the luggage at his feet. "Oh!" Bella blushed when Freddy picked them off the pavement. "But I don't have any money for a tip."

Tip? She wasn't about to tip Freddy for my work, was she?

43

"I'm sure we could arrange something," Freddy said. He tapped the wall of the stylish stucco building behind her and swung the luggage up the steps to the Fullerton Bungalow where she would be staying. Then without looking sheepish at all for taking all the credit for my work, he left with a cocky swagger to his step. "Text me," he said, "but only when you're desperate for my company."

She watched him go with longing in her eyes. Despite Bella's beauty, he'd leave her crying while he merrily chased after his next conquest. Wanting to save her from certain heartbreak, I gave her a bracing smile, an idea quickly taking form in my mind. "Don't bother with a tip," I told her—because I had one for her. "Freddy is terrible with money; too much hard living. Poor guy."

"What? Really?" Her eyes went wide at the intrigue, which I suspected would happen—she seemed the type to go for the bad boys. Revealing who he was wouldn't do the trick, but I knew what would.

"Yeah," I nodded. "It's tough watching a guy waste his life like that. He just needs a really good girl to turn him around . . ." Bella looked like she might be the one who wanted to do that, and I smiled because I was about to smash whatever attraction she felt for him. "He needs to find someone who gets him . . . out of his mother's basement, you know? I mean, everything he earns he spends on video games, pizza, and two-liter bottles of soda. He's gonna blow up like that guy from *Supersize Me*."

"Oh." Her nose wrinkled and she didn't look as intrigued.

"He gives girls his number and expects them to do all the work."

She stuffed her phone in her pocket, looking embarrassed. "How do you know?" she asked. "Did you date him?"

Now it was my turn to throw up a little in my mouth. My vivid imagination deserted me inside some weird scene that held my potential life with Freddy—instead of being me, I was this sweet, little thing—a little worn down, my shoulders hunched. I followed the brilliant Freddy around in my skinny jeans and high heels, desperately trying to get his attention. He'd call me fat while he flirted with other girls. The impression rushed through my mind like a near-death experience, and I backed away from Bella, shaking my head. I knew what would happen if Freddy chose that moment to make an appearance; I'd shove Bella at him, shouting, "Keep the girl; just leave me alone!"

Instead I gave Bella an enigmatic smile. "Let's just say he's a character. We'll leave it at that." With those mysterious words to serve as a warning, I retreated to the main building where I stole up the back, taking three flights of stairs to my room. As Austen had pointed out so rudely, mine was the crummy loft upstairs. No matter how quaint his parents tried to make the Morland Loft look in the advertisements, it was never rented out. And so Austen's parents ended up giving it to the staff for a meager monthly fee.

But I loved it—I felt like I lived in a tree house in the middle of a Swiss Family Robinson jungle. The loft had exposed rafters, and the palms brushed against the four windowsills on all sides of me. The birds nested on the roof outside. We shared this space together, which I was okay with as long as they didn't share their mites with me, too.

I collapsed into my beanbag and stretched my legs out in front of me, trying to process everything, but I could only concentrate on one thing. Austen was back. It was only for a month. My heart gave a little flutter. A whole month! I could actually see him again. And then what? I tried to be stern with my heart. Nothing should happen, and it wouldn't. Austen and I had both burned that bridge together—not only that, but we had thrown gasoline on that bridge and blown on it to make the flames burn hotter and brighter.

Still, even if any chance of a future had been ruined, I had every intention of being spitefully stunning while he was here; that would show him what he let slip through his fingers. I should take a shower. Do my hair. Put on some make-up. At least some lip gloss. *Starting now.* Except I couldn't get off my beanbag chair. I leaned my head back and stared up at the rafters.

Austen was lost to me, but it didn't mean that *all* romance was dead. I felt it. Things were a lot different here than it was at home. My parents had been realistic and longsuffering. My five older brothers were protective, and it was impossible for anything adventurous to happen to me when they guarded their little sister from anything too crazy. After moving here from Sacramento, I'd felt the possibility for adventure the instant I'd walked into the lobby of my new job.

Magic would happen at the North Abbey. There was a wedding in the works, after all—and it wasn't just a client's wedding, but a friend's—that made me both guest and professional, kind of a weird position to be in. But it didn't matter; even if Taylor's bridesmaids were hard to handle, at least Bigley might have some nice groomsmen in the ranks. Probably no lasting relationships, but as part-guest, I could get to know them when I wasn't on the clock. And of course, there was Bigley's best mate, Will Dancey. He might be fun. Dancey was a rock star with a tragic past, if anyone could believe the lyrics in his songs.

What was Dancey like? He'd be a romantic, for sure, but probably distrustful of relationships. I wouldn't even try to get past his defenses in a week—but we'd definitely have to share a *moment*.

Not everyone is familiar with "the moment," but it was one of my favorite theories, a little something I'd picked up from every Jane Austen flick I'd ever watched. The moment meant I had the guy's attention—it was that moment that I knew he was entranced with me while I was with him. It could be a look, a brush of the hand. It could happen in the middle of a dance or while playing soccer. It usually lasted only for a moment, thus the term.

Afterwards, the memory of that moment had to be carried around in my mind as evidence that romance truly did exist and that someday a guy that I loved would look at me like that every time he saw me. It would never dim. It would flavor his laughter and his heartache and his joy. His every emotion would belong to me, and mine would belong to him.

Maybe that made me weird.

Now I wanted to listen to Dancey's songs—they were just as sappy as I was. My London-Or-Bust, old-school suitcase that I used as my knickknack drawer was within grabbing distance, and I leaned forward on my beanbag to get to my iPod from in there so that I could download Dancey's latest album. Most of the songs involved love gone wrong, but the most popular one was heart wrenching. The girl that had inspired that one had left poor Dancey's heart a bloody pulp—likely she had stomped on it.

The song was called "Poppies." The melody drifted through my ears like a haunted memory from the past:

Don't go.
Dancing through London in a field of poppies.
Red like the color of your lips.
You're all I see.
Don't go.

I rested my head against the back of my beanbag, letting the music flow through me. Dancey felt what he sang. That's what I liked best about his music—everything he said came from the heart:

I smell the flowers in the mist of your hair.
Red like blood in a broken heart.
Kiss me again.
Don't go.

As I listened to the words flow into the chorus, I decided that the girl who had inspired this song had set Dancey's soul on fire, or he'd never care this much about her. It reminded me of what Austen had done to me. As soon as I came to that thought, I turned off the song.

It took the spider to force my legs into action. The insect poked a big, furry head from behind my shag rug, and I shot to my feet, scurrying backwards. The spider did the same thing on the hardwood floor, but went the opposite way until it disappeared behind my flat screen TV.

My hands were shaky, but since I was up, I headed for my vanity. It was a cute little setup with a mirror and a porcelain bowl sink. I took a flat iron to the auburn curls in my hair and dabbed some lotion onto my face. Austen would kick himself when he saw me. I'd look so good he'd wish every moment back with me to make me fall in love with him. Just as I was applying the mascara, my cell phone buzzed in my pocket. I looked at the screen and saw it was a text from Taylor.

COME DOWN TO THE ALLENHAM LOUNGE. REDD IS HERE.

Every romantic idea in my head fled at the name. Oh no. Oh no! Not Redd. While I had been falling all over Austen last summer, Redd had done his best to distract me. And no matter how much I tried to cushion my rejection, I had crushed him. My guilt consumed me.

Redd wasn't supposed to come to Taylor's wedding. We hadn't reserved a room for him, and Taylor hadn't said anything about her bestie crashing the festivities at the last second. I had pried very, very carefully to get that out of her. I had asked if anyone from the military was attending and she just looked at me blankly.

That was supposed to mean that Redd was not coming!

We hadn't even dated. Of course, it all depended on who told the story, but I never counted the evenings we had spent together as actual dates. I thought that we were hanging out. Taylor had been there, too, and I hadn't suspected that Redd would make a move, until he tried to kiss me. Redd had left last summer a very disappointed and embittered man.

My phone buzzed with another text from Taylor: HURRY. HE'S ASKING FOR YOU

Chapter 5

"A man does not recover from such a devotion of the heart to such a woman! He ought not; he does not."

—Jane Austen, Persuasion

Instead of going to the Allenham Lounge, I ran for the lobby, only thinking of Austen. Sure, he hated me now, but he'd have to see reason. He was the one who had gotten me into this mess, and he could get me out of it.

My feet pounded down the stairs and through the hallway. I flung open the door, knowing my entrance resembled more Ann-Marie's usual style than mine. "Austen. Austen! Austen!" I kept my voice to a harsh whisper.

Austen looked up from his books, this time with interest. I knew I looked crazy right now, but I didn't care. I raced to the counter and flattened against it, only inches from his face. "I need you!"

"I thought you said . . ."

"Not like that. Austen, the Captain is here!"

"The Captain?"

"Redd!"

"He's a captain now?" His voice lost interest.

"Yeah, he was promoted. That happens in the navy sometimes. You have *got* to pretend that you and I have something going on, so I don't look like a total loser." My eyes raced to the door between us and the lounge. It stood as a barrier between me and the captain's potential new girlfriend—I was sure of it. Even if I didn't like Redd, I

49

had rejected him, and if he knew that I was single and still available, well, then he'd rub it in my face and win. Sort of. Well, he would see it that way, and it killed me.

Austen punched numbers steadily into his laptop. I put my hand in front of the screen. "You're the one who talked me out of liking him!" I said.

He snorted. "No, that was you."

"Was it?"

Austen peeled my hand away from his screen. "You do have a mind of your own sometimes."

Yeah, I did, but I really thought that Austen hadn't thought that much of him, either—maybe because I had always misinterpreted everything Austen did back then. When Austen said Redd was a little off, that meant that Austen wanted to get together with me. Well, it didn't matter how wrong I was. I had looked for any excuse to drop the guy after I'd discovered he liked me, and when Redd proved to be such a poor loser afterwards, I was even gladder that I got out of dating him.

"Fine," I said. "It was me. I'm to blame. Can you do me the favor anyway?"

"No."

"What? Why?" I hated that my voice came out a whine.

His eyes danced mischievously at me. "You're mad at me. Remember? You're not even supposed to be speaking to me."

"Can we just put a hold on that for a bit?" Yes, I was throwing my self-respect out the window. It usually happened in situations like these. "You could at least pretend to be my boyfriend."

"Not a chance." He snickered. "This is going to be a lot of fun to watch."

I should've known he wouldn't play the knight errant. It wasn't Austen's style, and still . . . "I would totally do it for you!"

He laughed. "I know."

I really, really hated him right now. He checked out my face and laughed again. "Careful, you might spontaneously combust."

I changed tactics. "I'll pay you to do it!"

"How?" Now he looked interested. "You don't have a life savings—you just said you didn't."

I flinched, but before he could take any of his mean words back, I stormed to the door to the Allenham Lounge and ripped it open.

Captain Redd Wortham leaned against the fireplace, staring into it. The flames crackled and spit. The glow of it painted his cheeks gold. It was a dashing look with his intense eyes and his cropped, dark hair—it had red highlights like his name. Soft piano music, courtesy of Ann-Marie, played in the background. I listened to Taylor's merry conversation. She talked, of all things, about the weather to her cousin and her husband.

Since no one was aware I had come in, I studied the little group while they chatted and chuckled together. Reverend Eddy and Elly McFarey were a young, stylish couple, whose heads nodded in unison. Elly, Taylor's cousin, was, in a word, adorable. She had apple-red cheeks on an otherwise pale face and wore a colorful scarf and a short skirt with boots. Her vibrant red hair was her crowning glory. Her husband, Eddy, seemed more subdued in comparison. He wore black-rimmed glasses over clear blue eyes with blond, almost transparent lashes. He had a cool geek chic thing going with his lanky build, bow tie and suit jacket.

The gentle energy surging from the couple immediately put me at ease. The cousins were almost opposites. Where Taylor was wound tighter than hair in pigtails, Elly was calm and laid-back. She patted her cousin's hand in a friendly way; her touch had a soothing effect on Taylor.

My eyes drew back to the captain. He glanced my way, and his jaw tightened. Oh my. He was brooding, wasn't he? Unbidden, the image of a Jane Austen scene came to mind. I couldn't help it. Redd looked the epitome of a wronged suitor. The collar of his dark jacket was a little higher than usual. His khaki pants could pass as the breeches of a fashionable gentleman of the era. Due to all of his military training, his broad shoulders and narrow waist gave him a triangular look. He stiffened when he saw me. And then he did exactly what I thought he would do—pretended I didn't exist. He looked past me and nodded. "Austen."

Austen sauntered into the room, his eyes dancing with humor. "Redd, you came for little Miss Taylor's wedding?"

"She put a note in my invitation that I couldn't refuse."

Had she? The traitorous Taylor stood up, clasping Redd's hands in hers. I hoped she wasn't trying to set us up again, because if so, it would not go the way she had planned. She smiled like a certain bear with a honey jar. "Redd, you see, Jane has come. I told you she would if I texted that you were here."

"Interesting; she wasn't nearly as responsive to my texts," Redd said in his deep voice.

My face bloomed red. Austen gave me a considering stare, and I knew I looked the hypocrite since I had chided him about the same thing only an hour ago. "Is that so?" I asked. Redd's last text seemed like a big group invite. "I'm sorry. I thought I was part of some mass group text or I would've said something."

Austen smirked at that because I was proving to be just as big of a jerk as he was.

At Redd's disbelieving look, I remembered his other texts too late—he *had* hounded me with texts after our *sort of* break up—hardly any of which I'd returned. Oh dear, yeah, I was a coldhearted jade and now a liar. I remembered that I had tried to wean him off me by replying to his numerous communications with a text a day until that proved ineffective and I had to go cold turkey and stop texting him altogether. His last text before the mass invite had accused me of being dead.

And apparently I thought so little of it that I had immediately forgotten all about it because—well, to be honest—I always had these kinds of run-ins when it came to the dating scene. That, along with a terrible memory, made me quite the villain. I knew I made a lot of enemies, but usually it didn't come back to bite me so hard.

I mumbled something about being a bad texter, and Austen turned away from me, but not quick enough. His expression told me exactly how amusing he thought my predicament was.

Changing the subject was Taylor's talent, and she did it with a charming laugh. "Redd, dear, where are you staying while you're in town?"

Redd's expression smoothed into a pleasant one. "Just next door to here actually. I'm staying at the Kellynch."

Taylor made a strangled sound. "You are?" It made sense that he'd go to North Abbey's rival rather than be close to me.

"It's close to the action, but not too close," he told her with a wink.

"Well, there's no vacancy here," Austen said. "Jane stole the last room."

I gave him a warning look, but I shouldn't have bothered. Redd wasn't about to discuss anything "Jane" related. Instead, he smiled vaguely at the minister and his wife sitting across the room. "Did you drive all the way from Washington DC for the wedding?" he asked.

The couple chatted amiably with him about the differences of weather. Predictably, Austen got bored. "You know," he said, "if Redd wanted to stay here, Jane has a way of finding a place for everybody at North Abbey. It's like the fish and loaves—something for everyone. You should know that reference, Reverend."

Eddy looked up politely, but Redd continued his conversation with the minister's wife as if Austen hadn't spoken. Once again, I wasn't a subject that Redd wished to pursue.

Austen tried again. "Jane's also an excellent surfer. I think she gets that from all the instructors she's had."

Redd would know that I was a lousy surfer because he had offered to teach me, but again Austen's attempts fell on deaf ears.

Austen hid another laugh. I glared at him. Apparently, this had turned into a game to see how far Austen could push Redd before he talked to me.

"Jane," Austen said. "Is that a spider on your arm?"

I jumped.

"What?" Taylor cried. She propelled to her feet and danced around in her attempts to smash it. "Where did it go?"

The music came to an abrupt halt while everyone but Redd and me searched for the nonexistent spider. I was going to kill Austen for that one. He pointed my general direction, and Taylor brushed at me while trying not to touch me. Elly stomped the floor in her sleek black boots in an attempt to kill it, while Eddy watched on.

Ann-Marie stood up from behind the piano, her face pale. "Is it dead yet?"

"Yeah," I said, shoving everyone's helpful hands away. "It's gone. It's gone. Pretty much smashed dead."

Redd gave me a disgusted look and went to our little piano player who stood vulnerably by the bench. "Are you all right?" he asked her.

"Yes," Ann-Marie said in her most fragile voice.

"Did you need someone to turn pages?"

"I would like that very much."

Sure, the captain showed concern when I wasn't the victim. Austen coughed, and I knew it was to cover up another laugh as I stood, forgotten, in the middle of the room while everyone else patted themselves to ensure there were no creepy-crawly eight-footed creatures on them. Maybe that meant that I was excused?

I tried to slip from the room, but Taylor's voice stopped me. "You haven't said hello to Elly yet, Jane."

"Oh, sorry." I rushed to Taylor's cousin to remedy the situation. "I'm sorry for that poor introduction, Elly." I sat down on the couch facing her and her husband, Eddy. The couple both had very pleasant looks on their faces and exchanged the most polite conversation I'd ever experienced—possibly in my lifetime, most definitely since this morning.

Austen found the other side of the couch next to me, and after the minister and his wife gathered my life history, I listened to theirs, trying to ignore Austen's smirks and coughs.

"Do you know how they met?" Taylor asked.

I shook my head and scooted closer to Austen, having every intention of elbowing him in the ribs if he didn't stop laughing at the snub Redd had given me. "I don't believe you've mentioned it," I said.

"They were in-laws first," Taylor said.

"Uh . . ."

"Not like that! Their siblings got married first," Taylor said, "and Elly's new sister-in-law was such a pill. Elly couldn't imagine that Fran's brother could actually be so sweet."

"No, no," Elly countered. "Fran is a dear."

Taylor put a hand over her mouth in a fake whisper. "In Elly language that means that the two are barely on speaking terms. When Elly's parents went on a big European vacation a few years ago, Fran and Elly's brother decided to come over and house-sit. Elly was already staying at the house and going to school, so there really wasn't a reason, except Elly's brother and Fran wanted free rent. And Fran was so bossy, she took the best rooms in the house and refused to invite Elly to any of the parties she held *in Elly's own house*. Nice, huh? Almost like Fran thought Elly would steal her friends away."

That had Austen's attention, but then again, he was always indignant when he saw an injustice. "You didn't say anything to your sister-in-law, Elly?" he asked.

Elly's hands knit together. "I didn't want bad blood between us."

Taylor laughed. "Imagine how mad Fran was when she found out that her own brother fell for the girl she thought would steal her friends away from her."

"Oh no," Elly said. "It wasn't like that." Her pretty face pinched with discomfort. "Of course Fran wasn't upset."

Taylor nodded in true gossip fashion. "Fran was furious."

Eddy hid a smile. Apparently Taylor wasn't exaggerating his sister's rage, because he didn't contradict it. He put an arm around his wife and kissed her on the cheek. "I fell in love with Elly the moment I met her. She's the only one with the patience to listen to my boring sermons."

I realized that I had a cheesy grin on my face. This was why I loved romance—despite the pitfalls, the broken hearts, my pitiful attempts. Austen and I sat closer than we had before. I felt his warmth before I stiffened and edged away. I was still angry at him, and just to be clear, I leaned away from him.

He turned, his eyes darkening on mine. If I didn't know better I'd misinterpret that look as someone who was interested. But I knew better. It didn't matter if I had accidentally declared my love; Austen wasn't about to change his mind about me. This wasn't some 80's movie. Despite that fact, his hand went to my arm and I felt his thumb brush against my bare skin. His mouth opened to say something just as Ann-Marie finished another piece on the piano.

"Very good, Ann-Marie," Redd said in a powerful voice that interrupted the moment. "Remind me to come and listen to you more often. It might give me a reason to visit North Abbey once Taylor is gone."

Ah yes, another dig at me. Typical. I moved from Austen and his confusing "friendly" touches so that I could clear my throat. "We'll try to provide more entertainment for you soon, Redd. Maybe a trumpet, some drums."

He didn't laugh. Austen did.

"That's a compliment, Redd," Austen said after a moment. "Jane doesn't normally give anyone anything—her room, her time, her heart."

I fumed. "I gave you something," I accused in a low voice. "You're still wearing it."

His gaze followed mine to the offending item on his wrist. He shrugged. "It fits better on me."

Redd's eyes alighted on the bracelet, and his chin whipped up. I felt the full brunt of his displeasure from his glaring, condemning grey eyes, made more dangerous under brooding brows. A muscle worked against his sculpted jaw, which was actually terrifying.

Taylor had given me the bracelet. She had said something about how Redd thought it matched the color of my eyes. Had it actually been a gift from Redd then? The irony of my situation hit me—like a ten pound bar of iron to the face.

Redd shoved away from the piano. "I must get going." He looked everywhere but at me and I felt a little guilty.

Taylor stood, too, and smoothed out her skirt. "Already, Redd? You just got here!"

"Don't worry. I'll be back to kiss the bride."

"You'd better." She touched his arm. "You must come to all my parties. I know there are a lot of them, but you knew who I was when we became friends."

Redd kissed her cheek with an indulgent smile. "I wouldn't miss your parties for the world."

I frowned. Why was Taylor allowed the privilege of being friends—even before she was engaged—and I had to be the evil ex even though I never dated him officially?

"I don't know what will become of North Abbey when you are gone," Redd told her.

"Jane will be here." Austen patted me on the back, continuing his little game. "She's gearing up to be a great event coordinator."

Taylor nodded after a little hesitation, and I tried to take their fake compliments with grace. Redd turned to study an intricate vase on the fireplace mantle. "I will have to see for myself how well Jane fares after you are gone, Taylor."

With that, he shook the minister's hand and then Elly's, making his rounds around the room. Even Ann-Marie got a hug. She claimed it with gusto. When Redd found his way to me, his arms dropped to his sides and his gaze slid past me like I was invisible. It couldn't get any more awkward.

"Until we meet again," his voice came out gravelly, but he kept his emotions firmly in check. I saw them in his eyes, though, when he finally graced me with a look—they burned into mine.

I did my best to give him my cheeriest smile before he swung on his heel and left.

Chapter 6

"Shh. Surely you and I are beyond speaking when words are clearly not enough . . . I missed you."

"And I you."

—Jane Austen, Mansfield Park

Austen let out a low whistle as soon as we were alone in the lobby. Redd's beat-up Hummer sped past the great picture window of the resort. Austen turned to me. "That was rough."

I ignored him and headed for the front door. Churchell's Shack was part of the resort's setup. It was at the end of the trail just down the beach. I was due to coordinate for tomorrow's wedding brunch there.

"Hey Jane," he called after me. "Is someone going to release me from front desk duty here?"

"Yeah," I said over my shoulder. "Do you want to clean the toilets instead?"

He let out a laugh. "Is that what you're doing?"

"No."

"Good." I heard him gather up his books and laptop from the counter. "Then I'm going with you."

"Maybe if you were my fake boyfriend you could." I slammed the front door between us, wondering if that would do the trick. The wind blew through my hair, and I leaned my head back, listening to the waves in the distance.

"Fake boyfriend wouldn't have done you any good." Austen's voice made me jump. He zipped his jacket up to his neck and threw on the hood before shutting the door behind him. "The good captain couldn't keep his eyes off you."

"No, he couldn't look at me. There's a difference."

Austen shook his head. "It was all corner-of-the eye stuff. Believe me, the guy's not over you. I'm not teasing you this time—not that you aren't fun to tease." He gave a little chuckle. "Sorry, I couldn't help it back there. I love it when you get flustered—your face gets all red." He studied me and his eyes crinkled with amusement. "Yeah, like that."

He gave me a friendly nudge and I shook him off, trying to keep myself from flushing so he wouldn't tease me about it again. I knew what he was doing. This was his way of apologizing, but I didn't care if he wanted me to ease his guilt. I was tired of this emotional rollercoaster we had going.

I took off for the beach, and Austen fell into step beside me. He was really going to follow me to Churchell's, wasn't he? I mentally texted Ann-Marie to keep an ear on the front desk during her piano duty. Maybe I'd actually give her a real text later.

Glancing over at Austen and seeing his beautiful eyes on me, I sighed. "I think Redd actually hates me more than he did before, no thanks to you."

He shrugged and let it drop. But on further reflection, I knew Austen was right about the fake boyfriend. It would only be acceptable if Redd had brought a girlfriend; otherwise it would've been petty. The sand slipped and crumbled through my flip-flops on my way down to the beach. The sun felt good on my face and neck, and I tried to enjoy it.

"So, Redd is mad at you and you are mad at me," Austen said. "Who do I get to be mad at?"

My shoulders tensed. What relaxation I had gleaned from nature disappeared. I stopped myself from snapping back with a retort and took a moment to reflect instead. Redd held a grudge against me for the same reason that I had one for Austen. I couldn't be mad at Austen for not liking me. I could be annoyed that he'd led me a merry chase, but had he really? Or was he just being friendly in his own way, and I'd let my romantic nature take it to the next level? A guy wasn't really declaring himself until . . . well, he did. Before that, it was just speculation.

I cleared my throat. "You can be mad at the government. That's pretty popular."

He nodded. "I *am* mad." I looked over at him and was immediately sorry when he won my heart again with a wink. I lengthened my stride, and he matched it. He wouldn't let me dump him as easily as he had done me. I breathed out in resignation, deciding it was easier to be friends. I could use one right now. And if he was a fair-weather one? Well, I needed those too.

Digging my hands into the kangaroo pockets of my hoodie, I took the sand-covered steps of Churchell's Shack two at a time to reach its deck. The bar and grill was built to look like a tiki hut, complete with bamboo sticks. It had its own private pool on the deck, shaded with a thick foliage of palm trees in a mini tropical paradise. Besides servicing our guests, the shack also picked up business from the condos and other resorts from the area—namely the Kellynch.

Churchell Shack was nearly always hopping with customers, so I had timed my appearance an hour before the dinner rush. I pushed through the double swinging doors. The shack was just as open to the elements as the deck outside. The shutters on all the windows were open, and a soft wind lifted the fringe on the place mats. Bamboo rugs lay across a wooden floor. This place would be the hub for Taylor's brunch tomorrow. And Junie Fairchild, the owner, would be its caterer.

Junie moved a rag over her already-pristine counter. Her arms were muscular. She kept her long brown hair in a ponytail at the back of her head, with wisps escaping from the sides. She glanced up at me, no emotion clouding her perfect grey eyes. "You're here about the brunch tomorrow, right?"

I nodded and sat down, even though she hadn't given me the go ahead.

Junie and I were . . . frenemies, to put it accurately. It was weird, because she was everything that I wanted to be. She looked like she was ready to head out on a Safari—strong enough to take out a few crocodiles, but delicate enough that the men on the boat would never let her lift a lace-gloved finger.

I couldn't quite figure out what our problem was. Junie always kept me at a distance like she was hiding secrets that she didn't trust with anyone—least of all me. Everyone else loved her. Taylor had even taken Junie away with her when she left for Britain to see Bigley. I tried not to take it personally. I mean, I had never gone to Britain before and my luggage already said "London" on it, plus I loved any novel set in England. It should've been my vacation, but Taylor still insisted on taking Junie. Junie had a gift. If there was an employee award in a dig like this place, she would win it every month. Austen's parents were giddy around her. Freddy was, well, Freddy. And then . . . there was Austen.

Actual interest spread over Junie's face when she saw he was with me. "Austen! You're back!"

I didn't like how she said his name—almost like it belonged to her. I gave myself a mental shake, because it didn't belong to me either.

"Well, if it isn't Junie Be Fair!" he said.

That earned Austen a smile and a free soda. Junie Fairchild even added an umbrella to it. Besides being jealous, I should probably take notes, because I only got a complimentary-size cup of water. I choked on a laugh when I saw it.

"I just have some last-minute details to coordinate with you," I told her.

"Yeah?" She tossed the rag to the side to lean against the counter. "What's the guest total now?"

Taylor was famous for pulling switcheroos on us. It always made me look bad, but there was nothing for it. I put on a casual look. "As of today, two-hundred-and-ninety-five."

Junie nodded. "Fifty more then." She didn't look bothered by the change, not like she had when she'd first started her business—she probably even planned for it now. "I'll need more chicken breasts and barbecue sauce."

"I'm on it." I planned to ask how much, but became acutely aware that Junie wasn't paying any attention to me. She and Austen had some sort of visual conversation going on with their eyes. I coughed. "So, Junie Be . . . uh," I cut myself off—that was Austen's pet name for her. "I mean Junie, do you need anything else?"

"Nope," she said in her clipped way when addressing me, and then she sent a special smile to the guy by my side. "Austen, you didn't tell me you were coming to town." I felt a small sense of satisfaction that he had kept her in the dark, too. "How did Boston treat you?"

I hunched guiltily when I realized that these were all normal-people questions that I'd failed to ask him earlier.

He adjusted on his seat to get more comfortable. "It's dog eat dog out there, Junie Be Fair. I hardly had time to sleep and eat. The only exercise I got was biking to work."

"So, no time for dating?"

The question startled both of us. Austen was just worse at hiding it than I was. He let out a bark of laughter. "Hey, I got out. I wasn't a complete hermit."

"Then you're dating someone?"

"Why would I limit myself to one girl?" He winked.

"Oh come now." Junie leaned closer to him and put a gentle hand on his arm. "There's not some special girl worth settling down for?"

He said no! Why press him and test the fates, or he'd come up with a different answer—for the life of me I didn't know why I cared—it's just . . . I downed my complimentary cup of water in one gulp, all the while watching Austen narrowly. He laughed again. "Junie, there is no one as special as the ones I left here."

That was a really safe answer when talking to the two girls he had simultaneously and unknowingly led on while he had been here last time. I blew my cheeks out in exasperation. I had already forgiven him for it two seconds ago. Just so I wouldn't forget that, I looked away at the beach bums playing volleyball in the distance. The blond guy next to the net was cute. His long board shorts looked like breeches from the regency era.

"We definitely need to catch up on old times." I heard Austen say.

My attention veered back to Junie as she patted his arm before pulling away. "It's a date," she said in her throaty voice.

I jerked to the side and knocked my complimentary cup over. Dark soda spilled all over Junie's beautiful counter. I looked from the puddle to Austen's cup only to discover that Austen had covertly poured half of his soda into my cup when I wasn't looking—he probably pitied my little water cup.

"I am so sorry, Junie." I stole her rag and scrubbed at the spill. "I was just in a hurry to go. I have so much I need to finish before the wedding, and . . ." The counter was clean—wet, but clean. I put the dirty rag down and gave her a contrite smile. "Sorry, I really have to go."

I found my feet and didn't get two steps when Austen caught my arm—I was intrigued that his fingers could fit around my whole elbow. "Hey, I'm hungry. I've been stuck behind that counter for too long; can we get something to eat before going back?" he asked. "Come on, I know you're going to work through dinner, which will only make you more cranky." He smiled. "Let's eat."

Friends ate together, except I couldn't stomach him stealing the attention from every girl he met . . . and why did I care? "Sure, sure." I grabbed a menu and headed back to the counter, hurriedly perusing the food choices.

Austen steered me by my elbow. "Let's eat over there."

I nodded, letting him lead me wherever he felt like while I read through the menu. He shoved me at a booth and I sat down, finally noticing that he had cornered me behind a palm where I couldn't see the volleyball players from my vantage point. The old Jane would assume that he meant to get me alone, but I knew better now.

Austen settled down on the seat opposite me. "Now we can talk. Jane, I really want to talk to you. A lot has happened since I left."

He *had* found someone. I got scared. "A lot happened?"

"Well, yeah, but also . . ." He stopped talking and just stared at me. It made me wonder if I had something embarrassing on my face. I rubbed self-consciously at my nose. The corner of his lips lifted. "You look good." I knew that wasn't what he had been going to say. He laughed and abruptly changed the subject. "So you and Redd, huh? Why didn't that work out?"

I wasn't sure. If it had just been Austen that had stood in the way of that failed romance, then I'd probably be dating Redd now; but besides how obsessed Redd acted with me, the relationship had just kind of fallen flat. I shrugged. "He's cute, but I don't know, we just didn't click."

Spending time with Redd was actually boring. Since the moment in my childhood when I could grasp what romance was, I had imagined it as something so magical, so perfect, that I'd be willing to give up my single existence for it . . . but if being together with someone wasn't better than what I had now, frankly, I didn't want it.

What Austen and I had had was the closest thing that I could tag as an ideal romance—it made me feel fresh and alive. Of course, it had only been a figment of my imagination. As if on cue, Junie came by and mechanically lit the scented candle sitting in a bowl between

Austen and me. I suspected some evil ulterior motive on her part. Candles between Austen and me just felt wrong.

Junie put her hands on her hips. She was too good to write down an order. "So, what will it be?"

I gave her my menu. "I want the tuna sandwich."

Austen made a face. "I guess that means I'll take the oyster stew."

She left and he leaned closer to me. "Now we'll both have bad breath."

I couldn't help it—a laugh escaped my lips. "You are a romance killer."

"What?"

"A candle, and you're talking about bad breath?" I moved the candle around so that the flame sputtered in indignation. No matter how anyone tried to force romance, it never worked. Me with Austen. Redd with me. It was like romance wasn't in our natures anymore.

"Wait, I get it." I got excited as a new hypothesis on love sprang into my mind. I wanted to stand and pace while I worked it out, but since I was stuck in a booth, I settled for stuffing my legs beneath me to get some height instead. "It's not you. It's the times. When was the last time you were in a relationship?" When he looked blank, I hastily explained. "I mean a real, meaningful relationship. You probably never have. As for me?" I wrinkled up my nose, thinking. "Nope, nothing real. Now I know why!"

He stared at me. "You are the most fascinating person I've ever met."

Of course he wasn't being sincere at all, and it proved my point. "People are taking longer and longer to get married. And when they do? Well, divorces are taking over the country. And you know why? It's because once upon a time, romance meant something. People actually took the time to make that other person feel special. They brought flowers—not just flowers, the girl's favorite flower. The men knew which one it was, too. Do you know what my favorite flower is, Austen?"

He hesitated. "No."

"That's what I'm saying."

"And you're blaming modern times for that?"

"Of course I am. Now, when people date, they just do dinner and a movie. How do you get to know anyone over food and watching someone else live their life? And it's like we don't need each other anymore. We've got fast food, babysitters, our own jobs and lives. Our comforts have made us lazy and unromantic. We don't want to take the time to make moments special."

"Okay, I'll play." His lips were tight, and I knew I had struck a nerve. "Let's pretend that we were in a different time, shall we? I know what you're getting at. We're talking Jane Austen time, right?"

I nodded.

He grumbled under his breath, something about old girlfriends and being forced to watch the six-hour *Pride and Prejudice*.

"What was that?" I asked.

He flashed me a smile. "Where would you and I meet in this alternate reality?"

"A ball," I said automatically.

"So we meet at a club today instead."

"A club?" I leveled a look at him. "This isn't the movies. What kind of people do you meet at a club?"

"Usually losers. Fine, I meet you on the street."

"Oh c'mon. I'd be afraid that you'd steal my purse or that you're a stalker or something. The internet's not that much better. Remember, it's the majority of people I'm talking about here—not our confident friend Taylor—and I don't know you yet. The majority of people are like me: suspicious and afraid. No, online's not going to work for us, either."

"How about a party at a mutual friend's?" he asked.

"Okay, acceptable," I allowed. "It's close enough to a ball, but it still doesn't work the same. Assuming that you're the social type, you have *one* chance to make a good enough impression for me to accept you as a date—you have to at least seem normal. But I don't want to waste my time, so I also have to find you mildly attractive."

He gave me a slow smile. "I think I've got that one down."

"And you can't be a jerk," I matched his teasing tone, then sighed. He didn't get it. "That's why romance worked so much better back in the day," I said.

His eyes were on me. After a moment, he nudged me. "It's called a meet-cute, right? They happen all the time. They happen to me daily."

He knew about meet-cutes? Score one for Austen—those were on chick flicks. But now it was my turn to blow him away with my knowledge. I smiled. "You remember how we met, right?"

"Honestly?"

"You don't," I answered for him. "I know. Let me remind you: you said, 'Nice to meet you' and then asked me how my day was."

"Let me guess, you said, 'Fine'?"

"Brilliant," I said. "So we're the living example that not everyone has a great meet-cute."

"Hey." He held up his hands in a defeated gesture. "At least it wasn't a meet-awkward. It could've been a meet-get-out-of-my-face."

I nodded. "Sadly, there *is* a decided lack of good meet-cutes in the real world, which puts us back to our old courtship scenario. Say we didn't exactly hit it off at the ball the night before; they did this thing called a morning visit in the drawing room—it was like another chance to kick off a romance. All you'd have to do was pass the parent test, and then you could ask me for a drive in the park to get to know me better."

"And give you your favorite flower, which is?"

He got me there. "I don't know."

A dimple touched his cheek. "A cornflower," he decided for me. "They're everywhere in Cali. Very easy to find. Plus, they match your eyes. So I just pick a few on my way to your place."

I felt myself getting caught up in the romance of it. "Yeah, and then you'd ask me to dance at the next ball."

"Or a friend's party like we could do today." He was back to his same argument.

I shook my head, feeling my unruly curls escape from the sloppy knot at the back of my hair and bounce around my face. "Nobody dances nowadays. No, you'd already lose out because of that. Back then I could score two or three dances at a ball from you. Well, if you were a rake, and you would definitely be a rake."

"A rake?" he mouthed.

"A scoundrel," I translated. "And maybe after a few months of this, I'd allow you to be my official suitor."

"Or I could ask you out right away and not waste the time."

"Who does that?" I asked. "But sure, let's say you had the guts, it still doesn't work. Nowadays, you have to pass the stalker and jerk test I set up for you before I give you a first date."

"And if I pass?"

"Like I said; you take me out to dinner and we grill each other all night."

He leaned back in his seat, getting comfortable. "I can do better than that for a first date. Let's at least pretend I have an imagination. I'll take you out dancing or ice-skating or—stay with me here—to a movie. Two hours of being stuck together, we could even put the arm rest up for maximum closeness."

I liked that idea. Too bad he wasn't really thinking about me in this scenario. I also had to remind myself that Austen could get away with anything where I was concerned—especially now—but just some other normal guy that I didn't know? No, he'd have to court me for real or I would never let him touch me. "Yeah," I said, "but what if I'm tired or I hurt myself ice-skating or I have to get over the fact that you remind me of my ex? Or maybe I'm passing the time until the guy I really like asks me out?"

"You'd give me three dates at least."

"Great, so only three dates to give us the connection we girls crave, while we're both on the defensive. I mean, *oh no, this could mean marriage!* We're not friends yet, so we'll pick everything the other one does apart. We'd definitely have to give the performance of our lives to get anything going between us."

"Easy." He leaned closer to me. "It's called hormones."

"Okay," I said slowly, "but what if we actually wanted a lasting relationship? I'm talking something real here, Austen! Romance that would mean marriage and not a divorce? Believe me, fear always gets past the hormones. I know." I was pretty sure it had with us—well, if there had ever been anything with us to begin with. I wasn't so sure anymore.

"You think your way is better?"

"Yes! Courtship back in the day was fraught with romantic suspense. It gave you a chance to really get to know the other person before it got all confused with the physical. You'd ask to escort me to a play or on a drive in the park. If there were kisses, they were stolen. One or two before you asked my guardian for my hand in marriage. No more than that."

"Boring."

"Oh yeah?" I straightened. This was exactly what I was saying. "What does a kiss mean to you then?"

He was silent, thinking before he answered, "Well, it doesn't mean that I want to ask your guardian for your hand in marriage. Guys are just physical by nature. Girls need to stop confusing physical attention with a serious relationship . . ."

"Wait, excuse me? So, kissing and holding hands and whatever else you choose to do mean nothing to you?"

"It means something, just not everything you girls make it out to be." He looked flustered and grabbed my hand. "You feel that?" How could I not? I was very aware of his warmth on my skin. "Touching is just another way to get to know someone," he said

70

"And the commitment?" I asked. "Doesn't physical touch mean commitment to you?" He looked blank. Just as I thought; none of the excuses he'd found to touch me or the time we'd spent together meant as much to him as they did to me. "Wow," I said. "I knew that males and females were different—with the physical and the emotional thing. I get it, but you're so confusing. I blame you now. You're *the* courtship killer, Austen."

"Oh no, you can't pin that one on me. You're just making it a bigger deal than it needs to be. Romance isn't as hard as you want to make it."

"And you won't give true romance a chance," I countered.

"And you do? You wouldn't know what it was if it stared you in the face."

"Oh!" My whole body tingled at the accusation. He just called me out. It was so chick flick of him. Did he even know that? "What are you saying, Austen?"

"I'm saying that you only *think* you want a Jane Austen romance, but if you really had it, I know you—you'd hate it."

"Are you cursing me?" I asked—I was only half serious when I asked it, but still, I enjoyed the startled look on his face the moment the accusation left my lips.

He shrugged then gave a little laugh. "Take it as you will."

"Okay, fine," I said. "Then I'm cursing you back. I say if *you* really had a Jane Austen romance, then you would secretly love it."

"That sounds like a challenge."

"It is. We've both issued one, so now we've got to shake on it."

Austen's eyes crinkled up on the sides and he grinned broadly. "Any excuse to hold my hand."

I rolled my eyes and we shook. His hand left mine, and, just as I had thought it would, his touch left my skin all tingly. "You know we were meant to have this conversation since the day we met," he said. "Jane and Austen." He laughed, and I was sure it was at the irony until he said, "Now *that* would look good on a napkin."

The wind outside carried the sound of violins as I gaped at him. I was dimly aware that the violinists were playing a beautiful song under the late afternoon sun—a remake of a U2 hit. I wasn't aware that the musicians had been playing it before. I tried not to get caught up in it, telling myself that Austen meant nothing by what he said, when Junie came to our table and plopped my tuna sandwich in front of me. She took a little more time with Austen's oyster stew, arranging it artfully so that it looked like a true masterpiece.

Austen met my eyes. I wondered if he knew how much I wasn't enjoying this display of favoritism. "Thanks," he told Junie. She smiled and refilled our cups, then reached out and tousled his hair before she left us.

"Was that a Jane Austen romance?" he asked me under his breath.

I laughed and looked away. "No, not unless you're planning some sort of clandestine meeting after dinner." He didn't answer, and I panicked. "You aren't, are you?" After a moment he shook his head no. "You're not secretly dating?" I pressed.

He came closer to me, leaning over the table so that we were almost nose to nose. "How secret?"

"As in, you're both aware of it," I whispered back.

He shook his head and turned to his stew. He rested one hand on his cheek and watched me as if thinking. I finished up the first half of my sandwich. The violin music wafted into the little shack with the soft breeze. We were all alone at the sea of tables in the Churchell, which never happened. The scene couldn't be more idyllic for a Jane Austen romance. I didn't have the nerve to tell Austen that if we were in love this would be what it felt like.

"So," Austen broke the silence. "What's at stake? Usually there's something at stake when someone issues a challenge."

He was mixing Jane Austen up with chick flicks, but I decided to play along anyway. "I'll give you a candy bar." One of his eyebrows went up, and I shrugged. "I don't know—our hearts?"

"Sounds good."

The violins were silent a moment before starting up another song—this one had a Celtic feel. It was mysterious, alluring. It definitely set off my imagination. Even though I couldn't visualize Austen in the role of genteel suitor anymore, I could see that the shack tingled with romance. The flickering candle between us, the tavern wench.

"Can't those violins give it a rest?" Austen asked. "They've been at it the whole time we've been here."

Of course, he hated the same music that had mesmerized me. I smiled at the irony. "They're just practicing for tomorrow's brunch." I worked on the last half of my sandwich.

"Wow, I can't even think with that noise." He stood and reached over my head and closed the window shutters. "That's better, so where were we?"

"We were just about to ask for our checks." I blew out the candle between us. Between that and the violins, something had seriously played with my head.

Chapter 7

"But when a young lady is to be a heroine. . . . Something must and will happen to throw a hero in her way."

—Jane Austen, Northanger Abbey

The sky looked incredibly white the next morning, the leaves vibrantly green on the trees. No sign of thunderstorms like the news had so darkly predicted. Besides the stress of working on last-minute preparations for the brunch, it was a tremendous start to Taylor's wedding festivities. The party was well underway. The guests talked and laughed under the shade of the trees. Junie Be Fair-of-face, as Austen so liked to call her, was a hit. Her food was a culinary masterpiece—a savory selection of meats, finger food smothered in cheese or cream, and drinks with sugar iced on the rims of the glasses. Everyone complimented Junie on her beautiful assortment.

I glanced down at the white and red napkins on the table. Chuck and Taylor. Just like Austen had cruelly pointed out, the names looked terrible together. I gulped down a glass of pink lemonade to ease my suddenly dry mouth. It wasn't a sign. It didn't mean anything.

"Oh, there you are!"

I looked up to see Taylor's maid of honor coming at me like a model taking the runway with a vengeance. Her little puppy stared at me with beady, black eyes. "Are you sure there are enough chairs set up for this group?" Bertie asked.

"Yes, there should be."

"I just don't want to disappoint the bride. She is so nervous. I've never seen her this way."

I'd noticed too.

"She'd like more liver pâté on the table," Bertie added.

I nodded. "I'm on it."

"Taylor also said that she wants some strawberries. Do you have any chocolate to dip them in?"

My eyes slanted at her. Bertie wasn't using Taylor's name to get everything she wanted, was she? "I'm sure we have some chocolate," I said.

"And she's worried that flies will get into the food." Bertie waved over the food, warding off imaginary bugs. "There needs to be a better cover over this all. Taylor was worried about that." Bertie took a bite of a wafer dipped into the artichoke spinach dip. She savored it. "Mmm, definitely we need more of these."

Her eyes immediately grew big, and she swallowed it quickly before throwing her plate of goodies into a nearby trash bin. I figured out why as soon as a man approached the refreshment table. He was one of those pretty boys with blond hair and a mischievous grin to match. He wore board shorts and a tight white shirt that showed that he was also into the gym.

Bertie's attention was focused entirely on him. "Harry, it's been so long!" She batted her long lashes at him, transforming from queen bee to flirty girl in seconds. Bertie ran her hand carrying her wedding ring down the length of his muscular arm, and he turned on her with a laugh. "I am so glad to see you," she cried. "Actually I'm thrilled to see you—there was nothing else worth looking at before you came to the party."

His smile only got bigger and bigger as she proceeded to flirt outrageously with him, which forced me to do double-takes on her wedding ring. Each time, I was surprised to see that it was still there.

"Bertie!" a familiar voice hailed her. It was Mary. The bridesmaid was gorgeous with her ponytail down and her hair washed, but she still had a pale, drawn look about her. She came at us with an uneven walk.

Bertie took an involuntary step backward. "There you are," Mary called out. "Bertie. Bertie! Taylor is looking everywhere for you. She wants you to meet her mother. Mrs. Weston just got here. I can't get over how much she looks like Taylor—she hasn't changed at all. I thought she'd be all old and ugly now, but she's gorgeous!"

"Oh!" Bertie smoothed her hair and shocked me by handing me her teacup-sized puppy. "Just take her for a walk," she said. "My baby doesn't like sand in her fur, so don't go to the beach. And keep that dreadful cat away from her."

Before I could argue or ask for the rat-bear's name this time around, Bertie was off, her high heels clicking furiously against the pavement like a herd of zombies was after her. Mary reached for her tissues in her purse as soon as she spied the puppy. Her eyes flicked up to mine. "Hey, are you the event coordinator, too?"

"Yes."

"Then can you tell me why Taylor invited the Hayters?" She made a face that pinched her sour expression into something more unfortunate than before and sighed heavily, her hot breath hitting my face in an explosion of seafood aromas. "Well, there's no avoiding it now," she muttered. "There are so many people here, I guess. I can only hope the Hayters won't find me in all these bodies. I don't want to be seen talking to them."

I wasn't sure why Mary thought I was better company than some of Taylor's guests. She caught my shoulders in her claw-like grip and steered me around so that she could use my back to hide from the infamous Hayters while still getting at the refreshments. All the while she kept up a running narrative. "Henrietta was our roommate back in the day at Yale. And now look at her. She married a plumber."

"Mary." I held up Bertie's puppy. "You're getting dog hair in your hors d'oeuvres."

She gasped and let me go. I turned and, too late, met the eyes of the handsome stranger Bertie had been flirting with earlier. His blue eyes melted into mine. Before he could try to talk to me too, I gave him my cheesiest smile and disappeared into the crowd, intending to have some words with Taylor.

I was *not* a dog walker. And I did not help guests hide from other guests. Taylor had better tell her friends to back off. Not only that, but if I didn't convince Taylor to let Dancey stay at the Kellynch, I'd have to give up my room and sleep under Ann-Marie's piano tonight.

"Jane!" Taylor found me instead. She tugged on my arm. My complaints died on my lips as soon as I saw her face. She looked white with terror. Her mascara dripped down her eyes. "Freddy isn't at his post anymore. My friends are parking their own cars!" She dropped a huge pile of keys into my hand. "The cars are just everywhere. They're going to get towed soon if we don't do something. I called for a valet service, but they haven't gotten here. If Dancey drives here from the airport and has to park himself . . ." she let her horrified thought drop dramatically.

"Yeah, yeah. I'm on it," I said. "And Taylor?"

"Yes?"

Now was the time to tell her that Dancey could not have my room, but looking at her stricken face, I hesitated. Instead, I made a rubbing motion under my eyes, and she immediately took the hint and rubbed her face free of mascara. I turned and headed for the parking lot of the resort, puppy tucked under my armpit.

"Austen!" I rushed through the front lobby to the checkout counter. Austen was back at his laptop. Ann-Marie or Junie had just been visiting; the evidence was the pretty little array of food that sat like offerings all around him. I handed him the puppy.

"Oh no, no," he said.

"I have to. The valet service didn't show up and I'm in charge of parking cars."

"You? Really?" He was startled enough that I managed to get the puppy into his hands. "You can't even parallel park."

"Yes, I can!" I backed out of the lobby before he could try to return the little rat-bear.

He held up the cute little thing. "I'll find it a good home," he threatened.

"You do that!" I closed the door between us and headed for the car drop-off zone. "Any home would be a better home than the one she has now," I said under my breath—and almost ran into the valet that the service had sent. He reached out to steady me. My eyes ran over him. He was tall, had mesmerizing blue eyes, tousled black hair—I could only compare him to a beautiful, model version of Austen. He wore the signature black of a valet but looked better in dress code than any of them ever did. His eyebrow arched at me, and I laughed nervously. Since I had my feet firmly beneath me now, I pulled away from his helpful hands, noticing the dark scowl on his face. He really had the starchy valet act down.

I cleared my throat. "They only sent one of you?" I asked—it came out a little shaky.

He looked startled at the question. "Usually that's enough, so I've been told."

The moment he talked, he had my interest. His voice sounded like Bigley's, but not quite. "Hey, where are you from?" I asked.

"I grew up in Massachusetts, moved when I was eight." He stopped to stare at me suspiciously. "You want the short bio or the long one?"

I shook my head. I had heard that easterners were more stand-offish. Still, it was really attractive—his mannerisms brought a lot of Jane Austen movies to mind. I didn't have time to think too much about it. "That's super neat." Suddenly I was aware of how west coast I sounded. I decided that now wasn't the time to impress anybody. "Okay, well, come with me."

He hesitated a moment and followed after me. This guy had to be new. It was like he wasn't used to orders. I just hoped that he could still park cars. I reached the parking lot and groaned when I saw the mess. It was just as Taylor had described. It looked like one expensive traffic jam—BMW's, Porsches, Mercedes. The guests had parked everywhere they weren't supposed to. Parking enforcement would make bank if they found this.

"Okay, we have to work fast." I turned to my reluctant valet. "If the police get here, we're dead!"

"That's a bit dramatic, don't you think?"

I laughed. "You have no idea. Taylor is freaking out." At the mention of her name, his face cleared of expression. Of course, he didn't know who Taylor was. But he was getting paid, so I really didn't know why I felt compelled to explain anything.

"And who are you?" he asked in that stuffy way of his.

"Jane." I divided the car keys and gave him half. "Taylor's in charge. She told me to find you so we could take care of this."

He accepted the keys but acted like it was beneath him. I tried not to let it bother me. "No worries," I said. "I'll help you. I'm really sorry; this is going to be a nightmare."

"It's not quite what I expected."

"Sure, I know. It's just . . ." Another Lexus came around the bend and I groaned, snatching back the keys from him. "Actually, can you take care of that guest first?" Without waiting for his reply, I left him and headed for the nearest Audi and fiddled through the keys, trying to find the one that matched the luxury car in front of me. Only a few of the keys had the make and model engraved on them. As a last resort, I tried to press the unlock button on the keys, feeling like I was on a game show where the right key won me a car.

The last key unlocked the car in front of me with a neat little click. I shrieked. "Yes!" I jumped up in excitement just as the cute valet drove up next to me in the silver Lexus.

His gaze was focused, almost sultry. I had to remind myself again that we were on the job and to try not to romanticize him. I pointed to the trees above North Abbey. "We have to park up there on Oakham Mount, on the hill."

He gave me a quizzical look. "Taylor really asked us to do this?"

I didn't know why he kept questioning me. "Yeah. It's some weird city code. But if you just follow me up the road, I'll show you where."

I opened the red cherry beauty and slid onto the soft leather seats. This was possibly the nicest car that I had ever sat in—let alone driven. Putting the key into the ignition, I turned it and nothing happened. I checked to see if the car was in gear, but that wasn't the problem. I tried it again. Nothing. The beautiful cherry was dead.

The valet poked his head out of his car. "Is there a problem?"

I would've rolled the window down, but without power, I had to throw the door open instead. "It's dead. I can't get it to go!"

"You want me to push?" he asked.

"Very funny."

He stepped out of his car and leaned over me to push a button next to the steering wheel. The car started on demand. My mouth fell open. "You're kidding? Why would someone put a button like that into a car?"

A smile tickled the corner of his lips. "They're in the latest models now."

The valet was more experienced than I gave him credit for. And he was still leaning over me. And though I enjoyed it, we had a whole parking lot of cars to get through. "Thanks," I said. "Let's do this."

He squeezed my shoulder, and I made some sort of surprised sound as he went back to his car. I shut the door, my emotions all over the place. The faint scent of the valet's cologne still caressed my nose. I shook my head to break out of the spell it put over me and drove up the hill to the empty parking lot. The valet parked beside me, and I got out, motioning back to the trail that led down the hill. "It's going to be a hike from here. We're getting our exercise today."

"I don't doubt it." There was a hint of bitterness in his tone.

We walked back through the little Maple Grove trail while I kept stealing peeks at him. He was tall, athletic, and confident, not quite who I had expected to spend the morning with. "Well," I said, breaking the uncomfortable silence, "now I know why you do what you do. These cars are nice to drive." He gave me a long stare in reply and I felt my shoulders tense up. *Wow, he blew hot and cold.* I gave myself a mental shake and tried again. "What's the nicest car you've ever driven?"

He hesitated and for the longest time I thought he wouldn't answer, until he said, "A Lamborghini Reventon."

"What? Those even exist?" I laughed. "Where did you get a hold of one of those?"

"Paris."

"No way. First Massachusetts then Paris. You've been everywhere." After another wary look from him, I laughed. "Careful, I just might get your life history out of you."

That coaxed a smile from him, but no reply. I filled my cheeks with air and blew out. It was hard work getting the guy to talk. I gave up and, instead, opted for putting my hands in my pockets and pretending to be interested in the scenery.

"Surely you've traveled?" he asked.

His attempt at conversation startled me and I glanced over at him. "Just California. I haven't been anywhere. I mean, I like California—I'm from Sacramento—but I'm a little jealous of Taylor right now. I'd love to try out Britain . . ." my voice trailed off when he seemed to withdraw into himself again. I had to remember not to mention Taylor anymore. He must consider the boss the enemy. "Anyway," I said, "It's probably better that I don't travel the world."

"Why?"

"Well, because I don't want to be disappointed." I remembered Ann-Marie's theory and expounded on it. "It's like talking to a cute guy . . ." my voice trailed off. The new guy did not want to hear any theories on dating—especially Ann-Marie's.

"You know you have to finish that sentence, right?"

I turned to him. "We park the cars and then I'll finish that sentence. All right?"

He burst out laughing and met my eyes, shaking his head. It was like all his walls broke with that one action. Now he looked adorable. "You've got a deal, Jane."

I hid a smile. The sound of my name with that accent was better than chocolate. I turned back to the trail. Freddy had better not come back. I was really going to enjoy this morning with his replacement.

The clouds had gathered, getting bleaker and grumblier than an arthritic old man, but still the promised rain didn't come. We worked steadily through the cars, making neat metallic rows in the parking lot, but then it got a little tricky when the lot filled up. I stared through my windshield, trying to figure out our next move, when my new friend walked up to my window. I rolled it down and he gave me the bad news. "You'll have to parallel park to the side." I gritted my teeth and considered surrendering the expensive car to him, when he tilted his head. "You can parallel park, surely?" he asked.

"No!" I threw my hands up. "Could you do it for me?"

He shook his head. "Every girl must learn her way around a Mercedes."

I let out a little chuckle. The valet had been talking in this elevated speech all afternoon. "Yes," I said, "but she should *not* learn to do it in a Mercedes."

"She should *especially* learn in a Mercedes." He walked ahead of the car and guided me to park with his hands. I sighed and drove up to him. "Turn the wheel to the left, Jane. All the way, now reverse." I obeyed. "Now straighten it out."

"Are you sure?" It looked like I would hit the BMW in front of me if I tried it.

"Yes, straighten out. Turn the wheel to the right."

I did it, expecting to hear the crash at any moment. Instead the Mercedes cradled nicely into the spot between the BMW in front and the palm tree behind me. As soon as I was safely parked, I squealed and shoved open the door, leaping out of my seat, laughing and jumping. "Never before." I gave a fist pump. "That was my first time!" I almost reached out to hug my mentor, but threw my hands behind my back before I broke all professional boundaries.

He crushed me with a hug of his own and swung me around. Soon we were laughing. We joked and teased each other on our way down the Maple Grove trail for the fifty-something-or-other time that morning.

"I know it's really lame to be so excited about parallel parking," I said, "but someone was just teasing me about it and now I just proved myself." I made a happy skip and started walking faster. "That felt really good." I turned, seeing the valet's blue eyes on me. They looked as warm as I felt. We were definitely having a moment. I opened my mouth. "Thanks . . ." and then I stumbled over my next words when I realized that I didn't know his name.

I didn't know his name!

It would be awkward to ask now, especially after we just had a *moment!* I racked my brain on how to get it out of him. I'd get the valet to sign his name on North Abbey's receipt. That's what I'd do. If I was even bolder, I'd get him to put his number into my phone.

I wasn't that bold.

"Jane," he said. "You can finish your sentence now."

I almost thought he had noticed that I didn't know his name, until I remembered that I had promised if we finished parking the cars to tell him why I didn't like talking to cute guys. A few raindrops dripped down my face and I sucked in my breath. The rain made everything around us more beautiful. Junie would've set up the tents

83

by now to protect the brunch or Taylor would have another meltdown. I was glad I wasn't there for it. Lightning streaked across the sky, and the rain broke over us.

My nameless friend shuffled out of his sleek, black jacket and without asking, threw it over my head to cover me from it. He kept his arms around me and I moved closer to him, liking the feel of his strong arms around me. Surveying the parking lot, I saw that there was one more car left to park. It was a Jaguar. We had saved the best for last.

"I'll tell you what I was going to say after we park this one," I said. Maybe then I could distract him from my answer. It was embarrassing now that I liked him. I searched for the last keys in my purse.

He pulled them out of his jeans' pocket instead. "Want a ride?"

Grinning, I nodded. He opened the door for me and I slid into yet another beautiful car. He shut the door behind me, cutting the rain off as he made his way around the front to the driver's side. I leaned back, for a moment pretending we were in a phaeton drawn by two smart horses and we were on our way to a ball. I smiled at the silliness. I didn't have to imagine anything better than this moment. I had my own prince charming right here.

The door swung open silently on greased hinges and my attractive friend got in, the rain sliding down his nose and cheeks. I really wished I knew his name. He pushed all sorts of buttons on the console. This car had some special features. Seriously? Will Dancey himself probably owned this thing—no, rented it. Not even he would buy a Jaguar just for a visit.

I sighed. "I can hardly wait for this week to be over."

"Too much wedding for you too, aye?"

"Yeah." I looked away. "I just thought that it would be a chance of a lifetime to plan Taylor's wedding, but it's kind of a nightmare. Don't get me wrong. I love her. She's become one of my best friends since I came to work here; but sometimes she wants the impossible, and I don't know if I can give it to her."

He found my cold hands and pressed them between his fingers. "If anyone can do it, you can. You parallel parked, remember?"

The memory was enough to lift my mood. His hand left mine, and I stared at my fingers in sudden awareness—only Austen's touch could set my skin tingling like that. The valet started the ignition. A song from the radio blared through the surround-sound speakers.

Don't go.

Dancing through London in a field of poppies.

Red like the color of your lips.

You're all I see.

Don't go.

"Poppies," I groaned. It was Dancey's latest hit, but it definitely didn't fit my mood. I met the valet's eyes, and our fingers ran into each other on our way to turn it off. After a surprised laugh, he caught my hand in his and switched off the music himself.

"Thank you." I made a face. "I'm definitely not in the mood for *more* Will Dancey."

"What?" He broke into another smile. "Why not?"

I lifted a shoulder. "I don't know; life is so awesome right now and I don't want to ruin my mood."

"Predictable tragedy isn't really your cup of tea?"

I shrugged. "Maybe if Dancey stopped dating supermodels and dated someone down to earth, he'd be happier."

"Are you volunteering?"

I laughed. "No." I watched the rain slide down the windshield. He hadn't started driving yet.

"No?" he prodded.

I glanced back at him. He really wanted to know why? I flashed a smile. "I'm not comfortable living the glamorous life. I live in an attic and wear flannel to bed. Just being in his car is almost too much for me." I laughed. "No, really, I think this is *his* car. Let's just park it and get out of it."

He tilted his head at me. "*His* car?"

"The guy who wrote this song." I snorted out another laugh. "He's in the wedding party, so this car could actually be his. Ironic, I know. Anyway, I don't care if the car is insured for more than my mom and yours put together. I just want to get out and back on the trail with you. Expensive things make me nervous."

"Jane?"

"Yeah?"

His mouth firmed, and he peeled out of the parking lot, faster than I liked, but I breathed a sigh of relief as he took us out of the driveway away from North Abbey. That was, until he drove the opposite way from the Oakham Mount parking lot. "Whoa." My hands slid to the side of my seat to hold on. "Where are we going with *Will Dancey's* car?"

"Let's take it for a little spin. He'll never know."

"What?" I gritted my teeth. I didn't know this guy was the daredevil type. I shouldn't have said anything.

"You hungry?" he asked.

I found my seatbelt and clicked it on. "No."

"I am."

"What! No! We are not leaving North Abbey. Turn around right now."

"You said you wanted to do a little traveling. We could go to Vegas. Cross state lines."

"I think that would make this a felony. You're not serious, right?"

"Of course I am. Let's live a little. There's a little 'Chapel of Love' off the strip. It's my favorite. We could go meet up with the minister there."

"Hey! Not funny!"

His hands relaxed on the wheel, and I tried not to steal the steering from him. "You want to go back to the party?" he asked.

I was feeling a little ill at ease. "Yes. Most definitely yes."

"Then you have to promise me something."

Years of sibling training had taught me that was a bad idea. "You tell me what you're thinking first, and then I'll promise."

"I park this car if you let me take you for another drive."

My eyes went to his hands. The sinews stood out. They were nice hands, but a little too strong. I looked at his face, and I jumped when I saw that he was looking at me. His eyes weren't dangerous—they were crinkled in laughter. He had a strange sense of humor. But besides a rebellious streak, I didn't sense any killer vibes coming from him. In fact, I liked most everything about him. "When we're in *your* car," I said, "I'll go anywhere with you."

"I'll hold you to that."

"Wait!" I held up my hand. "I mean, as long as you let me drive."

He swung us into the road that made a circle around North Abbey to find the parking lot from the other side. We had been closer to the Oakham Mount parking lot than I thought. He turned off the ignition. "Now, finish that sentence you started, Miss Jane."

My mouth fell open. He remembered after all that? For a guy, that was saying a lot. After his little distraction, even I had forgotten that I owed him more information. I found myself playing with my hair—this was the strangest *moment* I had ever shared with anyone. "I don't like talking to cute guys," I said, "because it's always a disappointment. They're never as interesting after you have a real conversation with them, but," I laughed and turned away, "it was a little different with you."

Okay, heart-to-heart was over. I jerked open the door of the Jaguar and jumped out. We walked in companionable silence through Maple Grove back to the resort. I still didn't know his name, but I had a plan. The valets got their checks in the lobby. I just had to get my new friend to sign something. We had already scheduled a date and I couldn't call him, "*Hey You*" forever.

"Stupid Freddy," I grumbled. "I can't believe he didn't show up to work."

The valet shrugged. "I'm glad he didn't. I wouldn't have gotten to know you otherwise."

I flushed happily. We had reached the front door to North Abbey and I reached for it, but he wouldn't let me touch it. He gallantly swung it open for me, and I walked inside, dripping wet and wearing someone else's jacket—I remembered that final touch when Austen looked up from his laptop.

His eyes met mine, and then he glanced over at my companion. Austen looked confused. I dropped the collection of keys on the counter. "We got them all, no thanks to Freddy," I said.

"You got them all?" Austen's eyes veered to my companion again.

"Yeah." I thrust my thumb in the valet's direction. "We should hire him to replace Freddy. He's pretty good."

Taylor dashed into the lobby from the lounge, shrieking. "There you are! I was so worried." She opened her arms and I got ready for a hug—she never hugged me usually, but I braced for it anyway.

Her arms went around the guy next to me. "We called the airport. They said that your flight was in. We should've found you a service. You didn't have to drive. Why didn't you answer your phone?"

"It died on the plane," he said. "They mean business when they say to turn off your mobiles." His eyes found mine over Taylor's shoulder.

My heart thudded too loudly in my chest. I was pretty sure what his name was now. Austen coughed into his hand, his expressive face telling me what a mistake I had made.

"I thought that we had lost our best man." Taylor pulled away from her hug, still squeezing both his arms in her hands. "I see that you've met my friends already."

A dimple formed in his cheek. "Yes, lovely, lovely people."

He only looked at me, and I felt my stomach drop. I wasn't sure how to escape. It was only a matter of time before he blurted to Taylor just how much of a welcome party he had received at my hands.

"I'm glad you met Austen already," Taylor said; then she gave Austen a mischievous smile. "He'll be helping you put on a bachelor party for Bigley."

"Huh?" Austen hadn't been paying attention to Taylor—his eyes were on me—but at her words he gave her a look that meant she was overstepping her bounds again.

She shrugged with a sheepish grin. "I'm sorry, Austen. I didn't ask either you or Dancey before now, but who else could put on an amazing party but the two of you? Surely you don't expect Bigley's stepbrother to do it?" She giggled at the inside joke that I didn't understand. Not waiting for anyone else to respond, she steered our handsome friend past the foosball table, talking a mile a minute.

"Oh look," he interrupted her in that delicious British accent that I had foolishly mistaken as one from Massachusetts. "You have a foosball table here as well."

She grimaced. "Don't remind me of that game. It was awful. You made me look so silly." She turned to us with a conspiring laugh. "He pretended like he didn't know anything about the game and then he pulled a fast one on me."

He smiled. "I let you win."

"Dancey!" Bigley shouted.

And there was my big confirmation, not like I needed it. Bigley came through the door. His face had gone serious. "Is that what you did to steal my fiancé's heart? You lowlife." Dancey swung around to face his friend, his back to us. Bigley glared. "Why did you come anyway?"

Dancey's shoulders stiffened. "Because you invited me to come to your big, stupid, ugly, fat wedding!"

Bigley broke into a huge grin, and soon the two were hugging and slapping each other on the back. "How are you, old boy?" Bigley asked.

Taylor's and my eyes met in confusion. She broke away from them and joined Austen and me at the counter. "Jane," she asked under her breath. "Where did you decide to put Dancey?"

"Uh, yes." I touched my wet hair, knowing the curls I had taken such pains to straighten had gone frizzy. "We're putting him in the Morland Loft." I refused to look at Austen but guessed he'd think it was pretty funny that I'd be losing my room to the rock star.

"We're putting Dancey in the Rosing's House," Austen corrected quickly. "That's where he belongs."

My heart skipped a beat the same time Taylor's expression twisted into abject horror. She turned to her husband-to-be for confirmation. "But, but, Chuck, aren't your grandparents staying in the Rosing's House, dearest?"

Bigley abandoned his welcome party to come to his fiancé's side. He patiently rubbed her back. "As I was telling Austen earlier, hon, my grandparents are frail and want a quiet place to sleep. Austen suggested they go to the Kellynch across the way. It's much less drafty for them over there, and I agreed."

Austen had come to my rescue. Not only had he suggested that we use the competition, he even blackened the name of his parents' resort to do it—North Abbey was drafty? It certainly wasn't. Taylor's chin lifted, and she pierced Austen with an accusing glare.

"Hey, don't look at me like that," he said. "I'll make this easy on you. I work with Dancey on that special project that we talked about earlier, and you work with the Kellynch. Got it?"

She agreed more readily than I thought she would. "Fine. Great." She clapped her hands. The glint in her eyes showed she liked a good bargain. "Rosing's house it is." She turned to her guests. "Let's drop off your bags there, Dancey . . . before Austen changes his mind. Spit-spot, I'll ring for some tea."

Chapter 8

"I could easily forgive his pride, if he had not mortified mine."

—Jane Austen, *Pride and Prejudice*

"Will Dancey?" I asked. "*The* Will Dancey."

Austen looked down at the guest list. "Willard," he corrected.

"Willard?" I was going to pretend that really wasn't his name—it wasn't romantic at all. It had only been a minute since Taylor had walked off with my new valet, and I was freaking out.

Austen's eyes danced with bottled-up amusement, and I realized that he thought this was funny. He put down the lid of his laptop and studied me over it. "Looks like you've had your meet-cute."

"Oh no!" I held up my hand. "That was a meet-awkward. That was a . . ." I struggled, trying to remember how Austen had put it before.

"Meet-get-out-of-my-face?" he asked with a snicker. "Did you really make him park all the cars with you?"

"I . . . hey! It was an honest mistake. The service was supposed to send some valets. Why didn't any of them show?"

"Oh." Austen scrubbed at the grizzle on his face, looking a little sheepish. "Maybe that one was my fault. Taylor might've told me to call a service."

"And when I ran through waving a puppy around that didn't remind you to do it?"

Austen fiddled with the guest list. "I told Ann-Marie to do it. And then when I saw you out there with your rock star, I kind of

figured you had it handled. I didn't see his face until you two walked
in . . ."

"Just great," I complained. I realized something was missing.
"Hey, where's the puppy?"

"Ann-Marie."

And so the puppy went the way of the valet service. They were
both kind of floating out in space somewhere with Ann-Marie. This
was so typical.

Austen eyed my new acquisition that hung around my shoulders.
Dancey's jacket didn't exactly fit, but it kept me warm. His jaw
tightened. "It's not a total loss," he said, "looks like you got a jacket
out of it."

I leaned my head back and groaned, then trudged over to the
checkout counter, throwing my arms down over it. "Everything is
ruined. He was like this regular guy. A little bit stuffy, but . . . we were
actually having fun. We had this *moment*, you know."

"Moment?"

"The moment," I explained, feeling the pit in my stomach get
deeper, "is when a guy looks into your eyes and you look into his, and
something just happens between you—it's electric."

He frowned. "A telepathic moment? Sounds too sci-fi for you."

I rolled my eyes. I knew he wouldn't like *the moment* explainer—it
reeked too much of cheesy romance. "It doesn't matter now because
it's ruined. I can't believe it! We even set up a date together."

"You'd think the English accent would've tipped you off."

I groaned. "He said he was from Massachusetts."

"He lied?"

"No, Wiki it! I'm sure it's true. He was just some innocent
bystander dragged into my life. Maybe one of his parents came from
the UK and the family moved back to the motherland when he was
just a kid, I don't know. He honestly had no idea what this crazy
woman was doing to him. I don't think that he knew I had mixed him
up with someone else until . . . oh." My eyes grew wide with the

horror. "I dissed his song. It was on the radio. I can't believe I did that!"

Austen was laughing again. "And?"

I gave him a look of disgust. For a guy who said he didn't like girl talk, Austen was sure eating this up. "*And* he started driving really fast, and I thought he was stealing Will Dancey's car. I practically had to threaten him with jail—he said he wanted to take me to Vegas to get hitched. And he said he wouldn't take the car back until . . ." My sinking heart came back up to the surface and then shot into the clouds somewhere.

"Until what?" Austen prodded.

"I said I'd go out with him."

Austen's expression darkened. "Did you agree to that?"

"Um, yeah."

"Wow, you're the most stubborn girl I know and you decided to give some valet a chance because he threatened to take off with you in his stolen car?"

"It wasn't stolen." I smiled at the memory, seeing it all through a different perspective. Dancey had known I thought he was the valet when he asked me out.

Austen snapped his fingers in front of my eyes. "But you thought it was stolen. Didn't you think that was creepy? What happened to being suspicious of strangers?"

"Hey!" I defended myself. "It doesn't count when an accent is involved. It's an automatic point in his favor. And we had this moment. *A lot of moments, actually.* He showed me how to parallel park, and his hand kept touching mine. He said if anyone could pull off Taylor's wedding, I could. It was better than 'Roman Holiday'—I'm sure you don't know that movie, but well, he had these walls at first and then he really opened up . . ."

I knew that I had finally lost Austen when his eyes clouded over. "You know I'm not a girl, right? I don't want every detail."

93

Oh, now he didn't. "C'mon." I switched to my best southern Belle accent and drawled out, "You don't find accents attractive, sugarlamb?"

Austen took a moment to put his jaw away, and I was proud of my ability to actually reach him. "Is that the accent you used to get him to fawn all over you out there?" he asked, looking annoyed. "It all makes sense now." Mister meandered over the countertop, and he shoved the cat back. I noticed that Austen's eyes had a tint of red to them, and, too late, I remembered his allergies. Maybe some of that coughing hadn't been sniggering at my misfortunes. I almost took a moment to feel bad.

"All right, I'm sorry to mix you up in all this girl talk," I said. "I'll spare you the gory details in the future, but he's British! That makes a guy a hundred times more attractive."

"You said you didn't know that he was British."

I must've felt it—an incarnate sense found in girls everywhere. All my favorite heroes in Jane Austen movies had that accent; it was why girls everywhere couldn't get enough of them. And when Dancey talked he sounded just like—"You know what he is?" I got excited. "He's a total Darcy! No joke!"

"Dancey?"

I gave a little giggle when I realized the similarities in their names. There were other parallels too, like the differences in our social status and how I had misjudged him. "No, I said Darcy! He's only the most romantic man in all of Jane Austen-ville."

"Seriously . . . *that guy?*"

Yes. The king of all Jane Austen heroes—when Jane Austen invented him, she invented my heart. I settled onto the couch next to the silent TV. I flipped through the movies that Ann-Marie kept downstairs—most of them were romantic comedies and BBCs. "What do you know about Darcy?" I asked Austen.

He picked up his laptop and stuffed it into his backpack. "I happened to date a girl who made me watch the six hour *Pride and Prejudice*. It was traumatizing."

"Let me guess. You broke up over it."

He made a low groaning sound and joined me on the couch, making himself comfortable next to me. "I wasn't Darcy."

I smiled dreamily when I imagined Dancey's face in front of me—he blinked dark lashes over sober eyes. I sighed. "No one is."

"Except Dancey, it looks like." Austen slipped out one of Ann-Marie's movies, staring at the cover—the actress's hair was split down the middle with two sausage curls on either side of her head. It was a horrible look. He grimaced. "I don't get your bonnet movies. Why do you love them?"

"You wouldn't understand." Remembering that I had a wedding to put on, I dug my cell phone out and texted to follow up on the transportation to the rehearsal tomorrow. Freddy better show up tomorrow, or he was fired. I didn't care if he was some fancy decorated General's son. I glanced up at Austen, seeing that he was waiting for my explanation. "There are two kinds of people in this world. Jane fans and Jane haters. I'm a fan. You're a hater. I get it."

He pushed *Sense and Sensibility* back into the empty slot next to *Mansfield Park*. "I don't know the author's life story, but you're right, I'm pretty sure I hate her. Because of her, guys like Willard Dancey . . ."

"Will," I corrected quickly.

Too late, he caught on to my aversion. "Willard," he emphasized, "is just some snob that girls romanticize to be something deeper and more interesting than he really is."

"Girls do that for every guy," I said. "I'm sure lots of girls do that for you." Me, *for instance*. "You should thank Jane Austen and every other chick flick out there for making you look so good!"

I texted a reminder to our restaurant contact next. We had to make sure that our little budding performers from the wedding rehearsal were fed properly. Austen snatched my phone from me. "Did you hear me?" he asked. "The world is full of ordinary people with ordinary romance."

I smiled when I realized that I had finally found Austen's buttons. He seemed more bothered about this than I was. "People aren't ordinary to the ones they love, and their love isn't ordinary to them," I said.

"It isn't like what you see in the movies either," he countered. "If you keep thinking that love will be like that, then you won't find it. Ever."

"You keep saying that! But you know what? I think I just proved to you today that chick flicks *can* happen."

He mumbled something that sounded like, *"We'll see where that goes."*

"What? You know I'm not deaf, right?" I snatched my phone back from him. "Remember our little challenge? I did my part. I'm supposed to see love staring me in the face and like it, and you're supposed to enjoy a true romance. Your turn, Austen. I'm tired of doing all the work around here. Go find love."

"Jane!"

I shot to my feet at the sound of Taylor's voice. Austen stayed where he was, glowering. Taylor stalked into the room. If I ever thought Taylor looked upset before this then I was wrong—this was Taylor upset. She was shaking, and it could only mean one thing: she knew what I had done to her fiancé's best man. I forced my voice to remain steady. "Yes, Taylor?"

"You have to help me."

I gulped. "Right. That's why I'm here." I stepped around the couch and realized I was still wearing Will Dancey's incriminating jacket. I unobtrusively peeled it off my already-burning shoulders and tried to set it on the back of the couch before Taylor looked too closely at it.

"Something is missing!" Taylor turned in a circle. "I've tried to ignore it, but I can't."

Ever since I'd started working on Taylor's wedding, this had been the usual complaint. Though I was tired of trying to please Taylor, it was a relief that this had nothing to do with Dancey. "What's missing?" I asked.

"I don't know. I can't put my finger on it."

I couldn't help it. I turned to Austen for some kind of help. He looked clueless.

"Okay." I licked my dry lips and tried to reason with Taylor. "Does it have to do with the reception?"

Her face cleared. "Flowers." She snapped her fingers like she had it figured out. "They had to special order the Calla lilies."

"Lilies?" Austen asked. "You went for lilies?"

"Don't start with me, Austen," she said. "I have enough on my plate without hearing you get on my back for what kind of flowers I choose for my own wedding!" She turned a full circle. "We ordered the lights two weeks ago, right?"

"Yeah," I said. "I just talked to the lighting guy yesterday. He's ready to go."

"The photographer?" she asked.

"All set. I met up with her today."

She put her finger to her lips, muttering aloud as she thought of everything that could possibly go wrong at the reception.

"What about the T-Rex?" Austen asked.

Taylor looked confused. "A T-Rex? You mean, like a dinosaur?"

"Yeah, you forgot about scoring one of those really tough-looking dinosaurs for the party. I saw one at a reception once. I mean, not a real one, but one of those cool life-size, robotic ones. Nothing screams romance more than a big dinosaur."

"Are you saying that I'm overreacting, Austen?" her voice was cold.

He stood up and wrapped a comforting arm around Taylor's shoulder. "You're not being yourself, Taylor. You're calm, collected, cool under pressure—that's the Taylor we love. Stop stressing. You're here to do bride things—like eat food and kiss Bigley."

She stared at him, but I knew she hadn't processed a thing he'd said when she wriggled away to mutter, "I know what's wrong. The rehearsal tomorrow. Austen, I want you to be Chuck. Jane?"

"No." Austen shook his head. "She will not be you. I don't know where you're going with this, but if you think you're going to play dolls with us, you can forget that now."

I shot him a warning look—I didn't care if Taylor wanted to strap us to mini chairs and pour rank water from tiny teacups down our throats. If it got that crazed look off her face, I'd do anything. "Where do you want me, Taylor?"

"Stand here." She pulled me to stand next to Austen and studied us, her eyebrows lifting while she mumbled like a mad scientist in the middle of an experiment. Austen stood tense beside me, and I was quickly catching on to his nervousness. "Take her hand, Austen," Taylor ordered.

He hesitated a moment, then complied. He leaned over my ear to whisper, "She had better not make us kiss."

I choked on a laugh, but unlike me, Taylor didn't catch his aside. She was completely distracted. "Chuck is wearing grey with subtle pinstripes," she said. "The flowers are pink and white. Dancey has the rings. I'm missing something!"

"Love?" Austen whispered.

I elbowed him this time. "Stop it."

"What?" he mouthed. Then a little louder, said, "Taylor wouldn't hear a cement truck crash through the lobby—she's so caught up in the *romance* of the moment. Right, Taylor?"

Taylor glanced up distractedly, then pulled out a notebook and started writing furiously. She pulled open her phone and blasted the

"Wedding March" over us as she paced. Before too long, she disappeared into the lounge and plunked a few notes on the piano.

I closed the door between the two rooms to block Taylor from us. "Stop saying stuff like that, Austen!" It was really hard making a coherent argument with our hands together, and I jerked my fingers from his. Taylor was in the other room, and I decided the best thing was to tease Austen into a better mood. "Anyway, why do you care so much? You don't have a crush on Taylor, do you?"

He straightened. "I'm concerned about Taylor as a friend."

"That's sweet," I said. "Let Chuck worry about it. He's the man who *loves* her."

My light words didn't exactly have the effect that I wanted. The muscle on Austen's jaw twitched. Finally, he broke his silence. "Storms aren't romantic," he said under his breath.

That wasn't what I expected him to say. It startled me into replying, "Huh?"

"It's one of the lies from romantic movies that our little namesake Jane Austen started," he said. "What perfect man did our author friend marry anyway? I bet he wasn't half as good as Darcy."

"She never married."

"What? Why?" he sounded sarcastic. "No man could measure up to her creation?"

"How could you be so insensitive? Did you expect her to marry someone she didn't love?"

He made a face. "Wasting away from a broken heart isn't a happy ending. Sprained ankles aren't romantic either. Blizzards, debilitating colds, broken down cars. They all go under the same category. Not romantic."

"They *are* if someone saves you," I argued. "Preferably on a white horse."

"Oh yeah, like what happened to you last week?"

He knew very well that I had never seen a white horse up close—they were in short supply around here. "It doesn't even have to be white," I said, ". . . or a horse. It could be a beat-up car owned by a really nice guy who I just happen to like."

"Talk about settling," he said. "Who's the last knight in shining armor who fixed a flat for you?"

I refused to answer. There were too many times to count where I had been stranded and had to help myself. I took a deep breath. "That's only one lie," I allowed.

"Cinderella doesn't happen either," he said.

I smirked. "You're not even talking Jane Austen anymore."

"Rich guy drops everything for poor girl. Sound familiar?"

I frowned. I was particularly attached to *Pride and Prejudice* right now, and he knew it. "Aristocracy marries just that—other aristocracy," he said. "Social stations mean a lot more than you think. When have you gone for that stinky guy on the bus? And you know what else?" he asked. "Flirting gets you everywhere."

This whole conversation was putting me on edge. Why was Austen trying to rip my happy little rug out from under me? "I don't even know where you're going with that one," I said. "Are you asking me to flirt more?"

"I'm saying that it doesn't matter how deserving, quirky, or nice a girl is—the guy won't see her as a possibility until she lets him know she's interested. It also helps if she does her hair once in a while. A meet-cute only gets you so far."

"That's where you're wrong," I said. "A guy knows what he wants as soon as he sees it. If he's not interested in that girl, then flirting won't get her anywhere. That's setting her up for heartbreak."

"If she cuts the guy off and never speaks to him again, he won't go for her either—unless he's crazy. You into stalkers, Jane?"

"Austen!" This conversation was really hard to have with Austen so close, so I moved away from him. "What does this have to do with anything?"

"I'm saying . . ."

His voice was louder now, and Taylor pushed into the room as if on cue. She glanced up at us absentmindedly. I got ready for her lecture. "Oh, I'm sorry," she said. "You don't have to be my dolls anymore." She held up her notebook. "I'm going to take this to my room and see if I can figure out what's missing."

Austen took a few breaths before he managed to get something pleasant out of his mouth. "You do that, Taylor."

She ambled away from us. "Be nice to each other," she warned. The door swung shut behind her.

My eyes went back to Austen. "She heard you!"

"Good. Someone has to tell girls that chick flicks aren't real. You can't keep believing that if you're rude and mean that your guy will still give you undying loyalty. He won't. Love doesn't spring from a love-hate relationship. We're not in a movie!"

"I got it, Austen." I went back to the couch and found my cell phone. "Please say you're done already?"

"No, this is for your own good." He landed on the couch beside me and caught my hand again, forcing me to stay put with his eyes. Now he had my attention—this close, I could see that his right eye had a little freckle inside. "If a man is indifferent, he's not secretly in love with you." His words crashed me back to reality. "When a guy asks other girls out, he's not trying to make you jealous so you'll go out with him. He's not intimidated, and he's never going to change for you."

I finally understood what Austen was trying to tell me. It felt like a slam to the gut. "Is that what you think that . . ." I gulped before I incriminated myself again, "is that what you think *other girls* want from you, Austen?"

"I'm not talking about me; I'm talking about jerks that won't change for you." Before I could call Austen a jerk, he went off again. "It's as big a lie as finding out that the man you thought was your best friend was in love with you all along."

There were times I considered Austen my best friend, so was he implying that I didn't have a chance with him? I hated how he kept calling me on my mistakes. I tried to concentrate on what he was saying, but it was hard considering that my heart was breaking at his every word.

Austen looked like he was only getting started. "Love doesn't spring from funerals, or reunions—and especially *not* from weddings. Family functions are chaotic, and no one has the time to have a meaningful conversation with anyone there. Ever."

I felt my body go rigid, deciding that I had no intention of making that mistake with Austen ever again. "I completely agree."

I saw the regret in his eyes the moment I said it, and he let me go to knead his forehead. "Look, my point is that when I say that I'm worried about Taylor, that doesn't mean I'm in love with her, Jane. And when I say that Dancey is a jerk . . ."

Austen wasn't in love with me.

"Yeah." I really needed the sassy, best-friend "lie" right now—the one who featured in all chick flicks and let the heroine cry on her shoulder. Failing that, I was going jogging. Austen had just stomped on my heart again, which was stupid, because he had already rejected me. I had made it my rule to only be rejected once by a guy before moving on. It was the best way not to get hurt all over again, so I didn't understand why I kept doing this to myself. I had to stop feeling anything for Austen.

I made the mistake of meeting eyes with him again. The way he looked at me almost blew me away. All we needed was to cue the romantic music. He leaned too close, his focus concentrated only on me, almost like we were having "a moment." But we weren't.

"Jane?" he asked.

Before he could say more, Ann-Marie rushed from the lounge with a skip to her step and smiled brightly when she saw that Austen was still in the lobby, his arm on the back of the couch behind me. "Wow, Austen." She collapsed against the doorframe and sniffed the air. "Wow. I followed your scent in here. Do you bathe in that stuff? I could sniff you all day. You always smell so good."

I mustered up a bitter laugh to defuse my feelings. "And I was wondering if he actually took a shower today."

"That explains it." Ann-Marie peeled away from the door, not expounding on her elusive comment. She switched the topic. "What did you think of that cake that I brought for you?"

His eyes were on mine—they were full of confusion as though he couldn't figure out why I was so angry. He broke away to give Ann-Marie his attention. "Loved it. It was fantastic."

"Oh." She gave a little high-pitched laugh. "Don't say that word."

"What? Fantastic?"

"Mmm. You said it again." She landed against the door again in her laughter and we both stared at her. Only she would assign deeper meaning to a normal word. She brought her hands to her mouth. "If you knew why, you wouldn't say it."

He looked like he was about to laugh. "You're probably right."

"I'm just glad that you can't read minds," Ann-Marie returned.

"Why?" I cut in hotly. "Why *just* Austen? How come you're not glad that I can't read minds either, Ann-Marie?"

She smiled coyly. "I know what's on your mind, Jane. You're thinking the same thing that I am."

"No, you're on your own there." I turned on Austen now. He watched me warily. "You want to talk unrealistic entertainment?" I asked. "You can't tell me that your heart doesn't speed up when you watch your man-crush run over an exploding mine with bare feet while dodging bullets or blowing away a million bad guys when they take someone he loves?"

"What movie is that?" he asked. "I want to see it."

I ignored the question. "Admit it—you feel a little tougher coming out of that movie. So sue me if Jane Austen makes me more romantic. I don't want much. I want a guy who loves me. I want him to pick a flower out of the ground and put it in my hair."

103

He hesitated. "Even if he makes a garden out of your head, that doesn't mean love."

"That's where we disagree," I said. Ann-Marie watched us with big, saucer eyes and I glanced over at her. "Hey, and don't worry, Ann-Marie. Austen doesn't believe that guys can read girls' minds, so you're very, *very* safe. You have to flirt like mad to get anywhere, so keep it up."

With my hands coiled into tight fists, I shoved off the couch.

"Hey," Austen said.

I turned, only to have him push Dancey's jacket in my arms. "This belongs in the box of destroyed dreams and unrealized potential." He pointed to the "Unintended Gifts" basket near the register where pencil stubs, receipts, and other memoirs from cute men lay forgotten.

"No." I threw the jacket over my shoulder. "I'm not happy with the jacket this time—I'm going after the man."

It would be a matter of honor. After throwing down my proverbial gloves at Austen's feet, I took his taunt as a challenge and stomped out.

Chapter 9

"Fanny! You are killing me!"

"No man dies of love but on the stage, Mr. Crawford."

—Jane Austen, Mansfield Park

I needed a good jog to get Austen's words out of my head, but I wasn't able to escape my duties until later that night. I felt like a caged-up tiger. The first chance I got, I rushed out of my room in running shorts and a T-shirt. I fixed my iPod to my waist and zipped my green hoodie to my neck. Heat infused my cheeks when, for the hundredth time that day, I remembered what he had said. I knew what Austen was getting at: *Dancey was a jerk for liking me. He was the rich guy playing me . . .* If that was the case, then Austen had done the same thing to me, Mr. My-Parents-Own-North-Abbey.

Rage and embarrassment tingled through my body. So what if I was poor? I worked to survive. I didn't care about having expensive cars. I didn't have to pay for a house that I never got to live in. Entertainment wasn't necessary—I could easily provide that myself. Luxury foods would only be gone the moment I consumed them. When I didn't get as much in my paycheck as others got, I didn't complain. I enjoyed my job, and that meant that I could look at my annual income and say I didn't want riches anyway. I didn't feel sorry for myself, and I didn't expect anyone else to throw their money at me with some freak inheritance.

Sure, I had dreams like anyone else. We never had a lot of money growing up. My parents were both teachers in a school system raging with political intrigue, which meant layoffs every few years. Clothes were hand-me-downs from richer relatives, and soup for dinner was always on the menu. My brothers and I used to play a game where we'd pretend to fast-forward our lives into a future where we were rich snobs and we'd look back and say, "Remember when we were poor?"

Well, now I was halfway through my twenties and still poor. But worse, I realized that the rags-to-riches game meant more to others than I thought—Austen actually thought that my social status was a barrier to love. I sped out of the door of North Abbey to escape, feeling a weight lift from my shoulders as I broke free into the night. I headed down the trail leading through the grove of trees to the beach. Sand flew out from behind my sneakers.

There had to be more to life than this! A perfect man was supposed to be sweeping me off my feet. I wasn't supposed to be making a fool of myself everywhere I went or losing my heart where I shouldn't. It was hard for a romantic like me to take. I wished I could turn to Taylor for advice. That's what I had done since I had started work here. But the closer her wedding loomed, the more we had drifted apart. The stress was turning us into strangers, and now Taylor was too busy entertaining her posh friends. I broke free from the trees, breathing in the scenery. The ocean looked like it had been ripped from poster board and pasted against a dark sky. It roared in defiance.

"Just try to own that!" I wanted to shout to anyone who thought they were better because they had more than me. The moon, the ocean, the sky; it belonged to all of us.

Churchell's Shack glimmered in a blur of tiki torches and decorative lights. I jogged around the deck and stopped short of the stairs to stretch out my hamstrings on the sand. The sound of a party drifted out from the opened windows. Laughter and music. Most of these voices had to come from Taylor's wedding guests. Many of them I hadn't met yet. Austen had taken most of their keys yesterday and this morning. I didn't want to run into any of them. The partygoers dove into the pool. The water sprayed over the railing. I stepped away from it and turned to leave.

A few men streamed out from the doors. Girls latched onto them, giggling. The boldest of the gigglers jumped onto the guys' backs as they walked down the beach. I jogged past the late-night revelers. One of the men called out to me. "Hey, green girl!"

I looked down at my green hoodie. That had to be me. I didn't slow. "Fanny!" he called. "Hey Fanny." I slowed and glanced back. The guy talking to me was a shadow in the darkness. "You came!" He held his arms out to give me a big hug.

I backpedaled away, laughing nervously while holding my arm out to stop him. "No, uh, I'm not Fanny. You're mistaking me for someone else."

The man stepped into the light of a tiki torch. With a start, I realized that it was the cute blond Bertie had been flirting with at the refreshment tables before I'd had to leave to park cars that morning.

"You're not Fanny." He grinned at me as if it was a happy surprise. He was one of those guys who knew he was adorable. Pretty confident, too, which normally I liked. "Can I have a hug anyway?" he asked.

"Nooo," I said slowly. He also seemed a little too drunk to figure out personal boundaries.

"Oh, c'mon, green girl. I promise not to tell Taylor. She's your boss, right?"

Wait. He knew who I was? I was still smarting from Austen's words—social barriers didn't cross. Taylor's friends were rich, and I was Cinderella to them. Now I could see this handsome man for what he was—no matter the era. "We're getting a group together for a quick boat trip," he said. He stepped into the light, and I studied his tan face, noticing strong shoulders that matched his muscular arms. He must be one of those boys with toys—a boating, snowboarding, paragliding, adrenaline junky. "You can ride in the front seat with me," he offered.

"No," I cut off the invitation. Back in Jane Austen's day, this man would be an aristocrat giving the governess a hard time. Today, he was up to no good with the staff. "That's super nice of you to offer," I said just in case I misread his intentions, "but I need to check in early tonight. Wedding rehearsal is tomorrow." I shrugged and stepped back.

His voice stopped me from taking off again. "C'mon, you need to be more fun than that. Don't you have to earn your pay or something?"

Now I was sure I wasn't misreading him. I glared. "I think you have the wrong idea." My voice sounded harsher than I intended, but I wasn't in the mood for flirtatious banter. "You realize an event coordinator isn't some kind of escort, right?"

He laughed, his eyes taking me all in. "I didn't mean that. I'm sorry. Can we start over again? What's your name?"

I swung away from him, getting ready to end this conversation by bolting away. "Jane."

"Nice to meet you. I'm Harry Crawley. The groom's brother."

I stopped running in place. "But your accent?"

"I know. It's American. I'm Chuck Bigley's *step*brother."

I wanted to choke. I wasn't supposed to be cutting off Bigley's relatives. I forced my hand out to him to show I was willing to make a treaty. "Nice to meet you, Harry Crawley."

Sorta.

He took my hand, holding it a little longer than necessary when he shook it. If anything, it was flattering after Austen's *unflattering* conversation, but still I pulled back, trying not to yank my hand out of his grasp. I didn't want my escape to be too obvious.

Harry Crawley studied me. "You're different than the other girls here."

"Doubtful." My eyes went to the giggling bikini-clad girls who were pawing at his friends. I glanced down at my cut-off sweats. Okay, maybe I was a little different. "Well, I'm going to go finish my jog," I said, "but let the front desk know if you need anything."

"Wait, could I ask you something?"

I backed away. "Yeah, sure."

"Not here," he said. He stepped closer and took my wrist. Surrendering to the inevitable, I allowed him to lead me away from his friends to the little tables on the patio. "You're Taylor's right-hand woman, right?" his voice slurred a little.

"Yeah."

"I've got a surprise for the bride and groom at the wedding rehearsal tomorrow. You want to help us?"

My mind buzzed with the possibilities, and I sat down across from him at the table. Maybe this would help Taylor not be so uptight. "What were you thinking?"

"Chuck's always rubbing it in my face how he never does anything wrong." He guffawed. "What a lie. The guy just can't get caught. If his mom knew half the things he did, she'd stop threatening to disinherit him and just do it. Have you met her yet?"

I shook my head, feeling confused—Bigley was practically perfect.

"Chuck's mom makes Taylor look sane. No wonder my stepfather cheated on her." I grimaced at that while he rubbed his arm across his face. "So the guys and I thought . . . we thought we'd switch out Taylor's wedding ring for a cheap one from the quarter machine."

"Um, no." I put my finger up. "That's a pretty awful idea actually."

"He'd love it."

"But Taylor wouldn't, so I'm just going to have to tell you 'no' on that one."

"You're telling me 'no'?" He leaned back in his chair, a grin spreading lazily over his face. "You really are different from other girls."

109

"Not really." I felt myself getting irritated, "it's just that your idea's stupid." I squinted with remorse after the words came out. I had said that wrong. My present boldness had to do with going head to head with Austen earlier.

Harry Crawley laughed and took my unwilling hand. "You really don't want me to do the switch? Do you say 'yes' to anything?"

"Yeah, ice cream and chocolate."

It came out before I realized that it sounded like an invitation. He tried to stand up with my hand. "Okay, let's go."

"Hey!"

"How else are you going to make me behave?" he asked. "If you don't, I'm switching the rings tomorrow."

What? Was I on candid camera here? I took a deep breath. "Think about the most awkward date that you've ever been on and then multiply that pain by twenty. If you even think about doing a switch at the wedding rehearsal tomorrow, that's what you'll feel once Taylor and I are through with you."

"Totally worth it."

I jerked my hand from his and shot to my feet, the chair skidding across the sand behind me. "It's your funeral, drunk guy, but if you plan more mischief, be sure to give me the head's up, okay? I want to be sure to stop everything you do."

"So you're saying to give Taylor's ring back?"

"What?" My voice lowered to a harsh whisper. "You have it already?"

"You want to pat me down for it?"

"Strangle you is more like it!"

He laughed and leaned closer. "It was really nice to meet you, Jane. Next time I'll get you alone so we can really have some fun."

All my romantic ideals of finding love at Taylor's wedding fled out the door and instantly I was a hard woman. I gave Harry Crawley a cold smile. "You're a guest here, and I'm a professional. That means you and I will *never* have fun." There were social boundaries, after all.

I realized that I was parroting Austen's ideals, but I didn't care. I'd use them when they suited me.

"You have a beautiful smile." Harry Crawley pulled in even closer. "I'd almost say it was sweet."

"Artificial sweetener," I growled out. His face registered surprise at my retort, and I abruptly ended the conversation by jogging away.

The sand split under me, and the waves made an angry crashing in my ears that still buzzed with Crawley's disturbing flirtation. He was so drunk he probably wouldn't remember our conversation in the morning. And if he did? My thoughts went to Austen for help. I shook that thought away. This wasn't fiction, and he'd never play the role of my hero. I'd take care of Mr. Crawley on my own.

Chapter 10

"But then, if one scheme of happiness fails, human nature turns to another; if the first calculation is wrong, we make a second better: we find comfort somewhere."

—Jane Austen, Mansfield Park

The plucking and tuning of instruments filled the inside of the chapel. I picked at a muffin in the effort to get some nutrition out of it to fuel my tired body. Blinking swollen eyes at the group assembled at the church, I tried not to meet anyone's gaze. The problem was that there were so many people to avoid that it was becoming difficult.

Despite all my brave words, I was unsure of how my "moment" with Dancey would play out in the real world. The cold light of morning seeped through the stained-glass windows and made everything so practical. Austen's logical words against romance echoed in my head—add to that my conversation with Crawley last night, and it resulted in my confidence hitting an all-time low.

"Jane, Jane!" Taylor rushed over to me, looking flushed. "Jane, I'm so scared that I'm forgetting something."

"Leave your worrying to me," I said, fluffing her veil—she insisted on wearing it as her only ornament for the rehearsal. With her boots and flannel shirt, it was actually pretty cute. She should start a trend. "Just enjoy yourself."

"I can't," she whispered. Her eyes had a hollow look to them. The dark circles under them were looking more like bruises. "Chuck isn't here yet. He left with Dancey this morning." My stomach lurched at the mention of Dancey's name. With so much expectation built-up between us, the reminder of him seemed more like a threat now.

I shook my head. "Don't worry, Taylor. Bigley will come to the rehearsal."

"That's not what I'm worried about."

I searched her face. "Then what is it?"

She threw her hands into the air. "I'm not getting any sleep. I'm paranoid and crazy. I can't think straight. Is this what cold feet feels like?"

My heart sped up. *I had no idea.* I grabbed her arm and led her to one of the side rooms near the reverend's office. "Taylor, talk to me. What's happening?"

She wiped at the silent tears escaping from her eyes. "I love Chuck. I do. I want to be with him more than anything. He's the best man that I know—he's so sweet, kind, gentlemanly, thoughtful—"

"So, what's the problem, Taylor?"

"What if everything I want isn't right for me?" She choked over her voice.

I stared at her, not sure what I was really seeing. Taylor looked a wreck. Her normally immaculate hair was disheveled. Her lips trembled. Is this what love did to us? She was closer than she ever was to getting everything she wanted—what we all wanted—and the fear that it would somehow get messed up was making her crazy. I put my hand over hers. "Don't you want to marry Bigley?"

"Yes, yes, I do."

"Then you have to go for it, Taylor."

Austen popped his head into the room. Taylor was serious about making him my assistant and he looked anything but happy to be here. He studied Taylor's tear-streaked face, and I cringed, knowing he would see it all out of context and believe that he was right and I was wrong. He licked his lips, and I waited for him to tell Taylor everything he had told me yesterday. His eyes went to mine instead. "Chuck's here," he said.

He disappeared into the hall, and I turned back to Taylor, free to speak. "Don't you think you deserve happiness?"

She took my hand and clutched it. "I do. Please. Just keep reminding me that this will make me happy."

It took me a moment to take in what she'd just said. "Wait, Taylor."

She bolted out of the room so fast that I could barely keep up with her. Her face was now expressionless, like she hadn't just been crying—I envied the skill but was still worried about her. She patted down her hair, and as soon as she found Chuck Bigley, she looped her arms around him like he was her lifeline.

His hand found hers, and he turned so that she nestled into him—my traitorous heart melted at the sight, though I couldn't get what Taylor had said out of my mind.

"Hey baby." He kissed her, and then whispered, "I love you."

Or he could be whispering "elephant toes."

Why did Taylor call herself paranoid? About what? I took a step toward her and stopped short when I saw Crawley standing next to his stepbrother. He saw that I was looking at him and smirked, then took out a ring box.

I clenched my fist and ran into Austen. He steadied me, but his usual laugh was missing. Still, I couldn't help taking him into my confidence. "If I don't kill Crawley first, I want you to finish him off, okay?"

"What? Who's Crawley?" Austen asked.

"Chuck's stepbrother, Harry Crawley."

Austen's eyes narrowed at him. "Oh, that guy. Yeah. I checked him in yesterday."

"He's got some prank going on with Taylor's ring. And I don't know what to do about it."

"You want me to stop him?" Austen asked.

My heart fluttered at the suggestion. Austen was actually offering to help me. "I don't know what we could do, short of tackling him." I briefly considered the idea, but Taylor's stoic face changed my mind. Crawley laughed at something Bigley said, and I shuddered. "How can someone so nice be related to someone so awful?"

Austen shrugged. "Ask your biology teacher."

"Not funny. It's like I'm in the middle of a rom-com, Austen." He looked blank.

"A romantic comedy," I translated for him. "I had another meet-cute last night, but with the villain this time. I think you *really* cursed me with your little spiel against romance."

He looked surprised. "You think this is happening because of me?"

"If it is," I said, "I cursed you too. I can hardly wait for you to get yours."

"And what would getting *mine* entail?"

I waved my hand generously over the wedding party. The bridesmaids smoothed their skirts, the men chatted amiably. "Something like this—bride, reverend, tearful family, the works."

Austen rolled his eyes. "Sure, why not? Everyone looks so happy. Are you going to tell me what was wrong with Taylor?"

"She . . ." I stuttered to a stop. Austen was such a critic of romance—I could see him saying that it clouded our good judgment. He'd talk Taylor out of her own wedding when she only had cold feet. I tried to keep my uncomfortable misgivings to myself. Taylor deserved to be happy. "She needed my help with her veil," I said.

Austen didn't buy it—I could see it in his eyes, but I forgot about that the moment Dancey entered the chapel. My heart sped up. How could I ever have mistaken him for a valet? He walked with a feline grace, his stride confident. His clothes were understated and expensively tailored. My speeding heart turned into a runaway train. He looked too good—like a rock star . . . and my legs felt shaky when I realized he was looking back at me.

"You got any gum?"

I turned distractedly at the question, seeing Austen had asked for it. He didn't look happy. Right. He didn't trust Dancey. I glowered at Austen for ruining my moment. "No," I said. "What's your problem?"

"This wedding rehearsal for starters. Do you shout 'Ready-set-go' or is that my happy duty now that I'm your assistant?"

"I'm on it." I deserted him and found the reverend in the group. Eddy and his wife were tied up in conversation with the musicians, but as soon as they saw me approach, Eddy took charge of the whole proceeding. The reverend went to the front of the aisle, where the men joined him to wait for the bride. I was acutely aware of what Dancey was doing the whole time. He stepped next to Chuck Bigley, laughing at a few jokes. His eyes always veered back to me.

Feeling my skin tingle at the attention and not sure if I should be thrilled or terrified out of my mind, I clasped my clipboard and led the bridesmaids, flower girls, and Taylor to the end of the chapel. "Everyone in your places. Bridesmaids first, and then the bride, followed by the flower girls holding her train."

Taylor watched me expectantly, and I remembered that her father was coming in later tonight. I needed a fill-in. "Austen!" I turned and he grunted at my loud voice. He was standing right next to me. "Oh sorry," I said. "Can you give the bride away?"

Taylor treated Austen to a small, vulnerable smile. His expression turned sympathetic and he closed the distance between them in an instant, more gallant than he had ever been with me. He offered Taylor his arm. "I have such a beautiful daughter," he said.

"Not so fast, Austen," she said. "I'm older than you."

"Stranger things have happened."

I wasn't sure what. Keeping my eyes on the musicians, I set the stopwatch on my cell phone and nodded for them to begin. Their sweet music wafted through the room in response, and I motioned for the bridesmaids to make their way down the aisle. Even dressed in jeans and T-shirts, I imagined them as little ladies-in-waiting treading over the red rug of the church.

Bertie was at the front. Her arms protruded from her sides, her birdlike hands clawing the bouquet, seeming afraid someone might steal it from her. Mary was behind her, a stain on the front of her pale pink dress shirt. Her nose was red from rubbing it raw and still there was no sign of moisture on it. Last came Bella, her long blond hair piled high on her head in a messy knot. She drew looks from all of the groomsmen . . . except for the best man. Dancey only had eyes for me.

I flushed, not able to read his look. Was it true? Did he really think that I was that interesting? I wanted to get to know him better, but Austen's words against a possible romance between Dancey and me kept playing through my mind, making the doubts creep in. Maybe he was just bored and thought I was amusing?

The bridesmaids filed against the other side of the groom and joined Bigley's groomsmen at the front of the chapel. I waved Taylor to go join them, but instead she shifted from foot to foot. Austen looked worried. "Taylor?" he asked in a lowered voice.

"My bouquet!" she cried. "I put it in the car. It's not my real one—just a bunch of California poppies I found . . ."

Weaving around Austen, I found Taylor's other side and rubbed her back. "Just pretend you have it," I whispered.

The flower girls took my advice instead. The little blond twins pretended to lift her fake train. I made a mental note to pick the real train up today after the rehearsal. Taylor squeezed Austen's arm and made her other hand into a little fist as if she carried the bouquet. I hadn't expected her to take me so literally. Her hand shook.

Austen's eyes went to mine in silent rebuke before the two took off down the aisle. It almost looked like he had to drag her. Taylor was taking too long. The musicians reached the final notes of their song and had to start the *Bridal Chorus* again.

By the time Taylor reached Bigley, her smile was stretched tight and fake across her face. Austen relinquished her to her groom, but he didn't look happy about it.

117

The reverend reserved a kind smile for Taylor. Besides his priestly collar, Eddy was indistinguishable from the other men at the front. I was so used to the white-haired preachers we normally dealt with that it was a shock to see one who could take out the groomsmen in a game of basketball. He laid a comforting hand on Taylor's arm and turned to Chuck Bigley. "You wrote your own vows?" Eddy asked.

Bigley's focus was on his fiancé. "Yes, Reverend."

"Then please begin."

Bigley took a deep breath, his eyes tender on Taylor. "I, Charles Frank Bigley the III, take you, Taylor Missy Elizabeth Weston, as my wife. When I first saw that little dimple above your smile and the way your precious eyes sparkled like emeralds, I knew my life would not be complete until I uttered these words: I promise to be faithful, to hold you in the highest regard. Life will be hard, but it will also be beautiful. We will laugh, we will cry; there will be good times and hard, but whatever comes our way, I will never be sorry that you were by my side. Today, I make my promises in front of God, our family, and our friends, that I will always be true, that I will love you forever, and that I will dedicate my life to your happiness."

Taylor ducked her head and I knew that she was going to cry again. She took a moment to take back her legendary control before she sniffed and said, "I, Taylor Missy Elizabeth Weston, take you, Chuck Frank Bigley, to be my husband. You are everything I want," her voice broke. "My day begins and ends with thoughts of you—my dreams, my life, my heart I dedicate to you. Today, I make my promises in front of God, our family, our friends, that I am all yours: body, mind, spirit, soul. I vow to love you and do everything in my power to make you happy."

I sighed, feeling my fears wash away. Bigley would take perfect care of Taylor. Surely, Austen would see that this was true love. I stole a glance at him and saw him frowning. What was Austen's problem now? Bigley was perfect. The groom-to-be was all sweet smiles and kind eyes. He watched Taylor like she was something precious. Bigley held his hand out to Dancey for her ring.

With sudden dread, my eyes went to Bigley's stepbrother. Crawley met them with an amused grin. My heart dropped, especially when he slipped the familiar black box out of his pocket and gave it to Dancey, who did the hand-off to the groom.

Bigley snapped open the box. He glanced down, his eyes sliding back up to Taylor. He cleared his throat. "Let this ring symbolize the vows of our hearts, the commitment of our bodies, the joining of our spirits in holy matrimony. All that I am is yours."

He plucked her ring out of the box—*the perfect, non-trick ring*—and slipped it over Taylor's finger. I went limp with relief. Crawley found my eyes and winked at me. I leaned back against a pillar and took a deep breath.

Though this was only a rehearsal, Bigley kissed Taylor. She wrapped her arms around his neck and kissed him back as though her life depended on it. It was a little passionate for a church kiss. Austen took a step back from it. Dancey's eyebrows lifted.

I signaled the musicians to play again. Bigley took Taylor's hand, and they walked down the aisle towards me, their friends trailing at their heels.

"Great, great," I said, feeling the urge to rub my forehead free of the headache forming there. I had a lot of things to fix. "Let's go through this again. Bridesmaids, I want you to stand a little taller and keep closer together. Dancey." With a jolt, I felt the full impact of his eyes on me, and I tried to smile to ease the sudden racing in my veins. "Can you keep the wedding rings the whole time?"

He covered the few steps between himself and Taylor and with gentle movements, slid the ring from her finger. She wouldn't look at him—her hand tightened on her groom-to-be. Dancey glanced over at me. "Are you afraid her ring will run away?" he asked.

Something like that. I turned to the bride. "Taylor, you need to be a little faster down the aisle this time. We want you to meet Bigley just as the song ends. Just follow Austen's lead."

"I can't," she whispered brokenly. My heart thudded with a new, nervous tension until she said, "I can't without my bouquet. I need it. I don't know what to do with my hands."

"Oh, well," I shifted to find my new assistant. "Austen, could you get her bouquet?" I threw him the keys to the car Taylor and I had carpooled in.

His mouth was tight. Without a word, he brushed past me into the foyer, his footsteps echoing over the tiles until I heard the unmistakable sound of the front doors opening, along with a familiar and terse voice addressing him. "Where's Taylor?" Captain Redd asked. He had come as promised.

"She's in the chapel." Austen didn't bother to speak quietly. "We just finished the first run-through. Glad you're here. You can give away the bride this time." The scorn in Austen's voice revealed his distaste of the whole proceedings.

A few seconds later, Redd slipped into the back of the church in his full military regimentals. His presence only added to the pressure that formed a steady ache in my head. Taylor ran to him, holding out her arms. "Yes, Redd, please, give me away! You're like a brother to me. It just feels right."

Redd met my eyes over Taylor's head as if he blamed me for her strange, new vulnerability. He rubbed her arms to comfort her. "You have nothing to worry about, Taylor. I'm here now."

I was sure that was a barb aimed at me, but I didn't have time to brood over it. My phone buzzed, and I saw I had a text from Austen.

AUSTEN: SHE'S WORSE TODAY. TELL ME YOU'RE STILL NOT WORRIED ABOUT HER?

ME: SHE'S HAVING LAST MINUTE WEDDING JITTERS. IT'S NORMAL.

I stuck my phone back in my pocket and listened to the buzzing that meant Austen was madly texting me back. I ignored the texts for now. The musicians picked up their instruments and practiced another run through their prelude music. Since it was Bach, it shot me straight to a more romantic time period that I wasn't sure I should get lost in right now, especially when Dancey wouldn't stop looking at me. He might just see me as that strange girl who'd mistaken him for a valet, though I couldn't mistake the very real interest in his eyes.

The *very-married* Bertie took advantage of the lull to flirt wildly with Crawley. The bachelor encouraged her with scandalous remarks and roving eyes, but I wasn't as upset with him as I would've been had he gone through with his threat to sabotage Taylor's ring. Dancey leaned against the podium, his hands in his pockets. He broke his gaze from me and nodded at the chattering Bigley, but his attention was divided. Now he watched Taylor with Redd.

A sneeze next to me made me jump. Mary's hand clutched my arm in a firm grip. "You do not want to catch this cold," she said before she lost all breath to speak and gasped for more air. "The mucus is flooding my lungs. I can't get out the phlegm no matter how much I cough it out." She coughed in demonstration. "You should see the color that comes out of me."

I nodded and nodded until I was able to get away. As soon as I did, Bella sighed beside me, looking tragically beautiful. I followed her gaze to find Freddy at the back of the pews, holding Bertie's little teddy bear of a puppy. His broad shoulders made a straight line against the back of his seat, his eyelids lowered heavily over disdainful eyes. "Is he really so into video games?" Bella asked.

I grimaced. *This was for her own good. The last girl Freddy had played had left the state to be a nanny.* "Sadly, yes," I said.

"What about Chuck's brother?" Bella asked. "He's quite handsome."

Crawley laughed loudly and ran his hand down Bertie's bare arm. I shook my head. "He's one of those boys with toys. He'd dump you on the weekends and go drinking with his friends—and most of those friends would be girls—doesn't look like he cares if they're married either."

"Hmm." Bella let the sound draw out as she made herself more comfortable. "What about Dancey?" She watched me expectantly like I had become the authority on love. "What's his story? Who's the man behind the tragic love songs?"

"He's nice," I allowed. "A little hard to read. He blows hot and cold, I'd say, but more because he's distrustful at first, but then he warms up. He's a guy who might go for what he wants, I think, but he's written a lot of tragic love songs, so I think he's broken a lot of hearts—"

Bella cut me off with a giggle. "It's a good thing that he's so rich and good-looking then." She dimpled prettily when she caught sight of my stunned expression. "I'm just saying what everyone's thinking. A man must either be rich or good-looking to catch my interest. And if he's neither then he must be famous."

"Hopefully not as a mass murderer," I said.

She gave that a token laugh. "It seems Dancey has it all, doesn't he? That makes him the hottest guy here. Thanks for the advice, Jane. I'll do it." She broke off from me and headed for the rock star. Had I told Bella to go for Dancey? If I had, I was crazy. There was no way I could compete with the most gorgeous girl at the wedding party.

"Do you ever feel guilty?" Redd asked Taylor. As usual, his voice was too loud, as if he wanted me to overhear him.

"For what?" Taylor asked.

"Your dating past, all the hearts you've broken?"

Redd had reverted to torture via guilt trip. He stared at me. Why was it taking Austen so long to find the bouquet? I checked my phone and saw twelve messages from him. I groaned—he was not happy about the wedding. Before I could read his texts, I noticed that Crawley had managed to break free from Bertie and was headed for me with a mischievous grin.

Oh no.

"I've got to hurry Austen along," I told Taylor, tripping over my feet in my hurry to escape. "Start without me. I'll get you your flowers. But for now . . ." I plucked Bertie's bouquet from her hands and gave them to Taylor. "Just make do for a minute, Taylor. I'll be back. I'll be back!"

The musicians started up the *Wedding March* again just as I ran outside and found myself in the middle of a rainstorm. I gasped in surprise—besides the darkness, I hadn't even noticed it against the windows in the chapel. Austen leaned against Taylor's car, texting. Rain streamed down his face. His head lifted when I came outside. "No, stop!" At the urgency in his voice, I froze while he ran at me. "Stop it from closing!" The church door sealed shut just as his fingers scraped past the air over it.

He was all wet, his hair a sopping mess. "Didn't you get my texts?"

I thought guiltily of the twelve texts he had sent and pulled out my cell phone to see that most of Austen's texts had told me he'd been locked out. I knocked against the door, but the sound was lost against the heavy oak. Austen leaned heavily over me to protect me from the rain while I began to text everyone inside.

"I did that already," he said. "No one's answering."

It was like everyone had their phones off. "Well, how long can they possibly wait before they come outside to check on us?" I asked. "We can wait in the Lexus."

I hurried through the rain to get to Taylor's car, but Austen was already shaking his head when he caught up to me. "We can't—you gave me the wrong keys. Where's your white knight now? We could use a little help here."

"Hey, you're the one who cursed him into not existing."

He stared at me. The downpour turned his clothes into a second skin. Austen was lean from his biking and his hazel eyes were mesmerizing—they burned into mine. The attraction that I always felt

123

for him came back to haunt me. I tried to look everywhere but at him. When he wouldn't stop looking at me, sudden fear gripped me, and I checked out my dress to make sure that it was still black and made of heavy cotton.

Austen broke through my thoughts. "You got my first text."

That again. I leaned against Taylor's car, feeling the water pour down my forehead and drip past my lips. "Yeah, and Taylor is just fine!"

"Did you miss the way she kissed Bigley?" he asked. I hesitated. How could I not? Austen frowned. "It was like she was trying to convince herself that she was doing the right thing."

I gave a worried laugh. "You read *that* in a kiss? Now who's the romantic?"

"Kisses tell a lot, Jane. I know."

"Oh please. You wouldn't know what a kiss meant if someone smacked you with one."

I realized what I had said the moment that his hand went to my arm. He turned me gently to face him. His touch warmed me. Austen's face was only inches from mine, and for a moment I wondered if he meant to show me exactly what he thought a kiss should be.

"I know when the girl enjoys a kiss," he said. With a start, I felt his hands at my waist. "I know when she wants to be close and when she's lost in the moment." My eyes went to his lips and then back to his eyes, and I tried not to look like I wanted to kiss him, my thudding heart the only sound that came from me. Even with his arms around me, I shouldn't misread the moment. I shouldn't make the same mistake that I had before. Still, it felt good to be so close to him.

"When you kiss and when you feel it, that means something," he said, "not that desperate look I saw in Taylor's eyes."

The combination of the wind and my nerves made my teeth chatter as the cold wound its way through me. Austen's hands tightened over me when he felt it. "You're freezing. Come here." He pulled me against his chest.

His hands chafed my back and I silently called him out as a fraud—Austen had no idea when a girl enjoyed being near him. I never wanted him to let me go. I rested my chin on his shoulder to see if that told him anything. When it didn't, I smiled at the irony. "You're right," I said. "There's nothing romantic about a rainstorm."

Austen pulled back, his eyes trained on me. His hair was plastered to his face, and I reached up to push a strand back from his eye just as a frog rushed past my feet. I screamed. My hands landed on Austen's shoulders and I screamed again, trying to jump into his arms to escape the horrible, slimy thing.

"What are you doing?" He was laughing. "What was that?"

Embarrassment filled me and I tried to remove myself from his arms, but he wouldn't let me. "I just thought I'd try out one of those swing dance moves," I joked. "It's raining. Dancing just seems like the next step."

"You wanted me to dance with you?"

I searched his expression and found the teasing glint in his eyes. "Forget it," I said. "It's way too much of a commitment. Besides, I don't want you trying to read too much into it—that would just go wrong."

"Okay, I get it. No dancing."

I studied him, trying to see him as a character from one of my favorite Jane Austen romances; but no, he was just Austen. I kind of liked that. The doors from the church broke open as members of the wedding party spilled out into the rain—they must've finished rehearsal without me. I was annoyed at the interruption, but Austen straightened with relief. "Finally!" he said.

He put a hand on my back, leading me through the guests. We passed Redd on our way through the doors. The captain stopped short. His self-righteous eyes roved over us, not missing Austen's touch on my back. "I see you're working hard on Taylor's wedding."

Austen let me go to squeeze out the water from his already dripping shirt, and it spilled onto the tiled floor. "Thanks for letting us in, man."

Redd glowered. I refused to feel guilty. "We got locked out," I said.

The captain's full lips pinched angrily. "Together? How convenient for you."

Luckily Austen hadn't heard him. He was already heading for the chapel; the only thing left of him was a line of wet footprints in the foyer. Treating me to another accusing look, Redd rushed the other way. Freddy brushed through the foyer next, with Bertie's puppy tucked under his arm. He headed for Bella, who stood near the pastor's office, and bumped into her to fake an accidental meeting. Bella sucked in her breath, but before Freddy could start his smooth talking, she rushed the other way. Freddy stared after her in confusion. I had never seen a girl escape his charms so easily before, but Bella was in hot pursuit of Dancey.

She let out a giggle that put my teeth on edge. Her delicate hands smoothed out the front of Dancey's jacket, taking every opportunity to touch the bare skin at his neck. "Just make sure you don't drop Chuck's ring next time," she said with a flirtatious smile. "You'd think you wanted to keep the ring for yourself. You're not lonely now that your best friend is getting married, are you?"

Dancey's eyes drifted to me. "I'm never lonely."

"Is that so?" Bella's gaze shot from him to me, not missing the unspoken communication between us. "Well." She leaned closer to Dancey. "I can make sure of that. Your visit here doesn't have to be just about Chuck."

"It isn't." He patted her on the back and just like that, brushed off the most popular girl from the wedding party, coming for me instead. My hair was flattened against my forehead with rain, and I remembered one of Austen's realisms—*the man won't go for the girl who doesn't do her hair.* There was absolutely no reason for the rock star to

126

like me any more than a friend. I had embarrassed him when I mistook him for a valet, ignored him during the wedding rehearsal, and I certainly wouldn't have anything interesting to say now.

I shifted uneasily and untangled my curling hair from my face. "Hey." I couldn't quite meet his eyes. "Did you need your jacket back?"

"Yes," he said, "when I pick you up for a drive. Remember, you agreed to go anywhere with me."

The reminder made me laugh. Now Dancey fit the role of the valet that I knew and loved, not the rock star, and I immediately relaxed. I saw his lips tilt up in response. Dancey seemed to really care what I thought about him. Austen was right. It didn't make sense. Something else was happening here. "About that," I said. "You knew I had no idea who you were. Why didn't you say anything? It could've gotten you out of parking all those cars."

He considered me a moment, then surprised me by smiling. "I enjoyed being treated like a real guy for once. You were brutally honest."

I reddened when I thought about what I'd said about his song. I actually liked it, but it would seem like I was kissing up to him if I admitted that now. He leaned over me to whisper in my ear, "Remember, you agreed to go out with me when you thought I was a poor man with no prospects."

"Well, you did bribe me with a trip to Vegas."

"I'm not through bribing you. Tomorrow morning my car will be ready for you."

It was like he was setting up a drive in the park. This was so Jane Austen right now. I couldn't believe it, but the eagerness on Dancey's face convinced me that he was sincere. I nodded. "Yeah, but remember, I'm driving."

"You're not afraid that I'll steal off with you?"

"Are you kidding?" I laughed when a mischievous thought came to me. "I'm counting on it."

"Good. I don't want to share you with anyone else. Not with Taylor, not with your assistant." He lowered his voice. "I've had my fill of this wedding party—the guests chatter constantly about nothing. I'm not looking forward to that trite dinner party tonight. If I could, I'd steal you away from it."

"That hurts. I planned that trite dinner party."

"Then I'll behave for your sake." He picked up my hand and kissed it.

My mouth dropped after he strode away. He kissed my hand? Did people do that anymore? And he was a snob—it was strangely intriguing, especially since the snob thought that I was worthy of his attention. I gathered up the bouquets and corsages in the chapel and found my clipboard, only to stare blindly at my notes. Dancey was still interested in me. We'd had a meet-cute and a *moment*—the aftereffects of which had never lasted longer than a day for me in any other relationship. Dancey had gone through a lot of breakups. That meant this flirtation might only last the week he was here. Still, I was positive that I could enjoy the fun while it lasted.

Swinging my keys, I turned and met Austen's disapproving eyes. I shrieked, holding my heart. "Well, it's nice to see you too, *dear friend*. What did I do to deserve that look?"

"I thought I warned you about that guy?"

I laughed. "Oh c'mon, Austen. Let's not argue for once. I prefer to find out if a guy is a jerk my own way."

"So you believe me that Dancey is a jerk, but you're still giving him a chance?"

I stopped short. Had I said that? "Nooo," I said slowly, "but I will never know someone until I get to know them, and," before Austen went off on how the guy wouldn't go for me, I held up my hand, "and who knows? We just might hit it off."

"I didn't say that you two wouldn't." Austen looked disturbed. "When are you going out with him?"

"Not saying."

I brushed past him and was immediately sorry when I realized that he was just as wet as I was. His hand slid over my arm, and he squeezed my hand. "Can I, at least, ask you to be careful?"

"Oh, c'mon, Austen." I faced him, making sure he saw how confident I was about my decision. "You don't have to save the world—we're not so helpless without you. I might be a romantic, but I'm not stupid. Save your lecture for those who only use kisses as entertainment."

If anything, my brave words only increased the worry in his eyes.

Chapter 11

"It requires uncommon steadiness of reason to resist the attraction of being called the most charming girl in the world."

—Jane Austen, Northanger Abbey

All of our wedding rehearsal dinners took place at the Pemburkley Hall. Taylor's was no exception. The building had a Victorian feel, with ivy climbing over a latticed fence and curling around elegant pillars. The patios, both inside and out, were covered in jungles of flowers.

Austen and I sat in the middle of it all, putting together the decorations—ribbons, candles, lamps, garnish, candies. We had five hours before the dinner tonight to arrange them artistically on the dozen round tables set up in the middle of the room.

I took up some ribbon. "We're making bows first," I told Austen.

"Me? Make a bow?"

"What? Are your hands too delicate?" I asked in a mock challenge.

His jaw tightened and he got busy, making a bow that was far better than mine. I tried not to be jealous. We had an unspoken agreement not to bring up Dancey or Taylor. It was the only way not to fight, but I knew something was on Austen's mind by the way he kept frowning.

A slight wind ruffled his curly hair. The partitioned glass walls of Pemburkley Hall could be opened and closed to the outside world, and since Taylor had opted for the al fresco feel, the set-up crew had organized it so that, besides the roof, the rehearsal dinner would feel like it was all taking place outside.

Glancing over at Austen, I shifted uncomfortably. "And then we tie the flower to the decorative lamp," I said while I demonstrated.

The caterers came through the hall, bringing pots and ingredients. Pemburkley Hall had its own kitchen, off in a building to the side, where they'd prepare the dinner for tonight. Austen turned to the servers with interest. "Where's Junie Be Fair? She's catering tonight, right?"

I jerked a ribbon tight. "Why do you always call her that?"

He smirked, and, too late, I realized I'd given him ammunition. "You don't like me calling her 'Fair?' You jealous?"

"Yes, I'm the evil queen and no one else can be called fair."

"You just want a nickname for yourself," he said.

"Oh no." I shook my head before he could try to come up with one. "I'm adding that to a list of things to *not* talk about. No nicknames." I placed a candle inside the lamp I was working on.

"Wait, you have a list? You can't have a list of things I can and can't do," he turned thoughtful, ". . . unless I can have one for you."

He stole my decorative lamp and arranged some calla lilies and old fashioned roses around it. What else besides Dancey could he possibly not want me to bring up? My curiosity outweighed my natural reserve—like it usually did. "And what would you put on your list, Austen?"

He studied me, his hazel eyes clouded over with a look I couldn't read, and he wrapped another ribbon around a flower. "I'll come up with something. We'll play it by ear."

The musicians set up to the side of us. Working next to Austen, I let myself get lost in the peace of the afternoon. Before I knew it, we were both lying flat on our stomachs, twisting flowers into ribbons while listening to the musicians practice their music for tonight.

"Why can't musicians play Led Zeppelin at these things?" Austen asked.

"Maybe," I said sarcastically, "because that's not music; it's just noise."

He twisted ribbon into two more calla lilies before tossing them aside. "I want to elope," he said. I looked up quickly. "No offense to your career, but weddings are too stressful. I just want my friends and family to enjoy themselves. Maybe I'd throw a big cookout after I come back from my honeymoon."

"Hmm." I thought about the idea and imagined the most romantic elopement possible. First a proposal under a starlit sky, a hand taking mine, and then my beloved ushering me onto the nearest plane to a foreign country to seal the deal on a spur of the moment honeymoon. I smiled. "That does sound nice. Just get on a plane and go anywhere. Oh, I'd choose London! And then when I came back, I'd love to see everyone's faces when I showed them my ring and said I was married."

"London?" he asked.

"Nothing says romance more than London." *Or a guy from London.*

He frowned. "Don't even think about stealing my idea."

I finished up the last of the calla lilies and gathered them around me. "You're just mad because I made it better."

He sat up when I did and slipped one of the old-fashioned roses off my leg. Austen studied it before sliding it into my hair. "Oh, my version's definitely better."

I felt his fingers leave my hair. Austen could've laid a kiss on me and I wouldn't have been more astonished. I had told him that the flower-in-the-hair gesture was the most romantic thing I could think of. Why was he doing it now? To be nice—or was he using it against me?

My face was red—I felt it. Junie brought in cakes with the help of her fellow caterers. She had marbled the cakes with ribbons of frosting, and decorated the outside with a riot of real flowers and jeweled frosting. They were works of art.

Austen's lips went up when she passed him. "Hello Junie."

"Not Junie Be Fair?" she asked with a smile.

He shrugged. "Junie fits you better right now." He pointed at the flowers in one of the cakes she held. "The flowers bloom when you're near."

She giggled.

I groaned. Once she was out of earshot, I turned to him. "I think I preferred Junie Be Fair."

"No, nicknames are out. It's on your list." He picked up one of the lamps and put it on the table. He gave me a serious look. "I've figured out the first thing on my list. You can't wear red."

I glanced down at my red shirt. "Why?"

He leaned forward and whispered, "It looks too good on you. It's not fair to the bride." His eyes crinkled up to show me he was joking. He was such a flirt. He always was, but it didn't amount to anything if there was nothing behind it. "You can't wear it for another week," he said.

I stared at him, trying to put it together. The wedding party would break up at the end of the week. That meant no more Dancey. Was Austen that concerned about me going out with the rock star that he had to tell me how to dress with him? I would've taken the flower out of my hair and thrown it at Austen, but knew I could never perform such sacrilege. I cleared my throat instead. "I changed my mind, Austen; you can use nicknames." I stood up and shook out the candies in the bag onto the first table to show him how it was done. "And voila, we have our centerpiece."

"Sure thing, Mrs. Austen."

I frowned at the nickname. "Does that mean I'm taking on your first name or are you calling me a romantic like Jane Austen?"

He treated me to a bland smile. "You decide."

My shoulders tightened. I had to either let him torment me with a new nickname or not wear red for a week. "Fine," I said. "I won't wear red."

I went to work on the next table, and he helped me, placing a hand on my back whenever he had to get past me to get more flowers. I tried not to react. If a touch meant nothing to him, it meant nothing to me. The next time he did it, he didn't move away, as though he kept his hand resting on my back for the sake of convenience. Our movements quickly fell into sync after that, and the closeness between us felt so natural that it made me nervous. I didn't want to fall for him again, and I rushed off to get more lamps, keeping out of Austen's way so he wouldn't add further upheaval to my world.

That didn't stop him from making eyes at me from across the table. "Second thing on my list," he said. His lips turned up with humor, and I got ready for something outrageous. "No wearing your hair down this week. Put it in a tight ponytail."

"Back off!" Then I laughed. "What's your problem? If you're doing this because you're worried about me attracting the *wrong* attention, then I'm not doing it."

"It isn't," he said after a moment.

"Then why?"

"Your hair looks good up. You don't do it enough."

Now I *knew* he was lying. "Don't wear red because it looks good? Wear my hair up because it does—all so I can keep you from calling me Mrs. Austen? I'm calling your bluff—you'd never call me that in public. It's too much of a commitment for you. It's like you're claiming me."

"Hey, if the nickname doesn't work, I'll wear you down somehow. Don't forget, we'll be spending a lot of time together this week. I'm your slave after all."

I liked that idea too much, and now it was time to get my revenge. Leaning closer to him and standing on tiptoes so that our eyes were almost level, I smiled, feeling the breath of his lips against mine. "Try to wear me down and I promise it will backfire on you."

"I think I might enjoy that." His eyes were on my lips, and I was just as shameless, my eyes drifting to his mouth, then back to the unspoken promise that I read in his expression. I remembered what he'd said about being able to feel a girl's emotion behind her kiss. Would he know what I felt for him if I let this moment play through naturally?

My thoughts got caught in what he had said a few days earlier about how a kiss was meant to bring two people closer. There was no other meaning to it—no commitment, no promise of more.

And I was a romantic. Flowers in my hair meant something. Stolen glances. Long hugs. Holding hands—I was all about signs of affection. A kiss meant I gave someone my heart. Maybe that made me superstitious. Sure, it wasn't as bad as thinking a photograph could steal my soul; but I sure thought a kiss could.

And he didn't see it that way.

I lowered my lashes, feeling a deep disappointment pool at the pit of my stomach as I pulled away. His eyes mirrored that same disappointment, but he took on a casual look. "Does that mean we have a deal?"

It took me a second to realize that he was talking about the list; but it was uneven. I had only made one rule for him, and he had two for me. "I'll only do it," I said, "if you act the part of my perfect little wedding assistant for the whole week. No complaints or the deal is off."

"You got it." He sat back on the floor with the rest of the ribbon. "At least now I'm getting something out of it."

Before I could ask him what he meant, a little girl wandered into Pemburkley Hall. It was one of Taylor's flower girls. She sucked on the upper half of her hand, watching us with sober eyes.

Austen broke into an easy smile. "Looks like we've got a straggler. Text Taylor that we have one of her flower girls; tell her to bring us money in small, unmarked bills and we'll return the girl in time for her wedding."

I ignored him. "Hey," I asked the little girl. "You lost?"

135

She didn't answer and wandered over to us to point at the rose in my hair. "Pretty."

I had almost forgotten it was there. I plucked up one of the calla lilies on the table and slid it into her baby-soft hair. "Now *you're* pretty, too," I said.

She stood a little straighter, her lips puckering out, looking very self-important. Austen leaned back on his elbows. "And another romantic is born," he said.

"Don't blame me for that. She's a girl. It comes naturally."

"I can fix that. Here comes a spider." Austen's hand crawled toward the little girl, making it look like a big, fat spider. "He likes flowers," he said in a grumbly voice. He tried to steal the flower from her hair, and the little girl shrieked and smashed his hand flat. "That's what I'm talking about." Austen laughed. "I'll make an Amazon woman out of her yet."

She crushed his hand spider a few more times until I had to land on my knees and interfere with my own hand spider. It was a friendlier one and would dance in the ribbons and flowers to the beat of the wedding music until Austen's hand spider went to attack it. The little girl shrieked out a warning, but I made sure that my hand spider was fast and would dance away in the nick of time.

Austen couldn't take it. He wrapped his arms around my waist and slid me across the polished wooden floor, tucking me close to his side so that his hand spider could capture mine. With a start, I realized we weren't dealing with spiders anymore—Austen and I were holding hands.

"Austen!" I said.

"Don't worry," he told the little girl. "That spider won't get to your flowers!"

The little girl danced around us. "Thanksh!"

Austen looked sternly at my hand. "Be nice." And then he lifted up my fisted fingers and kissed the knuckles. My whole body went weak. His fingers loosed from mine, and he winked at me as if he hadn't just kissed my hand like a . . . like a man from my dreams.

The little girl sighed and brought her hands up in the air and twirled. "Now dance with her!" she commanded.

Austen watched me, the way Bigley looked at Taylor, the way my grandparents looked at each other, the way Darcy from *Pride and Prejudice* looked at Elizabeth. Before this moment, I'd never imagined that Austen would ever look at me this way. "There will be dancing tonight," he reminded me.

"Who wants to wait for that?" I asked.

"You're right; dancing is so dumb."

That wasn't what I meant, and he knew it. Still, the caterers were back with more food, and the last thing I wanted was to share this moment with any of them. I didn't have to worry. Austen freed my hand. Footsteps traveled behind us and I turned, seeing Junie carry in another platter of food.

Austen turned professional. "Can we help you bring those in?" he asked her.

She gave me a knowing look, and I tried to appear more closed off because I was confused again. Jane. Junie. Jane. Junie. No wonder Austen had to give her a nickname to tell us apart. Was she the reason that Austen had let go of my hand?

"Austen, I would love *your* help," Junie said.

I gathered the flowers so I could finish off the room. "Why don't you help her, Austen?" I asked. I broke off in a light laugh. "And while you're at it, make a list of demands she has to follow before you do it."

Junie made a sound of disgust behind me and came up to Austen, a seductive swing to her hips. "I did promise that you could take me out to lunch today, Austen. We could head out to the beach after you help me take in the last of the food."

Austen smiled up at her as though it was completely normal to end a flirt session with me to go on a lunch date with another woman.

Junie watched him possessively, and I finally knew why she hated me: Austen. Was he playing us both?

I dropped the rest of my flowers on the refreshment table and took up the little flower girl's hand. "I'd better return this little runaway before Taylor releases the search hounds. Have fun on your date with Junie, Austen."

My disappointment leaked through the memory of our earlier laughter together. It was so easy to get caught up in the magic of Austen. He made it so that I couldn't think about anyone else. I could feel Austen's eyes on my back as I walked away, and I knew I had to find a way to forget about him. So far the only person to help me do that was Dancey, and if Austen could go after someone else, then so could I.

Chapter 12

The glasses clinked together. Voices murmured. Soft music provided the perfect background for it all. Pemburkley Hall was completely transformed under the soft glow of the night. The little candles Austen had helped me stuff into the decorative lamps revealed faces that I was just beginning to recognize from the wedding party.

Since red was denied me, I wore a white dress with a flirty skirt. I had piled my auburn hair high on the top of my head and allowed the curls to escape down the side of my face. Taylor sat at the long table with Bigley at the front of the room. Her face was awash with a soft glow that I only noticed in women in love. Take that, Austen. Taylor was happy.

My heels clicked against the wooden floor on my way to the microphones. I tapped the mics to make sure that they were working. Everyone looked up at the noise, and I felt a flush of embarrassment creep up my neck. The tension from the guests was thick in this room, and I blamed it on the latest arrivals.

The Bigleys had come to town only hours earlier. Ann-Marie had breathlessly confided all the gory details to me. Bigley's mother had checked in only moments after his father had stepped in with wife number two. The first Mrs. Bigley had taken one look at the second

Mrs. Bigley and, without saying a word to her former husband, left for the beach, leaving instructions for Freddy to bring her luggage to her room without her. She hadn't returned to the main house.

Judging by appearances alone, Bigley's dad must like the blondes, since he'd married another one so soon after he divorced the first—though the second Mrs. Bigley looked to be a blonde in bottle only. The two women were near enough alike that they could be sisters, though years apart in age. Now all the Bigley women made a row of blondes to the left of their son. I wasn't sure how they'd managed the seating arrangement, since we had tried to keep the bickering group apart.

Mrs. Bigley the First had claimed her son's side. Bigley's father sat next to her, nestled tightly between wife number one and number two. Either Bigley senior had no idea that his former and present wives were at war with each other or he thought that he could keep the peace by pretending that they weren't. He smiled at the glowering women.

Mrs. Bigley the Second was tall and lanky; possibly a former model. She draped over Bigley senior's arm like a second skin. Though she had a smile that seemed pleasant, her narrowed eyes told a different story. Wife number one was shorter and stouter, with more wrinkles. She groomed her son with tight, rough movements, undoing his tie and redoing it. The poor guy looked stressed.

I left the mic and went to their table to lean over Taylor. My long necklace brushed her shoulder. "Everyone here?"

"Where's Dancey?" Bigley looked strangled by his mother's hands. "If we're doing speeches, I want him to say something."

"Chuck, dear." His mother smoothed down the invisible wrinkles on his jacket. "I don't want a repeat of your sister's wedding. Tell your father that he cannot have more than two glasses of Tequila sunrise if he's going to speak."

Bigley glanced over at his father, hesitated, and with his mother's unrelenting eyes on him said, "Dad, what's that you're drinking?"

The senior Bigley guffawed and held up his glass. "A sugarplum Martini. And tell your mother that I plan on getting quite drunk."

Mrs. Bigley the First swung around, dropping the pretense of using her son as a mediator. "Is that what you really want to do, Herb? Remember what happened last time."

"It's a wedding, Louise," Mrs. Bigley the Second hissed over her new husband's arm. "Try to act like a human for once."

Bigley's mother glared back. "Stay out of this, Carol."

Bigley senior laughed. His son, with his eyes trained on his elders, downed his drink in one gulp. Taylor's hand went to his sleeve, and she shook her head. Bigley forced a laugh, and suddenly I saw the similarity between him and his father. I didn't like it. I noticed the dark circles under Taylor's eyes. Behind that loving glow, her worry was eating at her. If Austen saw it, he'd misinterpret and spring to action.

"Okay, great." I clapped my hands. "Are the speeches all ready then?"

"We'll wait a little longer," Taylor said, nodding to her side where her mother sat alone at the far end of the table. Mrs. Weston had flown all the way from Massachusetts. She had dark features like her daughter, but the lines around her mouth showed that she pursed them often. Her lips were smothered in red lipstick. "Dad should be here any moment."

Taylor's own personal drama had gotten lost with the loudness of the Bigley's family feud. An empty seat between mother and daughter represented where Taylor's father should be sitting. Mr. Weston was finishing up a business trip in New York before flying in to attend his daughter's wedding between business deals—he should've been here hours ago.

I squeezed Taylor's shoulder. "Let me know when you're ready." Taylor's parents weren't big on the whole sentimental thing. After meeting them over the summer, I had decided that the severe couple could hold *"Baby, I Love You, But I Just Can't Smile"* contests and both come out as winners—or, in reality, big losers. I felt terrible for Taylor. "Is there anything else you'd like me to do?"

"No, thank you, Jane. We'll just wait."

Bigley reached out to give me a grateful pat. I jerked when he got my backside instead, and I tried not to laugh in embarrassment. Instead I gave him one of those reassuring smiles that meant I wasn't going to file charges.

Taylor fixed her fiancé with a look that I couldn't read. "When will Dancey be here?"

Bigley's eyes twinkled in what could only be a Herculean effort to restore his usual good humor. "I'm not worried. He'll be here soon." He reached out and touched me again, this time avoiding anywhere scandalous. He got my arm instead. "You look smashing, Jane, but this is Taylor's night. Try not to run away with the prince, Cinderella."

I nodded, having no idea what he was implying, and made good my escape. My stomach had been growling ever since I'd laid eyes on the hors d'oeuvres. Junie and I might be rivals, but it didn't mean that I didn't enjoy her food. My thoughts wandered to Austen, and I hoped I'd find him soon. I needed someone to distract me from the Bigleys. I stole a slice of chocolate cake and spiked a folded wafer delight with a toothpick.

"Oh, I hoped they'd let you come to this boring dinner."

I stifled a groan when the groom's stepbrother cornered me with his one-liner. Crawley had his plate piled as high as I hoped to have mine. "Of course I came," I managed a pleasant tone. "I'm in charge."

His eyes slid over me from the curls in my hair to my black heels. His gaze lingered on my fitted white dress. "Taylor should've at least insisted that you wear rags. No one will be able to pay attention to the bride with you dressed like that."

My stomach dropped, and it made me lose my appetite—that was the second comment on upstaging Taylor in the space of a minute, and it only mirrored Austen's accusations earlier. I angrily swiped more food from the table onto my plate, not sure if I'd be able to stuff any of it into my mouth now. "Why did you say that? That's not really something that a girl wants to hear. It's completely insulting."

"Is it?" he asked lazily. "You're always lecturing me on what's polite. You'd give Dear Abbey a run for her money."

"I'm not sure she'd survive you," I said. "Are we through here?"

"I hope not. Where are we sitting?"

I grimaced, hoping to pass that off as a dismissive smile and headed for the farthest table. Crawley followed me. He set his food on the table beside mine and left. Before I could think about moving, he came back with a raspberry punch for me. "You forgot this." He set it beside me and sat down. "See, I'm not all bad."

I allowed myself a nervous laugh. "I didn't say you were bad, Crawley."

"You just don't want to talk to me. I get it." He took a sip of his drink, staring at me like I was a particularly hard puzzle to figure out. "Do you want to blow off this party and go hang out somewhere, private?"

I almost choked on one of Junie's delicious pastries. "Now I know that you're teasing me."

A deep dimple played at the corner of his lips to show me that I was right on. I felt myself relax. "As a matter of fact," I said, "I do want to get to know you better. Tell me about your mother." *Wife number two*, I amended silently.

He straightened unconsciously and wiped a napkin at his mouth. "You really know how to ruin the mood, don't you?"

This time I burst out laughing, realizing that I actually felt more sympathy for Crawley after meeting the family. "I excel at ruining the mood, actually."

"It's a terrible habit."

I nodded. Romantics knew their stuff. A flurry of excitement at the other side of the room let me know that Bella had entered . . . in red. Her pearly white skin shone against the contrast. As soon as she met my eyes, I waved her over. I couldn't help it. She was pretty enough to catch Crawley's attention and smart enough to keep her distance, especially if I hinted at video games in her near future.

"Jane!" She made her elegant way to our table and eased down into the seat, smoothing her red skirt down. Her blond hair glistened in the candlelight.

Crawley turned into the perfect gentleman as soon as he saw her. "Are you hungry?"

"A little," she admitted.

He left to gather the necessary enticements to win her affections. I tried not to laugh—it was easy to distract Crawley from me. "I'm so glad I found you," Bella said. "Freddy is being a total nuisance. He said he wants to take me home—like I want to go to his mother's stuffy basement."

I coughed into my hand. "Let me guess. He tried to tell you that the place belonged to him?"

Her finger trailed over the scarlet tablecloth. "Yes, can you believe it?"

Harry Crawley placed a plate in front of Bella with the perfect blend of sweets and greasy meats. Bella took it gratefully. Her eyes zeroed in on Crawley with sudden interest. "You're Bigley's brother. How come you don't have his hot British accent?"

"A mistake I'm working on," he said, grinning at her with a sweetness I'd never noticed in him before. "We're stepbrothers, so I didn't grow up in Britain."

"Neither did Dancey." I said it without thinking, and their eyes went to me. I saw consideration in Crawley's. Yes, the loner rock star actually stooped to talk to me. I downplayed it. "I *think* he grew up in Massachusetts. It's on wiki somewhere."

A tinkling of glasses let me know that Taylor was ready for her speeches. Her father now graced her end of the table. His frown added to the collection of severe lines down his face. Dancey was still noticeably absent. It was ironic that his tragic figure could actually add cheer to the group.

"You'll have to go on without me, Bella," I said. "Take care of her, Crawley. I'm on duty."

I left them, feeling like a proud mother leaving her cubs. Crawley wasn't so bad, I decided—he was more of a jokester. And Bella was a sweet girl. I had misjudged both of them, which meant I was more than eager to throw the two together and enjoy their resulting happiness. Approaching the mic, I slid it out of the holder. The musicians took my lead and let their music die down.

"Thank you all for coming to Chuck and Taylor's rehearsal dinner." I winced inwardly when I said their names aloud, hoping no one noticed it sounded like the shoe brand. *Thank you very much for pointing that out, Austen.*

I licked my lips. "You number among Chuck and Taylor's dearest friends and family. Thank you for sharing one of the happiest, most important events in their lives. We are going to start out with a few words from Taylor's parents, followed by Chuck's. After that, we invite anyone who would like to stand and congratulate Chuck and Taylor on their coming nuptials to please do so."

Taking the mic in a firm grip, Taylor's father cleared his throat for his speech. I backed away and almost ran into Austen. The darkness shadowed his firm jaw. The candlelight made his hazel eyes gold, and my heart quickened at the sight of him. He was decked out in a white V-neck and dark jeans, his towering height giving me the security that I craved.

"The happiest event in their lives?" he asked me in an undertone.

Even his predictable disapproval was comforting. I glanced over at him, aware that his arm rested against mine. "That's generally what a marriage is," I said.

"It's supposed to be," he countered.

I gave him a warning look. If he was holding me to not wearing red and putting my hair up, then I was going to insist that he didn't rain on Taylor's parade. His eyes flicked over me. "You look good."

He didn't sound happy about it. Still, it didn't stop him from sliding a protective arm against the wall behind me.

Resisting the urge to ask him how his date with Junie had gone, I watched while Taylor's parents and then the Bigleys stood up to give their speeches. They were so proud. So happy. So excited. The moment failed to touch me like it normally did. It was all fake. The presence of Mr. Doom and Gloom beside me only made me notice the warning looks the parents shot at each other and at their children—the frowns, the slurred speeches, the shifting eyes.

Bertie stole the mic next. She also wore a flowing red dress. It sparkled under the candlelight. She put the microphone to her lips. There was a hard edge to her words, like she was staking her claim as best friend of the bride. "It's hard to believe that Taylor is leaving me for London. We've had so many adventures together."

Bertie expounded on her role in Taylor's life without including anything about Taylor—the speech filled me with sadness and made me wonder if Bertie cared about the bride at all. If Taylor didn't have her best friend, and she didn't have concerned parents, who did she have?

I glanced over at Austen, and he obligingly met my gaze as if he had waited for me to connect with him all night. I was the girl who thought that everything Taylor did was genius, and Austen pretty much thought the opposite. Taylor might have us, but she needed a better balance of friends.

Austen shifted, and I followed his gaze to find Dancey as he made his fashionably late entrance. The best man prowled around the perimeter of the room wearing a dress shirt with a few buttons undone. His hair was disheveled; not like he'd slept on it, but as though he'd run his hands through it while deep in thought—I couldn't help seeing him as some hero torn from the pages of my worn Jane Austen novels. He fit every romantic ideal I'd ever had.

He stepped into the spotlight just in time for Bertie to offer him the mic. Dancey shook his head once and dropped into the seat next to Bigley. His best friend was already grinning at his unconventional behavior.

Bertie wouldn't take no for an answer. She gave a hard giggle, straightening her ramrod back so that she seemed more imposing. "Now that everyone has heard from the bride's *best* friend, they want to hear from the groom's. Take it, Dancey."

Dancey didn't attempt a smile. "I have nothing to say."

The room went silent, and it felt smothering. Taylor's hands tightened over her napkin, and she twisted it.

Before it could get too awkward, I rushed forward and took the mic. "Well, *I'm* not about to pass up an opportunity to express my love for my friends." I had no idea what to say—I wasn't even expecting to give a pep talk at this thing. I tried to cover my hesitation with another flow of words. "Taylor, I just want you to know that I admire you so much. You're the sister I never had, and you know I've had my share of brothers."

Taylor giggled at that, and I tried to relax. "I remember the first time I met you—you were balanced on a ladder and two chairs to change a light bulb on a twelve-foot ceiling. It was really hard not to like you after that. You're so determined. It's a tremendous honor to follow in your footsteps—you do so much good here. I'll miss you. But I want your happiness more than anything," as I said it, I felt the impact of my own words, "and I hope you're happy . . ." Oh no, I realized that I was parroting Austen now. I avoided his cynical eyes. "I *know* you're happy. Of course you are. Anyway, Bigley sees it. He's a good man. Someone told me once that a kiss says it all. And since Bigley's the only one here who you've kissed . . . that way . . ." *uh, hopefully. What was I saying?* "I'm sure Bigley could tell us all how much you love him. And he loves you too. You're so lucky that you share that kind of love."

That was a disaster.

I smiled weakly at Taylor. Her eyes were bright with unshed tears—at least *she* didn't think I was a failure. Before I could slide the mic back into the stand for another unsuspecting victim to take, Dancey stretched his hand out for it.

After a moment's hesitation, I gave it to him. He handled it like an old friend—holding a mic was what he did for a living. "Are you sure your coworker isn't who you want for your best friend, Taylor?" he asked in his captivating British accent.

Bertie glared at me for that. I wanted to hold up my hands to defend myself, but Dancey wasn't through with us yet. Besides sitting a little straighter in his chair, he didn't stand. "You should listen to Jane, Taylor. You have love, you have everything. Your happiness means everything to those who love you. We'll support you no matter what happens." Even Dancey was sounding like Austen—hinting at something that I couldn't figure out. I felt like I was missing a few episodes in a mini-series. What did he know that I didn't? Dancey studied his best friend. "Chuck, it's not every day that a man finds love—you have everything that I want. And you did nothing to deserve it. I positively hate you."

Bigley leaned back and laughed at the joke. "At least you're honest, Dancey."

I gulped. When expressing affection, best girl friends said I love you and best guy friends said I hate you. Even though I had a lot of brothers, I still didn't understand how guys worked, but at least the groom shared Dancey's sense of humor. I could tell Taylor didn't. She was chalky white.

Unaware of any disturbing vibes, Mary grabbed a hold of the microphone next. She went on about how she put her health in jeopardy to attend the wedding because Taylor meant so much to her. I tried to sidestep from the action. As soon as I did, Austen found my hand in the dim room and folded my fingers over a glass. "Get Taylor some water," he said.

Turning, I saw Taylor was fighting tears again. I circled back to her and set the drink down in front of her. She gratefully tipped it back, swallowing the water like she couldn't get it down fast enough.

The poor girl was dying of thirst. I went to find more water and, spying Dancey's unused glass, stole his instead and set it in front of Taylor, who drank that too.

She wrapped her hand around mine. "Jane, could you see about getting a pitcher of water from the kitchen? Dancey needs his glass refilled." She smiled at me when I hesitated. "You can leave me; I'm good now."

I wasn't so sure about that, but sweet Bella took the microphone next. Crawley crouched on a chair near her, waiting for his turn—I was almost positive that the two had dared each other to go up. They were nervous, but at least *they* cared about the bride and groom. I spied Bertie glaring at the blond bridesmaid as if she had stolen Crawley from her—from a married woman? Everything was so confusing. I stepped back from Taylor, accidentally brushing past Dancey on my way out. He didn't acknowledge me, just glowered at the room. Something was wrong with him, too. After Taylor's violent reaction to his puzzling speech, I couldn't stand to look at him.

I reached the kitchen and blinked under the harsh florescent lights. The caterers busily put the finishing touches on little pastries. Junie headed the little army, her rosebud lips pressed firmly together. She had stripped down to a simple white T-shirt and cut off shorts. She was barefoot and balanced on the counter, trying to get more pots from the highest shelves. For a moment, she looked so free that I wished we could trade places.

"Jane!" Ann-Marie tugged me away from the pot rack over the kitchen island. I got a good whiff of peroxide. Ann-Marie had gone platinum blond for the occasion. She looked like a bombshell in her elegant scarlet dress. Taylor's wedding colors were the theme of the night. "Did you see him? The rock star. He's so dark and mysterious." She peered out of the kitchen at the wedding party in the Pemburkley. "He just says it like it is, doesn't he?"

"Yeah, real cool," I said, spreading the sarcasm thick. Taylor couldn't handle Dancey's candor in her fragile state. He was worse than Austen.

Ann-Marie gave a little shriek that made my skin prickle in alarm. "Wait!" she said. "He's coming this way. Dancey! He's coming. Oh!"

What? I ducked behind a tall cabinet, seeing Dancey push his way into the kitchen as though he had every right to be there. I turned away and grabbed a potato and pretended to be busy at the sink. I could feel his stare and hoped I looked busy enough so that he would find someone else to pester. He had his dignity to preserve, right? I turned the water on and scrubbed at the potato. From the corner of my eye, I could see his chest rising and lowering while he considered me. After too long, he turned to go. I squeezed my eyes shut, glad I didn't have to talk to him.

A shriek made me swing around. Ann-Marie crumpled into a heap of red skirts in the middle of the room, holding her ankle. "Oh! Help. My ankle. Help!"

"Ann-Marie!" I wiped my hands off on the nearest towel and ran to her.

She wiped at her dry eyes. "I stepped on my foot wrong," she moaned. I knew when she was faking, but, too late, I noticed that Dancey was more than willing to play her game.

"Are you all right?" Dancey moved closer. He wasn't looking at her—his eyes were on me.

I lifted my hands helplessly. "Ann-Marie, uh, has weak ankles."

Junie hopped off her counter and sauntered over to inspect the madness for herself. She rolled her eyes when she saw Ann-Marie conning poor Dancey with the ankle act. Junie probably thought that I had something to do with it. "Jane?" she asked. "Can't you take Ann-Marie somewhere else to *heal*?"

I blushed. "Yeah, just a sec."

"Yes, yes, I need someone to carry me to my car." Ann-Marie's eyes were on Dancey. "I'll never be able to make it on my own."

Dancey knelt next to her. "Would you settle for my hand?"

"I'm not sure," she said slowly. "Maybe you should check my ankle to see if it's sprained before I put any weight on it first?"

Dancey glanced up at me, and I noticed his eyes twinkled with amusement. "Jane, perhaps you should call for an ambulance. This girl is plainly too hurt to make it all the way home."

"It's too bad," I said, taking his cue. "There will be dancing tonight. So many cute guys. She'll really be missing out."

A look of genuine distress ran across Ann-Marie's face. "Maybe I should test my ankle first. I can't miss out on dancing."

"I don't know." I tapped her ankle. "Does this hurt?"

She sucked in her breath, but after a moment screwed her face into a brave look. "It doesn't hurt as much as I thought it did."

Dancey's large hands wrapped around Ann-Marie's smaller ones, and he helped her to her feet. Ann-Marie took a few experimental steps until she nodded in satisfaction.

"It's a miracle," Dancey said. "She can walk."

"And dance," she reminded him. "I can dance."

"Then you must save one for me," he said in his proper British accent.

She shrieked out a laugh. Dancey had just made a nineteen-year-old girl's night—maybe her year. My heart softened towards him, too. "Right now?" Ann-Marie asked.

"Not while everyone is still bidding their final farewells to the bride and groom," Dancey said with that same lingering bitterness from before. "Why don't you enjoy the rest of your night until I meet you later?"

She nodded and practically ran out the door, leaving me still kneeling at Dancey's feet. He smiled and wrapped his hands underneath my arms to help me up. I gasped at his strength. My feet hit the ground and he held me close, his face near mine, not letting me go. "Now you, on the other hand," he said under his breath, "I wouldn't mind carrying to your car."

"I don't have one." My eyes widened when I realized what I had just admitted—I didn't want to be the social inferior in this relationship. "I have a bike. I don't need one—a car, I mean." I was babbling now. "I live here, so . . ."

"Are you a mermaid who lives on the foam of the ocean, or are you a nymph in the woods?"

I relaxed at his teasing tone. "I'm the evil doll they keep in the attic."

"A treasure then." He released me, but stayed close, as though he was afraid I'd wander away. "I wanted to thank you for what you said to Taylor. She needs more friends like you."

"Why do you say that?"

"Her bridesmaids seem . . . interesting."

Oh. He was just as confused by Taylor's friends as I was. Maybe that made him worried for the groom. I gave him a reassuring smile. "Yeah. Taylor's nothing like them—she's stressed right now. That's all. I hope we can still keep in touch when she moves to London—she's not into long-distance relationships . . . which is why Bigley was so surprising to all of us who know her. It must be true love."

Dancey looked pained, and I realized that he didn't like talking about his best friend's relationship with Taylor. Did he not want to lose his friend to someone he saw as unstable or was he so miserable with his love life that he didn't like to see anyone else happy?

Crawley's voice drifted over to where we stood by the kitchen door. From where we were, we could see him standing by Bigley with the mic. "I look up to my big brother," Crawley said. "We might not be blood-related, but I want to do everything he does . . ."

"Come with me." Dancey caught my hand in his. "I need some air."

That sounded very intriguing. I let him lead me past Junie's watchful eyes and out the back door. Tiny decorative lights sparkled through the trees outside and glittered over the top of the pool. The waves from the beach muffled the speeches inside. Dancey led me to the railing that overlooked a patch of trees framing the bright moon as it rose over the crashing waves.

Dancey wasn't looking at the view; he was looking at me. His hand went to my hair, and he slid a curl from my carefully arranged updo. "You stand out from all those girls painted in red inside. You're stunning."

Austen would be frustrated to hear it—I could hardly wait to tease him about how his plan had backfired. Dancey's fingers gently massaged the back of my hand and I banished all thoughts of the overprotective Austen out of my head. "I didn't want to come to Bigley's wedding," Dancey said, "but I'm glad that I did, Jane."

His eyes went to my lips. He wanted to kiss me. Things were going too fast for me, which made me realize that I really wasn't into flings. I moistened my lips and decided to taint the situation with the ridiculous. "You always wanted to be a valet, huh?" I asked.

"I always wanted to be with a girl who didn't care who I was." His fingers caught my waist, and he pulled me closer. He smelled good. He was tall and manly and dressed really well—his arms felt like they belonged around me. His lips tipped up in a smile, and I knew he was going to kiss me.

Every girl instinct screamed at me that all I had to do was close my eyes and enjoy the moment. I cleared my throat instead. "Why didn't you want to go to Bigley's wedding?"

That killed the moment and I knew it. His hands loosened over me. "Weddings are—you know—they're depressing."

And now *he* had killed the moment—pretty much stabbed it, skewered it and burned the evidence. "You don't like marriage?" I asked.

"No. No. Jane, no. It's just that I know Bigley . . ."

Now I was worried. "He's not good enough for Taylor?"

"No."

My heart fluttered. "You don't think Taylor's good enough for your best friend?"

153

He laughed. "Are you through with accusing me of everything under the sun?"

The offense I felt on my friend's behalf made me all prickly, and I couldn't even meet his gaze because I was so confused. I shifted away from him. "Then why?"

"Because I'm a jerk. Hey, I'm sorry." He reached out and rubbed my back and I felt the prickles start to recede under his warm touch. Half of me wanted to pull away, but his eyes were beseeching on mine. "I shouldn't have said that. I haven't been the easiest person to get along with lately. I don't even know what my problem is. Do you forgive me, Jane?"

"I . . ." There was nothing to be angry about really—it's just that I wanted *moments* that added up to something. And if things like marriage and commitment really meant nothing to Dancey, then I didn't want to get involved, because our love was doomed before it started. I had thought that I could relax and just have fun, but now I realized that I didn't want another Austen.

Faint music from Pemburkley Hall reached us from inside. The uncomfortable toasts were over, and the dancing had begun. "Jane?" Dancey tipped my chin up so he could look into my eyes. "I promise not to talk like that anymore. I *like* being around you. You're different. You make me happy."

His charm was really hard to fight against. My doubts wrestled with my natural instinct to enjoy being with him. My smile won out. "You make me happy, too," I said.

Dancey looked relieved. "Do you forgive me?"

I nodded.

"Then dance with me?"

I studied his hand—the fingers were long and tapered, perfect for handling a guitar, perfect for holding hands. I accepted it and wasn't sorry when his fingers wrapped around mine in his strangely comforting touch.

The faint beat of the music followed his movements. It mixed with the sounds of the waves pushing up against the beach. He led me over the balcony, the music guiding me into his arms. The flickering tiki torches fought the dark enough for me to study his eyes that drank me in. It was like Dancey couldn't get enough of me, treasured me as much as I felt any hero should.

It wasn't long before Dancey went after his kiss again. His fingers strayed through my hair and trailed over my ears to my jaw, and there he held me captive with nothing but the force of his light touch. He didn't ask, but I didn't pull away this time, and he took it as permission.

His lips met mine, tentatively at first as if afraid I'd push him away. I wasn't sure of his intentions, but I remembered Austen's words—showing affection didn't mean commitment. It meant something else, an expressed interest—and I was interested.

Dancey's lips slanted over mine, and he deepened his kiss. My arms wrapped convulsively around him. I was afraid I'd fall if I didn't hold on. He became more confident, trailing kisses over my cheeks and neck. Then Dancey's kiss turned desperate somehow—almost like it was mirroring the kiss that Taylor had given Bigley at the wedding rehearsal.

I told my brain to shut off and enjoy the moment, but as soon as Dancey's grip tightened on me, I wasn't sure if he knew that he held me anymore. A girl maybe, but not me. It didn't make sense. Maybe I was imagining it.

And then I wasn't.

I pushed my hand against his chest. He gave me a curious look when I stepped back. I took a deep breath, not sure what to say. His fingers stroked my arm. His other hand was tangled through my hair. I knew that he wanted nothing more than to go back to kissing me again.

"Jane!"

I turned. Captain Redd stood by the kitchen door. I could only see his silhouette from the light of the kitchen, but his broad, unyielding shoulders told me his identity. "Are you out here?"

Dancey squeezed my arm and gave me a reassuring smile before pecking me lightly on the lips and stepping away.

"Oh, there you are, Dancey. Junie said you might be out here, too." Redd stepped further into the darkness. "Jane," his voice dripped with disapproval when he found me. I felt his condemnation pierce through my bones. Everything the captain thought about me had just been validated. Here I was lurking in the darkness with a guest when I was supposed to be running the show.

"Redd," I forced my voice to be light, but it was husky and it gave me away. I cleared my throat. "Did Taylor need me?"

"Yes. Right away." Redd ducked back into the kitchen, his shoulders stiff.

Dancey laughed beside me. "What's his problem?"

"I'm supposed to be inside." To my horror, I heard the stress come out in my voice.

He changed his tone. "I'm sorry. This is my fault." He started helping me with my hair—it was all over the place. "You should've left it down," he said. "It would've been less obvious."

"I didn't know that I was going to—"

"No, of course not. I didn't plan for it either, if that's what you're thinking." He laughed and managed to get some of my hair back up before bumping noses with me.

That got me to laughing too. "Dancey, you're a fast mover," I accused. "I shouldn't have come out here with you. You are too charming and I'm . . . well, I shouldn't have done that."

"What?" he asked me. "This?" He kissed me again, but this time his eyes were on mine, and I saw the tenderness behind his gaze. I must've been wrong about him before. I was letting my romantic ideals ruin a good thing.

"Yes, this," I said. And since the joke was too good to resist, I playfully pecked his lips with my own in a light kiss. He lifted me off my feet, stealing my breath away. Before setting me back down, he caught my ear with another kiss. The sound of it echoed through my hearing. My hair fell down around us. His hands had shredded through my carefully arranged hairdo again.

"It's hopeless," he whispered into my ear. "We'll leave it down for now."

"I can't."

Or all bets with Austen were off.

They might already be. For once, I didn't have to fantasize about love from a book because it was much more fascinating in real life. Not attempting to fix my hair again, Dancey took my hand possessively and led me into the party inside.

Chapter 13

"It is the greatest absurdity . . . . The folly of not allowing people to be comfortable at home—and the folly of people's not staying comfortably at home when they can!"

—Jane Austen, Emma

Carrying my high heels on the tips of my fingers, I stole through the hall that was outside the lobby, feeling the soft grey rug beneath my toes. Freddy headed the opposite direction from the lobby, looking tired. His dark hair was its usual messy perfection.

"Where's Austen?" I asked him as we passed.

Freddy gave me a long stare before answering. "Gone to bed . . . like any sane person."

That meant that I could sneak through the lobby to my bedroom unseen. Austen hadn't been at the party when I'd returned with Dancey. It was a good thing, because Austen was way too observant, and I didn't feel like fighting with him about Dancey right now. I was in the middle of my own argument with myself.

I tiptoed through the hall and pushed the door open, only to meet Austen's eyes at the checkout counter. He took one look at my hair toppling freely over my shoulders and turned to the girl sitting at the counter with him. "Hey, Junie Be Fair, look who the party spat out?"

Junie skewered me with a disgusted glance before ducking behind Austen's laptop again. She patted his arm, whispering something that I couldn't hear, and then before I could use the distraction to move through the room unnoticed, she left without saying a word to me. Junie was so full of secrets and drama. *I had mystery too.* I just didn't let everybody know it.

I gave Austen a tight smile and tried to slip past. His voice stopped me. "What did you do to Junie? I think she hates you."

"I think I breathe too much," I said. "It's highly offensive." I placed my hand on the doorknob rather than explain that Junie saw me as competition and it was all Austen's fault. The phone at the checkout counter rang.

"Wait." Austen pushed a button on the phone to silence it. "How did everything go tonight?"

I hunched guiltily. My emotions were so jumbled. "You didn't stick around at the party?" I asked.

"I lost interest after Dancey declared how much he wanted Taylor to be happy."

I gulped, trying to figure out a way to defend Dancey *and* myself for finding him so interesting. "Maybe Dancey just doesn't have a way with words."

"Yeah, because he doesn't make a living out of them," Austen said. "He can't even make it to his best friend's rehearsal dinner on time. Is he going to dump the whole bachelor party on me? I've got a deadline here. I've already wasted too much time plumping up Taylor for the sacrificial altar to the wedding gods."

I dropped my hand from the doorknob and returned to Austen, stealing the seat Junie had just vacated. "So you gave me the water for Taylor and then left, huh?" It was my way of fishing to see if he had seen me with Dancey—I didn't want him to think I was an idiot for ignoring his warning.

Judging by Austen's expression, he had no idea what had happened. Either that or he was giving me his best poker face. He shrugged. The phone rang again, and he stared down at it, looking annoyed.

"You going to get that?" I asked.

159

"No. It's after midnight." He hung the phone up again, his eyes going back to me. "At least Taylor's getting out of here while the getting's good."

Was he dissing my job again? "Why's that?"

"It's . . . well." He ran his hand through his hair, making it stand on end. I wanted to reach out and fix it, but forced myself to stay put. "How do you like your job?" he asked. "Have you ever thought of going somewhere else after Taylor leaves?"

My stomach sank. The night was going from confusing to worse. Had Austen's parents sent my former crush back to sack me? "Austen." I planted my hands against the counter. "You had better spit out what you want to say right now!"

"I just . . ." He stared at my hands. "I can get you references. You can go anywhere you want."

I couldn't believe it. Had he seen me with Dancey? Sure, it was unprofessional, but I could've at least gotten a warning first. I felt lightheaded. "You're firing me?"

"What?" He looked startled. "No! It's . . . this is all confidential. I can't say anything, but there will be changes at North Abbey, and I just want to make sure that you know you have options. That's all. You're talented. You could get anything you go after."

"I have ways of finding out what you're talking about, Austen."

He looked uncomfortable. "Probably not."

"Wait," I said as a sick feeling permeated me. "Junie knows what's going on, doesn't she?" I was almost sure of it. All the secret looks. The image of Austen sidled up next to Junie in the lobby, all cozy with my archrival, came back to haunt me. He had no intention of telling me the big life-changing news, but Junie knew everything.

Austen's brow rose in confusion. "Yeah, Junie knows. What's the big deal?"

Because he had confided in her instead of me, that was why. The two clearly had something going on. *And I had something going on with*

Dancey. I took a deep breath, trying to be fair about this. "Okay Austen, that's fine. Just tell me what's happening."

Austen looked like he'd rather swallow poison. The phone rang again. He tried to hang it up again, but I pushed his hand away. I realized that whoever was on the other side of that phone had instigated this whole conversation in the first place. The caller ID flashed across the screen. Colin Minster.

Why was Austen's cousin calling? He was a condescending, disgusting, rude . . .

I stood up, my hand hovering over the ringing phone. Austen's chin rose so that he met my eyes in a challenge. "Go ahead," he said. "Colin's been dying to talk to you. You want your next meet-cute, well, here's your chance. The phone's ringing. Answer it." When I didn't, his lips turned up. "C'mon, Jane. You've waited by the phone your whole life for a call like this. It's your big moment."

Normally the threat would be enough to make me scream and run away like a little girl, but Austen didn't want me to talk to his cousin. I picked up the phone.

"Finally!" Colin shouted out on the other side.

I winced. "This is Jane. How may I help you?"

"Jane." His irritated voice turned pleasant. "It's you! How is your stomach?"

His memory was impeccable. I always developed some sort of illness when he asked me out on a date. "I'm holding on," I said.

"I'm glad to hear it, since we will be seeing more of each other. Austen told you the good news, I'm sure?"

I glanced over at Austen, who looked anything but pleased. "He did," I lied. "What are your thoughts on it?"

"Naturally, I'm very conscious of what is expected of me—unlike others. As an investor in North Abbey, I feel it my duty to promote the establishment and its related businesses within the reach of my influence. In fact, Jane, I flatter myself that you will not object to my extended presence there."

161

"Colin." I was more confused than ever. "Are you staying here?" I winced at the horror that came out in my voice and tried to amend it. "We're happy to have you, of course."

"Is that a confession?" He sniggered then coughed. "I *was* hoping you'd put me in your confidence, Jane. You aren't dating someone new, I assume?"

"Not . . . officially," I stuttered. "But actually, yes, I think we're good enough friends for me to admit that—yes, I'm seeing someone."

He went quiet on the other line before muttering, "We'll see about that."

I glanced over at Austen. He was laughing silently. This was going nowhere. I was still in the dark, and if I wasn't careful, I was going to sign all my spare time away. "Colin, when exactly will you be coming to North Abbey?"

He sighed self-importantly. "I must trespass on your hospitality as early as tomorrow morning."

"Oh, no, no, no." I waved my hand even though he couldn't see it. "We're in the middle of a wedding, Colin. Every room is taken. The bungalows too."

He took a deep breath. "How is that possible?"

Trust Colin to be offended that we didn't keep a room vacant for him at all times. "What can I say?" I asked. "Business is going great."

"Really? I didn't have that impression. Austen seemed so willing to sell his half of the business."

"Sell?" I sank down on my seat, not sure if I heard correctly. "North Abbey?" I asked. Austen leaned heavily against the counter, watching me.

"I hope that my being your new boss won't change our relationship, Jane."

My hand tightened on the phone.

"In fact, my mind is made up," Colin said. "I intend to extend the olive branch to all the workers at North Abbey. You will be the go-between for myself and the workers there. I confess the allure of working with one of the greatest event coordinators in San Diego was one of the main attractions that enticed me to accept Austen's offer, since the place *is* quite a dive. But we'll make a lot of changes there . . . together." He smacked his lips. "Until tomorrow, Jane."

He hung up without letting me get another word in. I stared at Austen in horror. He was in the middle of holding up his hands like I would rip into him, but I felt limp with the horror of it all. "Austen, the business was supposed to go to you."

"We're changing management. Colin is soon to be the proud owner of North Abbey."

"And that's what you're doing here? You're making sure the transaction runs smoothly."

"Jane." He lifted his shoulders helplessly. "North Abbey is a money pit. Have you looked at the place? We're all appearances and gold paint . . . and even that is fading."

"But? But?" I stuttered as I stared around me at the Victorian rococo and carved cupids that made up the ceiling paneling. Sure, the place was old, but it was gorgeous like a priceless painting in a museum.

Austen abruptly cut into my thoughts, "After all the repairs we've had to do, we're making next to nothing in profits here."

He didn't believe in us. He was selling us out to Colin. Didn't Austen care about how darling this place was? We had met here—*okay, forget that. He didn't care.* But Austen had grown up here. Wasn't he sentimental in the least? My hand went to my forehead. Austen's practical approach was ruining my life.

"What will this mean for us?" I asked.

Austen avoided my eyes, packing up his laptop. "I'm sure everything will be the same."

As a rule, I didn't like change, but Colin would come and drive us all out . . . *and I would never see Austen again.*

"Well, great." I clapped my hands once, laying the sarcasm on thick. "What life would be complete without a Mr. Collins? At least I have my Mr. Darcy—there's nothing like a fiend to hurry me into his arms."

Austen stopped packing his laptop. "What?"

With a start, I realized I spoke the truth. "Hey!" I gave a hysterical laugh when I realized another correlation that my life had to my beloved books. "No way. We even have a Bingley here. Dancey's best friend. Our own Mr. Bigley. I'm all set for my happy ending!"

Austen was silent a moment. He knew the movie *Pride and Prejudice*. His ex had made him watch it. Even he had to see what an odd coincidence this was. "And I suppose you're the heroine?" he asked.

"Of course I am. I'm Jane!"

He wrapped his cord around his laptop in tight jerks. "Have you found out what inspires all those love songs Dancey writes, then?"

"What a good idea." I snapped my fingers like Austen had inspired me. "I'll ask Dancey about that the next time we meet. We were too busy dancing under the stars tonight for small talk. Hey, weren't you the one who said that I would never enjoy a Jane Austen romance? You were wrong. I do. You know what's even weirder, Austen? *You were wrong.* That's right—wrong. I think that's a sign, don't you?"

"Just like it's a sign that your name is Jane and my name is Austen." There was an edge to his voice. "By the way, it's not."

"You want to hear another sign?" I asked as if he hadn't spoken. "Dancey said that wearing white made me stand out from all the other girls in red and he *likes* my hair up. It didn't stop him from doing this to it though." I slid my hand through my messy hair. "I guess our deal is off, Austen. No need to help me out with the wedding anymore. I can handle it all on my own. Looks like you're getting out of this place just in time. We'll be sad to see you go."

I picked up my high heels from off the counter and marched out of the lobby, my bare feet slapping across the tiles.

164

Chapter 14

"You mistake me, my dear. I have a high respect for your nerves. They are my old friends. I have heard you mention them with consideration these twenty years at least."

—Jane Austen, Pride and Prejudice

I just wanted to make it to my room without crying. I had only one more flight left when I heard the raised voices in the hall from where I was on the staircase. Someone had beaten me to my crying fit.

"You don't love me!" The voice was female and hysterical.

"Mum." I recognized Chuck Bigley's voice immediately. "It was all a misunderstanding. Let me take you to your room. Is this your luggage?"

"This is your fault," she screeched. "What sort of woman are you marrying anyway? Why would she hire such a stupid bellboy? I'd fire him in an instant. In an instant!"

"Mum!" There was a note of desperation in Bigley's voice, and I felt sorry for him. "Taylor isn't responsible for the staff. She's the event coordinator. She's not even that anymore. It's Jane. You've met Jane. Nice girl. She'll make everything right. You'll see."

I hesitated on the stairs, wondering if I should go in and resolve the family crisis now that I was outed as the one responsible for whatever catastrophe happened while my back was turned. My hand went to the door leading to the hall. Taylor came up behind me. "I've got this," she whispered and patted my stiff back. "I can handle *Mrs. Bigley, the first.*"

165

Gone was the insecure female fretting over her wedding. This was the Taylor that I remembered. She squared her shoulders and saved me from the confrontation by marching into the drama that she was about to call her new family.

"Louise," she said, gushing in sympathy as soon as she came out into the hall. "Poor dear. I'll talk to Freddy myself."

In the time it took for the door to close between us, I saw Bigley's look of relief and his mother's suspicious eyes settle on Taylor. Both of them were still dressed up from dinner, but their clothes were wrinkled and sorely abused.

"That horrid bellboy of yours dropped my luggage off where Chuck's father is staying," Mrs. Bigley shouted. "Of all the stupid things. I walked into the room with that *woman* lounging on the bed."

I squinted in frustration. This was exactly the mistake we had tried to avoid when we'd heard that Mrs. Bigley hadn't dropped her married name. I thought I had warned Freddy to be extra careful not to mix up the former wife with the current one.

"I'm so sorry for the confusion, Mother." Bigley tried to soothe her in a voice I'd heard him use on Taylor. "How can I make this up to you?"

She snorted in response. "I should've known it the moment I stepped inside Netherfield Bungalow. The establishment was much too nice for you to set me up in."

"We have a much better place in mind for you," Taylor said. I listened to the swipe of a cardkey and the ensuing beeping as she unlocked the room we had actually intended for Bigley's mother. "It's the Price room," Taylor said. "The famous American actor stayed here in 1962."

"An actor?" Bigley's mother asked. The door squeaked open and she squawked out her complaints again. "Oh no. Unacceptable. Definitely not. This lodging is much smaller than what you gave your father. Chuck? Do I not mean as much to you? That is what this bedchamber tells me."

"Mum, you mean the world."

"I can hardly believe it. Is this how you prove your love to me? Who paid for your schooling when your deadbeat father decided to marry some aspiring actress who drained away his money? I ask you? Who is responsible for the life to which you've grown accustomed? Your honeymoon? Your tickets to Cancun? The money certainly doesn't come from your father's side, and this is how you repay me?"

"Mum, I love you. Keep all of your money."

"How noble of you, when it is too late to take anything back. How do I cash in on your plane tickets or return your education? Hmm? It was all a waste anyway. You hardly applied yourself."

"Louise," Taylor cut in. "This bedchamber might be smaller than the bungalows, but it's a relic of the original house and much more dear. Why must we compare diamonds to truckloads of glass? Look at the rococo carvings on the ceiling. The queen bed is a French antique Louis XV. See? This place is worth hundreds of thousands of dollars. We put you in a place that is closer to management. Help is only a phone call away. No waiting."

I grimaced, wondering if I would now be required to wait on Bigley's mother hand and foot. "I would like some tea," said Mrs. Bigley after a moment. She still sounded disgruntled.

"We'll have it sent up right away," Taylor said.

"I will take this *actor's* room," his mother said. "But I'm still quite angry at you, Chuck."

"Yes, mum. I'm sorry, mum."

The door closed, and I imagined that Bigley's mother was safely on the other side of it because Taylor and Bigley sighed out together. The shared silence didn't last long. "Freddy!" Taylor said in an urgent voice. I guessed she was on the phone. "You are in big trouble. Have someone bring Mrs. Bigley tea. I don't know, something European. Be sure to send it to Bigley's mother, not the former actress, and don't you dare show your face to her if you value your job. I doubt your dad could do anything for you after that."

Now that the crisis was over, I didn't need to eavesdrop anymore. Thinking fondly of my bed, I headed up the stairs. The next step groaned under my feet.

"Jane, oh, Jane."

I stopped, and Taylor opened the door to the staircase and motioned me out into the hall. She slid her cell phone into the waist of her tight skirt, glancing over at her poor husband-to-be. He looked haggard, his blond hair standing up like he had taken a beating in a pillow fight.

Taylor sighed at him. "Where were you tonight, Chuck? I looked everywhere for you."

"Yes, sorry about that." Bigley looked stressed, and I felt bad for him. He was stuck between two explosive firecrackers—his mother and his wife-to-be. "My . . . uh . . . brother wanted to tell me something of critical importance. It turned out to be a bit of nonsense about whipped cream and . . . uh . . . chocolate. Bachelor party stuff."

Taylor sighed at the reminder.

Bigley stared at his fiancé as if seeing her for the first time. He ran a hand through his hair, which told me how his hair had reached its present state. "I need some air, Taylor."

Taylor looked surprised. "What do you mean?"

"I just need to get out. I'll find Dancey. I'm choking in this tie. I have to go."

Without another word, Bigley rushed past Taylor and went down the stairs I had just vacated. Taylor's self-confident expression turned distressed. She headed blindly the other way, and I followed her down the hall, not sure if I should.

"Taylor, are you okay?" I asked.

She nodded, then burst into tears. "Oh, no, you're not okay." I threw my arms around her and hugged her tight. "Come on, Taylor. Let's get out of here." I helped her to her bridal suite in the Bennet room. It was a quaint suite, with an old fashioned vanity set up next to the bed. Taylor threw herself onto the patchwork quilt, her shoulders heaving. I sat next to her, rubbing her back while she cried her eyes out. A niggling worry played at the back of my mind that this was my fault.

"Chuck's father always enjoyed his life to the fullest," Taylor sobbed into her pillow. "He's made everyone else suffer for it." I rolled onto the bed next to Taylor so I could hear what she was saying. She sniffed. "He's a playboy—so, yeah, he didn't want a nag for a wife. He claimed to fall out of love with her: they were going different directions, they had grown apart. You know, everything guys say when they're desperate to get away. But Chuck's mom refused to let his dad go, wouldn't drop his last name, said that he was the one to blame when family functions were so confusing."

Romance gone wrong. I couldn't imagine the hurt on both sides. Nothing made me feel worse. "Maybe she'd feel better if she just let him go," I said.

Taylor shrugged. "Oh, it's her habit to hold on to him now, I think. She can't possibly love him still. I don't know if he ever loved her. You heard her—she had a lot of money and Chuck's father had a good time with it before he got bored."

"That would be heartless for him to do . . . even if Mrs. Bigley was hard to live with."

Taylor nodded. "From what I've heard, so is the second Mrs. Bigley. Carol's even more heartless than Chuck's mom and dad put together. Have you met her son, Harry? He's messed up."

I had changed my mind about Crawley, but Taylor needed to vent, and so I let her go on. "Things got a lot worse for Chuck after his father remarried," she said. "Mrs. Bigley can be a terror."

"Which one? The original or the new-and-improved?"

Taylor gave a hysterical laugh. "The original, of course, but the new, improved one holds her own in a fight, too. Let's just say that Carol makes sure that the original Mrs. Bigley knows that she is the new-and-improved, if you know what I mean? And yes, I feel sorry for

Chuck's mom, but I feel like . . . oh, Jane, please tell me that I'll never end up like *her*!"

"You won't. You're nothing alike." I gave her a side hug. "I don't think that you should live close to the in-laws, though."

Taylor was back to sobbing again. "They're all in London. London! I'll see her all the time. I love London, and now I don't want to move there. But I love Chuck, so . . . Anyway, it's a good thing that Mrs. Bigley approves of me. If not, then she'd never allow this wedding to take place."

I didn't have to ask which Mrs. Bigley she meant. Chuck's mother had made it clear in the hall that her disapproval held consequences.

Taylor squeezed my hand. "I don't care about money, Jane. I have enough of my own. Chuck does too, but his mother . . . she has a fortune that makes everybody kiss up to her. The money all comes from her side of the family. Though my soon-to-be-father-in-law squandered as much of it as he could, Mrs. Bigley—the original—owns the bulk of the shares in his businesses. Chuck's too. His mom holds her money over us like a threat. She says she'll leave it all to Chuck, but only if he doesn't turn out to be a lowlife like his father and marry some fortune hunter." She broke into sobs again.

Besides all the legal jargon and divorce talk, I felt like I was holding a conversation in the early 19th century. Fortune hunters weren't supposed to be an actual concern nowadays—I had thought they were a thing of the past.

"Chuck is always bending over backwards to please his mom. Sometimes," Taylor broke into a whisper as if afraid of saying the words that played on her lips, ". . . I think he cares about the money."

"No," I said quickly. "He loves his mom. That's all."

"But what if she says something against me? And what if Chuck listens? What if—?"

I tried to ease her worries. "He loves you too much to choose his mom over you."

Taylor gave a deep sigh and rested her chin on her pillow. "Chuck had better not think I'm anything like his mother, or I'm in trouble, Jane."

Chapter 15

"Seven years would be insufficient to make some people acquainted with each other, and seven days are more than enough for others."

—Jane Austen, Sense and Sensibility

I rummaged through the breakfast choices on the side bar. Everyone was asleep, and it was my chance to get some peace and quiet before Thursday began. I just needed to be alone with my thoughts. Taylor had cried herself to sleep last night. I wanted to talk to Austen about it, but we had just fought. My fingers wrapped around a container of yogurt, and I sat at the one table that made up the center of the dining room.

"May I join you?"

I glanced up and winced, not sure how Dancey would act after last night. I didn't know if I should play it cool or start where we'd left off—my feelings were all over the place. The harsh rays of daylight put such a cruel spin on reality. After Taylor's face-off with romance and Austen's plan to sell us off to Colin, I doubted anything too good to be true.

Dancey sat opposite of me and took my hand, playing with the ring on my finger—the crystal on it was my birthstone. His eyes didn't leave mine, and a smile tugged on my lips. I guessed that was a sign that he meant last night. "I couldn't sleep," he said.

"Me neither—I mean, that's normal for me though. As soon as the sunlight hits my face, my eyes just pop open . . ." My voice trailed off when he took the ring off my index finger and put it on my wedding finger. My heart almost fell out of my chest, and I managed to find the rest of my thought, "I can't really sleep when it's light outside."

"I can't sleep when I'm thinking of Jane." He met my eyes with his beautiful blue ones. His dark lashes swept luxuriously over them. "You're having *that* for breakfast?"

I glanced down at the yogurt forgotten in my hand. "Yeah, it reminds me of baby food. I mean," that came out wrong, "sometimes you like what you get, sometimes not."

"You want something more substantial?" he asked.

My hand tightened over the yogurt. "What did you have in mind?"

He gave me a wicked grin. "Anything that will get you into my car, Jane."

I was completely flattered. Despite my worries from last night, my heart raced at the thought of some fun. I had errands to run today—Lambton Marketplace, first off. Still, it would be great to have some company, especially Dancey's. "Well, I did want to pick up some mints for the bridal shower tonight."

He dropped his keys in my hand and then covered them with his own, his thumb caressing the inside of my wrist. "Let's go. I can't take another minute cramped up in this place."

I tried not to take that personally. His eyes on mine told me that he wanted to be with me, not that he hated the work I put into this wedding. "What about your friends?" I asked. "Won't they miss you?"

Dancey gave a light laugh. "I'd take a bullet for them, but that doesn't mean I want to hang out with them."

I laughed. "I should brush my hair first."

"I like your hair this way." He reached out and captured an auburn tendril of my hair, rubbing it through his fingers. I knew where this was going. We'd be kissing next, and if anyone walked in on us, I'd never hear the end of it.

I smiled at him and tried not to think about how practiced Dancey was in getting past my defenses. "Okay, but we have to be quick. Taylor is expecting me in a few hours to go over some final details."

"I'll deliver you in time, sweet lady."

I liked that. I nodded, and we left for his car. It wasn't parked in the same place as we had left it. Dancey had already been out on the town. I wondered if he had taken Bigley out last night to cheer him up.

Dancey was true to his word; he let me get in the driver's side. The leather seats felt as soft as butter, cushioning me like an overpriced beanbag. I pushed the button to get the car started, proud of my knowledge. The moment the car started, music blared through the stereos, flattening me against the seat. Dancey laughed and turned it down. I rubbed at my ears. "Do you always listen to it so loud? It's a wonder you're not deaf."

"Huh?"

Okay, so that was funny. Smiling, I reversed and enjoyed the smooth feel of his car, especially now that I knew it wasn't stolen. I went straight for the on-ramp and sped into the highway. Dancey pushed a button and the overhead window slid open, letting in a breeze that whipped my hair around my face.

"I think you're going to need these." He picked up some aviators from the side console, and I let him slide them over my nose, enjoying the feel of his fingers against my skin.

I had to admit it—racing down the highway in a Jaguar, wearing aviators, sitting next to Will Dancey, made me feel pretty cool. His arm draped around my shoulders wasn't that bad either. "Where to?" he asked.

I had an hour. I needed to buy mints, and all I wanted to do was race down I-5 and forget all my troubles—Taylor's unhappiness, Colin taking over the resort, losing Austen. I drove faster. Dancey's hand kneaded the back of my neck.

He turned up the music to fight the wind threatening to drown it out, and I laughed, realizing how it had gotten so loud before. "This is great!" I shouted.

"You should try it with the paparazzi chasing after you."

"One thing at a time!"

I realized that I was taking us to the beach. It would be the perfect setting for a date with Dancey. I could see the silvery waves crashing against the white sands. The sun was low in the sky, the air crisp and perfect on a pleasant San Diego morning. I decided against the heavily populated beach of La Jolla; I wanted Dancey all to myself. I swung a right and headed for the spot Austen had showed me—right off his parents' place.

Dancey glanced over at me, and I gave him a reassuring smile. "You hungry for something real? There's a bar and grill near here."

He nodded and played with my hair.

We reached Brightin Beach in good time. The waves washed over everything—the water sizzled under the sun, the foam glistening. Dancey's hand trailed down my arm, and he caught my hand before I could slide out of his Jaguar. "Jane?"

"Yeah?"

He kissed me, and for a moment I forgot why I had been in such a hurry to leave his car. I melted into him until he let me go. I sat back to gain my equilibrium.

His smile reached his eyes. "That was the first thing I wanted to do this morning."

I couldn't think of anything more romantic. "That must be why I love mornings," I said.

He laughed and got out of the car, going around the front to let me out of the driver's side. Once he had my hand, we walked companionably side by side. He guided my fingers around his waist. We traveled over the beach to Wickley's Pub, the warm sand trickling through my flip-flops. The crowd was thick around the restaurant—it had grown more popular since the last time I had been here. We slowed as we passed a thicket of trees where a sign that said *no trespassing* was hung prominently.

"What's in there?" Dancey asked.

"No idea," I said.

He tugged my hand and we were suddenly in the forbidding trees. My eyes went wide. Dancey was no longer the valet, but his rebellious streak was still there. I began to wonder how well I knew Bigley's friend. The minute I thought I had him figured out, he surprised me again. "Dancey. We can't be in here."

"What are they going to do if they catch us?" he asked.

"Fine us."

He shrugged. Of course he didn't care. It was just money, but what about a criminal record? He could get deported back to Britain. Jane Austen's Darcy would never do this, but Dancey wasn't as responsible as the *Pride and Prejudice* version of himself. He just needed a cause that made him truly noble; a younger sister like Georgiana to guard. "Dancey," I said, "tell me about your family."

"You really haven't googled me, have you?" he teased. "My parents divorced when I was eight, and my mom moved us back to Britain where she grew up. She died five years ago, and I'm an only child."

How sad. "But Bigley is like a brother to you?"

"Yeah."

"Did you take him out last night?"

His eyes found mine. "Why do you ask?"

"Well, Bigley said that he . . . well, his mom was being kind of overbearing. He told Taylor . . ."

Dancey nodded. "That he was going to find me?"

"Yeah."

Dancey looked away. "Chuck's a big boy. He doesn't need my supervision, even if I try to play the big brother." He laughed grimly. "I've been known to scare a few women away from him."

"But you'd never do that to Taylor, right?"

He gave me a strange look. "No, I guess you could say that Taylor is the closest thing I have to a sister."

That surprised me—he'd said some very non-brotherly things to her last night. "But Dancey, you've hardly talked to her since you've been here."

"She doesn't want to talk to me."

"Why?"

He shrugged. "We didn't exactly part on good terms when she left London."

I squeezed his fingers. He didn't know Taylor as well as I did. She was a fighter, but she never held a grudge. "But you know she's still not mad, right? She couldn't be. She wouldn't stop talking about you before you came. Taylor thinks you're great. She's just really stressed out right now. That's all."

"Any idea why?"

I hesitated, remembering our talk last night. I shook my head. "It's just the usual. She'll be fine."

He attempted a smile. "Let's not talk about Taylor." His hand trailed up my arm, and I laughed. Dancey was good at making me forget about everything except him. "I want to check out those cliffs," he said.

It was beautiful in the trees, but the *no trespassing* signs were making me nervous—of course, they *did* ensure some privacy . . . until the coast guard came looking for us. We hiked to some rocks framing an outlook. The view was beautiful. Dancey stood at my back, and we stared out into the frothy ocean. He put his arms around me. I sank into him and he rested his chin on the top of my head. "Are you happy at North Abbey?" he asked.

I stiffened when he echoed Austen's words from yesterday. "Right now I am." But I wouldn't be when Colin Minster took over. I'd have to plaster resumes everywhere just to escape him. With this economy, I wasn't looking forward to it.

"Would you ever consider leaving San Diego?" Dancey asked. "Maybe you could do some of that traveling you talked about?"

"I might have to," I said. "Are there any dives in Britain that need event coordinators?"

His fingers pressed into my stomach, sending flutters through it. "I might."

My heart sped up. Dancey worked fast. No wonder he got his heart broken on a daily basis. "Don't decide yet," he said, "but when I leave San Diego, I want to take you with me. A girl like you belongs in England with me."

That was *too* fast. I didn't even have a passport—let alone a visa. I laughed on the off-chance that he was joking. "The government might have something to say about that, Will Dancey."

"I'll wait for you. I can get around my people. We won't say that you worked for North Abbey. We'll make up some prestigious resume for you."

"Wait?" I asked. "What?"

He turned me so that he could devour me with his eyes and kissed me again—the fire he ignited through my lips spread through me in a happy glow. I couldn't think—let alone make any life-altering decisions yet. Besides the fact that he had dissed my dream job, one thought lingered—Dancey didn't want to leave me behind. Did this relationship mean more to him than I thought it did? The romantic in me screamed, "Yes!" I felt so happy, I could hug the world.

Foliage snapping behind us forced my head away from his. "Dancey?" I asked.

If that *was* the coast guard, I'd die a thousand deaths when they hauled us off to jail for trespassing. He studied my expression, and an inner gleam lit his eyes. I realized that he enjoyed the danger. He led me to a tree and pushed me down behind it to hide while he leaned against me to watch for anyone who might've followed us.

"What is it?" I asked.

"Shh." His lips were close to my earlobe, and I felt his smile tickle against my skin. He must think this was hilarious. I didn't. After a moment of awkward waiting, he squeezed my shoulder. "It's nothing, Jane."

A pop and a bright light startled me. Dancey groaned. "Or it could be that."

I straightened back up and he covered me, but not before I saw the photographer past his shoulder. She was a middle-aged woman, squeezed into tight little shorts and a plaid button-up. Her hair flew behind her in the wind, as did her fingers on the camera.

Dancey glared at her, looking the wronged rock star. "Why don't you go home, Jennings? Give me a private life."

"Who do you have with you?" Jennings demanded in a prim British accent. Had the lady followed Dancey all the way to America from London? The weathered woman looked insanely jolly about the whole affair.

I tried to hide my face with my hands, but it was too late. How much had this lady caught with her camera? Dancey gave me an apologetic look before turning to the photographer. "Don't publish those, Jennings. Please."

"Are you kidding? Do you realize how much this is going to make me—the troubled bad boy from Derbyshire finding redemption in the arms of a sweet little American girl?" She winked at me. "This bit of news will interest more than London, I suspect. All America will be glued to my gossip page. This will go viral."

My eyes went to her fancy camera, and she waggled a finger at me. "Don't you get any ideas, little girl. I've dealt with feisty Americans like you before. My pictures go straight to the cloud, so I won't be losing them this time around."

"This time around?" I asked. "Wait, what other feisty American are you talking about?"

Jenning's eyes crinkled up at the corners. "Don't you love how Americans talk, Dancey? They're so deliciously improper."

Dancey stepped in front of me, not looking amused. "Just give us a few days, Jennings, before you publish anything."

"When it's no longer news?" She tsked. "I don't think so."

I stared at Jennings and then the cliff. I supposed it wouldn't be right to push her off it. "We were just exploring," I said, adjusting my shaky legs so that I wasn't standing so close to Dancey. "Nothing else was going on."

Jennings' mouth thinned before she threw me a knowing look. "Stop protesting, dear heart, and enjoy your sudden fame. You've been thoroughly kissed, you little minx and you liked it!"

Had she caught that on camera? I remembered the breaking branches and winced when I realized it was possible. But maybe I'd be okay. Everyone in the wedding party would be too busy to tune into the news. Austen never did. But then I groaned when I remembered Ann-Marie. She always found time for social media. She'd blab this to everyone before I even got home. Taylor would be livid. She was protective of Dancey. Austen wouldn't laugh this time—I supposed I'd be labeled as an unprofessional. And then what jobs would I get after Colin threw me out into the street for refusing to date him? My stomach sank. I'd be doing retail before the week was out

"Wait, wait." I waved my hand. "I have a better story for you, Jennings." Dancey's eyebrows rose in surprise, but I was grasping at straws here. Taylor said that Dancey coming to North Abbey was a publicity dream. If business was so bad for us, then this could actually boost our popularity. Maybe Austen wouldn't sell us out to Colin. I took a deep breath. "If you agree not to publish any of those pictures just yet, you can have exclusive coverage of Taylor's wedding on Saturday."

"Taylor?" Jennings asked.

Dancey's dark expression turned furious. "No."

Jenning's grin widened. My eyes strayed to her camera. There was no telling what she had in there—but if it was too good, this wouldn't work. "I can see the headlines now," Jennings said. "Dancey finds a

180

crass American who connives her way out of trouble." She winked at me. "I like you."

I glanced over at Dancey. He stood shockingly still. Maybe he didn't like my crass American ways. Judging by the look on his face, I was sure he wouldn't be grabbing my hand after this. I tried to cut my losses. "Do we have a deal?" I asked the reporter.

Jennings nodded. "I believe, my girl, that we do."

Dancey gave a scornful laugh. "Jennings wants to cover some obscure wedding with subpar players that I happen to be attending? She wouldn't go for it if she had photographs more shocking than the two of us hiding behind a tree. Isn't that right, Jennings?"

Jennings looked secretive, but she shrugged. "The American girl offered me a deal that I couldn't refuse." Her eyes strayed to my hands. "Is that a wedding ring that you have on, dearie?"

I held up my hand defensively, realizing that I had forgotten to put my ring back to its rightful place after Dancey had played with it. "No—"

Dancey pulled me into a bone-crushing kiss. I was so surprised that I could barely react. His hands and mouth moved over me in what I knew would make breaking news. Jennings busily took photographs before Dancey pushed away from me with an angry violence. "Now, you've got your exclusive photographs, Jennings." He walked away from us both. "Forget covering Taylor's wedding."

I stared at him, so mad I could barely speak. Yeah, I had every intention of selling his fame to keep my face out of the papers, but he had kissed me out of anger. That didn't happen . . . except in novels. And now I was officially gossip fodder.

Jenning's laughter mocked us from behind. "The crass American is right, Dancey. The story isn't here. Is it?"

Wait, what was she saying? If the story wasn't here, where was it? My own Mr. Darcy—well, not mine; I wouldn't call him mine after this. But apparently the guy *did* have a protective instinct, just not for me. He didn't want the paparazzi near the man that he thought of as a brother. Dancey had depth. Of course, it didn't matter now; not for me. We'd both ruined whatever budding romance that lay between us. I had a talent for it.

Dancey had almost disappeared from the clearing, and I jerked to attention. Would he make me walk home? I still had to get Taylor's mints! I ran after him to catch up, but I couldn't speak to him. I was angrier than I thought as the injustice of what he had just done came to me. Little sparks of rage ran through me until I felt my hands shake. I wouldn't let him ditch me at Brightin Beach when I was the one who should do the ditching.

He wordlessly pulled his keys from his pocket and unlocked the Jaguar from a distance. Striding ahead, he jerked open the passenger side door and waited for me to get in. Not meeting his eyes, I dropped into his passenger's seat, trying not to say or do anything that I'd regret. I'd already made too many mistakes.

This was far from our happy little drive on our way over. How long had Jennings been trailing us to the place that I once loved? First Austen had ruined it with tainted memories, now Dancey. I guess I had a hand in its murder too. I now officially hated Brightin Beach.

Dancey dropped into the driver's side, the car sinking under his weight. I knew that he was mad. I was, too. He jerked the mirrors back into place. I crossed my arms. I was the crass American who didn't care about his friends and used his fame to get what I wanted. He was the guy who forced a kiss on me. We'd probably never go out again. He threw his arm around my seat so that he could speed back in reverse.

"Where to?" he asked, not looking at me.

I clenched my arms tighter around myself. "North Abbey." Forget the mints; my stomach tightened against the worry of what I'd find at home if this got out.

Dancey took me there. I glared at the palm trees speeding past. This was what happened when I went for someone that I hardly knew. Dancey didn't know that I'd never intentionally hurt Taylor. She was the one who had given me the idea in the first place—she hadn't actually been against the paparazzi taking a few snapshots. Of course, Taylor hadn't meant for them to cover her whole wedding, but it was much better than shadowing her big day with my scandal.

Examining my own motives, I realized that there had also been a lot of self-preservation in my pitch to Jennings, but so what? I wasn't as evil as Dancey imagined that I was. I'd used Dancey's fame to get the heat off me, but he had used me when he kissed me, so we were almost even . . . except I was starting to wonder if Dancey had played me from the beginning. How else could he toss me aside so easily after our first argument? Or maybe he had just put me on a pedestal and gotten upset when I fell? He might've believed that I was that sweet American that Jennings had first called me.

But I wasn't sweet. I was just normal, and as much as I hated it, I had panicked. Dancey was a romantic, just like me; but unlike me, he didn't stick through with his wild fancies when things got tough. The thing that killed me the most was that I should've known better. Dancey went through women like I went through dog-eared novels.

There was something about him that we all loved.

As soon as Dancey parked next to the curb of North Abbey, he touched my arm. It happened faster than I had time to think, and I whipped his hand aside before he could get a word in. His eyes were awash with the same regret that I felt. He reached over me to get my door for me. As soon as he got it open, the door ran into a male body standing outside the car.

"Hey there." A hand caught the top of the door and a face lowered down to peer at me. The man had slicked-back, dirty-blond hair and wore dark glasses. "So, this is what you've been up to, Dancey?" he slurred. "I thought you had business in L.A. today?"

I stared up at this new guy. Everything about him screamed slick, from his fitted grey Armani suit with a silky finish to the smoke dancing from the cigarette that dangled artfully through his fingers. "I heard Jennings was in town and got here as soon as I could."

183

Well, he was too late. The newcomer's eyes went from me to Dancey as if he knew everything. He treated me to a dry smile and put his hand out to me. "DeBurgy, Dancey's PR manager. And you are?"

Not this time. I pushed out of the car and made my walk of shame to the front doors of North Abbey. I squared my shoulders before going in. This was it, the moment when everyone's eyes would go to me, when the yelling would start. I pushed the door open and waited for the explosion. Ann-Marie passed me on her way to the piano. She disappeared into the Allenham Lounge and played a sweet little tune, so lacking in passion that I wondered if it actually had come from her.

My eyes traveled to the checkout counter. Austen hadn't come in yet. I wandered from the lobby into the lounge where the bridal shower would be held later today. Taylor busied herself with the decorations on the table. She wasn't supposed to be doing that. The setup crew should've been on it, but after a quick scan of her face, I decided that she wasn't in angry mode. I dragged my feet over to where she was working and tried to nudge her aside so that I could take over.

"No," Taylor said. "I like it. It calms me." She was working with the old-fashioned pink roses. Arranging flowers usually put a smile on Taylor's face, though I wondered about her sudden aversion to California poppies. They had been her favorite flower until she'd decided to get married. "Did you get the mints?" she asked.

"No."

"Good," she muttered, "I changed my mind about those." She gave me a weak smile. "I want those darling cupcakes from Bates."

"I'll make the call." I pulled my phone out with numb fingers.

"I haven't seen Chuck all morning," Taylor said. "He's probably embarrassed about what happened last night. At least his parents talk to each other, right? Mine don't even care enough about each other to fight." She glanced over at me. "What's the matter, Jane?"

I blinked up at her and forced my face to look pleasant. "I'm fine." But I wouldn't be once the word got out. "Uh, Taylor, how well do you know Dancey?"

Her face grew guarded—just like Dancey's had when I'd asked him about her. That must've been some fight. She shrugged. "Take away the fame and the money and he's just like any other guy." Her gaze turned sharp. "Why?"

I shook my head and made the call to Bates. After I had finished ordering four dozen cupcakes, Taylor was still waiting impatiently for my answer. I had been so caught up in my misery that I hadn't realized she was staring at me.

"You didn't go off with him, did you?" she asked.

I considered lying, but that would only make it worse when she saw the headlines. "We went to get mints at Lamberton Marketplace," I said.

"But you forgot them."

"Yeah."

Without a word, Taylor marched out of the room. There was a fire in her eyes and it wasn't directed at me. I gnawed on my lower lip, not sure what I had just done. My nails were the next to feel my abuse, and I wasn't even a nail biter. I decided to put my nervous energy to use and put the finishing touches to Taylor's bridal shower. By the time Taylor returned an hour later, I had ribbons and roses dripping from the columns, tables, and doorframes.

Taylor nodded at me, still furious, but she had a satisfied gleam in her eyes. A sense of purpose hummed through her as she straightened the tablecloths. I wasn't sure why. "Where did you go?" I asked.

She shrugged. "I went to visit an old friend, that's all." Her tone told me that it was useless to ask for more information.

"Did you need me to do anything else?" I asked.

"No, just come back at five-thirty. I want you to be here a half an hour before the bridal shower starts."

185

I waited for her to open up to me, but when she didn't volunteer any information, I left for my room, flushing like I had been caught with my hand in a cookie jar—a particularly vicious one that liked to snap off wrists.

Chapter 16

"You must really begin to harden yourself to the idea of being worth looking at."

—Jane Austen, Mansfield Park

I tightened the laces on my sneakers and tied them into a neat little bow. Knowing I had three more hours left before I had to go to the bridal shower, I had changed into my worn jogging shirt and shorts. These clothes definitely fit my style more than the fancy dresses I had worn to Taylor's parties. I didn't belong in luxury cars, or mingling with elevated company while holding a slender glass and attempting to make brilliant small talk.

Closing my bedroom door silently behind me, I made my way down the hall past the Dashwood room where Eddy McFarey sat on the bedspread and worked on his laptop. The reverend's suit was like a second skin that he never took off, though for the moment his bowtie had been tossed to the side. His wife, Elly, was hauling a bucket of ice into their room, still wearing her pajamas, the bottoms of which were rolled up to reveal a pair of black rain boots. She stopped to smile at me. "So nice to see you, Jane."

Eddy lifted his head from his work. "Hi, Jane!"

"You're doing wonders with my cousin's wedding," Elly said, touching my arm in her comforting way. "I've never seen such fabulous work. And believe me, I've been to a lot of weddings."

Her husband's occupation would ensure that. I was touched. I was so starved for compliments lately that Elly's words felt like a gourmet meal. "Thank you," I said.

"Elle," Eddy called out to his wife. "I want your advice. Jane, you too. I'm working on my sermon for next Sunday. I want to make a bowl of cream cheese fudge on the pulpit and leave out the powdered sugar so I can compare it to our lives without charity. Would making fudge in church be too distracting?"

I imagined powdered sugar flying onto his congregation.

With a wink at me, Elly turned to her husband. "Just be careful that you don't let me near the fudge after you put the sugar in, or I might attack it before you're through. Now *that* might be distracting."

"Hmm, you are distracting." He studied her with a smile. "I'll have to feed you more so that you won't ruin my sermon."

Despite the turmoil of my emotions that felt like someone had taken a concrete mixer to my heart, I appreciated how cute Eddy and Elly were together. I waved to them on my way down the hall. They were my proof that love could be good. It just never turned out for me, and I didn't understand why it was so hard. I hurried down the flight of stairs to the lobby and kept a lookout for Austen. I didn't want to run into him, and I especially didn't want to see Dancey.

My world was falling apart. With the loss of North Abbey and Austen, I felt like I was losing treasured memories from my past. And now with my failed relationship with Dancey, my future felt grim, too, as if I couldn't love. I was only left with the present, and that was closing in on me with the threat of Jenning's candid photographs.

I took off through the little thicket of trees making up Maple Grove as if I could outrun the troubles chasing me.

"Are you running away?"

With a start, I glanced behind me to see Harry Crawley at my heels. He easily caught up. I went faster, heading towards the silvery water washing up against the beach. When that didn't lose him, I tried to go painfully slow. But no matter how much I tried to shake Bigley's stepbrother, he kept up with my pace.

"Hey," he said. "I thought we made our peace yesterday."

We had. I even thought he'd make a cute couple with Bella. I
tried to relax. "Yes, we did. Sorry, my mind isn't here."

"Who is it with?" he asked. *Astute.* I glanced over and gave him a
weak smile. He'd know soon enough. The dread was killing me. "You
can trust me," he said. "I'm not so different from my brother."

I studied Crawley. They were only stepbrothers, but they both
had an open expression, the same eager blue eyes, that fair-haired-
child look. Bigley's dad really had married the same woman twice.
Knowing Crawley's life history with his two demon mothers made me
more sympathetic towards him. I took a deep breath and tried to
change the subject, "Speaking of your brother—where is he? Taylor's
worried."

"Nope, not giving out that information. Someone's got to cover
for him." He laughed when I made a face. "Have you seen his
mother?" he asked.

"Oh, so that's what's going on." Bigley was keeping a low profile
from his mom.

"We've been doing this since we were little," Crawley said. "I can
keep a secret. I told you that you can trust me, Jane. Talk."

I hesitated, but I had no one else to confide in. The concern in
his eyes loosened my tongue. I had to talk to someone. "I just made a
mistake," I said. "I should've known better. That's all."

"What did you do . . . generally speaking?"

"Um, well, I let someone get too close and he had no idea who I
was, so when I showed him my true colors, he didn't like it."

That was an understatement.

"So you're saying you took a chance at love?" He waited for me to
nod, and when I did, he smiled to himself. "Jane, you did the right
thing. How is anyone supposed to get together if they don't just go for
it?"

"Yeah, and it blew up in my face." I wracked my brain to figure
out what did make love work. "I think you have to sneak up on love.
Be a snake in the grass . . . and just be friends. At least at first."

189

"Is that what you do?"

"No." I shook my head, my mind going to Austen. "Actually, only guys can get away with that. Playing the friend card doesn't work for girls."

"What does?"

"Nothing . . . and I don't care."

We rushed over the wet sand, our feet making hollow indents behind us. His forehead wrinkled. "So you got hurt?"

I laughed, feeling the bitterness consume me at all the bad romance in my life. "Yeah, but doesn't everybody?" He was silent, and I realized that he was waiting patiently for me to continue. I had seriously misjudged Crawley. No guy listened like this. I felt like I could trust him. "So I like two guys," I admitted, "and I'm pretty sure one will find out about the other one really soon." Just the thought of Austen seeing the results of Jenning's photo shoot made my feet go faster.

"Two guys?" Crawley asked with some surprise. "I didn't think you were that kind of girl."

"I know." It felt good to get some of this rottenness off my chest. "But I'll get mine, Crawley. I'd say in about two hours I won't have to worry about either of them liking me. I'm a horrible person."

"No." He shook his head, slowing down. "Not you. You have stars in your eyes."

I twisted around and stopped running. "What?"

"You really do." He dimpled and reached out to brush my cheekbone with the back of his knuckles. "It's actually just in the corner of your eye—I almost missed it, but it sparkles when the light catches it. And when you smile, the whole world goes bright."

"That . . ." I felt my throat constrict at his kindness, ". . . that was a really nice thing to say, Crawley."

"It's the truth, Jane." He bumped me playfully with his arm. "A star doesn't belong in a cramped attic. Whatever you do with your life will be better than anything you can imagine. You can't help but go up, Jane."

With that, he flicked my chin in a consoling gesture and jogged away. My head whipped around to watch him go. I was completely dumbfounded. How poetic. How touching. He knew I lived in the attic and that I was a hopeless romantic? I leaned my head back and stared up at the clear blue sky. Was it true? If I believed in myself, could I ride this problem through?

I found my way back to North Abbey, feeling a little stronger and a lot sweatier. My confidence crumbled when I heard Colin's voice in the lobby. Taylor was with him, and I could tell that the two were arguing. I rested against the doorframe, trying to decide if I wanted to face Colin after all of this.

"We have a piano player?" he asked. "Just taking up residence here all day, playing who knows what? Why?"

"Ambience," Taylor answered. I peered around the hall. Her face was red.

Colin sat across from her on the sofa. He had frost-tipped his chocolate brown hair. His new bouffant style took crazy and out of control to a new level. It didn't mesh well with his hipster clothes. "It's an unnecessary expense," he said. "I want her out."

I pushed through the door to protest. Colin couldn't just sack Ann-Marie. She'd be heartbroken; and besides that, she needed the work. The guests loved her. "Colin!" I called out.

He gave me a sickly smile and mashed his hair against his forehead in a self-conscious way. The guy had an obsession with me that I couldn't quite figure out, and it didn't seem diminished today, though my hair was in a greasy ponytail and sweat had plastered my T-shirt to my body. I should've planned my entrance better than this if I wanted him to listen to me.

"I just heard you discussing our pianist." I gave him my most pleasant smile. "She's a gem. You wouldn't believe what the other resorts try to do to steal her from us."

191

"Do they?" He seemed suddenly unsure.

"Yes, yes," Taylor took up where I left off. "But of course, our Ann-Marie is much too loyal to leave us."

"Thank goodness." I waved a hand over my face in faux relief. "So were you just taking a tour of North Abbey, Colin?"

He gave a curt nod.

"Excellent." Hesitating, but then thinking of my coworkers' futures, I pulled forward and squeezed his arm to draw him away from the sofa, past the foosball table. "Business just thrives here," I said. "Have you seen the parking lot? It's full of cars."

"It hasn't escaped my notice—it's an unusual occurrence." He stopped short when he saw the "unintended gifts" basket at the checkout counter. "What is that?"

"It's just for fun," I said, rushing him past the stolen buttons, receipts, and other memorabilia. "Such a hit with the guests."

He let out a long sigh and stared at me. His eyebrows looked like dead caterpillars over watery blue eyes that held no expression. His mouth was molded into a permanent smirk, as if he was gloating over his newfound power over us. "There are so many changes I want to make," he said. "The feel is much too antiquated here; it's like a set from those old movies that my mom won't stop watching. I want a more modern atmosphere." Colin ripped open the front doors and Taylor and I helplessly followed him outside into the courtyard that led out to our quaint little set-up of cozy cottages. "I'll have to take a bulldozer to it."

"A bulldozer?" I asked. *Was he insane?*

"And a few employees won't fit our new image." He motioned in the direction of the beach. "Churchell's Shack will have to be torn down. I want a Frappuccino coffee house in its place."

"But . . ." I held out my hands.

Colin strolled down the walk until he almost tripped over Freddy in his bright red jacket. Unfortunately for Freddy, our bellhop looked much too lazy lounging in his golf cart. His disdainful glance rested on Colin's stocky frame.

Colin smirked. "There's no need for unnecessary employees," he said in a voice that failed at discreetness. "We will need to downsize."

I didn't particularly like Freddy, but now I was feeling protective of him; and besides, I had enough to do without taking on his job, too. After exchanging glances with a horrified Taylor, I rushed to repair the damage. "Colin, I respect your ideas, but I really think that we're going the wrong direction here. People come to our resort for the ambience. That's what makes us different from the others. Modern structures are a dime a dozen in San Diego."

"People come here from all over the world," Taylor added.

"Is that so?" Colin fixed me with his unwavering stare. "I hear we have our very own rock star staying here from Britain."

My back went rigid, but I nodded.

"I've always had a talent for singing," Colin said.

Taylor made a congratulatory noise at the back of her throat without quite meeting his eyes. Colin considered me a moment before placing his shaking hand at the small of my back. "Jane, I might listen to your ideas if you agree to take on a position as my assistant in all matters concerning North Abbey. I entertain the hope that you would work for us after the change, but . . ." He let the sentence hang cruelly before giving a long sniff, "I could only consider your suggestions if you were to take the helm here for many years to come."

I gulped.

He patted me. "Perhaps we can discuss this over dinner?"

There were so many things wrong with that suggestion. Freddy watched us with a little more interest than before. I stalled. "Now isn't a good time," I said. "But after Taylor's wedding, we could talk . . . if you're still interested."

Colin smiled brightly. "I'm certain that I will be."

Taylor's gaze slanted on me, but she kept her thoughts to herself. It was a usual occurrence these days. She turned to Freddy. "Put Colin's luggage in the Lucas Lodge."

Freddy straightened at the strange request. The Lucas Lodge was empty for a reason. It stank. We had suspected the Kellynch of sabotaging the most sought-after Bungalow at North Abbey by setting up a port-a-potty behind it for their renovation workers. Either that or their sewage actually was overflowing.

"Really?" I asked. "It's awfully close to—"

"Do it," she said with an evil smile.

It was a brilliant idea if it chased Colin away from his new acquisition. Maybe Taylor could save North Abbey, though certainly not my job. After the wedding she and Colin and everyone else would know the sordid details of my personal life. Despite all that, if I had any power left to save the home that I had grown to love, I'd help Taylor do it.

Chapter 17

"It is happy for you that you possess the talent of flattering with delicacy. May I ask whether these pleasing attentions proceed from the impulse of the moment, or are they the result of previous study?"

—Jane Austen, *Pride and Prejudice*

Ann-Marie's fingers danced over the ivory keys of the piano at Taylor's bridal shower. The pile of presents grew at the center of the table. They were wrapped in ribbons, decorated with stripes and polka dots and overly bright colors.

The Bigley women, both the "original" and the "improved," glared at each other from opposite sides of the room. The two had enough plastic surgery to make Barbie jealous. Crawley's mother wore her blond hair high on her head in a chic twist. Bigley's mother kept running her fingers through her short bob. Mrs. Weston, Taylor's mother, sat in the corner, lending elegance to the shadows with her long, dark hair. A thin line made up her ruby lips as she watched the women chattering around her.

Taylor was a nervous wreck, flying from one woman to the next like a momma bird bribing everyone to have a good time by dangling worms—or in this case, oversized cupcakes. The delicious confections from Bates were rapidly disappearing from the table.

Even the stick-skinny Bertie helped herself to one. She was in the process of trying to ingest it without getting frosting all over herself. "Are we ready yet?" her impatient voice cut through the room. As maid of honor, it fell to Bertie to direct the activities. "Sit down, Taylor. Sit down. No more chasing your tail."

Taylor lowered onto the seat that Bertie had set in the middle of the room. The other two bridesmaids took either side of her, Bella looking eager, Mary tired.

Bertie took charge. "Taylor," she said, "we want to know how you met Chuck. We want every detail. Spill it."

The younger ladies sighed as Taylor told her story. The older women looked uncomfortable, probably because the topic was how sexy their shared son was. Bella clapped her hands and squealed every time Taylor hinted that she loved the man she was going to marry. Mary sniffed despondently next to her, occasionally wiping a ball of tissue against her nose. She claimed to have a head cold. The tissues were wadded into a huge pile on the coffee table next to her.

"And you met Will Dancey while you were in Britain?" Bella asked eagerly. "Tell us all about him. I want to hear every scandalous detail."

Taylor's expression went cold. "He sings," she said and left it at that.

Bertie set her half-eaten cupcake aside and pushed her ramrod back even straighter. "I have the perfect plan. We should invite Dancey to sing at your bachelorette party tomorrow—"

"No!" Taylor cut Bertie off mid-scheming, though her raised voice unfortunately drew everyone's attention to her. She breathed out and attempted a weak smile. "He's in charge of Chuck's party tomorrow night and besides . . . Dancey wouldn't do that."

"Get your girl to ask him," Bertie said, motioning at me.

"My girl?" Taylor asked in icy tones.

"Jane." Bertie crossed one of her long legs across the other. "That's your name, isn't it dearie?"

I adjusted her dog on my lap—I didn't know her baby's name yet, so I guessed that made us even. "Uh, *Bertie*," I said, "why do you think that Dancey would listen to me, of all people?"

"Ah yes, he is a bit of a snob, isn't he?" Bertie looked gleeful at the thought. Her eyes raked me from head to foot, and I colored. Even though I had broken Austen's deal the night before, I had put my hair up in a ponytail again and wore a yellow sundress with a white cotton T-shirt, avoiding the more elegant red dress I had bought for the occasion. I wasn't sure why.

Bertie sniffed my direction. "I suppose he wouldn't lower himself to talk to someone like you—even with your face."

That startled me. Was that a compliment? I wasn't sure.

"Oh, but he *likes* her," Bella said. "I saw them together last night. They were helping a girl in the kitchen." She patted my hand bracingly. "Jane could convince Dancey to sing. Couldn't you, Jane?"

About a dozen jealous sets of eyes zeroed in on me again. Instead of distracting them from me, Taylor shrugged. "Jane does have a way with men. Remember my friend that I tried to set you up with last summer, Jane?" *As if I could forget.* "You know, Redd, the captain, the one in naval intelligence?"

"Naval intelligence?" Bella teased. "Isn't that an oxymoron?"

"Oh, he's no moron," Mary said in all seriousness. Before Bella could try to explain what her joke meant, Mary began a list of Redd's finer qualities. "He's quite intelligent I've found. In fact if I remember correctly, Redd Wortham comes from a very good family in Maine. I think his uncle owns a bank." She stopped, confused. "Are you sure Redd was interested in Jane?"

"No," I said firmly. "He wasn't."

Taylor snorted. "Jane had him wrapped around her finger, but she broke it off. She's picky."

I shook my head.

"Oh, I believe it," Bella said, looking proud. "She broke Freddy's heart. And her assistant's, too. His name's Austen, isn't it? He's so in love with her. I can tell."

I snickered at how ridiculous this was. "No, that's not true at all."

Bella clapped her hands, looking delighted. "Jane, you must use this power you have over men and get Dancey to sing for us!"

Not liking where this was going, I tried for a lighter tone, "I have no magical power over Dancey, Bella."

"Yes, yes, you do," Bella insisted. "He wouldn't speak at the rehearsal dinner and then after you spoke, he couldn't get to the microphone fast enough. And after he danced with you, you asked him to dance with the girl who hurt her ankle and then he did. Just like that." Bella gave me a knowing look. "Put a spell over our tragic little rock star, Jane. Tease him. Get him to do anything you want."

"I . . ." Glancing over at Taylor, I saw her preoccupied look. Bertie's eyes narrowed thoughtfully on me. Bella wasn't taking "no" for an answer and so I held up my hand. "Only if Taylor wants him to sing," I said.

I thought Taylor would say, "no," but she motioned for me to do her bridesmaids' bidding. "Yes, Jane, ask him," her eyes met mine in a challenge, "I'd love to see your power of persuasion."

Taylor was turning on me too. "He won't say yes," I said. "He'll be much too busy entertaining Bigley. They've got big kidnapping plans for the bachelor party Friday."

"Oh!" The original Mrs. Bigley fidgeted with the string of pearls around her neck. "Chuck will not do that. I will not allow it."

"Jane." Mary rubbed at her red nose, interrupting the squabbling. She adopted a pleading expression. "Would you please throw all these tissues in the garbage?"

I glanced over at the wad of tissues that she had wiped her nose with and tried not to make a face. With Bertie's puppy tucked under my arm, I fetched the garbage can and slid the tissues into them. I set the can near Mary's chair. Mary wiped another tissue against her nose and threw it on the table to make a new pile of crumpled tissues that looked suspiciously clean. "Jane," Mary said. "Bring me some water. My throat feels like it's on fire!"

Sure, it was. My hands formed fists. What a hypochondriac! I unkindly compared her to the one that Jane Austen wrote about in *Persuasion*. They even shared the same name—Mary. I stomped over to the water and slammed the glass on the table next to her tissues.

Bertie nibbled daintily on her frosting and, to my relief, took the attention off me by starting a bridal shower game. "How well do you know your husband-to-be, Taylor? Let's test your knowledge." Bertie took out a bag of oversized gumballs and a set of index cards from her Gucci purse. "We took Chuck aside and asked him a few questions. We'll go easy on you at first, Taylor. What's his favorite color?"

Taylor squirmed uneasily in her chair. "Green?"

"Yellow." Bertie elbowed me. "Jane, place a gumball in Taylor's mouth."

I almost laughed, then opted to hand Taylor the bag instead, refusing to play the role of torturer. Taylor popped the gumball in her mouth and started chewing.

"Now." Bertie rolled her eyes upward and took a deep breath. "When was the first time you kissed Chuck?"

Taylor blushed and tried to rush the story. "It happened at one of Dancey's concerts. He was standing by the soda machine."

Bertie looked confused. "Are you sure?"

"Yes, of course."

"Chuck said that it happened at the airport," Bertie said.

"No, it didn't. I . . . I know when I've kissed someone for the first time—especially if it was Chuck. Okay?"

"And he would forget?" the original Mrs. Bigley interrupted. Her blue eyes were hard like steel. "Chuck would know if he kissed you. He's not like his father."

"Excuse me?" the "new and improved" Mrs. Bigley lifted a finger and waggled it. "Herb has never forgotten when he's kissed me. Maybe it's not the man who's the problem." She looked smug.

"Whore," the "original" Mrs. Bigley said under her breath.

"What did you say?" her archenemy hissed.

199

"More?" I asked, purposely misinterpreting her. I tried to salvage the situation by shoving another oversized cupcake at Bigley's mother. "Here you go!" Even the lady knew she had gone too far and took the cupcake without complaint.

"Put the gumball in your mouth," Bertie directed Taylor.

"But . . . but, Chuck got it wrong," Taylor argued. "He didn't even pick me up at the airport. He sent Dancey to get me. I can't believe that Chuck forgot that!"

"Just drop it, Taylor," her mother hissed. The dignified woman tilted her head at the bickering Bigley females to communicate that their fighting was Taylor's fault. "Eat the stupid gumball."

Taylor looked miserable. Her eyes went to Bigley's mother in mute apology. "No matter where we first kissed," she said more contritely, "I'll never forget how I felt. He took my breath away—it was wonderful. He's so caring."

The original Mrs. Bigley looked unimpressed. She stuck her pert nose in the air. Taylor stuffed the gumball in her mouth, her eyes watering.

Bella took pity on her. "Harry says that Chuck has a terrible memory."

"Harry? Harry Crawley?" Bertie asked. She shot a venomous glare at the younger girl. "Why would you discuss such a personal thing with Harry?"

It made me remember that the "very married" Bertie had been flirting outrageously with Crawley the first time that I had met him—it had been one of the reasons that I thought he was trouble. "Harry and Bella are friends," I said in their defense.

Bertie snorted. "Friends? He doesn't make *friends* with females."

The "new and improved" Mrs. Bigley giggled. "My Harry's quite the player, isn't he?"

"I wonder where he gets it from?" Bigley's mother asked; this time there was no mistaking what she'd said.

The "new and improved" brought her eyes to the ceiling. "Do you have problems with how I raise my son, too? At least I let Harry live his own life. Your son can't breathe without consulting you."

The "original's" fingers wrapped around her oversized cupcake in a choking grip, and I cringed, hoping that she wouldn't smash it into the "new and improved's" face.

"Mrs. Bigley, you did a delightful job raising your son," Bertie's voice came out a purr. The insinuating way she said it distracted both Mrs. Bigleys from their bickering. They tensely waited on Bertie to clarify which son she had her claws on. "Harry is perfectly delightful," Bertie said with a coy smile.

The "new and improved" didn't look as amused as she had the first time she'd dismissed her son as a player. She tapped her perfectly manicured nails. "And how is that, Bertie?"

"We have an understanding, he and I."

"Mrs. Rush-Bertram," Bella said in stinging tones, "What sort of understanding would a married woman have with a man who doesn't make friends with females? Perhaps you only *think* you have an understanding."

Bertie gave her a dangerous smile, like a lioness baring her teeth at a younger, more attractive cub. "There is no doubt in my mind that we do."

Bigley's mother choked out a chortle and turned to her arch nemesis. "You still think you raised your son better than mine, Carol?"

The "new and improved" glowered at her husband's first wife.

Taylor held up the bag of gumballs as a distraction and tried to talk through the mass of pink goo in her mouth. "Aw we blaying?"

"Dear," Mrs. Weston corrected her daughter. "Don't talk with your mouth full."

Bertie glared at the more youthful and lovely Bella while shuffling through the cards in her hand. She read it. "How many children does Bigley want?"

Taylor picked up a gumball and stuffed it in her mouth without answering. Bertie pouted, her beautiful almond eyes slanting. "You didn't even try. Bigley said *he didn't want any.*"

The "new and improved" swung around to Bertie to belt out a laugh—it didn't go well with her sophisticated charade. "Are you sure about that? Did he consult his mother before coming up with that plan?"

"He certainly didn't think it through," Bigley's mother grumbled. "I'm sure on further reflection, he'd think better of it."

The "new and improved" snorted. "He'll likely come into some money that will change his mind soon."

"My son isn't as attached to my money as *some* are. I trust in his better judgment."

Crawley's mother rolled her eyes. "Then no grandkids for you, Louise."

"No kids?" Bella looked concerned.

Taylor lifted a brow, acting like she didn't care. "Awe wwwe dumb yet or awe we gonna keep goim until I doke and die?"

"The tissue paper game." I held up the roll of toilet paper that Bertie had set aside and that Mary had covertly used as Kleenex. Bertie glared, but I took over anyway. "Whoever makes the loveliest wedding dress out of tissue paper wins. Divide into groups of three."

The ladies all separated, the younger ones chattering happily. The mothers flat-out refused to participate. Bertie came up to me and dug a pointy elbow into my side. "What was that about, Jane? I'm in charge here. You're not even a guest."

My mouth firmed. I was sick of Bertie's cattiness. "Oh, I apologize," I said in a voice that implied the opposite. "We haven't been properly introduced. I'm the event coordinator for Taylor's wedding. I'm also known as Jane, Taylor's good friend. Nice to meet you, Mrs. Bertram-Rush."

She watched me narrowly. "You actually think you're in charge? I never would have guessed. Someone even halfway capable of her job would never let Taylor touch her own wedding. She's been half crazed with worry the whole time that I've been here."

"The whole time *you've* been here? How strange. Are you sure your presence has nothing to do with it?"

"Oh, don't get smart with me, missy," Bertie spat. "How about I get Taylor to send you back to your attic. That's where you live, isn't it?" She sneered. "I could fit my closet in there."

Everyone knew I lived in the attic? I tried to figure out who had blabbed, but knew it didn't matter anyway. There was nothing wrong with the attic. It was cute and cozy and I loved it. I was tired of proving that I was human to these backward people, anyway.

They all wanted me to know my place—like poor Fanny Price in *Mansfield Park*, constantly run to the ground by her aunt and her cousin Maria Bertram-Rush . . . . My breath caught in my throat. Too late, I noticed Bertie's eyes gleam in triumph at my reaction, but I was too busy reeling under the strange coincidence to care. First Mary and now Bertie were clones in a Jane Austen novel with names suspiciously close to the characters that they took after. A rush of nerves exploded through me at the thought.

Bertie sauntered through the ladies as they wrapped toilet-paper wedding dresses around their friends while they posed as live mannequins.

"Jane." Ann-Marie found me in the chaos and slipped me her cell phone. "You've got five texts. They're all from Dancey."

"Five?"

I exchanged Bertie's little teacup sized puppy with Ann-Marie for her phone, but before I could get through Dancey's texts asking Ann-Marie for my number, my phone vibrated. "That'll be him," she said with a little pout, seizing her phone. "I just gave him your number— that means he won't be calling me anymore." She sighed and squeezed Bertie's little rat-bear. "Did you get into a fight with him? That's so romantic. I want to do that. Making up is always so fun."

I gaped at her, feeling like I had been flattened by a four by four. Ann-Marie. Backwards, her name became Marianne—piano-playing, ruled-by-emotions, twisted-ankle-drama-queen Marianne from *Sense and Sensibility*. Turning, I spied Taylor in the chaos. There was a Taylor in *Emma* too. The heroine in that novel had set up her beloved mentor Ms. Taylor with the most pleasant man in the village. The two had been happily married . . . or were they? My gut wrenched at the thought.

And then there was Dancey.

My phone wouldn't stop beeping as it filled with texts. Ann-Marie's eyes were on mine. "He's trying to tell you sorry."

In ten texts? I opened up my phone and sure enough, each text said, "I'm sorry." He must have accidentally sent it ten times. The original Darcy in *Pride and Prejudice* had delivered a whole exposition to Lizzy about why he had done the things that he had done. But with such a non-descriptive text, I had no idea what Dancey was sorry about—that he'd kissed a crass American or that he had lost one?

"So." Ann-Marie licked her lips. "Are you off the market now? Because," she went on hurriedly, "I told Austen that I was interested in him last night, but he said he wasn't interested in me, but now that you're taken, he might . . . ?" She let the thought hang threateningly. "Austen is so cute. The way that his hair sticks up when he takes off his bike helmet is so adorable. He's got so much hair, you know. So thick and curly—I want to run my hands through it every time I see him. And his eyes. They're hazel, but sometimes they look yellow . . . I wish he looked at me the way he looked at Junie. Oh, Junie makes me so mad. I don't know what the guys see in her. Austen's always talking to her . . ." She hesitated. "What are you doing with that cupcake, Jane?"

I glanced down at the oversized cupcake in my hand. Sure enough, I had mangled it. "Ann-Marie," I said. "I think you should try to see if he's interested again. Guys like Austen need a kick in the pants."

She nodded.

"Very beautiful. What lovely ladies." The male voice sounded wrong in a room full of giggling females. The women turned to stare in irritation at the male intruder. Colin had made his appearance.

I pushed my cell phone into my pocket and tried to wipe the frosting off my hands.

"Oh, this one looks like a winner." Colin lingered near Bella who was covered in toilet paper, obviously judging the lady, not the dress, because the tissue hung limply over her arms in a mess. He hurriedly slid past Mary in her cleverly-crafted masterpiece.

"Jane." Colin predictably found me in the chaos. "Why aren't you slathered in toilet paper?"

I coughed over my laugh. *That sounded so gross.* "Ann-Marie and I were just cleaning up." I avoided Bertie's satisfied smirk when I gathered leftover cupcake wrappers and threw them into the trash.

"It won't be too long until you, too, are celebrating your own wedding," Colin said with a suggestive wink.

That got Bella's attention. She gave me a thumbs-up. I shook my head at her. "I doubt it, Colin. I'm one of those confirmed bachelor rats."

Ann-Marie sighed beside me. "That's easy for her to say. All the men are crazy for her and I keep waiting and waiting. I've tried everything. But you know the saying: 'Women are like apples. The best ones are at the top of the tree.' And the guys are just too lazy to climb up to us, so they just marry the ones who fall on the ground— you know, those nasty rotting apples full of worms."

I tensed as every married woman mentally stabbed us with their eyes. Colin added to the discomfort with his own unblinking stare. "I had better take up climbing," he said.

I gave an uneasy laugh. "No, I wouldn't want you to hurt yourself, Colin."

"Are you coming down from the tree then?"

205

In a way I was going down, but not because of Colin. I avoided the question, noticing that Taylor had waved me over. I escaped him to get to her side. "Did you need me?" I asked.

"Yes." She glared at the new owner of the North Abbey and lowered her voice. "I don't want *him* here, but I can't just ask him to leave. Colin basically owns the place, but . . ." she clenched her teeth, "get him out!"

Flirt to divert. It was low, but it was Taylor's wedding and I was already failing as her event coordinator. "Sure." I returned to Colin, feeling the dread a criminal might feel confessing to a murder. "Colin, I need to show you something outside."

Colin's eyes glittered with anticipation. "Jane, you turn more interesting by the hour. Lead the way."

I let him take my arm, feeling like the pied piper for unwanted men. "Jane," Mary said in an undertone. She stepped off a chair and swished her way towards me in a confection of toilet paper and duct tape. "What was in those cupcakes? My stomach feels like a ball of fiery gas."

"Flour, sugar, eggs."

"Oh." She groaned. "This feels worse than what I ate at Churchell's Shack at the brunch. My stomach felt like it was eating itself. What are you feeding us?"

I stiffened and lashed out, "Food. Would you like me to burp you?"

"Would that work?" she startled me by asking.

"Ask Bertie to do it," I said and left the bridal shower with Colin following after me. I was not cut out for this job. I didn't have Taylor's experience, and I didn't have the patience of Job; though once Jennings' photographs hit the internet, I *would* have the reputation of a scarlet woman. It wouldn't look good on my resume.

Once we were in the hall, Colin studied our surroundings with interest. "Where's the rock star?" he asked. "Is he staying here?" I cringed at the mention of Dancey and kept walking. Colin didn't seem interested in my answer. "I have a few song ideas that I'd like to discuss with him."

"I thought maybe you might want to see the game room, Colin." I led him there, hearing a game of billiards in play. Balls scattered and smacked against each other. Men's voices were low in conversation. A female laughed through the noise.

Hesitating at the door, I wondered whom I'd find inside. Word was that Dancey had business in L.A. today—I hoped that meant he wasn't back yet. Before Colin could mistake my lingering as an invitation to get cozy, I pushed inside the room. Bigley and Crawley were at the pool table. They both glanced up. Crawley's eyes filled with interest and I smiled at him, remembering his pep talk earlier. It was the only thing keeping me sane right now.

Even better, there was no Dancey and no Austen.

Redd rolled the end of his pool stick in blue chalk, not turning to me . . . as if he had some inner radar that told him to ignore me when I was near. Not surprisingly, Junie had joined the boys in their game. They were all dressed down in jeans, shorts, and T-shirts. Junie had ditched her shoes again. I was envious. She carried her pool stick like a spear over her shoulders, then swung it into place on the table like the tough chick she was before she executed a perfect hit. Two balls went into the side pocket. The boys groaned.

"You're making us look bad," Bigley said.

Junie caught him with her frank gaze. "Oh Chuck, you don't need me for that."

Crawley laughed behind them. Junie and Bigley knew each other better than I'd thought. I guessed it made sense since Junie had stolen my vacation to London with Taylor—they would've had plenty of time to get to know each other there. Bigley looked more at ease than when I had seen him last. His jacket lay over the back of a chair, his sleeves rolled up. Junie went for her next strike and scratched when she pocketed the wrong ball.

"Don't worry," Bigley teased her. "Mistakes happen."

"Only when I'm with you." She didn't look up this time. "I prefer to make my mistakes in the game where no one gets hurt."

Bigley shook out his shoulders like he was letting the trash talk roll off. It was his turn, and he took careful aim at a striped ball. It veered the opposite way, and he groaned.

"Maybe you should play on Junie's team," Crawley said with a laugh.

"Are you sure his mother would approve?" she retorted. "I'm not the kind of girl she likes."

I sucked in my breath. Junie was on one. She must've joined the crusade with Taylor to fight for Bigley's independence, but I wasn't sure if this was the best way to go about it.

Redd bumped fists with Junie as he passed her to the table. He stood needlessly close to her while he took aim. He pocketed the ball. With a start, I saw him watching me where he still crouched over the table. As soon as we met eyes, he looked away.

"Oh." Colin advanced on the game as if drawn in by a magnet. "I've played this before. I used to be quite good at it. Let's see." He picked up a pool stick and aimed it at one of the balls.

"Colin!" I tried to stop him. "You have to wait for the game to end. They're still playing."

He jerked up at my voice, his aim slanting and upending the entire game. The boys grimaced. Junie's eyes met the ceiling.

Colin didn't get that he was seriously overstepping bounds. "Let me try again."

Crawley snickered. Bigley leaned on his stick, shaking his head at me. His eyes twinkled. "What plague have you brought on us, Jane?"

I would've stepped inside the game room to join the brothers at the table, but Redd's glower stopped me. I hesitated at the door, though Bigley tried to wave me in. "Come talk to us. Crawley was just telling me that you're jogging buddies."

I smiled. "Really? We jogged together *once*."

Crawley teased me with a mischievous look. "The other time you ran away from me. That doesn't count?"

"Jane? Run away?" Redd asked bitterly. "That's so unlike her."

Crawley's eyes shot to him and then to me. A grin took over his face. "Is that him?" he mouthed to me.

I froze at Crawley's reference to my two love interests. I looked over at Redd to make sure that he hadn't noticed. Redd's attention was fixed firmly on Junie. He was taking extreme care with showing her the particulars of the game—overly so.

"No," I mouthed back to Crawley.

Crawley held up three fingers and raised his brows at me like he was shocked. "Three guys?"

"No," I mouthed back. I had no intention of stringing along three men.

Bigley's eyes ran between me and his brother.

Crawley tipped his head at Colin with a suggestive smile and then held up four fingers as if saying Colin counted as my fourth suitor. I tried not to burst out laughing.

"Jane," Redd's voice cut through our game of charades. "I'm glad to see that the years have been kind to you. Now you can get away with flirting with much younger men."

My face felt hot. I had almost forgotten that Redd saw me for what I truly was. Yeah, I got that the spell I'd once had over the captain was broken already—I got it a million times over. Still, *that* was hurtful. Harry Crawley was probably only three years younger, anyway.

Glaring at Redd, I could only see Captain Frederick Wentworth from *Persuasion*, some guy crippled by his bitterness because he had been jilted by a girl. The difference between me and the heroine in that book was that she actually wanted her captain, but . . . my thoughts cut off when I came to another realization. Captain Redd Wortham? Jane Austen had named her captain Frederick Wentworth. Their names almost rhymed. It was too weird.

Junie? Did she fit the pattern, too? I studied her. Junie raised her brows at me at the same time that I put her story together. She was so Jane Fairfax from *Emma,* Emma's not-so-secret archrival. "Fair" was Austen's shortened version for Junie's last name. It was all close enough to make me nervous. I leaned heavily against the door, trying to take it all in.

"Jane?"

I turned. Crawley put up five fingers and pointed to himself like he was the last member of my entourage of suitors. He gave his infectious laugh and the similarity hit me. Henry Crawford from *Mansfield Park.* That's who Harry Crawley was. His flirtatious ways said it all, even down to his surprising spurts of thoughtfulness and charm.

I was officially stuck in not one, but almost all of Jane Austen's novels!

Jerking from the doorway, I ran down the hallway for the lobby. After Colin had dropped by this afternoon, I had avoided the checkout counter, knowing that Austen would eventually go there to look over the rest of the accounts. I'd wanted nothing to do with him or his plot to give away North Abbey. Now I needed Austen like I needed my own breath. He'd better not ditch me now.

"Austen!" I called. "Austen!"

Chapter 18

"Sense will always have attractions for me."

—Jane Austen, Sense and Sensibility

I didn't feel real. I felt like I was in a novel where every girl hated me except my besties. And every man loved me—secretly, openly—villain and hero alike. It felt wrong. I needed something real. I needed Austen. I pushed open the door to the lobby and saw him right where I hoped he'd be. He was at his laptop, wearing earbuds, muttering to the music. Yeah. Ultra-normal.

"Austen!" I slammed into the counter in front of him.

He gave a helpless yelp and took out his earbuds. "Jane, you're talking to me again?"

He'd noticed that I had been avoiding him? It didn't matter right now. "Help me!"

"*You* want my help? Sorry, that's not gonna happen." He put his earbuds back in.

I reached over and tugged them out. He wasn't escaping me that easily. "Give me that guest list, Austen!"

"You are really controlling today." But he reached under the desk and slid it over to me. Meanwhile I shifted his laptop closer to me, minimized the document meant to destroy my world, and opened a word document so I could type furiously:

Ms. Taylor
Henry Crawford
Maria Bertram Rushworth
Charles Bingley

211

Mister Collins
Fitzwilliam Darcy
Mary Musgrove

"You want to see a cool trick?" I asked Austen. My voice dripped with sarcasm. "Compare these names to our guest list."

He looked confused, but he set the list next to the screen. "Fine, I'll play,"

"Okay." I started out my explanation, knowing this would sound crazy. "The names I just typed in are all characters in Jane Austen novels. I'll do the most obvious ones first."

"You told me this before," Austen complained. "Dancey is Darcy. Bigley and Colin are something. I can't remember."

"Yeah, no! Hey, I'm really freaking out here. Just look at the guests' full names!"

"Will Dancey, Chuck Bigley . . ." he read, "and Colin isn't on here."

"He's Mr. Collins—Colin Minster? It's opposite." I noticed Austen's confused look, "—I mean, it isn't perfectly the same, but it's still weird. And Dancey and Bigley just have different versions of the same first name. See? Chuck is really Charles in *Pride and Prejudice*. Fitzwilliam is like . . . Willard."

"Fascinating." His tone said differently. "Are you feeling okay?"

"No! You're not getting how crazy this is," I said. He smirked, and I waved my hands over each other. "No, *I'm* not crazy. Okay, maybe I am, but all their names are like the characters in Jane Austen novels. It's just creepy. You want to see the weirdest one of all?" I tried to find Bertie's name on the guest list. "Taylor's maid of honor is just scary. Bertie's nickname is her last name shortened. Her husband's last name is Rush. The character in *Mansfield Park* is Maria Bertram Rushworth because she married a man with the last name Rushworth. Bertie's real name is . . ." I skimmed through the list, "It's really Mariah Bertram-Rush." My knees buckled at how close they were, and I had to sit down.

"I wish I knew what you were trying to say," Austen said.

Now I knew that he was trying to be difficult. I took a deep breath. "Bertie's real name is almost exactly the same as the character in the novel."

He studied it. "Oh. Okay. Yeah, that is weird."

Good. I was getting somewhere. "Figure out Harry Crawley's now."

Austen turned to the word document, kind of laughing. "He's . . . Henry Crawford."

I breathed a sigh of relief. "Yes, yes!" Maybe now he'd believe me that the characters from Jane Austen novels were coming to life around me. "And then Taylor isn't on the guest list, but it doesn't matter because we all know that she's Ms. Taylor!"

"Taylor Weston?" he asked doubtfully. "It's kind of a stretch."

I cried out as soon as I realized another uncanny resemblance. "Ms. Taylor married Mr. Weston in *Emma*."

He finally cracked that smile that had threatened over his lips since I came in. "So you can take anyone's name and twist it like that? How many books did Jane Austen write anyway?"

"Only six. Well, seven if you count the one . . . . It doesn't matter. It's not just some weird coincidence that happened because she wrote a million books and has a million characters, okay? And there are more matches, too. Junie is Jane Fairfax. Mary Musswood is Mary Musgrove. And she acts like Mary from the book, too. She's a complete snob and always sick. Mary even says that she has . . ."

". . . a major case of hypochondria," Austen answered for me.

"No, but yes. Yes! And Captain Redd Wortham is Captain Frederick Wentworth."

Austen mimicked a buzzer sound at the captain's name. "Another stretch."

"It's not. Fred is Redd. They're both captains. Last names have 'worth' in them. Oh!" I pointed to the guest list. "Here's another one! We've got a character from *Northanger Abbey*!" I underlined Bella

Thorne's last name with my finger then typed in "Isabella Thorpe" to add her to the list of matches. "She's the beautiful, flirty one who gets into trouble with the men."

"In the book or real life?"

"Both."

He laughed. "I can't keep track of the real people, let alone the people they're supposed to be." He studied the guest list then looked triumphant. "You're missing two—the pastor and his wife."

Ed and Elly McFarey. In a moment, I had it: "Edward Ferrars— he's the clergyman who married Elinor in *Sense and Sensibility*. And that's all the guests at North Abbey!" I realized what I had just said and snapped by fingers when I found another Jane Austen reference. "Northanger Abbey!"

"Huh?"

"Never mind." He could only handle one thing at a time. "It's just really creepy, Austen. I feel like I'm in a novel. I think you really did curse me with all that talk about how our lives are not romances."

"Hey!" He held his hands up in mock defensiveness. "It goes both ways. We cursed each other. I said that you wouldn't enjoy a Jane Austen courtship and you said that *I* would."

"Well?" I asked. "Are you enjoying it?"

He laughed. "Seeing you like this? Enormously." Studying me— likely to see how serious I was about all of this—Austen dug his elbow against the counter and leaned closer to me. "Look, Jane. Do you realize things like this can't happen? Not really. These people aren't named the way they are because we cursed ourselves somehow. You think this is like some Christmas miracle story and all you have to do is a good deed and they'll just disappear? Because if so, you'd have a very angry Taylor on your hands. These people were named this way before you ever met them."

"But don't you think that it's such a coincidence . . . ?"

"That our friend Taylor has friends who have names that fit in a Jane Austen novel? Yeah. It's hilarious, but for all of her friends that do, I'm sure most of them don't. C'mon, Jane, you can't really be serious about what you're saying."

"Okay," I hedged. I wasn't ready to give up yet. "Explain why all her friends act like the characters?"

"Simple. It's like a horoscope. Anyone can fit any profile if you twist it around enough."

"Colin totally pulled a Mr. Collins earlier," I pointed out. "He crashed the bridal shower and then went into the game room and played pool in the middle of someone else's game."

Austen stilled. "He did what?"

"I know, bad for business . . . not that you care. And then Bertie told me to act my place or she'd send me to my room in the attic. That is so Maria Bertram-Rush. Dancey wrote me a super long text after our misunderstanding."

"Are you kidding me?" he sounded angry. "Wait, what misunderstanding did you have with Dancey?"

I waved his concern aside. "You're missing the point."

"I don't think so."

That was because Austen lacked imagination. He always did. It was partly why I had come to him. I needed his logic. I knew that I was being crazy—and it was his job to talk some sense into me. Noticing the angry glint that touched his eyes, I realized that he was actually livid on my behalf because of everything I'd been through. I was touched. I hadn't expected that.

Freddy pushed open the lobby doors from outside and strutted past the counter. Even as our bellhop-valet, he had the air that he was too good for us.

"Who's he?" Austen asked in a lowered voice.

I had it immediately. "Frederick Tilney . . . from *Northanger Abbey*. An arrogant rogue."

Austen would know the employee's full name: Freddy Tiney was a family friend. Austen went quiet and I knew he was right. This didn't mean anything . . . but if it did, at least I had saved Bella from

Freddy this time around, because the book version of Isabella Thorpe had ruined herself with Frederick Tilney. Now Bella was going after Crawley. Thankfully, my Crawford wasn't as bad as the original one.

No, he wasn't bad at all. I straightened. My imagination had completely run away from me this time. I really had been guilty of taking my theory too far. I breathed a sigh of relief that none of it was actually true.

"It's like playing *Where's Waldo* with Jane Austen," Austen muttered.

I laughed. Trust Austen to put this all into perspective.

Ann-Marie threw open the door to the lobby, holding Bertie's little teacup puppy. "Hi, Austen, I thought I heard you in here. I had a dream about you. Oh, Jane, you're in here too. Have you seen Will Dancey!" It came out a shriek.

"Willard," Austen corrected.

Dancey's first name didn't affect Ann-Marie like it did me. She practiced it over her lips. "Willard Dancey. You're so lucky that he likes you, Jane! He . . . is so hot! He just got back from LA. I saw him. He came by the bridal shower looking all brooding and sullen. You didn't make up yet after your fight, have you? How romantic. I know you love those kinds of guys in your movies, Jane, but he's real. I mean, he's a total . . . a total hunk! If I could get him alone for just a minute, I'd get him to write a whole crapload of happy songs. Yummy! We'd sing duets and kiss all day long."

Austen winced. "We've got a foosball table in here, Ann-Marie. That's the real secret to his heart—you heard what he told Taylor. Go at it."

Ann-Marie laughed and hugged Bertie's little rat-bear to her chest. "You could plan our wedding, Jane." She turned thoughtful. "No, forget that. Vegas is only five hours away. Do you know how easy it would be just to slip away with a guy like that and make it legal? All you'd have to do is convince him that he can't live without you. So easy. He's all over you. Did you see that car he's driving? You'd be saying, 'I do' before you knew it." She sighed. "Anyway, he asked about you, Jane."

Austen scowled.

Bertie's little rat-bear shifted in her hands and she shrieked again. "This puppy just keeps getting cuter and cuter! Don't you, puppy?"

I hid a smile. "Don't forget to return it to the owner."

She nuzzled her nose into the puppy's belly and then set her on the counter to dance her over to Austen. The puppy sniffed at his hands. "The boy smells good, huh?" Ann-Marie asked.

Austen patted the puppy's head. Between the rat-bear and Taylor's cat, we could start an animal shelter. "What's puppy's name?" Austen asked.

"Rat-bear," I said.

"No!" Ann-Marie screamed out. "I was thinking of naming her after you, Austen."

He looked uneasy. "That just wouldn't be right."

She giggled. "Oh, I forgot to tell you about my dream, Austen . . ." She went on for fifteen minutes about how Austen had saved her from bandits in an apocalyptic world and he was a vampire, and then it turned confusing from there because her mother forced her to clean North Abbey—but wow, Austen could kiss. She ended her long soliloquy by staring up into his eyes. "But wouldn't it be nice to kiss me?"

Austen looked dumbfounded. "I . . ."

When he couldn't finish that, she straightened. "Because someone told me that I should give you another chance."

I froze, knowing that I was guilty of that. Austen watched her helplessly. "I don't know if you should," he said. "Was I a good vampire or a bad one?"

Ann-Marie threw back her shoulders in a sigh. "Bad. Very bad—you couldn't even pull off a low V-neck." Her eyes went from me to him, and they took on a frustrated gleam. "Yeah, I get it. See you in my dreams, Austen." Balancing the puppy in her hands, she left.

Picking up his jaw from off the ground, Austen turned to me. "Who is she?" At my confused look, he clarified. "Who is she in a Jane Austen book?"

"Oh." It hardly mattered now. "Well, her name backwards is Marianne. *Sense and Sensibility*. Only . . ." I smiled, "Ann-Marie's like Marianne on speed."

He gulped. "Cool party trick." His fingers played a rhythm across the counter until he broke our silence to ask, "Okay, me? Who am I?"

That would be difficult. I put my fingers up like I was framing him with a camera and screwed up my eyes to see him as a character. "Well, you're a churchgoer—and Jane Austen had a lot of cute clergyman in her novels, so . . ."

"Stop." He held up his hand. "Don't hurt yourself. I changed my mind. Don't make me into a character. I honestly don't want a character."

"I can't think of one for you anyway."

"That's a relief."

Now my mind was obsessed with finding the answer. "You're too goofy to be Mr. Knightley."

"Wait, who?"

"The love interest in *Emma*. You're too young to be the colonel in *Sense and Sensibility*. Maybe Frank Churchill?" I considered another rakish suitor in *Emma*. "Loved him, but no, you're way too independent. He wanted his aunt's money. That made him a complete jerk. You're nice. Still, not as nice as Henry Tilney. Plus, you'd never put up with Henry's dad."

"Huh?"

"*Northanger Abbey*," I said. "You'd never do the stupid things Edmund does in *Mansfield Park* either."

Austen didn't look like he was following me at all. "Thanks?"

I wrinkled my nose. I kind of liked that Austen didn't fit any of the men in these novels. "No. You defy description. I'm Jane; you're Austen."

He groaned. "So now we're the authors of these people's lives?"

"I didn't say that."

"No, you just think we're cursed."

"Well . . ." I met his eyes. Austen was teasing me now, but since I had calmed down, I decided to play with it. "If you're cursed, too, then you'd need your own romance." Then it hit me like a stab in the gut. Junie! Secretive Junie whom Austen might actually have a thing for. "Do you?" I asked, unsure now.

He gave me a mischievous grin. "Maybe."

Just thinking about it put my teeth on edge. It was good that I was wrong about the curse, or every girl at North Abbey would be making the moves on Austen like the guys were with me. Bertie, Mary, and Bella didn't know how amazing Austen was, and I'd make sure that it stayed that way.

My phone buzzed, and I looked down at the text. It was from Colin.

COLIN: MEET ME AT CHURCHELL'S SHACK, WE NEED TO TALK ABOUT THE FUTURE OF NORTH ABBEY.

Austen plucked the phone easily from my hands. "Give me that."

"Hey!" I complained.

Austen typed off a text and thrust the phone near my eyes so I could read it.

JANE: WOULD YOU BE A DEAR, COLIN, AND CHECK ON TAYLOR? SHE WANTS YOU TO HANG FLOWERS AND RIBBON FOR THE BACHELORETTE PARTY TOMORROW.

I smirked. "Okay, yeah, send that."

Austen did the evil deed and handed my phone back to me. He took my hand. "Sit down, Jane. I think you've had a hard day."

He was right. I was so exhausted that I'd have let him take me anywhere. He led me to the sofa and we settled in front of the big screen TV. It was blissfully off for now. Austen faced me, looking contrite. "Jane, I'm sorry you have to put up with Colin. I know you're angry about it."

Well, my life had been shoved off the deep end because of Austen's rational decision. Losing North Abbey would affect my whole future. I groaned at the thought. "Why do you have to sell the place to Colin?"

"My parents are in the red, Jane. Taylor's wedding might bring in a little more money, but even after that, it will only mean that they owe a little less than they do now. The most I can do is get a decent price out of it. Colin's parents own a share in the resort and they're willing to buy us out."

Austen wasn't getting rid of the family business because he was bored with it. I had to remember that, even though I wished there was another way. I sighed and leaned heavily against the back cushions of the sofa. "We're losing our home to Mr. Collins," I grumbled.

His lip twitched up at the sides. "You're back to *Pride and Prejudice* again?"

"You don't appreciate how creepy my life is right now." I pulled out the Jane Austen collection from the side console. "I have to show you what I'm talking about before you try to lock me up in an asylum."

"Give me those," he said. "I'm confiscating these." He held the DVDs like they were dangerous weapons, then peered closer at one of the covers. "What's with her hair? That's so wrong."

"The hair can be pretty bad in the older ones; also in the latest *Persuasion*, but . . ." I stole *Northanger Abbey* from his hands and held it up to my eyes. "Adorably clueless girl finds love despite making all sorts of mistakes. She marries above her station though she has no money or family connections."

Austen looked wary. "Not a bad end," he said.

"Not a likely ending either, according to you. However . . ." I stood up and stuffed the movie into the DVD player and fast-forwarded it to one of Catherine's daydreams where two men fight over her and she is secretively pleased about it. "Personality-wise, I admit I'm a lot like Catherine because I love romance, maybe ridiculously so. Here's a fight she has with her main squeeze, Henry." I fast-forwarded it again. "He thinks that she is being over-imaginative and silly."

Austen leaned back into the couch, his eyes on me. "And that's us?"

"Not quite," I said, "Or we'd have this to look forward to." With a devilish laugh, I sat next to him and cut to the end where Henry declares his love for Catherine. With his arms around her, he told her that she wasn't so far off with her crazy theories.

"You're right. I'm wrong," Austen said. "I know the drill. Male loves female no matter what she does."

I elbowed him playfully. "I'm not through yet." I took out *Northanger Abbey* and put in *Persuasion*. "Here's a classic love-hate romance where girl loses boy and gets him back again." I cut to the part where the captain meets Anne again after his long voyage at sea. "She dumped him because he wasn't good enough—class distinction, money and all that, but now he's a captain in her majesty's royal navy."

I pushed play to show Austen a stiff captain ignoring the main girl, though it's obvious that she's the only one he can see. I paused the scene and turned to Austen. "Do you remember when I asked you to be my fake boyfriend?"

"How could I forget?"

"And?"

He shrugged. "It was kind of like that with the captain."

"Well, this movie says that I can get Redd back."

Austen stiffened. I climbed off the sofa and ejected *Persuasion* and put in *Sense and Sensibility*. "Guy goes for sensible girl," I summarized, "who keeps her distance and doesn't really flirt with him. He still falls in love with her. The other girl—who happens to be sisters with the sensible one—well, she *does* flirt, and she gets in trouble with the wrong guy."

I couldn't help it. I took Austen to the part where Marianne sprained her ankle and the perfect Mr. Willoughby carries her back to her cottage. "Even now it makes me all swoony," I said, "even if the guy's a weasel—he's a hot weasel."

Austen's eyes went to me and I hurriedly got to my point. "Remember when you said that a girl has to flirt to get a guy's attention? Well, you're right. Doing *nothing* doesn't actually work, except ever since we 'cursed' each other . . . I find that doing nothing works for me. I mean, what kind of girl gets a guy without flirting? And what kind of girl doesn't get anywhere with her flirting?"

"Do I have to answer that?" Austen asked.

"No, because I promise it won't be funny." I held up *Mansfield Park* next. "Classic Cinderella story. A poor relation is taken in, treated terribly—they put her in the attic—but then everyone sees how wonderful and sensible she is. She takes over the household and all the men love her—good and bad alike."

He gave me a look like I was far from Fanny Price's character description. "They love her because she's so sensible?" he asked.

"Fine, Fanny and I are only alike because we both live in the attic. And the guys are all going crazy around here. Crawley even noticed it. He accused me of having five suitors."

Austen caught my hand, tugging me away from the DVD player so that I sat down next to him. "Who are they?"

I counted the men out in my head again and realized that Austen was in that number, which wasn't true at all. "Sorry, just four suitors," I said. "Four, if you go by Jane Austen's definition. Wait, no five again. Jane Austen would count the fifth." With great daring, I pulled out *Emma*. "Best friend falls for his best gal pal. The one she loved was in front of her the whole time."

He was silent, watching me. "Show me," he said after a moment.

Surprised, I turned to see his expression. He was giving me that look again—the one that I couldn't read, but it was warm and it sent prickles of heat through my skin. If I didn't know better, I'd say that

Austen was getting in to this. "Okay," I said, not sure what clip I could trust him with. Maybe when Emma declared her love in the end. *No, too embarrassing.* Maybe the constant fights between her and Knightley. *Too close for comfort.* I finally decided on the party where Emma and Knightley dance and fall in love.

I was so caught up in the scene that I forgot that I was presenting this as a slideshow. Austen was quiet beside me—maybe bored out of his mind. I moved to turn off the movie when my arm brushed against his. I hadn't realized how close together we had been sitting. I cleared my throat and met his eyes. He was still watching me, and I noticed the little gold flecks in his eyes, the stray freckles on his face, the curve of his lips.

I took a deep breath. "But that would never happen."

"Why not?"

Instead of scurrying to put in another movie to cover up the silence, I was mesmerized by the moment. That's what this was—a *moment!* So much more seemed to rest between us than words.

"Do you want it to happen?" he asked hesitantly.

"I . . ."

"Who will you dance with?" He grinned self-consciously when he butchered the line we had just watched Mr. Knightley say from *Emma.*

It took me a moment to recover, but I knew Emma's line by heart. "With you," I said, "if you will ask me."

"How shocking," he said, going completely off-script. "The both of us alone here. Think of what we could do? If anyone caught us together, they'd force us to get married."

I gave a weak laugh to catch my breath.

He picked up the last movie in my pliant hands, his fingers brushing through mine. "There's one more," he said.

Of course it had to be *Pride and Prejudice.* He put the movie in this time. I remembered that he knew this one because of his ex-girlfriend. "Poor girl marries a rich guy," Austen summarized for me this time, "who loves her no matter how mean she is to him. She gets everything she wants."

I picked up the remote, toying with taking the movie to the scene where Darcy dives into the water, but so far that hadn't happened. I knew what had. I took us to Darcy's first proposal to Elizabeth. Darcy told Elizabeth that he loved her against his will. Then they fought and the two parted in anger.

I paused the scene, realizing that I had nothing to say about it.

"Did that happen with Dancey?"

Glancing over, I found an irate Austen. The emotion behind his words startled me. I'd expected teasing, maybe a suggestion to enjoy my little Jane Austen romance while I had it. Not this. I didn't normally kiss and tell, except once my little dalliance with Dancey hit the internet, I'd have no choice. If Austen was mad now, he'd be a lot more so when he found out the truth. I didn't know how to break any of this to him. Maybe I already had?

"Okay." His hand went around mine again, startling the words away from me. "You need to get out of the house. We both do. You are *not* having a Jane Austen romance." That sounded suspiciously like a command. "I'm going to prove it. You like dancing?"

I nodded.

"Good. I'm giving you a splash of real life. I promise it's a lot more fun."

Chapter 19

"There is nothing I would not do for those who are really my friends. I have no notion of loving people by halves, it is not my nature."

—Jane Austen, Northanger Abbey

We walked into the Barton Club. The music blared from the speakers, though it couldn't drown out the talking and chattering from the occupants inside. It was a good distraction from my own thoughts. The waitress found us a booth, and I lowered gratefully into it.

Instead of taking the side facing me, Austen cornered me on my own bench, putting his feet up on the opposite side. "We are only going to talk about normal things tonight," he said. His eyes danced with promised fun, and he brought his arm around me to give me a bracing squeeze. "We're not talking about dating or Jane Austen or business or . . ." he thought for a moment, "cross-stitching."

"Fair enough." And now I couldn't think of anything to say. "How long are you in town?" I asked.

"About a month, maybe shorter. Depending . . ."

On how long it took him to assess the value of the place; but we weren't supposed to talk business. "You still working with the kids at the community center?" I asked.

"I've seen them once since I've been here. We played some beach volleyball."

I'd be disappointed that he didn't invite me—I liked those kids—but Taylor's wedding got in the way of everything: another forbidden topic. I was really struggling here.

"Hey, Jane." Austen's arm left me so he could nudge me. "Have you been out to the beach lately?"

"Just to jog, but not as much as I'd like."

"Whatever happened to your learning-to-surf idea?"

"Oh, that!" I rolled my eyes. "I can't get it. Taylor and Ann-Marie tried to show me after you left, and they gave up. They said that I'd never learn."

"Maybe I should get you back in the water."

If he were here for long enough. That felt like something we couldn't talk about either. I gave a non-committal shrug and changed the subject. "Are you liking Boston?"

"The water's too cold. The beach is only for docking ships. It's pretty for cycling though, and the fall is amazing. I've never seen such vivid colors—you'd love it. You should come up and visit me."

He'd have to be good at long-distance relationships for that. I pulled out my phone. "Just a second; I want to check something." I texted him. His phone vibrated, and he pulled it out and laughed when he saw my message.

ME: CAN YOU USE A PHONE NOW?

Pursing his lips, he typed something in. I read it as soon as my phone registered the message:

AUSTEN: NOT WHEN THE PERSON IS SITTING RIGHT NEXT TO ME.

Before I could text him back, Austen stopped me, bumping his foot into mine. "About that," he said. "I'm sorry."

Sorry that he wasn't interested in me enough for a long distance relationship or sorry that we had argued about it? I had assumed that I had read too much into the relationship, but now I wasn't so sure. I took a breath and tried to find out. "What was that about, anyway?"

He shrugged, running his finger over the tabletop. "I couldn't get out of here fast enough. I've worked at North Abbey my whole life, and there was no way I wanted to carry on the failing family business. I just wanted to leave it all behind."

"What about me?"

He looked troubled, like the question pained him, but still he answered. "I thought it was easier to not leave anything I cared about behind."

So he forced himself not to care. And now that Austen had exhausted all his options in Boston, he thought that I would just be waiting around for him to pick up? The romantic in me didn't want to be second choice, and neither did the logical side—second would just be dropped again for *the best*.

"And now?" I asked.

"I can see that if I care about someone, that's not going to work."

I warmed at his words, at the same time forcing myself not to fall for them. If I could believe his story, he had left me and stewed about it for eight months. And where did that leave Junie? They seemed pretty close. Austen would have to prove he meant what he said. And if he failed me again, that would hurt—my heart *and* my pride.

Austen looked up, and I followed his gaze to see Chuck Bigley. The blond Brit was guzzling down a brandy at the bar—a far cry from the self-confident man that I had seen in the game room earlier that night. Far too many buttons were unbuttoned on his white shirt, and his suit pants were wrinkled. Dancey's publicity manager, DeBurgy, lounged next to Bigley, watching the dancers at the club. My heart sped up nervously, and I wondered if Dancey was hanging out with both of them tonight. A quick scan of the room told me that Dancey had ditched his friends again. I was glad.

Bigley set his glass down and DeBurgy laughed at something he said. The publicity manager was a polished man who dressed in tailored suits that accentuated his broad shoulders. Unlike Bigley, he seemed on top of his game tonight. The gold rings on his fingers told me that Dancey paid him well. DeBurgy caught me staring, and elbowed Bigley with a knowing look. Taylor's fiancé swung around and, with a big smile, motioned for us to join him.

We waved back, but Austen wasn't moving, and I didn't feel like crawling over him to say hello. After Taylor's fiancé saw we weren't coming, he headed for us instead, taking his glass with him like a security blanket.

Before he reached our table, Austen tilted his head at the groom-to-be. "He's *not* one of your suitors, right?" he asked under his breath.

"Of course not."

Bigley took a seat on the bench opposite us, unwittingly forcing Austen to move his feet. He gave me his famous smile. "Jane, I was beginning to think that you never left North Abbey. And here I find you at the Barton Club. Good girl. It's about time you let your hair down."

I felt sheepish and touched my hair. I had left it in a ponytail. "And yet, it's up," I said and laughed awkwardly. I glanced around the darkened room, past the flashing blue and red neon lights on the dance floor. "Where's Taylor?"

"She's off doing what brides do."

It was an evasive answer. I tried to ignore Austen's suddenly watchful eyes and fished again for some conversation. "It's hard to believe that the wedding is only two days away."

Bigley grimaced and took another drink. "I can only hide from the women for so long. They'll kill each other if I don't make an appearance Saturday morning."

"To your wedding?" I asked, getting worried.

"Of course, to my wedding. That's what people do, get married, don't they?" Bigley didn't seem quite right, but when he finished the last of his drink, I knew it was the brandy talking. He motioned for a waiter to fill his glass up again and to leave the bottle. He threw the amber liquid down his throat. "My stepbrother won't stop talking about you," he said once he had breath enough to speak. "But Jane's a pretty girl, isn't she?" He directed that comment at Austen.

Austen was taken aback and glanced over at me. "Gorgeous," he shocked me by saying.

Bigley gave a drunken laugh. "You know what Harry did? He made a bet, if you believe it, that he could get Jane to go for him." He shook his head. "He doesn't know Jane very well—she's too stubborn for that."

I gaped when I realized the implications.

"A bet?" Austen asked in disbelief. "People do that?"

I went stiff. "No, Austen, it just happens in books. Henry Crawford made a bet to his sister like that in *Mansfield Park*."

I was sure Bigley had no idea what I was referencing, but he gave me a shrewd look over his glass and flashed another big smile. "The bet backfired on him. My stupid brother—he's the one who's fallen for you."

And Austen was my witness. He never would've believed this moment if he hadn't seen it with his own eyes. Bigley leaned over the table to pat my arm. "Why don't you put him out of his misery, Jane?"

Things were just getting weirder. "H-how would I do that?" I asked.

"Take him out. Just for a night, I don't care where as long as it's far away from me."

I gave an uneasy laugh. "He's really fun to hang out with, but I'm really busy . . ."

"Going on drives with Dancey?" Bigley's eyes turned cold. He must've heard that from DeBurgy. Turning to the side, I saw Dancey's publicity manager watching us narrowly from the corner. As soon as we met eyes, DeBurgy smirked. Girls surrounded him, and he wrapped his arms around them both.

Glancing back at Bigley, I saw that his expression was open, his smile innocent enough. The man lifted his glass to Austen. "Or do you prefer clubbing with the help, Jane?" He said it with a laugh, but the way his eyes roved over us felt wrong.

Austen lifted a brow. "The help?"

Bigley failed to notice the dangerous turn in Austen's voice. He nodded drunkenly. "Just show my brother a good time, Jane. There's a good girl. It's not too much to ask. I'm pouring a lot of money into this wedding—most girls wouldn't complain." He winked at me. "Keep it on the sly if you can. Mum won't like a scandal and there won't be. If you help me out, Taylor doesn't have to know what you've been doing on company time."

Austen leaned forward. "What exactly are you accusing Jane of doing?"

"What?" Bigley looked surprised. "She hasn't said anything to you? I thought the two of you were *friends?*"

I tensed, trying to shield myself from the gossip bomb about to explode about me and Dancey. I tried to avert it. "Chuck," I said. "Thanks for the head's up. I'll think about what you said." *I had no intention of it.* He couldn't treat me like his servant. Still, this was Bigley—likely he was too clueless and drunk to get what he was saying.

"Just a little advice from someone who knows his best friend too well." Bigley took a fortifying swig of his brandy before giving us another grin that was quickly losing its charm. "Dancey isn't serious about you, Jane. He likes to leave women behind like dirty laundry— the guy's a publicity nightmare. Poor DeBurgy; he's overworked. I don't blame him for keeping such a close eye on things."

"DeBurgy?" Austen asked with an edge to his voice. "Who's that?"

"Dancey's PR guy." Bigley pointed out the self-assured man in the corner. "He puts out a lot of fires. The guy earns all that money he makes. Look at that suit."

"That's really his name?" Austen asked again. I wondered why until I realized the significance. Lady de Bourgh was the name of the biggest snob in Jane Austen novels—and since she wrote a lot of snobs, that was saying a lot. De Bourgh had tried to control Darcy's social life in *Pride and Prejudice* too. I was impressed that Austen had recognized it.

"His name is really DeBurgy?" Austen asked again.

Bigley kept nodding. "He flew down here to keep an eye on Dancey. We all know Dancey loves the women. You should've seen him with Taylor."

"Wait, wait." Austen looked flustered now. "Did *Dancey* go out with Taylor?"

Bigley's expression hardened—it looked odd on his normally pleasant face. "Some best friend, right? He backed off once he knew I meant to marry Taylor. Guess I ruined his fun."

"Dancey has a thing for Taylor?" I asked.

Bigley snickered in the face of my cross-examination. "Dancey has a thing for *all* women. He doesn't care about anyone but himself. He's meant for royalty; certainly not an American. Of course, that doesn't stop him from playing around." His eyes met the ceiling in disgust. "I even saw Dancey with your piano player tonight."

"Ann-Marie?" I asked.

"Is that her name? She ran from him crying. Dancey has a way with the chicks."

I saw the concern in Austen's eyes. It sparked my own. "When was this?" I asked.

He shrugged. "Before I came here. It was Dancey's classic "use them, throw them away" trick. I wish I had his talent."

I didn't realize that I was breathing so hard until Bigley slammed his hands against the table to stand, startling me from my thoughts. "My brother might be a little thoughtless," Bigley said, "but he'd never play you like that, Jane. Not now, anyway. I'll pay you well."

Austen stood up at that, his chest expanding. "You talk like that any more, Chuck, and you're going to get punched in the face."

"Huh?"

"Why would you tell Jane how to live her life with me around? Are you dumb or do you think I'm as big a jerk as you are?"

Bigley gaped at him, but I had a feeling that he was too drunk to comprehend anything Austen was saying except the "punch" part. He muttered something about getting another drink and stumbled away.

I became aware that I had jumped to my feet sometime during the argument when Austen turned to me. "I thought you said he was nice?"

"Well, yeah . . ." My mouth worked before I could get anything out of it. With the way Bigley had acted just now, he should've been named after the villainous Wickham from *Pride and Prejudice* instead. Of course, in our world we would know him as Wicky or Wickhemmy.

"He—he was supposed to be—supposed to be Charles Bingley from *Pride and Prejudice*," I stuttered. "The nice, friendly guy."

"I think you're way off."

My gaze flew to Bigley, who was flirting it up with the waitress. DeBurgy laughed behind him and egged him on. "DeBurgy?" I mouthed. "The same one from—?"

"I *know* who DeBurgy is," Austen growled.

"How? She's a minor character in *Pride and Prejudice*!"

"My ex was obsessed with the six-hour version, remember?"

I collapsed back to my seat to think this through. I rested my head in my hands. "I thought that our Harry Crawley was nicer than Jane Austen's."

"How could you have possibly known?" Austen sat down beside me, his broad shoulders hiding me from the crowd.

I felt numb as all my superstition came back to haunt me. "In *Mansfield Park* Crawford wanted to make Fanny Price fall in love with him because she hurt his vanity, and then he ended up falling in love with her instead."

"That's fake life," Austen said, "and this is real life."

I wanted to believe it as much as Austen did, but now I half-expected all the Bennet girls to descend on me with a flurry of gossip and girl talk.

"Is this why Taylor keeps crying?" Austen asked. "Jane? Did you hear me? Does she know what kind of a guy Bigley is?"

It looked like our Bigley was a drunk whose mother controlled him by threatening to take away his inheritance. I glanced over at Bigley with the ladies at the bar—he was a womanizer, too. And his stepbrother was Henry Crawford from another book. "I'm sorry." I kneaded my forehead. "It's really hard to think with my life unfolding like a novel."

Austen grunted out in exasperation. "And you've just had your first misunderstanding. How long do you plan on dragging that one out?"

I realized that he was talking about our resident rock star. "Oh, that. Seriously, I don't plan on talking to Dancey ever again."

"Or you can just ask him what Ann-Marie was doing with him and ask Taylor what they had going on together and get all the facts . . . at least then you'll know the truth."

"What? That Dancey's a snake!"

"That's what a snake told you," Austen said, jerking his thumb at Bigley.

I got suspicious of Austen's motives. "Why are you defending Dancey?"

"I like this little thing called truth—as much as I want to throttle the guy for messing with you."

My heart melted a little at that. At least he wanted to protect me. How sweet . . . and logical. Austen was so unlike any romantic hero I knew—he didn't let misunderstandings cloud his judgment. And he actually trusted me to talk to Dancey. Once again, he defied fiction.

"Jane? Are you okay?"

I nodded.

He scooped up my hand in his, looking into my eyes. "Jane, I promised that you would have fun tonight, and we're going to do it. Dance with me?"

I nodded vigorously. We pushed from the booth and I followed Austen out. He took my fingers and lifted them to rest on the curve of his broad shoulder. I liked the feel of it—the muscle there felt strong. After everything that was happening, he felt like an anchor.

Once we reached the dance floor, he swung me close. Nothing felt better than to be in Austen's arms. The DJ played some oldies remix. It was fast and hardly romantic, but it helped me forget my troubles. Austen had a few moves of his own, and they involved swinging me until I laughed and then holding me close so that the breath caught in my throat. His arms were strong and comforting. I felt like I belonged in them.

I lifted my chin to see his hazel eyes deepen on me like they were drinking me in. Austen rested his cheek on my ear for a moment as if thinking. "Can you forgive me for not being a romantic?"

It took me a moment to understand what he was saying. Could he forgive me for being one? All of my sins came back to haunt me. To top them off, I was still waiting for the paparazzi to publish the photos and ruin everything that I had with Austen. "Only if you return the favor," I said.

"How?"

Anything I said would ruin the dance, maybe even destroy the fragile truce we had set up for the night, so my hands tightened over him instead. "If you let me do this," I said; then I brushed my lips across his cheek in a light kiss. I drew back to smile at him.

Austen reached up to trace the outline of my jaw. His light touch sent tingles over my skin. "I don't know if I should allow that—we might cause a scene on the dance floor." His eyes burned into mine as though he wanted to return my kiss, but he pulled me in for a hug at the last minute. The feel of his arms against my back felt more intimate than a kiss. As the music faded into the next song, he pulled away and gave me a smile that did something magical to my heart. "Are you hungry?"

I tried to clear my head to concentrate on my stomach and realized that I was starving. I wasn't sure when I had eaten last. I nodded, and he took me to get some refreshments. We ordered drinks and nachos dripping with cheese and salsa.

Austen knew my favorite soda without asking. We sat at the counter and talked about everything except the troubles that weighed most heavily on my mind—the doubts about my relationship with Austen and the strange curse taking over my life. The night was almost over when I turned and met the eyes of the dreaded sea captain.

Redd sat across the bar, his normally straight back hunched over the counter. Junie was next to him, and they talked in low voices. She played with her hair, undoing it from her bun and rearranging it on her head in a movement that I recognized as one she did when deep in thought. I looked away. I didn't want to become the next topic of their serious discussion.

As if on cue, my phone vibrated in my pocket. Austen's must have too, because we both checked our phones at once.

ANN-MARIE: I SEE YOU!

I glanced over at Austen. "Did you . . . ?"

An uneasy smile touched his lips, and he scanned the room. "I think we're about to get an Ann-Marie attack."

"Jane! Austen!" She hugged Austen from behind and then ducked under his arm to stand between us. She looked terrible. Her face was all red, her eyes puffy from crying.

I got angry at Dancey when I saw it. "What happened to you?"

Her lip trembled. "I hate men." She flipped her hair defiantly so that it hit Austen. "No offense, Austen."

"Trying not to take it."

My arm went around her. "What happened, Ann-Marie?"

Her lip trembled. "I don't want to talk about it. Not now. Not ever."

"Okay, okay." I nodded and imagined the worst. "We'll take you home."

She shook her head and wriggled free from me. "No. I'm going to have a good time tonight if it kills me." She searched the room, only to brighten visibly. "Hey, there's Harry Crawley!" She waved through the crowd at him. "If anyone can make a girl feel special, he can."

My hand went to her wildly waving one to stop her. Crawley was the last person I wanted to see right now. He was with his friends, scamming the joint for girls. He wore a button-up with nice jeans, his blond hair a premeditated mess around his ears.

"Hey, Ann-Marie," I said. "Why don't you stay here with us?"

Her eyes narrowed at our nachos, then passed over me to Austen. "No thanks."

"Ann-Marie, Crawley's not . . ." I struggled how best to put it, "I don't think he's on the hunt for nice girls like you."

"What? You mean like girls who aren't exciting?" She looked angry.

"Uh, no."

"Ann-Marie," Austen cut in. He looked protective. "The guy's a jerk. Don't talk to him."

Ann-Marie went limp like a noodle. She stared up at Austen with a slightly open mouth. "How sweet, Austen," she practically cooed. "I love it when you're jealous. It makes me realize how much you care." Her hand went to his arm.

He looked exasperated. "Yeah . . . as a *friend*, Ann-Marie; as a friend."

"Friends don't do that," she insisted,

"Yes, they do," I said.

Her big eyes were fastened on Austen. "Friends don't smell like sandalwood cologne, either." She sniffed him as per tradition and batted her eyes up at him in pure enjoyment. "Delicious. I can sniff you all day." Her hands clamped over his arm. "I'm going to put you in my pocket and take you out and inhale you when I need my Austen fix."

"You know what, Ann-Marie?" Austen jerked away. "You're on your own; but if you don't listen to us—"

"Yeah, I get it. You warned me." She gave a hard laugh and headed for Crawley.

I popped a nacho in my mouth, watching her meander her way to certain failure. She then proceeded to attack Crawley from behind with the same hug she had given Austen. "Looks like she's on the rebound," I muttered through a mouthful of chips.

Austen looked worried as we watched Crawley fend her off for a bit. I glanced to the side to see Redd's eyes on me again. They were pointed and full of self-righteous anger. *Seriously, get over it already.* With everything going on, I felt like I was on a speeding train, seconds away from a wreck.

I jumped when Bigley joined Redd at the counter and then Bigley watched me, too. After a few words to Redd, he turned to Junie. She didn't look happy, and her fingers twisted through her napkin. I really hoped that Bigley wasn't saying anything about me. It made me wonder how well Junie knew him. Had she seen this side of Bigley in London when she had been there? Just like a villain entering the stage for the final act of a play, DeBurgy wandered over to the group as well, an easy laugh on his lips. If I had any doubts as to the subject of their conversation, those cleared when Redd broke from the talking to direct another glare my way.

This time Austen was on to him. He leaned over me and caught Redd's angry look with one of his own. Redd flushed and turned. Austen swallowed his mouthful of nachos. "What's Bigley doing with your favorite person?" he asked.

"Junie or Redd?" I lowered my head to sip on my soda.

"What? Now you're angry at Junie? Aren't you worried what Bigley's saying to her?"

237

Yes, actually. Bigley whispered something to Junie, and she relaxed enough to laugh. Her eyes went to me, and they gleamed with satisfaction.

"I don't particularly trust Junie," I told Austen.

"Why?" His voice turned lecturing. "Just because you think she matches some kind of villainous profile in your books?"

Junie slid her hand under Redd's arm, and then her free hand found Bigley's arm, too. If she had a third, it would go to DeBurgy. I swallowed hard, knowing Austen would never believe that she had it out for me.

"What can I say?" I asked. "She plays a great archenemy."

Crawley's hands landed on the counter between Austen and me, his fingers splaying out. His eyes danced devilishly when they met mine. "Help me, Jane. I'm throwing my life in your hands. That girl doesn't take prisoners."

Ann-Marie! It was true, but . . . I felt my own lips tug up in a smile, at the same time that Austen's turned down. Despite everything Bigley had said, I couldn't help liking Crawley—the guy could always make me laugh. "I didn't think you ran away from girls," I said.

"Just one. The other I'm running after."

I wanted him to be talking about Bella. She was sweeter than me, gorgeous, and way more his style.

"We just talked to your brother," Austen said. He still looked irritated about it.

"Yeah." Crawley's smile didn't dim. "He's a jerk."

Wait. Did Crawley know what Bigley had done? Austen and I exchanged glances. "He wanted Jane to keep you busy," Austen said, clearly digging for more information.

Crawley threw his head back in a laugh. "He said he might do something like that. What was your answer, Jane?"

"I . . ." He had tried to blackmail me, and smeared his best friend's reputation to do it. Still, Crawley wasn't taking any of this

238

seriously, so maybe it had all been a joke. "Hey, if you're really that lonely," I said, "we'll hang out with you."

"Hang out?" Crawley remained standing, but his manner was still laid-back. "I doubt Chuck mentioned hanging out . . . and it wasn't a group invitation, was it, Jane?"

He did know. How twisted was that? "Does he always play your matchmaker?" I asked him.

"No; I've never met a girl I couldn't charm, but I'm running out of time here. We only have two more days left."

"But . . . but, who does that?" I sputtered.

Crawley shrugged, laughing a little. "I told you that Chuck's just like me. Only he doesn't get caught. Good thing too, or his mom would cut him off without a penny, as the old-timers say in Britain."

"I didn't realize you were foreshadowing."

The silence that took over Austen had gone dark and moody—especially, I knew, because the talk had gotten so far out of the ordinary. Still, Crawley acted like it was all just a big flirt game. Maybe it was?

"Don't you like Bella?" I asked.

"I'm done with her. She isn't exactly hard to get," he said. My hand itched to slap him on Bella's behalf, but the glitter of sudden anger in his eyes stopped me. "Besides," he said. "I don't appreciate girls being thrown at me as a distraction."

I thought I had been doing them both a favor—I could see now that I was wrong. Crawley broke his gaze with me to watch a blond head moving through the crowd. Such shiny, long locks could only belong to Bella. His lips turned up in a smirk. "Not that she isn't hot. Maybe you prefer that I get my kicks elsewhere?"

Austen lurched in his seat, and my hand found his under the counter to get him to stand down. I could see how it would all play out if he didn't: Austen would flatten Crawley, Bella would go to Crawley's rescue, and Crawley would leave with the girl as promised.

But I had a different scenario in mind; I knew the villain from the
book, and it gave me an idea.

Luckily, Austen responded to the pressure of my fingers, as
confusing as it was. He settled back in his seat, and I popped another
nacho in my mouth, chewing slowly before answering Crawley. "You
know, I could never go for a player." I kept my voice light. "You have
to prove that you're serious about me."

And then I'd throw Bertie at him to show that he never would be.

Crawley looked confused. "We only have two days . . . ?"

"And ours would be a lifetime commitment," I threatened before
tossing another nacho in my mouth. Those words were a death toll on
any relationship suggested by a player.

Austen's eyes went to the ceiling, and he breathed out slowly.

"I wonder what our kids would look like?" I asked. "I've always
wanted eight. I hope you can support them all. What do you do for a
living?" If he were a gentleman, I'd throw a glove at his feet to show
that I was calling him out to a duel.

"I prefer to enjoy the moment," he said through tight lips.

"I can't," I said brightly, "unless I know you're for real. Are you?"

"And how do I prove that?"

"That's your job, Crawley. Figure it out."

Crawley didn't look happy, but then after a moment of tense
waiting, he returned my false smile—the confidence behind it made
my stomach rub nervously against itself. "I think I can manage that,"
he said and left, marching past Bella like she was invisible.

I breathed a sigh of relief. Austen's eyes sought mine. "Do you
want me to finish him off?" he asked.

"Aren't you curious to see what he comes up with?"

Austen didn't look amused. He made a low guttural sound in his
throat to show his irritation and stood to search the dance floor.
"Where did Ann-Marie go?"

Heads bobbed around me, making a wall that obstructed my
view. The force of my gaze did nothing to part them so that we could

find her. Austen's hands found mine, and he steered me back to my barstool. "Stay put," he said, and he let the crowd swallow him so he could hunt for our friend.

I waited for about five minutes. Another five made me wonder if Austen had been kidnapped by Ann-Marie. I checked my cell phone for a text. Nothing. Even if I tried to call Austen, he wouldn't hear it in this noise. My hand went to my aching head. I had to get out of here soon or Bigley might find me again. I hopped off the barstool.

The second I did, I ran into Junie. She grunted in surprise. Whatever she'd been holding toppled to the floor. "Oh, I'm sorry." I landed on my knees and gathered fistfuls of the napkins she had dropped. I noticed one of them had been scribbled on. Before I could see what it said, Junie plucked it from my hands, holding the napkin over her stomach. I knew better than to ask her what it was. It was clearly a secret, as usual.

Junie avoided my eyes. "I'm going home," she said. "I'm tired. I'm tired of all of this!"

I noticed deep circles under her eyes. Her eyes glistened, and I realized she had been crying. "Junie? What's happen—?"

"Don't ask me!"

"Junie?" Austen pulled from the crowd, and she burst into tears and fell into his arms, clinging to him in a long hug that made me uncomfortable. She broke away just as dramatically and rushed away. Austen watched her go, looking helpless.

"What did you do to her?" Austen wasn't asking it. It was Redd. He towered above me, his body tense with indignation.

"You were with her last!" I shouted through the noisy crowd. "What did *you* do to her?"

"Hey," Austen held up his hand. "Knock it off. Both of you!"

Redd's eyes didn't leave mine. "Junie was just fine until she saw you, Jane, and that sobered her up real fast. Then she ran off." Because she had seen me with Austen? I turned to him, but he just stared worriedly after Junie.

241

Redd wasn't through with me. "You don't care about anyone but yourself. That won't make you too many friends."

"What is wrong with you?" I shouted. "What do you have against me?"

"Someone has to stop you from ruining everyone's life."

"Who is *everyone*?" I asked.

Austen's arms wrapped around my waist and he pulled me back from Redd. "Sorry, Captain." Fury laced through his words as he fought yet another battle for my honor. "We don't have time for this. This happens to be *my* night with Jane."

Redd's cold expression froze his jaw into a chiseled and arrogant line. He dipped his head at us in farewell. "I wish you both the best. No doubt you deserve each other."

Austen didn't look back at Redd's offended departure. Instead, he headed for the exit with me in tow. The weird techno music cut out when the door slammed shut behind us. Fresh air hit my face in a blast of wind that rushed through the garden of swaying California poppies. The flowers only reminded me of Taylor.

Redd's accusation burned in my ears: *You don't care about anyone.* If he was talking about Taylor, his words held some truth to them. I should've been a better friend or I'd know what was going on now.

Austen headed for his car in the crowded parking lot. "What happened with you and Redd? If you say that you only broke up with him and ignored his texts, I won't believe you."

The shock of our encounter wouldn't leave me. "I'm cursed. I wanted romance and now I'm getting flooded with it."

"What's really going on?" Austen asked.

"My life is playing like a book, and I don't like it!" Judging by the sound of irritation that escaped his lips, he'd drill me with more questions to get to the root of this. I beat him to it. "Do you and Junie have a thing going? Was she running from you? Is that where you disappeared for ten minutes?"

242

He went silent and pulled the keys from his pocket when we reached his jeep. "She hasn't been acting like herself the last few days."

I leaned against the door, crossing my arms. "Have I?"

"You always act strange, but . . . not more than usual, not like . . . everybody else." He groaned, his keys clanging against his sides along with his hands. "Five guys? Seriously. I never liked Chuck—but I had never been so close to a barroom brawl. And Crawley? No offense, Jane, but I just don't understand why every guy is after you."

"It's not my fault. Try being a girl sometime."

"Who's the fifth guy?" Austen asked. "You've got Dancey, the captain, Crawley; Colin's after you, too, I've seen it myself; but who's the last guy?"

Austen. He was the *only one* who counted. And he had the least interest in going after me. His eyes were on mine as he waited for me to say his name, and I struggled to answer. "Use your imagination," I said.

He sighed and took the other side of me, leaning back against the jeep door. He crossed his arms in imitation of me. "Chuck was flirting with the waitress," he said in a quieter voice. "According to your theory, that shouldn't happen. It's out of character."

"But we never knew Bingley intimately in *Pride and Prejudice!*" I tried to work it out. "We never saw him behind the scenes. We only had Lizzy's perspective the whole time."

"No, no," Austen said. I felt the pressure of his fingers as he gently took my arm and looked me in the eyes to show me that he was serious. "I'm trying to prove that we're not in a book. Don't you get it? Losing the family business to Colin? That's reality. Seeing the groom cheat on your friend two days before her wedding? That *is* life, Jane." It was like a dam had broken inside of Austen's mouth and he was spilling everything that he'd kept back from me. "There's nothing more real than jealousy and disappointment and heartache. Now you see things for what they are. Just accept it: life sucks."

Dark clouds rumbled threateningly in the sky. A few stray drops of rain spat down on us. "You think this is normal?" I asked. "If anything, the whole Bigley thing turns us into a bad soap opera—because, Austen, real life is full of laughter and love and feeling happy."

"And then it's gone."

I was stunned. My ideals got me hurt a lot, but they had also cushioned my falls because I hoped for the best. Austen's logic would never help him the same way. No wonder he didn't take risks. "Is that why you won't fight for North Abbey?" I asked. "I just thought you didn't want it, but . . . are you afraid of losing?"

His lips curved up like he thought that was ridiculous. "Afraid? No, I'm not afraid."

"So you just don't care? Do you care about anything? What about me?"

He actually looked hurt. "I may not be as passionate as you are, Jane, but that doesn't mean I can't feel."

"Show me." It came out before I thought too much about it, and then I wriggled uncomfortably. I might as well have dared him to kiss me. I felt like I was in fiction again, and I held up my hand. "No, no, don't, I don't want to add to the drama going on right now."

"Good," he said, "because I'm not going to kiss you just because you challenged me."

"No, that's something that I would do." *I would . . . if I had no pride.* Plus, I didn't want to scare Austen away. He meant so much to me now—like he was part of my family, a part of me. My pride didn't matter. "Oh, forget it," I said and turned to him to slide my hands through his curly hair. Austen froze as I stood on tiptoe to plant my lips over his.

Austen responded almost immediately. He pulled me closer and made me forget all my wild fantasies about the perfect kiss, because this felt real. The rain beat harder on us as his breath became mine.

His intentions mine. His loudly beating heart was mine, too. I fell back from the kiss, trying to catch my breath.

"That's what it feels like to be crazy," I managed to get out.

"That's nothing." His hands cradled my throat; the water from the rain made his fingers slip down to my shoulders. "You want to know what it feels like to be practical?" He gently touched his lips to mine, giving me a kiss that felt like he was breathing me in.

I stepped back again, my heart ready to explode. "How was that practical?"

"Because it came from me."

Yes, practical. All of my confused thoughts from the day centered and made me realize how wrong all my Jane Austen talk was. I had something better than a fantasy written in the pages of a book. I didn't want to believe that this spark between Austen and me had happened because of some curse. It couldn't be . . . because I'd do anything to make it real.

The rain pouring over Austen's face glistened under the street lanterns. He regarded me for a long moment before holding me close and kissing me again.

Chapter 20

"But he told you that he loved you?"

"Yes . . . no . . . never absolutely. It was every day implied, but never professedly declared. Sometimes I thought it had been-but it never was."

—Jane Austen, Sense and Sensibility

I practically skipped down the hallway on the way to my room, my heart singing. Kissing Austen felt so right. We belonged together. He was the Yin to my Yang. He was logical. I was emotional. Together we made *Sense and Sensibility*. The superstition that I was caught in a Jane Austen novel was far behind me now. I had something real to hold on to. My smile felt too big for my face.

I passed Taylor's room and heard crying. I stopped, my heart settling back to its normal place. Poor Taylor. While I was on cloud nine, she was feeling all alone. Now that I knew about Bigley, I realized why. This time I would be a better friend. I took a deep breath and knocked on her door.

"Just a minute."

I knew Taylor was trying to put her face back together, but I didn't want her to hide her feelings from me, so I just pushed open the door. Elly sat on the bed next to Taylor, rubbing her cousin's back. "Hi Taylor," I said. "Uh, how is everything going?"

Taylor motioned me inside, and I closed the door. The moment I did, she gave a long, shuddering sigh. "My parents are in the middle of a cold war, Jane. My dad said that he can't take being stuffed into a tiny room with my mom and he's going to the Randall Bungalow."

I panicked. "But it's in the middle of renovation."

"My dad doesn't care. He just packed up his bags and left to go camp out in the middle of all that plaster and wet paint."

"But . . . but . . . but . . ."

"You don't want to get in the middle of that war, Jane. It's cold. You should see my parents fight—they're nothing like Chuck's parents. They don't need words—just looks and sighs. It freezes the room. If I could've given them separate places to sleep without being too obvious, I would've. They can't spend longer than two days together without my dad running off on business." Taylor groaned and turned to her cousin, who watched her with a look of sweet concern. "Why am I surrounded by dysfunctional relationships, Elly? I just want a good marriage like yours."

The cute little redhead wrapped her arms around Taylor in a tight hug. "You can. You will."

My heart started to race when I realized what they were saying. This was my cue to tell Taylor about her jerk of a fiancé, but I took one look at the tears streaming down her cheeks and lost my nerve.

"Chuck means everything to me," Taylor said. "If I lost him, I wouldn't have anything."

I forced my hand up. "I have something to say . . ."

Elly's expectant eyes were on me, as were Taylor's red ones. I opened my mouth to let it all out: *Bigley is a mean drunk: he tried to pay me to go out with his brother, he flirts with waitresses, he thinks his best friend is a louse and still asked him to be his best man.*

It would break Taylor's heart, but we were running out of time. Taylor looked so vulnerable, so sad. It made me wonder if she already knew about Bigley. "I know it hurts you a lot that your parents are fighting," I said, "but is there anything else bothering you?"

The tears came anew and she scrunched up her pillow. "I'm trying to put my heart back together, Jane; trying to look at everything

247

logically so I can move on. I look at my parents' wedding pictures and I see . . . they were so in love. They had one of those fairytale weddings, you know. But . . . but fairytales aren't real. I know that now."

She did know about Bigley.

Taylor reached for my hand and squeezed it. "I don't want you to make the same mistakes that I have."

"I won't," I said, "but Taylor, you're not married yet. It's not too late."

She looked confused. "What are you saying? Chuck has his faults, he does; but I wouldn't throw it all away on a dream. Love isn't a magic wand that fixes everything."

No, it wasn't. As she talked, I couldn't help but think about Austen. It made things exciting that we were so opposite, but it could also work against us. Still, our differences weren't as serious as Taylor's problems with Bigley.

"Even if love isn't a fairytale," I said, "you can still expect certain things—"

"No." Taylor sat up. "No man will change for you. It isn't fair for either of you to expect that. You have to see him for how he truly is."

Everything that Austen had ever told me came spilling back into my mind. Austen said that best friends didn't fall for each other. And kissing, hugging, handholding, romance in general? It didn't mean as much to him as it did to me. Did that mean I was settling like Taylor was?

"My mom knew exactly what my dad was before they got together," Taylor said. "When they traveled all over Europe and made all those big plans to change the world, she knew that he really lived for business. He always put it before her. There were warning signs, Jane."

I was all about signs—if a guy couldn't stop looking at me or was too nervous to talk to me, he liked me. Usually the signs worked for me, not against me. As much as I wanted to enjoy the memory of my first kiss with Austen, I examined it through his eyes of logic. I had kissed Austen first. Sure, he'd responded, but what did that mean to him, anyway? He was still planning on selling North Abbey and getting out of here.

"Do you really want to live your life in denial?" Taylor asked.

I glanced over at her, confused. Even if her words fit my situation, we were talking about her situation with Bigley, not mine. "Taylor." I eased down on the bed to sit down beside her. I couldn't let her turn this on me again. "We've got to talk about this."

She gave me a look of longsuffering. "This is about Dancey, right?"

That caught me off-guard. "No, not Dancey . . ." I remembered something significant. "He's a part of this, isn't he? Bigley said that Dancey liked you. Wait, did you two have a thing?"

"A thing?" She gave me a stern look. "Dancey plays people, Jane. Sure, he's a really great guy, but he's always going to be Dancey, you know?"

"And you don't like that?"

"You can't go for him," she shouted. She clapped her hands to her mouth as if she had shocked herself. She lowered her voice, "I mean you shouldn't go for him. He might like you now, but oh, just seeing that he's doing the same thing to you that he does to every other girl makes me so mad! He won't change for you."

"What? Wait, I wasn't talking about Dancey before. Were you?"

"Yes!" She looked furious. Elly's lips twisted in worry. Our previous conversation flashed through my mind and it made a lot more sense. Taylor had thought that she was warning me against Dancey the whole time. She didn't know about Bigley.

I took a steadying breath. "Taylor, this is about your fiancé, not Dancey. He was drinking tonight." Seeing her confused look, I hurried through my words. "I mean, he drinks a lot! Did you know that?"

She started to laugh . . . hysterically. "Oh no you don't, Jane, don't turn this on me."

I made another desperate attempt. "He's not very nice when he drinks."

"Chuck? Oh, I can't believe that I'm hearing this." Taylor's eyes met the ceiling. "Patient, good, kind Chuck? Did Dancey put you up to this?"

"No. What? No! I can have my own opinions. Tonight, Bigley tried to pay me to go out with his brother."

Taylor exchanged glances with her cousin, and Elly cracked a smile. "Well," Taylor said. Her lips turned up, too, and she swiped three tissues from the boxes and dabbed them all over her face in an attempt to clear off all the moisture. She was no longer crying. "I'm sorry, Jane. I might have put Chuck up to that. I told him that I was worried about you and Dancey. I'm sorry."

"What?" Now I was angry. I couldn't believe that Taylor would mess with me like that.

"Crawley's nice and cute," Taylor said. "Why wouldn't you be interested in him?"

"Oh, I don't know!" I practically shouted. "He said some really creepy things about Bella. He said she was too easy."

"So, he's observant."

"Bella is your friend!"

"Yeah, but Dancey is Chuck's best friend and it doesn't mean he trusts him. We know our friends, Jane. I would never wish Bella or Bertie—or Mary, for that matter—on Chuck's brother."

"But you would wish him on me?" I asked.

"Yes; I like both of you very much."

That was very sweet but completely unnecessary. "Well, even if you thought this was the perfect set-up, I'm taken. Austen and I were in the middle of a date."

"Austen?" Taylor sighed and brought her fingers to pinch the bridge of her nose like she had a headache. "Jane. You have a talent for going for the wrong guy every time. Austen isn't interested in you. We all know that. Have you seen him with Junie? Do yourself a favor and actually go for someone who likes you."

I couldn't believe that I was hearing this. I stood, feeling my emotions curl into pain. "That was harsh, Taylor."

"As harsh as telling me that Chuck is up to no good two days before my wedding? What did you expect would happen if I listened to you?"

My mouth flopped open. I wanted her to know the truth. Bigley had also been flirting with the waitresses, too, but it seemed trite to bring it up now, as though I wanted revenge. Taylor had officially shot the messenger.

Taylor put her hands on my arms. "What you saw tonight was Chuck trying to make me happy. He probably warned you off of Dancey too?"

"Yes," I mumbled. "He wasn't very nice about it."

"That was also my doing. I'm sorry, Jane." She hugged me and I took it, feeling stiff. "I'm the one who isn't the nice one," she said. "It's not Chuck's fault. I told him to scare you away from his best friend and I didn't care how he did it. I was worried about you. We only did it because we care. Can't you see that I care?"

"Yes, but Dancey and I . . . we don't have anything going on right now. Austen and I . . ."

Taylor sighed and deserted me for her dresser. Her restless hands went to an assortment of flowers in a vase—they were leftover from the bridal shower. "Can't you give anyone else a chance?" she asked. "You did this to Redd, too. You're letting your crush on Austen stop you from getting into a real relationship."

"Hey, what we have is real." I wasn't planning on sharing the intimate details of my romance because I wanted to keep it to myself and savor it for a while, but I was in a crunch. "Austen and I kissed tonight."

251

Taylor's sharp gaze pinned me. "Did he say he was going to stay here with you then?"

"Oh c'mon, like he's going to change all of his plans because of one kiss?"

"You said it." She took my hands in hers again and rubbed them. "Jane, it was only a kiss. Of course, Austen would want to kiss you—it's you. You're amazing. But that doesn't mean he's changed or anything has changed between you." She turned to her cousin for support. "Tell her, Elly. Tell her to go for the man who might actually take this somewhere."

"Elly married the man she loved," I interrupted before Taylor's cousin could say anything. "Of course Elly would want me to go for that too. She found true love."

"And I haven't?" Taylor asked in chilly tones. "Elly? Tell her."

Elly looked uneasy. "I think, Jane, that the more sensible you are when you follow your heart, the better off you will be. But, I also think that the choice is yours. No one should make it for you, because you're the one who has to live with it."

I didn't want to think about tomorrow, but what if I got so caught up in today that I threw my tomorrow away? The fact that I didn't want to make a choice wasn't good. I groaned. If Taylor couldn't see Bigley for what he was and I couldn't see that Austen wasn't taking this anywhere, did that just mean that love made us stupid? I wanted to enjoy the moment that I had with Austen, but it was hard now that the moment was breaking apart. I was mad, mad that Taylor had a point. Austen had a point too. So did Bigley and Redd and Elly. They all had a point.

Don't go for Dancey. Don't go for Austen. Go against your heart.

I pulled away, fighting to remember why I had come. I still had to help Taylor see the truth, even if I had a hard time facing it myself. "If you knew that Bigley was a jerk, would you still marry him, Taylor?"

"No."

At least that.

But maybe Bigley wasn't a jerk. Taylor lifted a brow at me as if making a point. She was the strong one who sent her fiancé on impossible tasks and he did them. And I was the one holding on to a dying relationship because I was desperate to make it real. I couldn't argue that I knew more about love than Taylor did. She was the one getting married, not me.

The only thing that I knew was that Crawley was a jerk. Okay, maybe I wasn't so sure of that now that I was armed with important backstory. I'd have to peel back the layers of confusion to see the truth, and I wasn't there yet.

I wished that I had the ideals of Jane Austen to fall back on. Everything was so clear when I could open a book and read it all in black and white. Then I could know who was good and who was bad; but Austen had taken that away from me. Now that I had to look at everything logically, including Austen, it was ruining my relationship with him.

Chapter 21

"Know your own happiness. You want nothing but patience; or give it a more fascinating name: call it hope."

—Jane Austen, Sense and Sensibility

DANCEY: WE NEED TO TALK.

My heart sank when I saw the text from Dancey that morning. I sat heavily on my bed and tried to decide what to do. I had managed to avoid him yesterday when he'd gone to L.A. on business, and then Austen had wiped him from my mind when he'd kissed me. *Yeah, Dancey and I needed to talk.* I had to find out if what Bigley had said was true—for a lot of reasons.

Taylor was getting married tomorrow morning, and if Bigley was a big fat liar, then I'd have to figure out how to talk her out of it, not help her go through with it. Add to that the stress of the bachelor and bachelorette parties tonight; Taylor's besties were getting harder to handle.

I wandered around my room to get ready for the day and picked up a brush and ran it through my hair, trying to figure out what I was going to do. I had played the field. I hadn't meant to, it had just happened. And now there were a lot of hearts on the limb here—including mine—but the one I kept going back to was Austen's.

But it wasn't sensible going for him—according to everything Austen said about relationships, we didn't stand a chance. The romantic side of me thought there was no problem in dropping everything to go after him, but the sensible side that was growing stronger told me that was a very bad idea. It hadn't worked last time and had ruined our friendship.

My phone vibrated again, and looking down, I saw that Dancey was making another attempt to contact me.

DANCEY: YOU REMEMBER JENNINGS, THE REPORTER? SHE AGREED TO YOUR DEAL. SHE WON'T PUBLISH OUR PICS IF SHE GETS EXCLUSIVE COVERAGE OF TAYLOR'S WEDDING. TAYLOR GAVE US THE GO AHEAD. IT'S ON.

I felt limp with relief. Photographs of me locking lips with Dancey wouldn't be plastered all over the web. Taylor had fixed everything for me. I didn't deserve it, but she had. My stomach clenched at the close call. And then I had another thought: why would Jennings agree to my deal? She didn't seem the type to do charity work. Dancey and I did have to talk. I picked up my phone and texted.

ME: I'M FREE FOR LUNCH. WE CAN TALK THEN.

A flood of adrenaline rushed through me after I sent it. I would be seeing Dancey again. The hours we had spent together had been exciting, but compared to what I felt for Austen—it felt hollow now . . . like a fling. I didn't know that a romantic like me could do flings.

Throwing on my favorite hoodie and slipping on some flip-flops, I left my room and ran down the stairs, taking them two at a time to the lobby downstairs. Shoving open the door, I spied Austen just like I had hoped. But instead of working away at his laptop, he had flopped down on the couch with the remote, watching *Pride and Prejudice*—the short version. I stepped quietly into the room just as Darcy asked Elizabeth to marry him for the second time. This time she accepted him. Darcy had won her love by his good deeds, all their miscommunications had been cleared up, and everything was forgiven; especially after Elizabeth had taken a tour of the big house she'd get if she married him.

Austen, meanwhile, was tying ribbons for party favors. Taylor must have enlisted his help yet again. He was better at the creative side of things than I was. My gaze drifted to his hands. They were rough, but gentle, etched with a few scars that marked everything he was— and they had been in my hair last night.

I cleared my throat. "Austen."

He jumped guiltily and fumbled with the remote to pause it. I hid a smile. His was sheepish. "Well, I think that's enough Jane Austen for one morning," he said.

"Did you watch the whole movie or did you fast-forward through it?"

"This is the fifth Jane Austen movie I've watched in a row." At my startled expression, he shrugged. "I didn't sleep last night."

"Why did you do that?"

"I wanted to know how crazy you were." He smiled and stood up. His thick hair was a mess. His eyes were red from lack of sleep, but they were focused on me. "Besides a little daydreaming from the *Northanger Abbey* girl," he said, "and some matchmaking from *Emma*, I can't find a character for you. Sorry."

I sat at the counter across the room. "I have the same problem with you."

"I'm not dashing enough?"

"You're . . ." I struggled for words, "you."

"Hmm." He closed the distance between us and found my hand, looking mischievous. "And there's more bad news. No matter how I swing it, I can't find any trace of wickedness in Bingley when I watch *Pride and Prejudice*. Unless it's just an act, our Bigley is way off."

I searched his face for a hint of irony and caught it in the twinkle in his eye. "Well, the guy in the movie was just the actor," I said. "Maybe he couldn't quite get Charles Bingley right."

Or our Bigley's only sin was that he was weak. Taylor said she had talked Bigley into doing what he'd done last night. I wasn't sure if I bought it.

Austen's eyes were on mine, and I was having a hard time thinking about anything else. "But it's weird," he said, "because

256

everyone else is spot on—even down to the red regimental coat that Freddy wears as a bellhop. Mr. Collins is a sniveling weasel, Maria Bertram-Rushworth is a snob, Crawford's a player."

"Yes, but a likeable villain," I said.

"Disagree," Austen said.

"The one we know said some really nice things when we were running on the beach together."

"And he helped your brother move up in the army so he could win your love. Yeah, I saw it in the movie—Crawley's only working you. Also, I think I've watched enough *Pride and Prejudice* to know I shouldn't let you go off with Dancey again."

His thumb rubbed over my fingers. My eyes went to his—they smoldered. The way he watched me was the way I had always dreamed that he would. I was beginning to think that Taylor was wrong. This could work. "So," my voice came out throatier than usual, "what's the verdict, Austen? Am I crazy?"

"It's a fictional delusional disorder. I've seen it before."

"What's the cure?"

He kept a straight face. "I have a whole team of specialists working on it as we speak, but the only treatment we know of is highly dangerous."

"I'm willing to risk it if it means living a life free of my paranoia."

Austen leaned heavily across the counter, closer to me now, and I knew he meant to kiss me again. "If it doesn't work, the treatment might make it worse," he warned.

I couldn't keep down the smile. "What did you have in mind?"

"You should spend time with someone who doesn't bring on the fictional delusions; some quality time. Maybe lunch?"

That was taken by Dancey. "Well . . ." I reddened when I realized the mess that I had gotten myself into. Those photos of the two of us were still floating around somewhere if I didn't take care of them. What would Austen say if he saw them?

"I can't do lunch today." Not tomorrow either—that was the wedding . . . if it still happened. And if it didn't happen? The photographs were going up. With horror, I realized that I was in a moral dilemma. "I can't do lunch the rest of the week actually," I told Austen. "I'm going to have to take a rain check on the treatments."

He straightened, his hands still on mine. Now I felt like a criminal; with his eyes searching mine like that, I was sure he meant to gauge my feelings towards him. I needed his help in our intervention with Taylor, but if we succeeded . . . I might lose him. I tried to figure out a way to come clean. "Austen?" I rallied my nerves. "Things are about to get crazier around here, I think."

The phone chose that moment to ring. I tried not to take it as a sign as I broke away from him to answer it. Ann-Marie's breathless voice was on the other end. "I can't do it!" she wailed.

"What can't you do?" I asked.

"I feel deathly ill . . . like my heart doesn't want to go on."

"You've got a broken heart?" I ventured.

"Yes, yes! I can't get out of bed. I feel all feverish and weak . . . ever since I talked to *him*."

"Who?"

"Don't make me say it. My throat closes up whenever I try to say it. I have it bad, Jane."

"Ann-Marie!" I wanted to have sympathy for her, I did, but this was not the time for dramatics. I could barely wing everything with her here. "I need you! Quit acting like you're dying of the bubonic plague and come to work. You can tell me what's happening when you get here!" I hung up the phone when she started talking about her fluttering heart.

"*Sense and Sensibility*," Austen muttered. "Right? When Marianne gets a broken heart and almost dies after being out in the rain."

"Uh, yeah." I turned back to him, gathering my wits. I was just about to admit my wrongdoings again when Bertie rushed into the room. One of her arms cradled her puppy; her other arm swung like a pendulum beside her. She shoved the cute mat of fur into my hands. "Where's Harry?" she demanded.

"Not here."

She came nose to nose with me. "He doesn't care about you, you know."

That had come out of nowhere. "Are we still talking about Crawley?" I asked in some confusion.

"Of course we are!" she cried. "Don't get into your mind that you have some sort of future with him—he's just doing what he does to everyone, playing the field, and he's playing you!"

"Is that what he did to you, Bertie?" Austen asked casually. I shot him a look of respect. *Very perceptive.* Austen leaned against the counter, looking tired from his all-nighter.

Bertie glared at him. "Who is this? Wait." She raised a hand in a dismissive gesture. "No, I am tired of dealing with Taylor's employees. Harry and I were very happy before you came along, little girl. Don't get any grandiose ideas. He's only amusing himself with the staff."

I couldn't believe I was hearing this. I felt the dog's tiny tongue lick my chin in a reminder that I was doing her mistress a favor. "Are you kidding me?" I ground out through clenched teeth, "Do you really want to leave me alone with your dog after accusing me like that? I don't want your stupid boyfriend or your adulterous life. Now take back your cute little puppy!"

Bertie huffed and marched out of the lobby just as quickly as she had come, still leaving the poor, nameless pooch behind. I stared after her. "For some reason, everyone is acting according to script. If things go the way the books do, Bertie is going to run off with Crawley. Bella will get into trouble with Freddy. And Colin will try to get me alone in the drawing room for some kind of proposal."

Austen gave a grim laugh. "I'd like to be a fly on the wall for that one."

"Of course that won't happen." I paced the room, not able to cast off my growing superstition. "Even so, we'll play it safe. If we can stop everyone before they do what they are supposed to do, then that's how we'll survive the next few days."

Austen watched me like I was going crazy again. I tried to ignore that as the room came alive with guests. Mary coughed and sputtered and choked into a tissue, and Colin came in through the front door, looking smarmy—every hair carefully misplaced in his bouffant style, the front of it slicked back against his forehead.

Mary came within range first. Her hands landed on the counter, and she took a deep, gasping breath before she managed enough air to speak. "My stomach is trying to claw its way through my skin," she announced. "It's ripping my intestines apart until I give birth to a monster."

That was very descriptive. "How would you like me to help?" I asked.

She sighed. "I can only pray that I make it to Taylor's bachelorette party tonight."

So far Mary hadn't allowed her ailments to stop her from any of the parties, but I made soothing sounds anyway and promised faithfully to be concerned about it. Mary took that as validation of her unhealthy state, and her voice grew weaker. "If I don't make it, tell Taylor that I value her friendship and everything that she has done for me."

"Are those your last words?" I asked, feeling like maybe I should fetch Reverend Eddy to deliver her last rites.

She hung her head and lowered her shoulders in exhaustion. "We shall see." She limped away as if she had contracted a broken leg from her visit in the lobby. Austen nudged me. "What character is she again?"

"*Persuasion*," I said under my breath. "The sickly sister."

Austen watched her leave for the breakfast room. "That's the only one that I didn't see last night, but now I feel like I have."

"Jane." Colin tried to claim my attention next. His voice gave me a prickling sensation, and I turned, taking in the glory of his matted hair. "If you want to take a more active role in the future of North Abbey," he said, "we have more business to discuss . . . in the drawing room."

It was just as I'd predicted.

Austen interrupted the moment. "We don't have a drawing room."

"The room off to the side with the piano, then. It has a picturesque window."

"Before you do that," Austen said, "I think there's a matter that only you can clear up, Colin. A woman in the breakfast room is in desperate need of your help."

Colin tilted his head. "The one who was just in here?"

"Yes, that beautiful damsel in distress. As up-and-coming owner of North Abbey, you are the only one she will trust with her needs. She said so herself."

Colin seemed taken aback, but then he dipped his head with a smug smile. I could barely believe my luck, but Colin was taking the bait. "We'll talk later," he promised with an indulgent nod at me, then left to take care of Mary. I didn't know whom I felt sorrier for.

I gave Austen a grateful smile. "Austen, you are my hero." I gave him a hug before the moment could be stolen from me again.

"I have to tell you something." We both said it at the same time and laughed—I noticed his was just as nervous as mine, which made me more nervous.

"Go ahead," I said.

"It's just that . . ." his hands caught mine like before, and my knees went weak all over again. "When we talked about being cursed earlier, you acted like I thought being in a relationship would be a bad thing, but this feels great . . ."

"Oh." The word came out with my breath. Austen was declaring his feelings for me. My worries over my predicament with Dancey took a smaller role as I tried to enjoy the moment for what it was.

"If you could forget those five suitors while I'm here," he said, "and just concentrate on me, I want to make everything up to you. I won't make fun of how you see things just because I think differently. To be honest, Jane, I'd like to give you everything you want."

"Oh." I struggled to find something more meaningful to say, but everything got lost in my feelings. I just wanted to stay here with Austen forever.

"There you are!" Taylor rushed into the room, and we stepped back from each other, seeing Taylor's beseeching eyes. "I hoped you'd be down here. Did you talk to Dancey, Jane?"

I stared at her. I thought she didn't want me involved with Dancey. "Uh, no, not yet," I said. "Why? Did he say something?"

"Yes!" she shrieked out happily. "He agreed to sing at our bachelorette party. I'm annoyed that you ignored my advice . . . but I'm still glad that you can get him to do anything you want."

"Can she?" Austen asked. His eyes probed mine.

Taylor's interested gaze went to him, and I knew that she was looking for any signs that he was taking this relationship more seriously than before. "Yes, he's a really good guy. Dancey has charities. He worked closely with the victims of that last hurricane. He's great like that, but he can be stubborn, and Jane has a way with him. I think he really likes her." Her eyes had a hard glint, and I knew the speech was entirely for Austen's benefit. "So thank you, Jane." She hugged me. "I thought he wouldn't do it."

I met Austen's eyes over her shoulder and pulled back.

"Austen." Taylor turned to him. "Has Dancey talked with you about the bachelor party yet?"

"It looks like he's been busy with other things."

"Well, Dancey can't be in two places at once, Austen, so that means that you'll have to head up the party on your own tonight."

Austen looked annoyed. "What a surprise."

Taylor cringed under his sarcasm. "Oh, Austen, I'm sorry for everything that's happened around here, and I'm sorry that I've been acting so Bridezilla lately. It's just pre-wedding jitters. Will you forgive me?"

Austen didn't answer immediately, and I hurried to cover up the silence. "Of course," I said, "it's just that—"

"Your groom isn't acting like a groom," Austen finished brutally for me. He crossed his arms. "How well do you know him, Taylor? Tell us why you've been so unhappy. Does it have to do with your fiancé?"

Tears glittered in her eyes. "No, none of that is Chuck's fault. Didn't Jane tell you? I put him up to what he did last night."

I wanted to run away at the repeat confrontation, but I knew Austen was better at handling this than I was. His arm went around her and he patted her back. "Then tell us what's wrong." Taylor's mouth worked, but nothing came out. Austen changed tactics. "We're asking as your friends because we care about you. We trust your judgment, and if you tell us to leave you alone, then we will, but last night Chuck wasn't acting like the guy we thought he was."

"Jane told me that he had been drinking. We already talked about this." Her eyes searched mine out. "Jane, tell him."

"We did talk," I admitted begrudgingly.

"You see?" Taylor nodded. "And no, Chuck isn't perfect. He's really good at putting on a pleasant face around strangers, but he has problems. The drinking, certainly. You've seen his mom. So controlling. And sometimes he really drives me crazy. I drive him crazy, too—I can be bossy and demanding, but—but we have an understanding . . ." Her eyes shot to us like she was afraid we'd judge her for what she was about to say, "We're happy together and we'll work it out eventually. But thank you." Taylor's hands found both mine and Austen's. "I appreciate good friends like you . . . and now I'm respectfully telling you to go take a running leap off a building, okay?"

I laughed uneasily. Austen nodded, but I could tell that he wasn't happy. Taylor smiled at him. "Did you finish those party favors?"

I picked up one of the glittery masterpieces to show Taylor in an attempt to ease the tension. "Here they are!"

"Thank you!" Taylor kissed me on the cheek and then gave Austen the same treatment. "I don't deserve the two of you. You're wonderful!"

I felt unsettled. Taylor seemed too calm—as if she was getting ready to play martyr. "If you need us, Taylor," I said, "we're both here for you. We'll do anything for you."

She cracked a smile. "Anything?"

I remembered Crawley. "Within reason."

"Oh good." She patted my cheek. "There's my Jane. I was starting to get worried." Her phone buzzed, and she slid it out of her purse to check it before putting the phone up to her ear. "Hello Elly, is your husband at the church?" She waved distractedly at us, and we listened to her iron out more wedding details on her way out the door.

"I guess she knows already," I said.

"And this is how chick flicks ruin lives," Austen said, shaking his head. "What is sensible about waiting until after a wedding to iron out differences? The guy *won't* change for you."

My mind went immediately to my relationship with Austen. I wanted him to make more commitments—not so that I could fulfill some strange, romantic fantasy, but so I could be sure that I wasn't resting my hopes on nothing. Was it unwise to bank a future on Austen if he didn't do that?

The clock against the wall ticked out its unmerciful passing of time. The morning was going by too fast, and I needed to get some errands done before I met Dancey for lunch. "If Taylor changes her mind, she knows we'll help her out," I said. Austen wasn't pleased by the verdict, but there wasn't much either of us could do. "I'm off to pick up the food for our bachelorette party." I brushed past him.

"Hey." He found my hand and forced a smile just for me. "You forgot something."

"What?"

"Me." He pulled me back to him and then surprised me by kissing me. His arms held me tightly and his lips found mine. I clung to him, not wanting to let him go. If this was the passion Austen was hiding, it was worth the wait. I felt his lips turn into a smile, and he pulled back. "Have you figured out your favorite flower yet?"

"Just the one you gave me."

"Cornflowers," he murmured. "Beautiful like you. Of course, you know I won't be happy until you come up with your own, right?"

"There are too many to choose from." I shrugged, realizing Austen knew everything I did about myself, and grinned. "You like my favorite soda. That's a good start."

He moved my hair from my eyes. "I want to talk to you again today. Are you sure you can't slip away for lunch?"

I couldn't take the guilt anymore. My breath wouldn't come out right. "I can't do lunch because I have to talk to Dancey." There, it was out.

If Austen was disturbed by the revelation, he didn't show it. "You'd better not talk to him like I talk to you." He said it lightly.

That forced an awkward laugh out of me. He didn't know how right he was. I wondered if the reporter had destroyed those photos yet. I'd make that one of my first demands. "You see, Bigley wasn't too far off," I started to explain, "uh . . . about me and Dancey. We . . ."

Austen put a finger to my lips. "You don't have to confess anything to me. All I care about is what you do now."

That made me feel tons better, except I wasn't sure what I was supposed to do now. What did I have going with Austen anyway? "Yes," I said, "but best friends don't fall for each other. You said it yourself. Men aren't secretly in love with you, they don't just fall for you when you haven't flirted with them, and there are no love-hate relationships."

I could have gone on, but Austen had gone stiff. "If you don't mind," he said, "if that's my voice in your head telling you that we won't work, I prefer you exorcise it out."

"Then you were wrong?"

He took a deep breath and changed the subject. "So what are your plans with Dancey?"

"The usual. I'm just getting rid of any baggage we might have, and I'm clearing up tragic miscommunications, like you suggested."

"You need to stop listening to me. I'm the naysayer and you're the romantic. Let's keep it that way. Besides, didn't you say that we need to throw everybody off their script? This lunch is starting to sound way too close to that scene when Darcy proposes for the second time."

The proposal scene had been the last thing that Austen had watched when I had interrupted his Jane Austen fest this morning. Now that he mentioned it, Taylor had just cleared up a lot of things about Dancey. What if Dancey did the same when we talked? Was I falling into a second proposal trap? The way things kept happening around here, I couldn't guess what I would feel from one second to the next. Only one thing gave me comfort—Austen's logic. "You said that all of that was in my head," I said.

"And now I'm saying to take my voice out of your head and listen to your own."

"Does that count for what you just said now," I attempted to joke, "or . . . ?"

"Jane! Just promise me that whatever decision you make will be based on how you feel and not how you *think* you should feel."

He didn't know what he was asking. It could completely turn on us in the end.

I held his hand hoping it wasn't for the last time. "Thank you for your trust in me." Because I didn't trust myself.

Chapter 22

"He had suffered, and he had learnt to think, two advantages that he had never known before..."

—Jane Austen, Mansfield Park

I sat down at the table in Churchell's Shack, waiting for Dancey to arrive. The ocean crashed against the beach, mingling with the voices from the lunch crowd. As far as meeting times, this was as safe as I was going to get. I refused to fall for a classic Dancey seduction.

Dancey pushed open the saloon-style doors and came in swaggering, looking exactly like the rock star he was. He would've fooled me into thinking that he didn't have a care in the world, but when he reached my table and took off his shades, the imploring look in his eyes went straight to my heart.

"Jane." He sat down on the opposite bench from me. "Can you please forgive me for how I behaved?"

It wasn't quite what I had expected, but I was grateful for the apology. I nodded. "I have to apologize too. I went into survival mode. Bargaining with Taylor's wedding was probably a bad idea."

He shrugged. "We'll do it. Nothing newsworthy is going to happen there anyway. Jennings contacted me. She sent me the photos." His contrite gaze wavered on me, and he broke into a grin. "They were pretty good."

I blushed, not understanding his change of heart—I suspected it had to do with Taylor. "What did Taylor say to you?" He affected a look of unconcern, but I knew he cared more than he let on. "None of this makes a lot of sense. I mean," I spread my hands out, "I still can't figure out why the reporter went for it."

He took a deep breath, and I realized that he knew why. Dancey looked to the side. His publicity manager, DeBurgy, had taken up residence in the corner next to a potted palm. The man took advantage of the fresh air by lighting up a cigarette. Dancey reached a hesitant hand out to touch mine. "There are too many people here to talk. Can we go someplace a little more private?"

As long as I could withstand his charms—I studied his face: the classic profile, his sapphire-blue eyes, the lips that I was far too familiar with. I had to at least hear what he had to say.

"Jane, is he bothering you?"

I swiveled and found Colin—a perturbed expression on his face. His gaze ran over Dancey and he jumped back, startled. "Oh, I didn't know it was you." His mouth turned up into a goofy grin, and he bobbed his head, not meeting Dancey's eyes. "At last, I meet the famous singer. I've heard your songs on the radio. They're all right. In fact, I have been known to sing a song or two. My mother told me that I should've gone on to be a singer myself."

He sang a few warbled phrases to prove it. It felt like a bad serenade. It definitely caught DeBurgy's attention from across the shack. The man dangled his lit cigarette while he stared at us. Ash dripped to the ground. It gave me an idea.

"You know, Colin," I said. "DeBurgy is the man who made Dancey who he is now."

Dancey cocked his head at me, his eyes widening in confusion. "Yup," I said. "I bet you could just go up to DeBurgy and see if he's interested in signing you as his next star."

Colin held his heart. "I couldn't do that. Wouldn't I need an introduction?"

Dancey bit down a smile and managed a "No."

Colin left us immediately.

"Genius, Jane. Let's go." Dancey took a proprietary grip on my hand and, with his eyes on Colin while the man accosted his publicity manager, he led me carefully to the door. I met Junie's disapproving eyes as we passed the counter. Great. I hadn't planned for any witnesses, but as long as we had one . . . I ordered two sandwiches from her. I wasn't facing this on an empty stomach.

Dancey came behind me and threw some cash down, mumbling something to Junie about keeping the change. We took our bounty outside in its neatly wrapped paper. A last glance behind me found Colin still pestering a harassed-looking DeBurgy.

The warm sand slid through my flip-flops. The palm trees swayed in a breeze that wrapped my white skirt around my legs. We walked until the crowds started to thin and the water became unfit for surfing and swimming, with too many rocks to disturb the waves.

Still, it wasn't far enough for Dancey. He kept on doggedly until we reached an alcove shielded with boulders and washed-up debris. Dancey kicked off his shoes and collapsed onto the sand next to a patch of weeds choked with wild California poppies and blue cornflowers. Dancey patted the sand next to him, indicating that I sit down beside him. I hesitated a millisecond before joining him, but I kept my flip-flops on.

"I never meant to hurt you, Jane."

I tensed. This sounded like a break-up speech, and even though I had half expected this meeting to end that way, serious talks always made me nervous. "I'm sorry for my part in this too," I said. "At least we figured out we wouldn't work before you wrote a song about me." I smiled to cover up my lame joke.

He looked stunned. "Jane, I didn't say anything about us not working. We fought—that doesn't mean I want to end it." My hand rested on the sand next to his, and he laced his fingers through mine. I hadn't realized we had been sitting so close. "Before you say anything, let me explain. I'm not used to women like you." He laughed self-consciously when I felt my face redden. "You say everything that's on your mind. So, I think it's only fair if I return the favor. I didn't want to come to this wedding." He breathed out a bitter laugh. "I didn't think that I wanted to try for love again. But when I met you, I realized that I could still feel. I could love again. I just want the chance to do that with you. I want to get to know you, Jane."

I didn't know what to say, or even what to think. Dancey had the ability to steal any girl's heart that he chose, and he picked me? Not to insult myself, but I felt like an unlikely target—especially since I hardly knew him.

"Why didn't you want to love again?" I asked.

He gave me a rueful look. "Your heart can only break so many times before it hurts to think about love again. And the last one . . . ?" He sighed. "It almost ruined me. Jane?" He reached up and rubbed his thumb across my cheek. "You and I aren't so different. And I don't think you're immune to me, either. We can make each other happy."

There was one benefit Dancey had from his rash of broken hearts—he had more experience with getting into trouble, because that's what this felt like to me. Austen came up in my mind as a barrier between me and Dancey's charm, but my doubts were eating away at that too.

Just like Dancey, Austen would be gone from North Abbey. Austen could hardly wait to leave the miles of sand behind him. At least Dancey had invited me to come with him. Austen had left me before. Logically . . . logically, he would do it again.

But logically, Dancey would also dump me. And that was the problem with having Austen's reason invade my mind, because according to him, nothing would work—nothing that I wanted, anyway. But I couldn't control the future, so why think about it too hard? I just had to figure out what I wanted.

"Ann-Marie was crying last night," I said. "Do you know why?"

"I was comforting her, but it only made her cry harder. She likes some fellow on your staff."

Austen. "Yeah, he's a heartbreaker," I said.

Dancey drew back from me, his hand brushing over the bed of weeds next to us. A few orange poppies stood out from the green. They were Taylor's favorite. It was a shame she didn't use them for her wedding—there were plenty here. He plucked out one of them and gently slipped it into my hair. It made me breathless.

"I'll cover you with poppies if they gave your heart to me," he said.

I recognized the lyrics from his latest heartbreaking song. His eyes warmed on me, and his hands trailed through my hair. "We can do anything we want together. We have a future. I can feel it."

This was what I had always wanted—before I was old enough to read and appreciate Jane Austen. It was the romance that I had dreamed about. My whole life was spent living in my dreams rather than real life, and now real life was calling to me; life could be better, perhaps, than what I imagined.

Seeing Dancey's earnest gaze, the way he leaned, I knew that all I had to do was surrender my worries and enjoy being with him like I had before. This was the romance that I felt would last forever . . . but I didn't want it from Dancey. I wanted it from Austen—simple, down-to-earth, definitely not-smooth-talking, commitment-phobe Austen. Tilting my head at Dancey, I remembered the first time we had kissed. There had been a moment when I'd known that he couldn't see me. Not really.

"Who broke your heart?" I asked him.

"What?"

"Whoever it is, she still holds the pieces. You never got them back from her."

He traced my lips with his finger. "That would make perfect lyrics for my next song." He took a deep breath and dropped his hand. "She . . . it's over between us. She wanted to play it safe, and

I'm definitely not safe. We're still friends, and I can't see her without wishing that things had been different."

Sudden understanding washed through me. I knew why Dancey didn't want to go to Taylor's wedding. The reporter's talk about that other sassy American girl who'd broken her camera; why Jennings now wanted exclusive pictures of Taylor's wedding. I knew what the reporter hoped would happen. She wouldn't get it . . . unless I helped it happen.

I slipped the California poppy from my hair. Dancey had written them into his song. "These are Taylor's favorite." I put it back into his hand. "They would look beautiful in her black hair."

His jaw clenched, the muscles ticcing involuntarily. I was fascinated—jaw clenching seemed so novel-like. "Does she know how you feel?" I asked.

He looked miserable. "When we first met, I was so taken by her. I've seen a lot of beautiful girls, Jane, so this wasn't purely physical. I mean, it felt physical but also spiritual."

Those were definitely the words of a poet. Austen would never put it like that, but he didn't need to. I nodded for Dancey to continue.

"Chuck couldn't make it to the airport to pick her up. He asked me to do it. It was freezing outside, so I put on a wool cap and sunglasses—I didn't want anyone to recognize me. She was wrestling with her bags. I didn't know such a slender girl could carry so much; the straps were all over her. She was so organized about it. A little girl mouthed off to her mom, and when Taylor was through with them, they were both smiling—it's funny what I remember. When I came up to her, she thought that I was Chuck. I don't even know how it happened, but she threw her arms around my neck and kissed me. And just like that, she had my heart." He flushed guiltily. "I kissed her back."

Of course, they had the perfect meet-cute.

Dancey covered his face and groaned. "She was there for my best friend, and we were all over each other. I still feel terrible about it."

I recalled Taylor's bridal shower when she'd said that her first kiss with Bigley had been by a soda machine at one of Dancey's concerts. It made sense that she would remember who had really kissed her at the airport.

"When I told her who I was, she was so mad. But," Dancey laughed at the memory, "I was so stupid that I couldn't stop making it worse for myself. And you know what happens to Taylor when she gets all worked up; her nose wrinkles like . . ."

I listened to Dancey go on about Taylor. He talked about the foosball championship where Taylor had begun to thaw towards him. He'd ruined the moment when he'd stolen another kiss. "It made sense when she told me that poppies were her favorite flower. You know the word 'poppy' where I'm from also means a smart and hot girl?" he asked.

Shaking my head, I listened to him talk about the song he'd written for Taylor—it was after she had accepted Bigley's marriage proposal. His emotions had bled onto the paper as he'd tried to make the words purge her from his life. When Bigley had started acting up—drinking and flirting with other women—Dancey had discounted his anger at his best friend as just wanting Taylor to be happy. But he had been jealous. Terribly, terribly jealous.

I had misjudged Dancey. We all had. My prejudice had marked him as a player, but his romantic streak ran just as deep as mine. He actually had a list of things that he loved about Taylor. Her flashing eyes. Her temper. Her throaty laugh.

Yeah, I was the rebound. At the same time, I was relieved to be free. Thankfully, I had listened to my gut instincts before this had gotten out of hand. I picked a blue cornflower from the weeds and rubbed the soft petals between my fingers. They reminded me of Austen.

Dancey stopped talking as if he had just realized what he had done. His mouth moved, but nothing came out.

I turned to him. "Dancey, I'm glad you told me."

Remorse stole through his expression. "I'm sorry, Jane. I didn't know how deep I was. I thought that I could move on. I have to move on . . ."

I shook my head. "You can't do that. Now that I know how you really feel, you owe me."

He looked wary. "How?"

"I want you to steal Ms. Taylor from Mr. Bingley."

Chapter 23

"We all know him to be a proud, unpleasant sort of a man; but this would be nothing if you really liked him."

—Jane Austen, Pride and Prejudice

I flipped open my phone and texted Austen after I parted ways with Dancey.

ME: MEET ME IN TEN MINUTES AT CHURCHELL'S SHACK.

The sand was getting in my shoes, and I ripped them off and dumped the sand back to the beach where it belonged. The bachelor parties were tonight. The wedding was tomorrow. We didn't have much time to sabotage this thing. I had left a confused Dancey behind. He wasn't so keen on my idea, but I didn't need his cooperation. I needed Austen's brain.

My buzzing phone signaled that Austen had written me back: I'M ON MY WAY.

A warm feeling permeated through my heart and shot energy into my limbs at the thought of Austen coming for me. Dancey had told me that I was insane for suggesting he steal the girl he loved the day before her wedding, but I wasn't through with him yet. Taylor loved Dancey back. I was sure of it. And no girl was safe until Dancey was off the rebound. I would be doing everyone a favor.

I ran up the steps at Churchell's Shack and shoved into the crowded place, not stopping to look for danger—namely Colin, Redd, Crawley, or Bigley. Honestly, I couldn't keep track of them anymore.

"You're here again?"

I hunched my shoulders, seeing the dirty blonde femme fatale scrubbing at the counter. "Hi, Junie." I sped past her and found a seat beside a fern. It was my traditional rendezvous spot with Austen. I fiddled with my phone a bit more as twenty minutes or so passed with no sign of the man I was crazy about. I was ready to wriggle out of my seat with impatience until I saw his lanky figure on the beach in the distance. He wore a Henley shirt and board shorts, and I drank in the sight of him.

He tackled the steps to the shack in the same manner that I had and cleared the doorway, his eyes roving over the crowd until they lingered on me. His smile was inviting. Everything about him looked and felt great. He greeted Junie in his usual charming way and wound through the tables to greet me. "Jane." He slid into the bench, facing me. He studied me like he was assessing if I was the same girl he'd left. I was. Sort of.

"Austen, what took you so long? I was afraid you fell into quicksand on your way over here."

"Worse." He pushed his hair from his face. "Taylor wanted me to cancel her subscription to Em's Matchmaker's online dating site, and I got stuck on the phone with customer service. They tortured me with call-waiting music. Twenty minutes! It took me twenty—no, twenty-two minutes to get a refund! I'm shaking." He lifted his hands. They were hardly shaking.

That didn't make me feel any better. "How much did you get back?"

"Fifteen dollars." He saw the look on my face and broke into a laugh. "It was the principle of the thing! They had her on automatic renewal!"

I snickered. "Okay." That's what I liked about him—he didn't give up. I needed that. "I guess it can pay for lunch. I just met with Dancey."

He looked tense. "Yeah?"

I reached for his hands, not able to stop from touching him any longer. "And you were right about everything. Taylor is unhappy. Dancey is unhappy. We need to help them."

"Them? When did this become a *them* thing?" Before I could explain, he shook his head. "No, no, I'm not helping Taylor get away from one jerk to go for a worse one."

"He's not a jerk! He's just misunderstood. We got it all wrong. You told me to find out the truth about him and I did. Dancey was on the rebound."

"With you?" he asked. I hesitated, and he threw back his head, his eyes meeting the ceiling in exasperation. "I can't believe this. So you're not interested in him. Great, but there are easier ways to get rid of a guy. I'm sorry, but I can't forgive him as easily as you can. He's on his own on this one."

"What about Taylor?" I asked. "She's in love with him. You saw her this morning—she's willing to sacrifice herself to the wedding gods because she's so depressed. She doesn't care if Bigley isn't the one if she can't have Dancey."

"That makes no sense."

"Well, it must to her, because she's doing it."

He studied me. "Even if Dancey was the right guy for her, what makes you think this will work?"

"Because every romantic bone in my body says so. If the guy wants the girl back—he chases after her. It's how it's done. He runs after the taxi. He follows her on a plane. He'll lay down all his money, his need to be right; he sacrifices everything. He'll die for her!"

His lips turned up, but he bit the smile down. "If he's dead, he won't get the girl."

"Oh yes, he will . . ." I struggled with my words, especially when I saw that he was getting that stubborn look. "Austen, why don't you help me instead of being such a cynic! Yeah, normal people don't follow the pages of a romance novel. I get it, but this isn't my story or yours. This is Ms. Taylor's. And she doesn't belong with Bigley. She belongs with Dancey."

"Can you hear yourself?" he said. "Taylor made her decision. She told us this morning. She's going through with it, and there's nothing we can do to change that. This isn't a book, Jane, this is real life and these are real people. We can't make these kinds of decisions for other people."

"The story's in our hands," I argued. "We're Jane and Austen— it's what we do. We're the ones who live vicariously through other people's more exciting lives because we're too afraid or too cynical to live it ourselves."

"Whoa! What?"

"There is no way that we are going to end this badly," I continued as if he hadn't said anything. "We're going to have our happy ending."

He stilled, and I wondered if he was about to declare his feelings or if he even had any for me besides a mild flirtation between jobs. A myriad of emotions passed through his eyes, but instead of sharing any of them with me, he licked his lips. "What's your plan?"

"Well, first things first." Taylor and I had a similar problem, and I hoped that it didn't seem like I was talking about Austen and me instead of our friend, because that would be awkward. I plunged ahead. "Taylor doesn't think that Dancey loves her. He needs to show that he cares, or she won't go for him."

"Okay, and how do we do that?"

"That's the hard part." I thought a moment. "A romantic gesture is good—like reliving a special moment that they shared together, or if Dancey repeats something significant back to her that she said to him first—which we can't help him do because we're doing this without either of their knowledge."

"Besides, it's redundant and unoriginal."

"It's called being thoughtful," I argued.

He readjusted himself in his seat. "What about the usual—turn down the lights, burn some candles, throw around rose petals?"

"This isn't a wake." I laughed at his provoked expression. "What if Dancey came in like some kind of white knight to save her . . . somehow?"

"So what do we do?" Austen asked. "Throw her out into the ocean and half drown her and then he has to nurse her back to health?"

"Let's avoid killing her," I said.

"We put someone she loves in danger—we throw her cat in a tree so Dancey can save it."

I giggled a little at his sarcasm. "How about he saves her family from ruin?"

Austen grimaced. "No one can save *them*."

"Okay, put a hold on the *saving* plan for now. We let Taylor see Bigley for what he is . . . and that Dancey loves her, and then find out who she goes for."

"How?"

"There's this lady with the paparazzi—her name is Jennings. Dancey and I agreed to let her take exclusive pics at Taylor's wedding."

"Why would you do that?"

I wriggled uncomfortably. "I don't really want to talk about that right now." His eyebrows went up, and I rushed hurriedly past that topic. "But the point is that we have the paparazzi on our side. They can get anywhere. She can follow Bigley and take pictures with him flirting with whomever he flirts with—the maid, the bartender, whatever, as long as it breathes. You have a bachelor party, right? You can do it there."

"Getting pics at a bachelor party is low."

"It's all we've got."

"You're forgetting one thing," Austen said. "Taylor knows who Bigley is; she forgives his drinking and everything already. You said so yourself—this isn't about Bigley, this is about Dancey."

"Then the paparazzi can discover Dancey loves Taylor."

"How?"

"I don't know, but I have a few ideas. I've got the lyrics to his latest song and a great meet-cute at the airport to work with . . . if I *accidentally* leaked that info to Jennings."

"Jennings?"

"The reporter."

"Ah yes, the mysterious reporter," he muttered.

"And then we compromise them."

He looked confused. "Besides spy movies, I'm unfamiliar with that phrase. Compromise them?"

"It's from the Jane Austen era. Basically we put them into a romantic situation and as soon as they give in to their feelings then we catch them in the act and force them to marry. Well, they'd marry in Jane Austen's time, but in our time . . . Jennings will get her exclusive pics. If Taylor is still willing to take Bigley after what he's done, he won't take her! What do you think? The pictures will be out there for the world to see. She will be thrown into Dancey's arms."

Austen was silent for a moment. "Have you been compromised?"

My lips tightened. "Not yet."

He reached for my hand. "Remind me to fix that."

That threw me off balance. Austen was turning into a romantic, which I liked . . . but it also confused me. He wasn't the romantic type. "Jane." His fingers trailed a pattern over my skin. "You realize that this is a horrible plan."

"Can you think of something better?"

Austen sighed and turned, staring blindly into the lunch crowd. "Taylor would kill us if we did this. She'd slice and dice us and serve us up cold at her wedding breakfast. Besides," he put his other hand over our entwined ones. "It's not nice. How would you like it if someone sabotaged your wedding?"

Noticing Colin to the side of us, I shrugged. "Well, it all depends on who I was trying to marry."

I watched DeBurgy lean over the counter. Colin was busy buying him drinks and getting ignored. "You know," I said, "Colin can sing a song or two." Austen looked confused. "We have our distraction," I said as way of explanation.

Junie plunked two waters at our table and a plate of nachos. We hadn't ordered them. I would've suspected a change of heart, except she looked unfocused; more than unfocused. Her lips trembled, and her face was all red.

"Junie?" Austen turned to her. "Are you all right?"

Junie's eyes rested on him. "I'm fine."

She rushed away, and my heart sank. She didn't like that I was with Austen. He glanced over at me, and I knew he wanted permission to follow her. "She doesn't look good," I said. "You—you can go after her if you want."

He smiled. "Jane, no matter what arch-rivalry you've got going with Junie, you're a good friend to her." He startled me with a quick kiss before heading after her.

Still feeling the pressure of his lips against mine, I watched Austen approach Junie, my emotions all over the place. He put his hand on her shoulder so that she turned to face him. After talking for a bit, she hung her head and broke down, covering her face with her hands. Austen hugged her. I wanted to believe that there was nothing between them, but the tender way that Austen held her made me suspicious. His hand smoothed her back. And Junie? Well, she clung to him like she'd never let him go.

I gulped, realizing that my own life wasn't running as smoothly as I wanted. After too long, Austen broke away from her and headed back, his jaw set firmly. He didn't sit across from me this time, just stood there at my table and glared at nothing. "I'm in."

"You're in?" He talked to Junie and just like that, he was going for my plan? He was fuming. My eyes searched her out in the crowd, and I saw that she had returned to polishing the counter, her eyes on the rag in her hand.

Austen gave a hard laugh. "You don't want me to give an acceptance speech, do you? I'm in. Let's go sabotage Taylor's wedding."

Chapter 24

"Well! Evil to some is always good to others."

—Jane Austen, *Emma*

Pemburkley Hall hopped with music and laughter. Taylor's bachelorette party was well underway. The glass wall partitions had been opened to give the party a more airy feel. It let in the night sky with its twinkling stars and fresh ocean breeze. Streamers sprayed over our heads like a big waterfall. Big tissue-wrapped poppies, twisted with the real wildflower, adorned the tables—so far Taylor hadn't noticed that I'd put them out.

I was in shorts and a T-shirt, looking less-than-festive compared to the other female guests, who were dressed in leis with grass skirts and wraps over swimming suits. They carried drinks with little umbrellas propped merrily inside. The pool had been opened for the occasion. The hot tub bubbled beside it, ready to boil the next occupant lobster-red.

Taylor stood next to the refreshment table near the Bigley women, pointing out the little fish fillets and fried calamari. Her laughter was too forced, her smile too tight. Everything about her convinced me that we were doing the right thing. Austen had reported via text that Dancey had also arrived at the bachelor party at Churchell's Shack across the way. Taylor planned for him to come to Pemburkley Hall in an hour to sing. Austen and I were going to make sure that we made it a private concert.

Picking up my phone, I texted Austen.

ME: TAYLOR IS BY HERSELF. CAN I MAKE MY MOVE?

Austen didn't answer back right away. Two bites of ice cream and three pretzels later, my phone vibrated.

AUSTEN: NOT YET. THE TARGET HASN'T TAKEN THE BAIT.

That meant that Bigley wasn't flirting with any of the waitresses at the party. Once he did, Jennings would be sure to get the appropriate photos. It was low, but we had to save Taylor from herself.

I popped a cashew into my mouth, chewing absently. Besides our mission to stop this wedding, I had a lot on my mind—mostly Austen. After talking to Junie, he had acted differently. Maybe I was imagining their deep connection, but did it matter? Austen was giving the resort away to Colin so he could leave us all behind. I could try to chase Austen across the country, but what if that wasn't what he wanted?

Taylor played with the umbrella in her drink, dunking it and biting on the end of the toothpick. Her nails were bitten down to a jagged edge. The beautician would fix that tomorrow, put concealer under her eyes to cover the dark shadows, apply a little more color to her pale cheeks. If we didn't help her, Taylor would be completely done up so that no one would see the pain beneath all her make-up.

I texted Austen one-handed.

ME: IF THE TARGET DOESN'T TAKE THE BAIT, I'LL GO PLAY BAIT. I'M SERIOUS!

This time my phone rang—apparently the threat meant a call to action. I answered it. "Austen?"

"Absolutely not."

I smiled—at least he was protective. "It probably wouldn't work anyway," I said. "He knows me and he hasn't tried anything yet. I'm not his type."

"Bigley's choosing to play the good guy at his own bachelor party." Austen grunted out his annoyance. "It's probably because, uh . . . the waitresses here are all over fifty."

I groaned. Taylor might love Dancey, and he might love her back, but neither would be willing to hurt Bigley if he wasn't uncovered as the player that he was. I readjusted the phone against my ear. "I'm thinking Taylor might've had something to do with hiring them."

Austen gave a little laugh. "The bachelor party's a bust. I don't even see Crawley—he's wandered off somewhere."

My neck prickled and I turned to make sure he wasn't standing behind me. He was the last thing I wanted to deal with tonight.

"I see Dancey," Austen said. "I'm going to send him to the rendezvous spot, all right? You just find a reason to get Taylor to leave the party."

I took the challenge and clicked off the phone. Taylor was talking with her bridesmaids by the hot tub. The ladies dangled their matching manicured feet into the water. Taylor sat down and edged her legs in with theirs. Bertie sat a head taller than the group, her hand clutched tightly to her muff of a dog. I was afraid of getting close just because she'd stuff the rat-bear in my hands. Ann-Marie wasn't nearby to take the brunt.

Bella looked glorious, as usual, in her florescent-pink bathing suit. She swung her mane of shining hair against her back. Her lips were set in a pout that hadn't been there at the club yesterday. Mary sniffed but didn't have a tissue. It was dangerous to get close to any of them, but I had a mission to accomplish.

"Are you talking about my car?" I overheard Bertie ask as I walked closer. "Oh, please. It was a gift. My father has no sense. It's only a Chrysler Mercedes knockoff. All looks and no drive."

"Your father spoils you," Taylor said.

Bertie tittered. "You can't expect my husband to do it all. He can't tie his own shoelaces without tripping."

Taylor didn't look amused. "It's surprising you even got married if you feel that way about him, Bertie."

Bertie thrust her finger out so that her diamond glittered under the lights. "All men are the same, honey. You give them what they want and they give you *everything* you want."

Mary stared enviously at Bertie's ring. "Your husband does make a lot of money."

"Please," Bertie said, "not enough for me."

"Good thing you love him so much," Taylor said pointedly.

"And you know so much about love, Taylor?" Bertie narrowed her eyes at her. "Chuck doesn't give you many gifts. But Dancey . . . he'll perform for your party. I didn't see that one coming. Does he have a crush on you?"

"That was Jane's doing," Taylor said.

I froze by the table next to them, not sure if I wanted to walk in on this.

"Jane?" Bertie's lips curled in distaste. "What does any man see in her?"

"Oh no, you don't," Bella snapped—the beautiful girl dripped with venom. "No more talking about Jane—she's not all that, you know. She can't have all the guys."

Taylor blinked in confusion. "What guys?"

"I don't want to talk about it." She crossed her arms. "No one can steal a man from me, especially some girl who could stand to lose a few pounds."

I was shocked that I had turned into the most unpopular girl at the party. All three sets of eyes belonging to Taylor's bridesmaids turned to dissect me at the table in a decidedly unfriendly gaze. Before I could defend my weight as curvaceous, Bertie's dog was in my hands. Mary followed up with a medical order. Bella ignored me, with her cute nose pointed in the air.

"Taylor . . ." I managed to find her in the group, trying to ignore the stinging insults. "Dancey has something he wants to tell you—I think he wants to iron out the details for the performance tonight."

Taylor reddened when she saw me, but she didn't move her legs from the hot tub. She gulped a few times. "He's done this before in front of much bigger audiences. I think he'll be fine."

"He won't sing unless you talk to him—that's what he said."

Her mouth gaped open. "Are you serious?" She jerked angrily from the hot tub, her legs dripping across the patio. "Where is he?"

"By the Longburn Lagoon." Or he very soon would be.

"What? What is he doing there?"

"I don't know. He said to wait for him while he gathers his things."

"Oh, honestly." She wrapped a towel around her legs, her black hair curling against her neck. Her green eyes shone especially bright; I hoped with excitement. "I'll be back." She shoved her bare feet into her flip-flops and set off at a brisk pace.

The puppy licked my chin. Before I could text Austen that Taylor was on her way, Bertie's voice stopped me. "You might have Taylor fooled, but none of us are."

I glanced over at her distractedly. "What?"

Taylor's bridesmaids all glared at me. "You're trying to sabotage this," Bertie accused. "Aren't you?"

I stiffened, trying to pull out her meaning before I gave anything away. "Taylor's bachelorette party?"

"You're trying to sabotage Taylor's wedding. Don't pretend that you don't have something for Dancey. This is Taylor's special occasion, and you're trying to steal all the attention from her."

I glared. "Don't I have to lose a few pounds for that?"

Bella paled and refused to meet my eyes.

"Oh, no, no, no." Mary looked nervous and placed a hand on the skinnier lady's arm. "Now, Bertie, Jane would never go for Dancey. He's a big rock star and she's just a party planner."

"Um, thanks for that, Mary," I said, telling myself that she meant well. "You see? So none of you have anything to worry about. I'm only doing my job, girls. I think we can all agree that we want Taylor to be happy for her wedding."

Bertie gave me a slow, mocking smile. "Then I suggest you get out of her life."

That was enough. My hands curled into fists. "And leave her to a vulture like you? I don't think so." I turned on my heel to put some distance between us to stop myself from doing something I regretted when I heard the loud splashing that signaled Bertie was pulling from the tub to come after me. If I walked away now, it would only look like I was running away from a twig in a bikini. Bella was right. I was a big girl—at least compared to the paper-doll Bertie. Maybe I'd sit on her. I swung around to face her.

"After everything Taylor has done for North Abbey?" Bertie growled out. Her knobby fingers dug into my arm. "It must sting to leave all her hard work behind for you to ruin it all."

"I've worked to get where I am, unlike some people." I peeled her hands away. "I think North Abbey will be fine. In fact, once you're gone, we'll all be very, very happy."

"That's until I get you fired."

"I'm pretty sure that I'd still be happier than any of you. Look at you, glaring and gossiping—so bored of life. How sad for you; your money and looks got you nowhere."

Mary looked confused. "What is she saying?"

"I don't know why Taylor puts up with you," Bertie sputtered. "She's always been a horrible judge of character."

"You can say that again," I said. "By the way, I forgot to tell you. Your daddy sent your adult diapers with your weekly check. We put them on your bed with your mint that you're going to throw up later tonight."

I pushed away from her to make good my escape, but now my thoughts were all over the place. That had been an awful, unprofessional thing to say, and I hunched guiltily. I was doing all sorts of crazy things tonight, and I was due for a fall. I did have Taylor's best interests in mind, didn't I? Depending on how the cards played in the next few hours, I was about to do the nicest or jerkiest thing that I had ever done in my life . . . if this worked. Everything centered around "if." *If* Taylor was in love with Dancey, *if* he loved her back, *if* love was enough to bring them together, *if* Bigley was as big of a lowlife as we thought he was, *if* my romantic ideals were right. If. If. If.

Suddenly all of this seemed much bigger than me. A yipping in my hands made me aware that I had also taken off with Bertie's dog. Sighing, I tried to find Bertie. I should probably apologize too, but she had stormed off, no doubt to tattle on me to anyone who would listen.

Swinging back around, I ran into Crawley. I backpedaled several steps. He held a microphone. "What are you doing?" I asked.

"I'm proving I'm serious about you."

"No, no, no, you don't want to do that."

Laughing, with his beautiful eyes crinkled up at the sides, Crawley put the mic to his mouth. Lights and music followed the motion. I turned and saw Ann-Marie by the sound system. She stuck her thumb up at me.

Crawley started to sing a rocked-out version of "Poppies," of all the songs to sing. Dancey had better not hear or he'd leave the meeting spot we'd arranged for Taylor and come here to jerk the mic from his best friend's brother. The women shrieked out happily and cheered.

I texted an SOS to Austen.

ME: WHAT DO I DO? CRAWLEY'S SERENADING ME!

AUSTEN: MUST BE TRUE LOVE. GO FOR HIM.

I didn't appreciate his sarcasm. To the side of me, Crawley's mother clapped and sang along. Bigley's mother covered her ears. Squaring my shoulders, I tried to sneak away.

Before I could get too far, Freddy hissed into my ear. "I play video games, huh?" I cringed as I came face to face with our resident baggage handler. All Freddy's bored looks had been wiped from his face, leaving only his accusing glare. "Thanks for smearing my name; now Bella won't look at me. These manly hands have never touched a controller in my life."

"Never?" I asked. "You're really missing out."

"Real funny, Jane. Maybe I'll return the favor. Everyone knows that you have it bad for Austen."

"So does Austen," I tried to sound flippant. "What are you going to do, tell him?"

He smiled wickedly. "I heard a few things about you."

Now he had my attention. The best thing to do was to grovel for mercy. "I'm sorry," I said, but then looking at Bella's upturned face while she watched Crawley from the crowd, I knew I didn't feel sorry at all. "Did I ruin your chance to mess with another girl's head?"

"Not at all. I'll just mess with yours now."

Bertie's puppy shifted in my arms, and I ran my fingers over her furry ears. "Hey, let's be friends. Take a puppy. We'll call it good."

Freddy left me without saying another word. I was a little worried, despite my joking. The problem with having dirty laundry out there was that enemies were more than happy to air it.

Crawley finished up his song and released the mic to Ann-Marie's waiting hands. He strode towards me. More music rushed through the speakers to replace his singing. At least we weren't left in awkward silence.

"Great job, Crawley," I said.

"Harry," he corrected. "You always call me by my last name, Jane. We're not football players."

The closer he got to me, the farther I held Bertie's puppy out between us. Unfortunately the thing was too small to do much good. Crawley looked down at it. "Wait, is that Pudgy?"

Pudgy? That's what Bertie named her? If the poor thing even tried a diet, there would be nothing left of the puppy. I brought Bertie's pet to my chest. "Yeah, Pudgy and I are pretty close now."

"No, her name's Puggy. I said 'Puggy,' as in Pug—not that there's an ounce of Pug blood in her. Come here, little girl." His hands went to me. I froze, and he took the puppy from my hands. He laughed when she went crazy with excitement.

It left my hands with nothing to do. I crossed them across my stomach. "At least her name isn't 'little rat-bear.'"

He gave me a complimentary smile. Apparently the joke wasn't funny to everyone. He kissed the puppy's head. "You are so adorable." His eyes were on me.

"That's what I think, too!" Ann-Marie stuck her face into the puppy's belly, her red hair in Crawley's face.

Time was running out. Taylor had to be at Longburn Lagoon by now. I didn't know if Dancey was there, too, but we needed to lead Jennings over there to take her pictures. I desperately tried to think of a way to distract Crawley. "I lost Bertie," I told him. "If you could find her and give her back her puppy, I'd be grateful forever."

Crawley looked disgusted by the idea, which meant they were probably on the outs. Ann-Marie did too, and she came to his rescue. "I put Taylor's cat in a room off the foyer," she said. "You can just put Puggy in there and they can play together."

Crawley looked to me for permission, and I hurriedly gave it. He left to fulfill my last request. Ann-Marie watched him go and turned back to me. "He's yummy. You're letting him get away?"

"No," I nudged her to go after him. "You've got to catch him."

"Jane!" She gave me a furious look that took me aback. "What am I? Do you just think I'm some idiot that you can send off to bug the people that you want off your back? You made me think I had a chance with Austen. I thought you and I were friends. Do you even see me as a real person?"

I felt terrible. The accusation compounded the shame that I was already feeling and I began to realize that I did some pretty stupid things. "I'm sorry. I wasn't thinking."

A big smile engulfed her face at my admission. "No, you don't, but I'm still going to do it." She rushed off after Crawley, leaving my heart racing at the emotional rollercoaster. I tried to stuff my guilty feelings away so I could worry about them another time. I had a party to flee.

Leaving the laughter and chatter far behind me, I rushed through Maple Grove and dialed Austen's number. He answered after one ring. "I was just about to call you," he said. "The target has taken the bait."

"Really?" I had never felt more relieved. More than before I needed to be justified for what I was about to do. "Who is Bigley flirting with?"

"I can't see. Just a sec. Let me get closer."

"Jennings is there, right?" I asked. "She'll have to take the pictures quick because we have to lead her to where Taylor and Dancey are meeting. But not right away. I want Dancey and Taylor to have a moment first. You know, one of those deep connecting moments where the girl knows the guy loves her and will do anything for her. When their eyes meet and—"

"Uh oh."

My heart jumped at the alarm in his voice. "What?"

"It's Junie. She's with Chuck."

Austen would never let Junie get involved in this. "Why Junie? Wait, they don't have something going on, do they?"

"Jane. We don't want compromising photographs of her with Chuck. She'll get fired."

He really cared about her, and despite my misgivings about Austen's relationship with her, I knew he was right. "Okay, we can't let that happen." I tried to figure out a way around this. "Where's Jennings?"

"No idea."

"Just throw some sleazy girl at Bigley until I get there."

"Easier said than . . ." his voice trailed off. "I just saw Jennings. She has her camera."

My heart lurched. Junie would really have a reason to hate me now. I hadn't meant to put her job in jeopardy. "I'm coming, Austen. I'm coming! Figure out a way to stop Jennings!"

I shut off my phone and took off at a run to stop the biggest disaster of my lifetime. The sand attacked my flip-flops and I kicked them off so that I could make record speeds to Churchell's Shack.

Cigarette smoke filtered through my nostrils as soon as I ran up the rickety wooden steps to the bachelor party. DeBurgy stood near the top stair, puffing away. The guy wore another fitted suit, though he had loosened his tie.

The deep laughter made a huge contrast to Taylor's party. I looked past the game tables full of cards, empty bottles and bowls of chips. Bigley's dad was already passed out. Redd watched his heaving chest with pursed lips. Most of the men I didn't recognize, but I saw Eddy wandering through the tables, snacking on peanuts and mints. Taylor's dad was noticeably absent.

DeBurgy blew more smoke into my face and glared at Jennings. Dancey's publicity manager had sniffed out the paparazzi easily. "A girl at a bachelor party?" He waved his cigarette the reporter's direction.

Austen was trying to distract her with a big steak. Jennings wore a glorious maroon jumpsuit with a belt at the waist. I had to give it to her; she gave the party some class. This camera was even bigger than her last one.

I tried to search out Bigley in all this mess, and found him standing by the pool. Sure enough, Junie was there and the two talked in low voices. My blood boiled as my suspicions took form. Sure, Bigley had gotten to know Junie when Taylor had taken her to London, but to a blueblood like him, Junie would always be the help. Bigley was taking advantage of her. Jennings peered at them over Austen's shoulder.

I felt DeBurgy's hand at my back. "Go work your magic, event coordinator. Avert disaster."

Bigley reached for Junie's hand. I ran at him full speed. Jennings lifted her camera and I screamed out, making Bigley jump in alarm. Junie turned towards me, but their hands were still touching. Before

Jennings could get any shots off with her camera, I shoved Bigley into the pool and fell in with him. We splashed hard. The water ran past my ears, and I sank to the bottom, holding on to the struggling Bigley the whole time.

I broke out of the water, hearing the pictures go off around me. Bigley splashed beside me. "What was that, Jane?"

My fingers loosed over his soaked shirt and I swam over to the side of the pool. "Just part of the bachelor party fun," I shouted over my shoulder.

Austen reached for my hand to help me out. "Not quite what I pictured," he said.

"Me neither," Jennings said, coming our way. The material of her jumpsuit flapped around her legs like a tent. She cocked a brow at me and gave me a sour look.

I half-expected to see Junie join in with the glares, but she had disappeared. DeBurgy, too. I came out of the water, my hair dripping with the rest of my body. "These aren't the photographs you want, Jennings."

She laughed, which meant my mind tricks weren't working on her. "Oh, they'll do for now, unless I can find better ones?"

"You'll get those at the Longburn Lagoon," Austen told her in an undertone. I knew working with her was killing him. He watched her like she would grow fangs and devour us both.

"I was already there," Jennings said in a smug voice. "I found nothing but a foosball table covered in poppies and some violinists playing a song by our favorite mutual acquaintance. Is this some sort of joke?"

Bigley wiped the water out of his eyes. "What are you talking about?"

He wasn't drunk like I thought he'd be. I turned to him. "What were *you and Junie* talking about?"

He gave me a long stare in reply. It was all I needed to know. I bent my knees and pushed off the floor of the deck, racing down the flight of stairs to get back to Pemburkley Hall. I had to find Taylor and bring her to Dancey. A noise beside me alerted me that Austen had caught up. He raced beside me.

"Let's drop this, Jane," he said. "You tried everything that you could, but this isn't working. Let's just go back to the lobby before everyone finds out what we did and we lose all our self-respect."

I only ran faster. Bigley had been flirting with Junie and he had been completely sober when he'd done it. I wasn't going to let Taylor marry that guy.

The music got louder through Maple Grove. The singer wasn't Dancey, but I had known it wouldn't be. I turned the corner into Pemburkley Hall and found Dancey staring at the singer across from him. Dancey held a few forgotten poppies in his hand while Colin sang his heart out.

"Dancey," I called. His eyes drew to mine. Austen stiffened beside me. I'd forgotten how much Austen hated the guy. This was going to be awkward.

Dancey motioned at the overly passionate singer. "What is that?" His British accent emphasized his disdain.

"Colin," I answered. "Dancey, you were supposed to meet Taylor at Longburn Lagoon."

"She wasn't there, just a foosball table and . . ." He held up some of the poppies we left there.

"Yeah, yeah." I nodded and picked up my phone to text Taylor. ME: WHERE ARE YOU!

A few seconds later, I got a text back from her. TAYLOR: MY CAT! MISTER IS STUCK IN A TREE!

But that plan had been shelved. It went under the potentially harmful category. Austen's eyes were on me, and I hesitated before grabbing Dancey's shoulder to shake it. The singer turned from Colin's appalling performance. "Taylor's cat is in trouble," I said.

"Her cat?"

Austen's expression went dark. I held up my hand before he could blow our cover. "Let me figure out where she is." I hoped that this was fate working for us instead of against us. I dialed Taylor and put the phone to my ear. "Taylor," I said as soon as she answered. "Where are you?"

"Outside. Just past Pemburkley." She sounded frustrated.

I took off to where I thought she might be, picking my way through the grove of trees. Dancey and Austen followed close behind while Taylor recounted her troubles: "I never got to the lagoon to talk to Dancey. Colin passed me on my way and told me that he was taking Dancey's place tonight. There was no way I was going to let him ruin my party, Jane! I went back, but Bertie stopped me and said . . . well, never mind what she said. And Crawley was singing that awful song in the background. Dancey must've put him up to it. I'm so mad! I finally got Bertie to stop complaining and left to give Dancey a piece of my mind, but then I found Mister crying from the top of a tree. Poor Mister! I've been trying to get him down, but Bertie's dog is making so much noise that I can't think."

We took a bend in the pathway to see Taylor on the phone, holding a hand out to her cat who dangled from the lowest branch. Taylor was a few feet too short and couldn't reach Mister. Bertie's puppy circled the tree, yapping happily. Thinking back on Ann-Marie's idea to lock the two animals together, I realized too late that that hadn't been a good idea.

Dancey rushed to her side. She saw him coming and clung to his arm. "Help me, Dancey! Help me!"

"I . . ." he looked down at his leather flip-flops. "What do you want me to do? Throw my shoes at your cat?" She gave him one of her exasperated looks, and he amended his words. "We'll climb the tree. Anyone wearing decent footwear?"

I was barefoot. Looking over at Austen, I saw his feet were bare too. They weren't before. I smiled slowly. "Dancey, you'll have to rescue Taylor's cat."

Dancey sighed and approached the tree. Taylor watched him breathlessly. Just as Dancey placed his hands on the tree, Bigley came from the shadows, his wet hair plastered back from his head, his shirt clinging to him after falling into the pool. He looked just as good as that six-hour *Pride and Prejudice* version of Darcy after his dip in the pond. My worried eyes went to Taylor.

"Dancey?" Bigley laughed at his best friend. "You're not going to try to climb after that cat, are you? Grab the pokey little puppy; I've got this." The moment Dancey gathered the puppy in his big hands, Bigley pulled the grilled Calamari from his plate of snacks that he had clearly snuck from the bachelorette party and now he dangled it under the cat. With no yapping puppy in the way, Mister trailed down the tree and claimed his prize.

"Naughty cat!" Taylor lectured. "Poor cat!" She went to Bigley to claim Mister. "I was so worried. Come here, baby."

Flashing light followed by a popping in the darkness told me that Jennings was getting her pictures. Bigley smiled to himself and wrapped his muscular arms around Taylor, kissing her for the camera with their cat between them. I glared. The scene looked far too precious.

Austen nudged me, making my hands fall from my hips. "He's not all bad," he said.

My mouth hung open. "But . . ."

"He saved the cat. He's a hero."

Clearly he was being sarcastic, but Taylor was impressed with him, and that meant our plan was ruined. She covered Bigley with kisses. "Oh, thank you! Thank you!"

Clapping and laughter followed the romantic scene. A small crowd had gathered near the tree. Many of Chuck and Taylor's friends and family had escaped the Colin show to watch the drama unfold in Maple Grove.

The original Mrs. Bigley drew her brows together, annoyed. "Why is my son all wet?"

A deep, masculine voice answered her with a snort. "Jane pushed him into the pool." The observation came from Redd. He glared at me from the shadows.

Taylor looked shocked. She pulled from Bigley. "What? Why?" *Because her fiancé was flirting with Junie.*

"Where's my baby? Oh there's my baby!" Bertie ran into the circle to reach Dancey, using every excuse to touch him while she pet down her little dog's ears. "Come here, honey. Jane!" She turned to me once she had her puppy in hand. "I gave you little Puggy to watch. How did she get out here?"

I wasn't about to punish Ann-Marie for helping me. I lifted my shoulders. "I'm sorry. She got away."

Taylor's hand grew still over Bigley as she watched me get accused of everything. Unfortunately, DeBurgy chose that moment to make his un-timely appearance. He pulled his cigarette from his lips, looking bored as he took in the scene. "It's just a cat anyway," he said. "Can we go in now and eat?" He gave me an appraising look, and then his eyes slid over me to Dancey. "I think we should leave these two lovebirds alone."

Dancey didn't answer DeBurgy; he swung around and strode back to the party. I couldn't believe that he was giving up so quickly. Our Darcy could still get the girl. It didn't matter if she was nothing like Elizabeth from the books. I didn't believe in fate like that anymore. Taylor and Dancey were meant for each other.

He was disappearing into the trees. I ran to catch up to him. "Dancey, Dancey." When he kept walking, I stepped in front of him to stop him from getting away. "If she knew you loved her, she wouldn't go through with this."

"Jane." His hands went to my shoulders and he set me to the side. "There's a time to give up. So, give up. Now." He walked past me.

"What about your song?" I called out in desperation.

"It made me a lot of money. Now stop trying to help me. I'm fine."

Taylor caught up to Dancey. Her suspicious eyes ran between us. "Are you leaving, Dancey? You promised you'd sing. I *need* you to sing."

Dancey stopped walking. "Why?"

"I need you." Taylor sounded desperate.

Dancey looked miserable. He kept his gaze focused firmly on the lights coming from North Abbey in the distance. "No, Taylor, you either take all of me or none of me. There won't be anything in between. Not anymore."

Taylor went silent. Dancey met her eyes then. When Taylor didn't move, he pursed his lips and pushed away from the both of us. She watched him leave the party until he was a speck on the beach. "He said he would sing." She sounded heartbroken. "How did this happen? Who let Colin get a microphone anyway?"

I slowly raised my hand, though I did it behind my head—it seemed less incriminating.

Taylor's eyes welled with tears. "You pushed Chuck into the pool. You sent me off to Longburn Lagoon. I don't get it. You let Bertie's dog run off. Bertie said that you were trying to sabotage my wedding. But you wouldn't do that. I know you better than that, right? Jane?"

"She was probably trying to get some good photos for the paparazzi," Redd said behind us. As usual, he had impeccable timing. "I saw her talking to that reporter tonight."

A tear slid down Taylor's cheek. "Jane? Is that true? Answer me."

I felt awful. "Your fiancé is cheating on you," I said.

Taylor gave me a look that froze me to the core and swung away, marching over the sand. "You're fired," she shouted over her shoulder.

Redd looked shocked. That same shock ran through me.

"Taylor." Austen sounded breathless behind us. He had run over from the group that was still congratulating Bigley. "You need to listen to Jane. She—"

"Austen, you're fired too."

He looked taken aback. "You can't."

Austen had a point. Technically, Taylor worked for his parents, but she was too mad to care. She tripped over his shoes in the sand and picked them up. Glaring, Taylor threw his shoes back at him. "I just did it, Austen," she shouted. "And you're not invited to my wedding either. That goes for the both of you. I don't want either of you in my life. You got it? Good. My life isn't a game. It's over!"

Chapter 25

"Perhaps it is our imperfections that make us so perfect for one another."

—Jane Austen, Emma

Austen's arms were perfect for hugs. We sat on the beach soon after getting fired. I rested my head against the crook of his shoulder. His thumb brushed against the bare skin on my arm.

I slumped in defeat. "It was my fault. I shouldn't have made you go through with it. What am I, five?"

Squeezing me closer, Austen tried to comfort me. "Our brains don't connect until we're twenty-six, so if anyone asks, we can just blame it on that."

I sighed. "I failed Taylor because I was short two years?"

"At least you cared enough to get fired. Not many people would do that."

Austen wasn't making me feel better. I laughed darkly at our predicament. He did too, then sobered when he looked down at me. "It's not too late, Jane. If Dancey loves Taylor, he'll own up to it. He won't give up."

I pressed closer to Austen, wondering if that was true for us. "You know, if you tried to make me feel better about tonight, I wouldn't complain."

His arms tightened around me. He gave me a soft kiss. I closed my eyes, rendered completely powerless by his gentle touch. I had meant for him to say something comforting, but this was good, too. I smiled. "I know what will make you feel better," he said. He untied the bracelet that I had given him from his wrist. "You've been missing this, I know."

I tried to stop him from putting it on me, but the temptation to have him play with my wrist made me give in. Soon, I wore our bracelet tied with a neat little bow. "Jane," he said, his eyes turning devilish. "Do you still think we're cursed?"

"If we are, then we should do it more often."

He kissed me again, this time more thoroughly. His fingers slid past my ears and trailed past my face as he pulled slowly away. "Which book are we in?" he asked.

"Jane Austen didn't have kissing scenes." I cracked a smile. "Maybe it had something to do with their breath back then?"

"Then I'm glad we're not in one of her books."

I pouted. "Don't say that. She'd give us a happy ending. It's hard to come by these days."

"You're trying to curse us again." Austen gave me a quick peck on the cheek. "We can't have that. If you talk that way, I'll have no choice but to throw you in the water."

"You're not strong enough."

"That's it." He picked me up and I gasped, feeling the air lift under my feet like I was flying. His arms made me feel as light as Bertie. "Oh, you'll be sorry!" I laughed. "I'll break your back. I was just told tonight that I'm too curvaceous." I tried to wriggle away, but he had a firm grip on me. "Austen! I do not do night swimming."

"What happened to your spirit, Jane?" He ran for the waves with me in his arms, and I screeched, holding him firmly around the shoulders. I wasn't sure where he got the energy, but it was contagious. He set me down in the water and the waves lapped around my ankles. "Have you had enough yet?" he asked me.

Of course I hadn't. This was too much fun. "No!"

He grasped me around the stomach from behind and dragged my ankles through the waves. It felt lovely. Austen lowered my feet back into the water and held me against his chest to give me a kiss near my ear that rocked me from head to toe. "You know what I love best about the waves?" he asked. "They just keep coming. That's what I like about you—you don't give up. Even if it gets us both fired, I wouldn't have you any other way."

"You weren't really fired," I pointed out.

"No. You want to live off me?"

"Who do you think I am? Bertie?" I splashed him and ran away from him through the waves. He chased after, and I turned and splashed more water at him. Before he could take me down, I tackled him first. The waves crashed over us, and we pulled out of the water, our hair glistening in the moonlight.

The lights from the tiki torches flickered on the deck of Churchell's Shack. Its ghostly light beckoned from the distance. Junie would be inside cleaning up after the bachelor party. I shifted, trying to make out the details of Austen's face—I didn't get much. "Why did you decide to help me after you talked to Junie?" I asked him. "What does she have to do with this?"

Austen helped me stand up out of the sand. "She was upset. It had something to do with Chuck. She didn't go into details."

"You didn't pry?"

"Why would I do that?"

We were so different. I could pry. "Let's go in, Austen. We'll say we're helping the cleanup crew because we feel so bad about what we did, and then we can get everything out of her before it's too late."

"And then Taylor orders our execution." His eyes rested on me. "At least I can't complain that my stay in San Diego was dull."

"If you keep talking about going away," I muttered, "I'll throw *you* in the water." Austen just laughed. I took that as a challenge that I'd take him up on later. I trudged through the sand, my wet clothes dragging me down. Finally we reached steady ground through the means of the deck. We entered Junie's brightly lit shack. It was empty, but littered with bottles, peanut shells, and dirty dishes. Junie would be back to clean it before morning.

"If you wait for her here, Austen, I'll go to the main building. Whoever finds her first does the interrogation—we'll do it right this time."

Austen ran a hand through the back of his wet hair. "Can't we just raid the fridge and eat all the leftovers?"

"Yeah, make sure you clean the fridge while you're at it."

He smirked. "I think I'll just set up the single light bulb over a rickety chair. I've got an interrogation to do." He dragged a chair from the bar and fell into it, clearly having no intention of following through with anything that he said.

A laugh tickled through my throat as I set off down the beach to Maple Grove. I felt all tingly from Austen's touch. Maybe it was our adventure in the waves, but I couldn't stop smiling. I had just gotten fired and I still felt great. Austen really knew how to cheer a girl up.

Picking through the roots growing through Maple Grove, I reached the courtyard in good time. The overhead lights lit the cobblestone pathway. I didn't want to run into anyone after what had happened, but I was desperate to find Junie. I hadn't the faintest idea of where she could be.

By the time I smelled the cigarette smoke, I knew it was too late to retreat. A sleek silhouette blocked the door to the main building where DeBurgy had set up watch. No one could get past the publicity manager without being seen, but I still had a right to be here. Straightening my shoulders, I brushed past him.

DeBurgy reached out and caught a string of my wet hair. My T-shirt and shorts were still dripping. "Were you shipwrecked?" he asked.

I pulled away, but the moment my hands rested against the door, I had a sudden thought. I glanced over at DeBurgy. "I thought you were staying at the Kellynch next door?"

He nodded once. In the shadows, his heavyset eyes made dark sockets in his face, giving him a skeletal look. "Let's take a walk," he said. My breath caught at the strange request. The lit ash of his cigarette made an orange target in the darkness. He pointed with it to one of the side courtyards. "There's a pretty garden over there. You can take me on a personal tour."

I refused to see the similarities to his request and the one the actual lady from *Pride and Prejudice* had given to Elizabeth. In that one, Lady de Bourgh had tried to lay claim on Darcy for her daughter. I was done with feeling superstitious about my life. Besides, going off with DeBurgy into the dark seemed like a very bad idea.

DeBurgy must've sensed my hesitation because he smirked. "You're looking for Junie, aren't you? You don't have to tell me; it's written all over your face."

"What makes you think—?"

He cut me off, "I sit in the corners at every party, at the bars, the cafés, and I soak everything in. People talk when they drink too much or when they're miserable; when they think no one else will listen. I've got eyes and ears, Jane. These eyes know who you're looking for. And my ears hold the information you're dying to get your hands on."

The guy had enough flair to do shows in Vegas. I stared at him, still not sure what to do.

He snorted. "I'm far too busy to seduce inexperienced girls in a courtyard after dark. Are you coming or not?" DeBurgy headed languidly for the courtyard, and though I was tempted to leave him hanging so I could ruffle his confidence, he had the information that I wanted. Taking a deep breath, I pulled from the door and followed him.

"Dancey has a habit of making my job difficult," DeBurgy said once we reached the garden. The palm trees hung over us in silent shadows. "He always had such poor taste in girlfriends." This was said in a sneer. "He's young and reckless; makes poor choices in friends." He took a long pull of his cigarette, his gaze leveled on me while I gagged on his smoke. "His best mate can't keep his hands off the women—especially under his mother's watchful eye. The fact is, I don't care if the groom wants to hijack a plane of monkeys. I don't care if you or Chuck's mother or his fiancé is upset about it—I don't want Dancey mixed up in this nonsense. You see?"

"He already is," I said.

DeBurgy made a sound of impatience. "What would you say if I could get your job back; find you a better job even?"

I was surprised at the offer—it wouldn't come free. "For what?"

"Forget about ruining your friend's wedding. That's not very nice for a girl like you to do anyway; not very professional either. Taylor doesn't want your help. We all know that."

My heart raced. DeBurgy must think I had a chance at stopping this thing or he wouldn't have bothered to intervene. He flicked the ash from his cigarette, staring down at me.

"I don't get it," I said. "You said that this is the same information I'd get if I talked to Junie?"

"She's not going to talk to you, Jane. We came to an agreement earlier tonight—the terms of her conditions are between her and me. I offered her a position elsewhere, and she jumped at the chance."

My mind went to the abandoned shack where I'd parted ways with Austen, the food and dirty dishes everywhere. It had been Junie's pride and joy only yesterday. I felt oddly sad that she wasn't returning, then frustrated. DeBurgy's meddling was proof that she had real information that could help us.

DeBurgy touched my arm, then drew back at my wetness with a scowl. "You care for Dancey, don't you? Jennings wants to uncover a story on his relationship with a practically married woman. Taylor doesn't need that. Think of the shame she'd feel reading those headlines during her honeymoon? It would be all your fault, but we can fix the trouble you've started. We'll work together."

I felt like I was talking to a boa constrictor who was trying to convince me to strangle myself—he made it sound really good. "We can get the paparazzi off Dancey's back," he said. "I can pull out the big guns, hold a press conference, make some charity contributions. All you have to do is play the role of Dancey's girlfriend—strangely enough, you are the lesser of two evils. We can't have him stealing his best friend's fiancé on the eve of his wedding, now can we?"

"I can't pretend to be Dancey's girlfriend," I said. "That would break Taylor's heart."

"Are you kidding me? She's looking for any excuse not to feel guilty for leading on my client."

"Why don't you just ask Dancey to back off?" I asked.

"He refused."

I almost gasped in my relief, but kept it down under DeBurgy's close scrutiny. Dancey's refusal meant that he still liked Taylor. He was going to fix this. I shook my head, not able to keep back my smile. "Sorry, DeBurgy, we don't have a deal."

I tried to walk off, and he followed me like an offended shadow. "You would pass up such an opportunity?"

"Hey, it's not going to work anyway. You said so yourself, Dancey has it bad for Taylor."

"He's protective of you." DeBurgy threw his cigarette on the grass and stomped on it in his agitation. "He'd go through with it if he thought it might save your reputation as a professional. Dancey asked me to destroy the photos Jennings took of the two of you together."

That stopped me in my tracks.

DeBurgy stepped in front of me. "Just think of poor Taylor if she saw them. So sad, so betrayed. And Austen? He's a man—we all feel jealousy and do stupid things we regret later on. Lucky for you, I hid the photos with the bellhop for safekeeping."

"Freddy?" I asked. DeBurgy put the KGB to shame. How did DeBurgy know that the guy hated me?

"You fix my little PR problem," DeBurgy said, "And I make *your* problem go away for good."

I stepped back and decided to buy myself more time. "What are you waiting for? Set up the press conferences." I raced away to find Freddy. I wasn't sure if he'd be home yet or still packed away in the lobby. I tried the latter first, and found Redd sitting stiffly on the couch. The military set of his shoulders gave him away. He stared at the blank TV. I didn't want to talk to him, but I was desperate. "Have you seen Freddy?" I asked.

Redd's sleepy eyes widened as soon as he took me in. "Jane!" He stood up, and the napkins that he held slipped to the ground. I noticed that there was writing on them. Before I could get too close, he took a firm grip on my shoulders and looked steadily into my eyes. "I got you fired. I am so sorry."

"That's fine. Have you seen Freddy?"

"No, it's not fine. I've been doing some thinking. I don't like myself this way. I feel like I'm being forced to act a role that I despise. I can usually let go of a failed relationship."

"No one is acting themselves right now." I took a moment to free him from his guilt. "You're forgiven, but you could really make it up to me if you could help me find Freddy."

He frowned. "He left with Bella somewhere."

I almost choked on a gasp. "She's in trouble. We have to save her." Redd straightened at my words like any officer in the navy would at such a call to action. I ran for the Fullerton Bungalow where she was staying. We careened through the courtyard just in time to hear Bella's scream.

Redd barred me from entering. "Jane, stand back." He crashed into the door, and the hardwood stopped him with a jolt; it sounded like he was running into a tree. The reinforced timber we used at North Abbey didn't budge. Bella screamed again, and Redd shoved his shoulder against the door, shouting out in the confusion.

"Use the handle," I reminded him.

He went for that next, and it turned easily under his hands.

I rushed inside after him, and we found Bella in the middle of tackling Freddy. She threw her fists against his back and beat him over the head with her glittery purse. "I'm going to kill you, Freddy Tiney!" Bella screamed. Her hair was a mess. Mascara ran down her face, making her look like an 80's rock star. The warm fire in the living room crackled in the fireplace behind her, mocking her with a cozy scene straight from a Hallmark movie.

Redd easily pulled Bella off the struggling bellhop. She pointed a manicured nail at Freddy. It was chipped. "Freddy, you're a horrible disgusting creature. You may not live in your mother's basement, but you should!"

"What happened?" I asked.

"He had these photographs—ooh—and he said such awful things. What a turn-off! Being a jerk doesn't impress the girls, Freddy!"

"Where are the photographs?" Redd asked.

"There." She pointed to the crackling fire. "I threw them in there and then Freddy got mad. At me! Me? Told me he knew I had a nose job, recognized one when he saw one. What a freak!" She glared at him. "It was just a little nose surgery, Freddy! What a horrid basement creature you turned out to be." She held her hands out to me, and Redd released her so that she could hug me. "Thank you, Jane, for warning me away from him. I'm so sorry for all the things I said about you. You were right about everything!"

"Thank you for destroying those photographs," I managed through her strangling grasp. The girl was as strong as a bull. I could see now how she had gotten the best of Freddy.

She pulled away, her golden hair falling every which way. "After everything you've done, how could I *not* help you?"

I knew the destroyed photographs weren't the end of it, but I was still touched that despite Bella's resentment, her first instinct was to protect me.

"You're not fat either," Bella assured me. "I was horrible for saying it."

"Well," I felt my lips tip up. "I *am* curvaceous."

I heard a snap behind us. Freddy had taken a picture of Bella with his phone. He breathed out heavily, his eyes indignant, and I knew he didn't like being bested by a girl. "Now who looks like a basement creature?" he growled. He held his phone up, showing Bella at her worst. Bella made a weak, strangling noise. Her hand fluttered to her heart. Freddy smirked. "How about I post it online? Make a meme out of it. By the time you get to it, it will be viral. No man will have you."

The phone was out of his hand halfway through Freddy's speech. Redd smashed it against the wall. I heard the delicate pieces inside crunch. The glass over the screen cracked like broken ice, and then the screen went black.

Redd was amazing, just like the hero he was meant to be. He glanced back at us as if vaguely aware that we had witnessed his valiant act. "I hate anything viral," he said. "Everyone is always sharing it on Facebook, calling each other Nazis. A complete waste of time."

Bella fell into his arms. "You saved me. I would've died. Just died. Ruined! Such a thing—such a thing would've been worse than death."

A fate worse than death was the phrase she was looking for. Bella arched her neck back and kissed the taller man. His arms tightened around her, and he dutifully kissed her back. Her hands went to his hair, and he escaped long enough to wipe her face clean of mascara. She giggled and kissed him again, getting lipstick all over his face.

Freddy glowered beside me. I felt like he was the bumbling villain in a bad movie and I was his awkward sidekick. I shifted. "Well, Freddy and I are going now," I said, averting my eyes from the passionate couple.

Bella waved at me behind her back.

"He owes me a new phone," Freddy grumbled.

"You'll have to get a new job, too," I told him as soon as we were out on the patio. "Bella was a guest here. Even your dad can't get you out of this one."

"What good will that do you?" he asked. "Those photos of you aren't gone for good."

"Then I'm taking you down with me, Freddy. Living in your mom's basement will be the least of your worries!"

Something sinister snapped in Freddy's eyes, and his bored, devil-may-care attitude turned into an evil glare. He lurched forward, his hands closing the distance between us.

"Jane!"

I turned as Bertie came out from the Southerton Bungalow, interrupting Freddy's possibly murderous intentions. I had never been so glad to see her. She held her little rat-bear in a crushing grip. "What was that all about?"

Freddy was completely acting out of character! "Freddy was just putting out some fires," I said, giving him a warning glare. "Weren't you?"

Freddy's eyes twitched, and he dropped his hands back to his sides. I noticed that they made powerful fists. "Hmm," Bertie said, "well, I'd like you to send up some fresh towels."

I gulped. "Sure."

Freddy's face had turned a molten red, and I wondered if he would explode in front of my eyes. "Well, what are you waiting for?" Bertie said. "I'd like them warmed if that's not too much to ask for in this backwards place!"

Freddy swung around and marched the other way. I shivered. No way was he getting Bertie fresh towels—I was just glad for her waspish ways, or he would've killed me. Bertie held her puppy out to me. When I didn't immediately take Puggy, she stomped her foot. "Jane, I'm waiting!"

Did Bertie not know I was fired? I cleared my throat and wove a nice little story for her. "I can't take poor Puggy. It's part of North Abbey's new regulations. They're very strict. You'll have to walk Puggy yourself."

Now it was Bertie's turn to look like she might strangle me. "Very inconvenient! It was possibly the only thing the staff was good for!" When I didn't budge, her lashes lowered in heavy annoyance.

"Then if it isn't against North Abbey's *new* regulations, I need you to play messenger girl for me. Harry Crawley isn't answering my texts. Go find him. It's vital he find his brother for me. Now that Chuck is marrying my closest friend, we'll be seeing a lot more of each other. I think it's only proper we get to know each other over drinks."

I stiffened. That was a very bad idea. She had to know that Bigley was at his worst when drinking. Had Bertie given up on Crawley and decided to take advantage of his stepbrother? It seemed she had or why else would she do this? After her little rendezvous with her best friend's husband, she might even expect gifts. Despite all that, she brought up a good point—maybe the best way to figure out what was going on with Bigley was through his brother.

"You know where Harry Crawley is?" I asked her.

"That's why I'm asking you to find him." Bertie slammed the door, leaving me staring at it.

I had last seen Crawley with Ann-Marie. I texted her on the off-chance that she knew where he had gone.

ME: HAVE YOU SEEN HARRY CRAWLEY?

A minute later, she answered.

ANN-MARIE: HE'S WITH ME. WE'RE BY LONGBURN LAGOON.

That got me worried. I didn't want anyone else to find our romantic foosball setup, and I especially didn't want Crawley to be there with Ann-Marie. I took off for the lagoon. It was in the middle of Maple Grove, in a clearing overhung by palm trees. There was an elegant bridge over it and a Chinese garden off to the side. I heard the foosball game long before I saw Crawley hunkered over it. Ann-Marie shouted out when she got a score.

"You're not getting away with that," Crawley said.

He had orange petals all over in his hair; so did Ann-Marie. The two had clearly gotten into a fight with the California poppies. Crawley seemed to have gotten over me, too; his eyes were only for Ann-Marie. I was tempted to scold the two for letting the dog and cat escape and then hijacking the foosball game, but they looked so happy. At least they were getting something out of my hard work.

"There you are," I said. They glanced up with brief smiles and bent down again to concentrate on the game. "So, Bertie is looking for your brother," I said.

Crawley's shoulders stiffened. "Why? She's a succubus. I don't want her anywhere near my brother."

A succubus? Very apt description—my respect went up for him tenfold. "Well, good," I said. "You're protective." I remembered everything that he'd said at the rehearsal dinner. "You seem to love Bigley a lot. Is your stepbrother a good guy?"

"Yeah," he answered quickly. "He's just going through a hard time right now."

"Why?"

He shrugged. I could tell that he wasn't concentrating on the game anymore. Ann-Marie made another score, and he wordlessly marked the point on the scoreboard.

"He doesn't want to marry my friend, does he?" I asked.

The game stopped. Crawley looked up, his eyes wary, his hands frozen on the handles. "Who told you that?"

It was a lucky guess. "Can you tell me why?" He was silent, and I tried harder to get him to talk. "Is it his mother? Does she have something to do with it?"

"She—she . . . look, there's a reason my stepdad couldn't get along with her, okay? Taylor's just the first girl that Chuck's mother ever approved of. Chuck likes her too."

"Who was the girl his mother disapproved of?" I knew as soon as I said it that I had guessed what really happened. Crawley had a hunted look. "Oh c'mon," I said, "are you trying to protect Mrs. Bigley the First? She's been rude to your mom all week." I cleared my throat and pulled out the big guns. "She called your mom a whore."

"There was a girl he liked." Crawley's eyes filled with self-reproach when it came out. "Don't say anything to Taylor, okay?

314

Chuck could see that Dancey had a thing for Taylor anyway, so my brother didn't think it was that big of a deal. He left his best friend alone with Taylor and thought that would take care of everything."

"Bigley loves someone else," I breathed. It all made sense.

"Chuck had it bad, so bad that he let it slip to his mom, even talked about marrying her. His mom freaked out, said she'd disinherit him, said she'd even take Taylor over some girl with no money or a good family. When Chuck got home from that, he didn't know what to do; but he found Taylor crying on his couch, and she told him that she had gotten into a fight with Dancey. So Chuck made his move and asked her to marry him. He tried to make everyone happy, but he did a lousy job of it. And now Chuck's a stupid drunk like his old man."

As if I didn't have enough to worry about, now I had to add to that the shared fates of Bigley and some mysterious girl from England? Still, the solution seemed so simple. "Why does your brother care if he gets disinherited?"

Crawley looked grim. "He's worked too hard to lose everything. He's completely dependent on his mother. If he loses her approval, his businesses go under. People lose their jobs. He'd have to give up everything to marry the girl he loves. I warned Chuck. I told him to stop his dependence on his mother before she pulled something like this."

What a tragic, beautiful love story. "We have to do something," I said. I remembered the insane prank Crawley had planned when we'd first met. "Help me steal Taylor's ring tomorrow."

He laughed. "What?"

"I can't go to the wedding. You've got to do it for me."

"You really are a mover and a shaker. I knew it the moment I met you."

"I told you that Jane was." Ann-Marie skipped next to him. "She's one awesome chick."

Crawley put his arm around her, and I smiled, liking this side of him. He studied me, his blue eyes narrowed into thoughtful slits. "I'll see Bigley tonight. I don't see how it will help, but give me the word and I'll do what I can."

"Oh." My heart lurched in excitement and I squeezed his arm. "I knew you wouldn't let me down. Do everything in your power to stop this wedding, and I'll do the rest." I ran the opposite direction, then dug in my heels to spin back around. "Put the foosball table away when you're done, will you?"

Crawley groaned, but he wore an amused expression. Ann-Marie poked him in the ribs as a reminder that there was more fun to be had, and they went back to their game like I had never been there. I was glad that Crawley's love for me was so forgettable. The two made a perfect match; both of them were devilish little imps.

Honestly, I didn't know what stealing Taylor's ring would do, but it was my last attempt to delay the wedding. DeBurgy's threats still hung like a cloud over my efforts. I had nothing left to do but to find Bigley. It was his turn to get the Jane treatment. He was the only one who I hadn't tried to force my reason on yet.

Chapter 26

"There is safety in reserve, but no attraction. One cannot love a reserved person."

—Jane Austen, Emma

I felt some déjà vu on my way to my room when I saw Elly hurrying to Taylor's bridal suite with a bucket of ice. Elly wore her boots with her rolled-up pajama bottoms again. I loitered outside the hall, at war with myself. What a terrible friend I had turned out to be. I wanted to comfort Taylor, but wasn't sure what sort of welcome I'd get.

Taylor and Elly talked in low voices. "You have to follow your heart on this one," Elly said. "I can't tell you how to feel, Taylor. It just happens."

"And then what?" Taylor asked. "I become like Chuck's mother? Or my dad? I can't be like them. What am I doing, Elly? I'll hurt everyone. What I want is too crazy, too illogical. I can't trust this."

My heart thumped out an irregular rhythm. Taylor could be talking about anything, but what she was saying was enough to make me want to stay around and help if I could.

Elly made soothing noises. "It's not crazy if it's right. Love might make you feel like you're in a rollercoaster, but it also feels secure, like it will last forever."

"On a rollercoaster forever? I don't want that."

Elly laughed. "You know what I mean—love is exciting and comfortable all at once."

"It makes sensibility sensible," I said at the door.

The cousins turned as one to look at me. Both of them sat on the big patchwork quilt on Taylor's bed. There was just enough room for me. I waited for Taylor's verdict to see if she'd let me join. "Jane!" She rolled out of her bed and came for me, her arms enfolding me in a protective circle. "I know why you did it. I get it, but it's unacceptable. How are you going to take over weddings here if you try to break up all the brides and grooms you don't feel love each other enough?"

My throat felt tight. "Our friendship means more than my job, Taylor."

"What makes you think that friends do that?" Taylor pulled away from me to give me a stern look. "You see things so differently than I do. I can't ask you not to care, but can't you turn it off for once? You're not fired anymore, Jane. You're not, but Elly will get me ready for my wedding tomorrow, okay? I don't want you to try to talk me out of this anymore."

"Taylor, I just want you to be happy."

"Just open your eyes!" Taylor looked contrite as soon as her sharp words came out, and she moderated her tone somewhat, "I knew what would happen with Dancey if I ever got together with him. I didn't have to see it for myself to know that he'd never be faithful."

She reached over and handed me a manila envelope from her bed. I knew they were Jennings' photos. "DeBurgy?" I asked.

"Yes."

And Taylor had still taken me back as a friend and an employee. I had been thinking up explanations for days and wondered if the one I had would at least get Dancey out of trouble. "We were on the rebound, Taylor—though neither of us knew it. He thought he could forget you. I thought I could forget Austen, but neither of us could."

"Jane, Jane, stop. I know." Taylor hugged me again. I felt horrible. This misunderstanding was so cliché. We were supposed to be more sensible in life. "I don't want to talk about it. I'm giving you another chance because we're friends," Taylor said.

"Dancey?" I asked.

Taylor glanced over at Elly, and the two seemed to be having some mental argument before Taylor's hand tightened on my arm. "I told him to leave and I meant it."

She had told me to leave too, but here I stood unfired. "Taylor?" I tried to reach her, knowing I was fighting a battle on rocky ground. "If you won't think about Dancey or yourself, then think about what Bigley's going through."

Taylor sighed and paced the perimeter of the room, her hands clasped tightly together. "You heard about that, too? I suppose I have DeBurgy to thank for that." She sat next to Elly. Her cousin's green eyes were downcast. "Chuck told me about her tonight," Taylor said in a subdued voice. "I know that he cared about . . . someone else, but we're willing to make it work."

"You can't!"

"Jane," Taylor's voice was soft, sad. "You've got other things to worry about. Austen knows about the photographs, too."

The envelope felt heavier in my hand. The fire in my heart built to a raging storm that would not break until I felt my hand around DeBurgy's throat. I was going to kill him. Taylor's voice made me realize I was halfway out the door and heading for someone completely different. "Jane, where are you going?"

"Austen!"

I hurried down the staircase, not knowing where to find him. I didn't have time to talk sense into Bigley anymore. He was stupid enough to make his own decisions. Taylor too. I was out of charity with everyone, especially Dancey, who had done more than his share to implicate me with those ridiculous photos. Why did he have to hire such a stupid PR nut like DeBurgy, anyway?

I decided against Churchell's Shack. Since I knew DeBurgy was handing out photos in the courtyard like candy, Austen would've gotten them there. I headed for the Wood House where he was staying. It was a horrible lean-to on the side of North Abbey. It was aptly named, since it looked just like an old log cabin. A lone figure sat forlornly on the steps. By the time I was close enough to figure out that it belonged to Junie, she reluctantly stood to greet me, her lower jaw trembling. She wouldn't meet my eyes.

"Junie?" I slowed down, not knowing what to do with her. She looked so sad, but I didn't think that she'd take a hug. I noticed her luggage to the side of her. It was the same luggage that she had taken to London when she'd stolen my trip with Taylor last fall. DeBurgy had said that Jane had taken his deal, whatever it was. "You're leaving?" I asked.

She nodded, her fingers clenching and unclenching like she couldn't figure out where to put them. "Thank you, Jane, for throwing Chuck into the pool. It probably meant nothing to you, but it meant everything for me." She lowered her head against my shoulder and broke down crying. "If you hadn't been there . . ."

Jennings would've gotten her photos to replace mine. Stupid paparazzi. I couldn't believe that I had tried to put someone in the same position that I was in now. It had been horribly thoughtless of me.

"DeBurgy talked to me," she said, "and he told me that you didn't care for Austen, not like you should. I saw the photos of you . . ."

"Those aren't what they seem," I tried to defend myself.

"Austen deserves better. He's kind and good, everything a girl would want." A tear slid down her cheek. "You've never treated him like you should. Please don't hate me, Jane. You know what's been going on, what I've been feeling, don't you? I know you know."

"I know that I know too." It was lame, but how else could I respond? I felt prickly with dread. I had always known Junie had something for Austen, but he had dropped all of that for me. Now that he knew about the photos, all that might change.

"I never could see myself with anyone else," Junie said. "Maybe that's wrong. I know I'm not the only one who loves him. I know what you feel about him, too, but I don't care anymore. I don't care what anyone thinks. He wants me back. We're leaving here tonight."

"Tonight?" My heart shouted out in protest. Austen was being too rash. If he just gave me time to explain, he might stay here with me.

"Please, Jane," she said, "I didn't want to hurt anyone. I'm sorry! Tell Taylor in the morning. You're the only one who knows. She deserves to know too."

"You're running away together?"

"Secret's out, Jane. We're in love." She broke down crying.

This was Junie's big secret—just like her counterpart on *Emma*, she was running away with her Frank Churchill—except her Frank Churchill happened to be the guy that I was crazy about. I knew that Junie didn't like that we were dating—her crying spells, her glares, trying to forget her pain by using Bigley. The anger and sorrow boiled inside me. I hadn't saved Junie from the paparazzi for this—Junie and Bigley had so much in common; I should've let them rot together.

She touched my shoulder. "I'm sorry, Jane, but nothing will stop us now."

I couldn't react; I felt weak from all the emotions charging through me. "Did Austen tell you that?"

Austen came from the darkness then, his shoulders stiff. He had changed from his wet clothes and wore a jacket. He didn't speak to me, his eyes only on her. "Are you ready?"

She let him take her luggage. Her hand still rested on my arm in a final farewell. "Please, don't be mad. It's better for everyone this way. You'll see."

I rallied my last bit of fight, afraid of living a life without Austen, so afraid that it would make me do anything, even beg to keep him with me. "Austen?" I clutched his arm. "DeBurgy gave you the photos?"

He pulled away. "I don't want to talk about that right now, Jane. I've got somewhere to go."

"With Junie?"

"Yeah, and we're late."

I didn't want to chase him all the way to the airport declaring my love, but I would if that's what it took. "You said yourself that misunderstandings were lame, Austen." I couldn't believe that I had to throw his words back at him, but I was desperate. "You said people should find out all the facts before they do something stupid."

"You want to talk stupid, Jane? Do you really want to talk stupid?"

Wait, was he calling me stupid? I stiffened. "Hey."

Remorse filled his expression. "That's why I don't want to talk about it right now. I'll say things that will hurt both of us. I'm too mad to think."

And too mad to listen. There was nothing that I could do. I'd lost everything. My regret couldn't take anything back. Maybe Dancey was right—there was a time to give up. If Austen didn't care about me, then I didn't care about him . . . except I did. The thought tortured me. I couldn't lose Austen, everything that he was to me—the laughter, the love, the hope. I couldn't comprehend how terrible life would be with only tainted memories and thoughts of our unrealized future together, but I dreaded a life without our love. More than that, I mourned the loss of Austen. He meant more to me than any friend. He felt like my family. The part of my soul that kept a part of him couldn't let him go. I doubted I ever could.

I turned from him and Junie, not able to see where I was going. I couldn't run anymore. My legs felt weak, and I could barely put one in front of the other. Austen walked away, taking everything from me. His footsteps, the lowered voices—all usual noises took more meaning and burned into the night. Real life felt too heavy. It felt yucky, painful and hopeless. Exactly as Austen had described it.

I wasn't sure how I made it back to my room, but as soon as I closed the door behind me, I found my luggage, the one with "London" written across it. It used to be that leaving San Diego for some romantic countryside was the only thing I could think about. Now I threw everything I owned inside luggage I had never used before. It was strange that I was using my dreams from yesterday to pack up my dreams of today.

If I helped Taylor into a loveless marriage, it would go against everything that I believed in. Weddings were happy, the beginning of something wonderful. It would kill me to go to this wedding tomorrow. Even if I could force myself there, I would only think about losing Austen and what we could've had. He had no right to go off on a romantic elopement without me. I had stolen that idea from him fair and square. A hysterical laugh escaped me at the memory. He had been so logical about his plan, and I had completely ruined it by putting my romantic spin on it. Life was so much better spent together. How could there be an Austen without a Jane?

I broke down crying. My belongings were quickly disappearing from the room that I had grown to love. I really *did* have next-to-nothing to my name. The room looked as bare as it had when I'd had to find a room for Dancey. Austen had saved me back then.

My hand went to the bracelet that he had tied to my wrist only hours earlier. A rush of pain and regret stole through me, and I forced my thoughts elsewhere. I concentrated on my luggage, instead. It would be difficult to keep my escape quiet in the middle of the night. Using all my inner and outer strength, I dragged the heavy luggage from my room and down the stairs. I felt I was taking someone else's belongings down to the lobby one last time.

I walked into the familiar room downstairs and saw a guest waiting next to the front doors with luggage. I recognized his sleek, black jacket—I had worn it on the day that we had met. "Dancey?"

He turned. "Jane?" It felt like fate was throwing us together again, but life wasn't about "fate." I had Austen's logic to thank for that. In reality, Dancey and I were both losers in love. He stepped closer to me and handed me his cardkey.

323

I took it, not wanting to explain that I was leaving too. Clutching it, I saw the "unintended gifts" basket to the side of me. I loosened Austen's bracelet from my wrist and dropped it in. My eyes stung again, but I refused to give in to more tears.

"Jane?" Dancey was at my side. "You're upset. Come here." He wrapped his arms around me, and I fell against his chest, crying out my sorrow and frustration.

"The photos?" he asked me. He took out a handkerchief and wiped at my eyes. I nodded, unable to get a word out without crying harder. "Me too," he said. His eyes went to the basket.

I turned away from it. "It's where you put useless items left behind by people you care about. It's a stupid tradition. Usually, it doesn't mean anything. It just means love is fleeting. That's all."

After a moment, Dancey reached into a pocket and threw a poppy into the basket with my bracelet. His eyes went to my luggage. "You're leaving too, aren't you?" he asked. I nodded, and his chin tilted stubbornly. "My car is waiting outside. Let's go."

At least I didn't have to call a taxi. We headed out into the passenger drop-off area, and I allowed him to help me to his car. The jaguar glistened under the light like before, but it didn't feel as impressive. It carried Dancey's sadness. He threw my luggage in the trunk, but before closing it, his mouth lifted in a smile. "Your bags already say London on them."

I sniffed, not wanting to talk about my stupid dreams. He opened the passenger door for me and loaded me in. I watched him walk around the front of the jaguar, knowing that each step that took us from North Abbey took me farther away from ever seeing Austen again.

Dancey got into the driver's side. I played with my fingers. "When does your flight come in?" I asked him.

"In two hours. I just booked it. Yours?"

I wiped at my eyes. "I don't have one yet." In fact, I wasn't even sure if I wanted to leave town, but running far from this pain seemed like a good thing.

Dancey took a deep breath. "I have an extra ticket. I wouldn't mind leaving DeBurgy behind. He can take the flight after."

I glared through the windshield. "You know he gave everyone those photos, right?"

"Was that him?" He started the car and put his arm around me so he could back up. "Looks like everyone has our best interests in mind. The poppies on the foosball table were a lovely touch, by the way."

I smiled sadly, remembering the great time I had had putting it together with Austen.

"You care about Taylor a lot," he observed.

I lowered my head and nodded. I felt his hands in my hair as he tried to comfort me. "So why are you skipping out on her wedding?" he asked.

"She fired me, then unfired me, but . . ." I sighed. "You're one to talk. Taylor will be upset you're leaving, too."

"She told me to go home. I don't have a choice."

"You could've taken her with you," I muttered.

He laughed grimly. "You don't have a passport, do you?"

"Nope, I can't go anywhere."

". . . except to Vegas."

I lifted my head to look at him. He had that same desperate look he'd had when he had been standing on the balcony with me before. I understood it now, because I felt it too. "But if I took you from Taylor's wedding," he said in an undertone, "she would never forgive me."

"She wants you at her wedding, too," I said, "even if she told you not to come."

We sat there for a moment while I wrestled with my hopelessness. Dancey looked torn. He rested his elbow on the steering wheel, pushing his dark hair out of his tired eyes. It would be easier to make a dramatic exit. Every romantic scenario screamed for me to run away from my misery in a huff and do something crazy that would make everyone sorry for what they'd done—but in real life, people stayed put and toughed things out.

After a moment, I handed Dancey his keycard. "Sometimes we have to do hard things for the people we love."

Dancey stared down at it. His beautiful eyes cleared from the storm that had hijacked them earlier. Peace slipped through his expression, and he popped the trunk to release my luggage. He left his car and helped me drag my things back up the stairs to my room.

Chapter 27

"Well, my comfort is, I am sure Jane will die of a broken heart, and then he will be sorry for what he has done."

—Jane Austen, *Pride and Prejudice*

The morning came too fast. The birds chirped outside my window, and with nothing in the loft, I felt like I was camping. I took my time getting ready to go. Everything but my dress for Taylor's wedding was crammed into my "London" suitcase. This was the time to make myself look glamorously unavailable, strikingly hot, but . . . I wasn't really into it. I stood in my pajamas, staring at the sad girl in the mirror. I put more mascara on. Waterproof.

Something hard plinked against my window. I cringed at the sound, thinking the window would break, and when another clatter followed the first, I hurried to my window and peered down at the grass below. Austen stared up at me. He was in his suit, his white shirt untucked, his collar open. "Jane, get down here!"

I grappled with the window and shoved it open, but when I looked down at the grass, I didn't see him anymore. I had only a few seconds to wonder if I had gone crazy before the doorknob to my bedroom turned. It was locked. The knob-twisting turned into impatient knocking. As soon as I got the door open, Austen came storming inside like a raincloud. His tie dangled in his hand.

I clung to the door in shock. "You came back."

"I'm not going to leave until we stop this wedding." He took a hurried tour of my room, his eyebrows going up when he stared at the bare walls.

"Austen?"

He glanced back at me. "I forgive you; now let's go."

But he hadn't forgiven me, not really . . . unless he hadn't gone through with his elopement with Junie. I studied him, noticing that he still looked on-edge. He took a steadying breath. "This is the most idiotic thing that I've ever done, but that's the way things are supposed to be, right? Sacrifice everything for love?"

I felt lost. I had no idea what he was saying, but he was talking about how love could solve all life's problems. He was the illogical one now—it left me without a role in his life.

"So we lost the fight," he said, pacing the room. "We screwed everything up, but that was yesterday, not today. We haven't lost anything today, not until we go out there and throw it all away. Then we can go back to normal like none of this ever happened."

Nothing would ever be normal again—especially after that terrible speech. I realized I was pouting, literally pushing out my lower lip. I bit my lip to keep it from misbehaving. His eyes roved over my pink-striped pajamas. "Hurry. Get dressed."

"Are you talking about going to the wedding?"

"What else did you think I was yacking about?" He gathered my off-white dress and stuffed it into my arms. The cotton swished through our hands as our fingers came into contact. I never thought I'd be so close to Austen again. As if aware of it the same time I was, he stepped back from me. "We're going to stop a wedding," he said. When I didn't move after that, his hand went to my back and he nudged me closer to the door. My legs and self-respect took over from there, and I rushed into the bathroom, clutching my dress close to me.

Taylor had thought it would be darling for the wedding party to have dresses fashioned in a Greek style, and mine was no exception. As soon as I pulled my head of auburn curls through the collar and stared at myself through the full-length mirror, I shrank back. I didn't see Greek at all. With the high waist and flowing fabric, I could've stepped from the pages of a Jane Austen novel. Austen would notice as soon as I walked out of the bathroom.

"Jane?" he called. "Why is there nothing in your room?"

That would be harder to explain than the dress. I rushed out of the bathroom to distract him. As soon as his eyes fell on me, instead of the scorn I expected, they filled with admiration. "You look beautiful. Is your plan to cause a scene while I steal away the bride?"

He almost sounded like the old Austen, except he wasn't mine. That made him a much different Austen. He pushed past me into the bathroom and used the mirror to work on his tie. My hands itched to help him out with it, but I kept them down firmly.

"Jane," he called. "You really need to put up some pictures in here."

Before I could answer, he came out of the bathroom and rushed me out the door, down the stairs, and to his Jeep in the parking lot. His car had been stuffed with surfing gear the last time we had been in such a hurry. It still was . . . and with biking gear mixed in with that. I wasn't sure if I could fit inside with it all.

"It's fine," he said, reading my expression. As if to prove it, he helped me into the passenger side. It was a tight fit, and he had to arrange my dress around me, tucking this way and that. He found a bicycle crane near my feet and threw it into the backseat, then returned to tucking in the flimsy material of my dress. His fingers tickled me with his rough efforts, and I slapped his hands away. Normally I'd grab him and kiss him, but the thought of Junie stopped me.

He pulled slowly away. "All right and tight?"

"Yes." I clicked in my seatbelt. "I'm all tucked in, Mommy. Let's go."

Austen gave me a meaningful look that made my toes curl in delicious anticipation. Normally that expression was followed by a

329

kiss, but he slammed my door instead. I silently reprimanded
for still being such a fool for him. The Jeep dipped when he
driver's seat. I sensed that he was fighting his own inner battle
because, though he kept his hands firmly on the wheel, he was
concentrating on the road at all. His eyes kept finding me on ou
to the church.

We'd crash if we weren't careful. "Austen," I said. "Slow dow
We're not late."

He did, but I still felt jittery. "You ever stop a wedding before?"
he asked. "I'd prefer we do it the least-dramatic way possible. During
what part do we object?"

I tore my gaze from the road, my hands tight on my seatbelt.
"What?"

"You know, during the wedding ceremony? When will Eddy say
'object now or forever hold your peace' and then we run in shouting
like crazy people?"

Tension ran through me at the thought. "I don't think that
actually exists in real weddings." It hadn't happened in rehearsal. "No,
that's just Hollywood." I was starting to have second, third, and fourth
doubts about crashing Taylor's wedding, and it made me wonder if we
were doing the right thing. "Sometimes, Austen, we have to do tough
things for the ones we love . . ." I began.

He snorted. "What do you think we're doing?"

My speech had worked better on Dancey last night. Austen
parked the car in front of the church much faster than I felt
comfortable with. The parking lot was packed with cars—many of
them the same ones that I had parked during Taylor's brunch.

I pushed open the car door, hearing the birds in the trees. A dog
barked in the distance. Austen's door slammed behind him, and I
followed him up the stairs to the church. He pushed the chapel doors
open. I got ready for him to shout out, "I object," but the ceremony
hadn't started yet. No groom. No bride. The guests were all there, but

I couldn't find a bridesmaid or a groomsman among them. The musicians played Pachelbel's Cannon in the background.

I turned to Austen. "I'll find Taylor!"

"I'll get Dancey."

We split up, searching through the guests and finding no one that could help us. I'd have suspected that we had crashed a fake wedding except the Bigleys took up a whole pew of blondes on the groom's side. Taylor's mother sat on the bride's side of the church. Taylor's father wasn't there—he'd be with Taylor. Redd sat in the pew at the front. That's where I found the first bridesmaid. Bella lounged against a pillar, giggling and drinking in Redd's every word.

I rushed down the aisle to reach her. "Have you seen Taylor?"

A dimple touched Bella's cheek. "She's with Elly, getting ready."

"Where?"

"I don't know. Elly said to wait out here."

There were a few rooms I could search. Since Taylor had fired me, she hadn't told me where she'd be. Mary traveled through the side foyer, ripping up tissues in her nervous hands. Bertie was there with her little dog, too. She leaned close to a blond male wearing a fitted grey suit. I stiffened when I recognized the subtle pinstripes I had picked out from Macey's. The suit belonged to the groom. Bertie was all over him. Fortunately, Bigley wasn't flirting back; not that she needed any encouragement.

I raised my hand and called out, "Bigley! Bigley." When he didn't hear me, I tugged on his arm. He turned, and I found that I had a hold of his stepbrother instead. "Crawley?"

His friendly eyes crinkled up at the sides. "Well, there you are. I wanted to tell you that I got Taylor's ring." Then he leaned down to whisper in my ear. "I got the groom too . . . safely hidden away."

A rush of horror filled me. He hadn't actually kidnapped him, had he? That was definitely taking things too far. "When you say you have the groom, Crawley, I hope that you aren't talking about anything sinister."

"Only if you want me to be."

The guests in the chapel were getting restless. "Are you going to tell me what you actually mean?" I asked.

"No, I'm going to keep you in suspense . . . just like everybody else."

I was afraid of that. Eddy walked past the musicians up to the front of the chapel, taking his place at the pulpit. "Welcome, beloved guests of the bride and groom. Today we gather for a happy occasion."

Or not so happy.

Elly slipped in through the back of the chapel, her crystal earrings dangling. Taylor would be ready to walk down the aisle, too. Bertie, Mary, and Bella disappeared from the side foyer to take their places with the bride at the back. I imagined Taylor in her veil, with her bouquet of old-fashioned roses, her flower girls holding her train that had been especially lengthened for the occasion. And then I imagined her heart breaking when she thought Bigley had deserted her at the altar. I meant to talk her out of this, not humiliate her. My eyes raced to the front of the chapel. The groom should've taken his place there by now with his best man—both of them were nowhere to be seen.

"Crawley." I shook him. "Where's the groom?"

He didn't answer, though his eyes sparkled with some inner joke. I saw Jennings in the back pew. She wore a marvelous cream-colored dress suit. She clutched her camera and studied the gathered crowd. She wouldn't hesitate to make Taylor's private shame public.

I picked up my phone and texted Austen: I THINK WE MIGHT HAVE A BIG PROBLEM.

Elly gave the reverend an encouraging nod as soon as she found her seat. Her husband met her eyes and smiled before opening the ceremony. "Today we are here to celebrate love. When love is in its holiest and purest form, it is sacrificing. It fills us with hope. It is everlasting. This love is not only what a husband feels for his wife, but the love that one feels for a child, for a parent, for a brother, for a sister. Love brings out the best in us all."

The doors in the back weren't opening. I got another sneaking suspicion—if I was right, then Crawley was far too efficient. "Hey, where's Taylor?" I asked through gritted teeth.

Crawley gave me a distracted look. My worry turned into real fear. I dug my fingers into his arm. "Did you take Taylor too? You can't just kidnap the bride and groom from their own wedding!"

He let out a bark of laughter. "Jane, please. It wasn't that complicated. You put the idea in my head. It didn't take much work after that."

Eddy was still talking about love, his eyes straying to the doors now. The musicians repeated the last few bars of Pachelbel Canon like they were a skipping record while they waited for their cue to start the wedding march.

"This'll be good. Be patient." Crawley patted me on the head and strutted to the front of the chapel, confidence lifting the powerful line of his broad shoulders. He looked for all the world like he was entering a high-fashion dance club, not like he was about to demand a ransom for the bride and groom. Instead of getting a mic, Crawley cupped his mouth with his hands to make his announcement: "You're a few hours too late to watch the wedding. My brother, Charles Frank Bigley the III, ran off to Vegas last night to get married there instead. Turns out the bride and groom are tired of everyone's interference in their lives, so they both eloped."

I gasped. That wasn't what I wanted them to do. What was Crawley thinking? Jennings' camera went off, catching horrified expressions and a few grins from the crowd. She couldn't have gotten better reactions if she had planned them.

Bigley's mother propelled to her feet. "Take that back, Harry! That is a horrid trick to play! Get me my son!"

Mrs. Bigley the Second stood up, bristling in behalf of her own son. "How dare you blame Harry for this? It isn't his fault, Louise, it's yours!"

"How is that?"

"You're a control freak! You drove your son to this."

Bigley's father tried to pull both ladies down by their designer sleeves. "Now, now." His hand missed his second wife several times before grasping her expensive purse. His slurring speech betrayed that he'd had too many drinks that morning. "Chuck's a hopeless romantic. Just got impatient."

The scathing glare his first wife directed his way should've been enough to sober him. "I didn't come all the way from London just to miss my own son's wedding! You call Chuck back here this instant! Harry?" She turned to him. "Do you hear me? Do it before I rap some sense into your thick skull! You're just as thick as your mother."

Harry Crawley met her glare with a smug smile. I was furious at him, too. He helped them do this? It made no sense for Taylor and Bigley to run away the night before their wedding . . . unless they were both afraid of getting talked out of it. That would officially make this my fault. My gut wrenched at the thought. First I had lost Austen, now Taylor.

The Bigleys bickered loudly and I stepped toward them. "Stay out of this, or we'll get skinned alive," Austen warned me. His hands were on my arms. Before I could turn to him, the doors in the back flipped open and the bridesmaids came spilling through, their eyes and mouths wide with shock. I knew how they felt.

Taylor's dad marched down the aisle at the head of the group, his eyes on Crawley. "Where's my daughter, boy?"

Elly stood up, clutching an envelope close to her stomach. "Uncle George, Taylor ran off to Vegas. I'm so sorry."

Taylor's cousin would never lie. The two really had gotten married. There was nothing Austen or I could do to stop them now. That still didn't explain why the best man had disappeared unless he had already figured out what had happened. My heart hurt for him. "Where's Dancey?" I asked Elly.

Her hands trembled, and she looked more nervous. "Dancey is with Taylor. They eloped together."

The chapel went silent. Sweet relief spilled over me. Of course, that's what Crawley meant—Taylor had eloped with Dancey. How could it be otherwise? Dancey must've convinced Taylor to go with him after he'd helped me upstairs with my bags. I tried to imagine the romantic scene and failed to get past their "Hello."

Taylor's dad looked over at his wife. No reaction crossed her expression. "Did you know?" he asked her gruffly. Mrs. Weston frowned harder, not answering him—that was a big "no." Her fingers tightened on her purse.

Mr. Bigley leaned back, both his elbows resting on the back of the pew. He looked thoroughly entertained. "Then who did Chuck take to Vegas?"

"Not Taylor," Crawley said with a laugh.

Bigley's mother collapsed back into her pew. She groaned. "He took that little tart. I told him not to marry her!"

My own legs felt weak as I tried to process everything. Crawley had given his stepbrother one last pep talk that had convinced him to disobey his mother—I just hadn't thought it was possible, especially since Bigley had kept it secret that his London love was in town for his wedding. I remembered all the times that he had disappeared. Had he gone to see her? It seemed Vegas was the way to go. Austen would've taken Junie there last night, too. I wanted to cry at the thought. Unlike the rest of them, Austen had come back to torment me after tying the knot.

"Well, that was anticlimactic," Austen whispered next to me. "We didn't have to do a thing."

"Herb! Stop laughing!" Bigley's mother screeched. She threw her purse at him. "Go bring my son back."

"Which girl do you expect me to bring back in my collection of runaways?"

"Taylor, of course! She agreed to marry my son! Talk some sense into her."

Bigley's father let out a crass laugh and glanced over at Taylor's father. "I'm not sure what Mr. Weston would say to my kidnapping his daughter."

Taylor's stern father lowered onto the pew next to his wife, his expression inscrutable. It was infinitely more terrifying than the original Mrs. Bigley's growing temper, though she turned redder the more her former husband talked. "We'll make it a shotgun wedding," Mr. Bigley said. "What say you, Eddy; you ready to perform the thing?"

Eddy took a steadying breath. He had found his wife's side and put a comforting arm around her. I spied her long, red hair as she hid her face against him.

"This isn't funny, Herb!" The original Mrs. Bigley was throwing a fit now. Her hair and dress still looked perfect, but her face was now the same hideous hue of her dress. "That ungrateful girl allowed that rock star to seduce her with his fame!"

"And what of Chuck's current wife?" his father retorted. "Who seduced her, do you think?"

"Not my son! She seduced him. If he doesn't come back, I'll cut him off without a penny."

"Come now, Louise, open your purse. We've a new a daughter-in-law to impress."

Laughter rippled through the crowd, the loudest coming from Colin who sat directly behind the Senior Mr. Bigley. Colin had landed a new suit jacket for the occasion and tamed his wild hair. Besides his habit of not meeting anyone's eyes, he blended in surprisingly well with the other guests. DeBurgy crouched in the pew next to him. He didn't look happy under the flashing bulbs of Jennings' unruly camera. I froze when his gaze pierced me through.

"No, no, no!" Mrs. Bigley made a sound of disgust. "Herb, this girl Chuck married is not acceptable."

"She's our daughter now. Of course she's acceptable . . . if any of us are, you harpy."

The dark temper emanating from Taylor's father turned into confusion the more he watched the Bigleys fight. Any normal person would rejoice that his daughter had escaped a bad situation, and maybe he was starting to get a clue. Taylor's mother pushed from the pew, glowering darkly at her husband. She flipped her black hair behind her shoulder and exited the scene without a word.

"Austen," Ann-Marie shouted over the raised voices. She came at us in a sparkling silver dress. "There you are. I haven't been able to get you off my mind all day." She stroked his arm and gave him her usual flirtatious smile. "Do you want to know what I've been thinking?"

Austen's eyes darted from me to her. "No?"

"Are you sure? I keep playing it over and over in my mind and it's really good."

He broke into a laugh. "Then I'm *really* afraid."

Her more-boisterous laughter joined his, and I seethed. I had thought Ann-Marie was through with her crush on Austen. Her hand squeezed his arm. "I was thinking that you should give Jane some loving. She doesn't like it when I flirt with you. I think she's jealous—she must not know how much you like her."

My throat tightened. I couldn't even grace Ann-Marie's joke with a smile; my heart felt dead. I had lost Austen forever. Of course he didn't like me—he had married Junie. Ann-Marie let go of Austen when she caught Crawley watching her. "You troublemaker, Harry! You like to cause scenes, don't you?"

He strolled over to us, looking bored. "Don't you?"

"Yes." She skipped over to him and wrestled his hand from his side. "Let's make another one."

With an unholy grin, Crawley caught Ann-Marie in a kiss that didn't belong in any church. His stepmother shrieked out a complaint and swept out of the chapel on her heel. The expression on his own mother's face darkened.

Austen stared at the passionate couple. "You sure Bigley's stepbrother isn't Wickman?"

"Wickham," I corrected. "And no, I like him much better than that villain from *Pride and Prejudice*. He's definitely Henry Crawford from *Mansfield Park*."

"He's a villain too," Austen pointed out.

I smiled.

"At least someone is getting some action at this wedding!" Crawley's stepfather called out. He had found a flask somewhere in the vicinity of his pockets, and he chugged it down. "Eddy, use your wedding certificate. Make an honest man out of my Harry. Will you?"

"Dear!" his wife complained—she no longer looked amused.

Eddy forced his grin back down. Elly snatched his hand, either for comfort or as a warning—I'd never know, but since he was the reverend I guessed it was a reminder for her husband to keep his role as the spiritual leader.

"Does anyone object?" Mr. Bigley called out. He had worked himself into a drunken fervor. "No? Good." He took another drink. "Cheers!" His raucous laughter echoed over the murmurs from the departing guests. His present wife rolled her eyes and sank into her seat.

"Jane!" Bertie's heels clicked madly beneath her as she barreled through the aisle to find me.

"Run for your life," Austen said. When I didn't, he squeezed my hand. "There's my girl. Be strong." And with that, he followed his own advice and took off through the throng of people. Before I could get too miffed, I saw that Colin was his target—Austen was off to finish the deal with North Abbey. Now I wanted to cry.

"Do something!" Bertie poked me in the ribs. "You call yourself an event coordinator?" I swung around to face her. She glared at me. "Usually when I go to a wedding, I watch someone get married!"

All the stress from the morning culminated and I snapped back at her, "In this case, you watched someone avoid the same mistake you made, Bertie. Taylor married for love. It happens sometimes."

Bertie's bitter complaints died on her lips. She tugged on the low décolletage on her dress, though it revealed nothing but the stark bone in the middle of her chest that heaved out her indignation. "Taylor will hear about this."

"Leave your complaints outside. Don't let the door hit you on your way out."

Bertie's magnificent eyes narrowed on me before she jerked away. I noticed that Mary had been standing behind her the whole time. I bristled, getting ready for another attack. The woman had dropped her sick act and looked confused. "Why would Taylor not marry Chuck? He . . . he has everything. Handsome, charming, rich."

"Unsettling as it is, wealth and attractiveness isn't the fountain of all happiness in a marriage. What do you need? Another box of tissues? A medicine cabinet? CPR?"

Mary dropped her unused tissues into the garbage can behind us. "I love my husband," she said. I felt my anger melt away at her earnest words. "We actually went through with the wedding—it wasn't much; not what I'd dreamed. We never had a lot of money; certainly not as much as my friends have. Even the Hayters have more. You know, that roommate from college? I used you to hide from her at the brunch," she reminded me, "the one who married the plumber."

"Yeah, yeah, I remember," I said. "Plumbers actually make a lot of money."

"I know! And I married an accountant who had a crush on my roommate before he even looked at me—she didn't like him back, so I always thought I was second choice. Third choice after Anne!"

"Who?"

"That's not the point. Now we have four boys who drive me crazy, but they don't drive him crazy. I don't drive him crazy, either. We're happy." I wasn't sure where Mary was going with this until she said, "Poor Taylor. Poor Chuck. What would it be to have what they have?"

I didn't think that Bigley had a very good home life. Taylor didn't know what it was like to have her parents talk to each other, but I had a feeling that everything would work out now. "Taylor's going to be okay," I said. "Dancey really loves her."

Mary nodded. "I think my husband loves me too—I know he does. He's a good man, Jane. Thank you for the party. I'm going home to my family now." Her chin tilted up, and she left with a new confidence in her step. I hoped that her pristine minivan would soon be filled with the sound of her boys' laughter and forgotten goldfish crackers crushed underfoot now that she realized what most mattered. She passed Austen on her way out. He was still deep in conversation with Colin. I pressed my lips in worry while the two shook hands. I knew that meant the end of North Abbey.

"I knew I hated weddings, but this tops the cake," DeBurgy said. I looked over my shoulder and saw him standing behind me like the devil he was. His irritated expression was still intact. "I see that absolutely none of you listened to me."

I glared at him. "Well, that's Americans for ya." He gave me a disgusted look and refused to answer. I struggled to keep my breath even, knowing he was behind Austen's grudge against me. "I think you're through here, DeBurgy," I said. "You've already done the worst that you could possibly do."

"Then you don't know me very well. I have much worse in mind. I am most displeased."

My ears rang at the familiar line—it happened to be the last one uttered by Lady de Bourgh herself in *Pride and Prejudice*, and now I was hearing it from the worst snob in all of England. DeBurgy scraped past me, his breath hot on my face. "You are about to feel the worst of my displeasure, Jane."

Perfect villain. Just like a book, everything neatly fit together like the pieces of a puzzle: perfect beginning, perfect ending—except Austen. He should've been with me. And he wasn't. He might as well be a daydream for all the good it did me. He'd take me in his arms, sweep me off my feet, declare his love with a kiss. But in reality, he talked with Colin in low voices. He hadn't chosen me, and now we had to say goodbye.

DeBurgy pushed his way into the conversation between Colin and Austen. His face morphed into a pleasant expression before joining in. I couldn't figure out what mischief DeBurgy was planning. He had already ruined everything for me. But as DeBurgy talked, Austen glanced back at me and, even more troubling, turned away when our eyes met. A few more excruciating minutes passed before Austen patted Colin on the back and broke from DeBurgy to return to my side.

"So?" I asked.

He studied me in return, his heavy lids shuttering his expression. "So?"

I tucked my hair behind my ear, feeling miserable. This was worse than the last time I'd told him goodbye. I smiled bitterly at the irony. "So, you should text me when you're in Boston," I said.

Austen's eyes sharpened on me, and I knew he saw through my brave act. He nodded. "I'll be sure to give you the full itinerary of my trip."

His sarcasm was hauntingly familiar—too much of this reminded me of what had happened last time when we had tried to say goodbye. I wished I knew how to rewind our relationship between then and now, back to when we had been crazy about each other.

A snapping camera behind me reminded me of what had driven the wedge between us. "You gave me an empty chapel to photograph?" Jennings complained. She wandered the chapel, snapping a few pictures of the stained-glass windows while making caustic comments. "I'm not sure I got the best part of the bargain, Jane. Do you know how popular I would've been after my last photo-shoot? You and Dancey made a gorgeous couple."

Her words plunged daggers into my heart, and I turned to see what damage it had done to what was left of my relationship with

Austen. My stomach sank when I saw that he was already gone. He had left me for Junie.

"You know why I did it, right? Right? Jane, are you listening?" Jennings waved her hand in front of my eyes. "I did it all to take down DeBurgy. I'll take pictures of empty chapels all day if it means getting back at that conceited pinhead-in-a-suit."

I lowered onto the pew on the front row, vaguely aware that Jennings and I were the only ones left in the chapel. "What did he do to you?" I asked.

"I don't like him. He destroys people—I give them flavor."

"You worked as a pretty good tag team this time around," I said. "DeBurgy found those photographs you took and gave them to the man I wanted to spend the rest of my life with. Now he won't have anything to do with me."

"That man with you earlier?" Jennings' face turned into a row of hard lines, her pursed mouth spread across her face along with the wrinkles in her forehead, every bit of her scrunched up in thought. "He still loves you," she said finally. "I saw the way he looked at you—he can't get enough of you. I'm not a tabloid writer for nothing. I can sniff out tragic love stories from a whole chapel away."

What a lie. It was also Jennings' job to weave a story that would sell—I knew better than to believe her now.

"Jennings," Elly interrupted us out of nowhere. She had been so quiet that I could've taken her for a church mouse. She held out a manila envelope—I recognized it as the one that had held those hated photographs. "Taylor wants you to have these."

Jennings snatched the envelope from Elly's hands, ripping off the top. I stared at the floor, not able to do this anymore. Jennings was wrong about Austen. He didn't care enough about me to say goodbye. My cell phone vibrated with a message, but I couldn't look at it.

Jennings slipped photographs out of the envelope. "Willard Dancey," she breathed. The photograph was of him, but this time I saw that his arm was around Taylor and he was kissing her.

"A picture of the happy couple," Elly explained.

"I had high hopes for those two after she broke my camera," Jennings said.

Elly blushed in Taylor's behalf. "My cousin's full name is Taylor Elizabeth Weston—for when you do the write-up. If-if . . . you do a write-up, I guess."

"Taylor Elizabeth?" Jennings couldn't keep back her satisfaction. "Her parents are fans of the movie star, I take it?"

"Actually her mother named her for Elizabeth in *Pride and Prejudice*."

I startled at that, at the same time that my phone vibrated. I turned it off.

"That's not all." Elly handed Jennings her last envelope. "This is Mr. Charles Frank Bigley the III, with the new Mrs. Bigley . . . the third; or shall we say, Junie Bennet Fairchild-Bigley. Looks like Taylor and Dancey ran into them at the strip—Chuck stole Dancey's idea to elope."

I gasped, my reality spinning so much that it rocked my world. I could scarcely believe it. "Junie Be Fair?" I asked. "B" stood for Bennet—Austen had known that and never put it together that she could be Jane Bennet from *Pride and Prejudice*? "But, but . . . ?" I stared at the photographs in Jennings' hands. The couples posed in front of the "Chapel of Love" on the brightest strip in Vegas. They smiled broadly. And why wouldn't they? They had played us all for fools.

Austen had taken Junie to the airport to meet Bigley, not to marry her. What a big, stupid misunderstanding. So where did that leave Austen and me? I scrambled for my phone. DeBurgy said that we would feel his displeasure. He couldn't have done anything worse than the photographs—I hoped not. I stared at the screen on my phone, my fingers shaking. Sure enough, there were twelve messages. All from Austen. I flipped through them.

AUSTEN: I AM WALKING TO THE DOOR.

AUSTEN: I AM WALKING THROUGH THE FOYER.

AUSTEN: I SAID GOODBYE TO THE REVEREND.

AUSTEN: HUGS FOR EVERYONE. FIRST A BIG HUG FOR MRS. BIGLEY THE SECOND AND THEN A BIGGER HUG FOR MRS. BIGLEY THE FIRST, COULDN'T GET HER TO SMILE. I'LL KEEP WORKING ON IT.

AUSTEN: REDD PATTED ME ON THE BACK. HE'S HOLDING HANDS WITH BELLA.

AUSTEN: I AM WALKING DOWN THE STEPS.

AUSTEN: I'M GOING TO MY JEEP, LISTENED TO AN AWESOME STORY FROM FREDDY ABOUT YOU.

AUSTEN: ONE STEP.

AUSTEN: TWO STEPS

AUSTEN: THREE STEPS.

AUSTEN: TWELVE STEPS.

AUSTEN: I AM WAITING FOR YOU ON THE HOOD OF THE JEEP.

Austen had promised to give me the itinerary of his trip and there it was. Jennings was right—he still liked me. I interrupted her conversation with Elly. "I've got to go. Someone's waiting for me outside."

Jennings burst out laughing. "Give that cute boy a kiss for me." Her cackle followed me out of the chapel. I couldn't get outside fast enough. The wind from the crisp morning air hit me as soon as I rushed out the church doors to find him. The wedding guests lingered near their cars under the sun, gossiping and joking about the non-wedding. Austen sat on the hood of his Jeep, his head down. I got another text on my way to him.

AUSTEN: I'M GETTING HOT. A LITTLE BORED.

"Austen!" I called.

He put down his phone. I saw he was laughing at me. I looked down at my dress. I knew I looked very Jane Austen-esque. Despite everything that I had learned during the last week, all my beliefs in romance and happy endings stared back at me from the folds of fabric in my skirt. Sappy dreams of love weren't true, and yet they were happening anyway. Austen sat on the hood with his suit and tie. I didn't have to imagine that he looked like the man of my dreams—he just was.

I hurried down the chapel steps . . . and ran into a guy and his dog. The leash got tangled around my legs. I clawed at the leash in my haste to escape. "Oh, I'm so sorry," I said and looked up to see an abnormally attractive man.

"Quite all right," he said. His warm eyes found mine. "Do I know you?"

This scene could've come straight from my daydreams. "No, no." I untangled myself, glancing over at Austen. His head was tilted at me. I excused myself from the handsome dog-walker and tried to cross the street. The latch on one of my Greek sandals broke, leaving my right foot completely bare. I desperately scrambled around to find the sandal and saw an exotic-looking man holding it. "Is this yours?" he asked.

"Uh . . ." I was stuck in another meet-cute. I stepped backwards and ran into a dumpster. My arms paddled through the air as I felt myself tip into it. Another man wearing a tie and vest rushed forward to save me from my fall. He was muscular and athletic, and reached me far too fast. With sheer force of will, I forced myself upright without his help, my pulse rushing. The guy with my sandal stepped tentatively toward me, and I picked up my skirt and deserted them all, running for Austen like my life depended on it.

I reached him in a matter of seconds and leaned heavily against his jeep, trying to catch my breath. That was a close one—a million meet-cutes coming at me at once, and still I had managed to elude them all for the man that I adored. I grabbed his hands. "Austen! I thought you and Junie eloped."

"What?"

"It was a misunderstanding. I get that now."

"I was just taking her to the airport."

"I know, I know! I thought she was taking the deal she made with DeBurgy, and you were mad at me, so I thought . . . but I didn't know that the B in her middle name stood for Bennet."

He shrugged. "Yeah, it's a weird middle name."

"Well, Junie is like Jane Bennet from *Pride and Prejudice*, so of course she'd want her own Charles Bingley." One of Austen's eyebrows sketched up, and I held up my hands to defend myself. "I get it; we're not stuck in a novel anymore, but you want to hear something even stranger? Chuck's middle name is Frank! That also makes him Junie's Frank Churchill. Weird, huh?"

"He gets another character?"

"Yeah, from *Emma*. And she's his Jane Fairfax—you always did call her 'Fair.' It makes sense that she'd elope with him."

"Wait. She married *him*?" he sounded irritated now.

"Yeah, it's awful, but they looked so happy in their photos, and maybe they'll be fine. And here's the other thing, Austen. I was selfish before. I've made so many mistakes, but I understand that now. I shouldn't ask you to keep North Abbey. You should sell it. It's not your dream, it was mine."

Austen's forehead crinkled. "No, no, this is all wrong. This isn't how it goes. We're not supposed to be this way." He slid down from his jeep, picking me up by the waist and setting me on the hood where he had been. It left me breathless. His arms stayed around me. "As you were saying."

I had a harder time concentrating now—I felt like I was in the middle of an iconic love scene. "I wanted you near me," I said, "but I couldn't be happy for you when you were following your dreams. That's not what real love should be. I'm happy for you, Austen. I'll support whatever you decide to do."

He laughed. "Great, because I'm going to need your help at North Abbey. DeBurgy came through with his threat." I waited in dread to hear what DeBurgy had done. "Colin's not taking the resort," Austen said. "DeBurgy signed him on."

"Wait, for real?"

"Yeah, DeBurgy's making Colin a rock star—he whisked away our buyer. What a low move, right? He thinks he's ruined everything, but, Jane, I was going to withdraw the offer to Colin anyway. Dancey's marriage will bring enough publicity to keep us popular for a long time." Austen loosened his tie in his excitement, then set it on my lap and took my hands. "Let's stay and fight for the place, Jane. You and me together."

"But you don't want to be here," I argued.

"I know what I want." He trailed a finger down the side of my face. "I'm just not the romantic guy you've been dreaming of—not even close to it."

"I like reality a lot better."

His eyes glittered with mischief. "But we had such a lousy beginning," he said. "Even you said our meet-cute was lame."

My lips twitched at the memory. "It was a terrible first meeting," I said.

"I can explain that. One look at you and you tied my tongue—I couldn't be clever at all." My heart went all gooey at the admission—how cute! I didn't care if it wasn't true. I'd tell my kids that story for decades. "And then we fought during our end-cute the first time we tried it," he said. "It wasn't cute, or the end, at all."

"I'm glad that it wasn't the end."

A smile touched his lips. "Is there any hope for us?"

I put his tie back around his neck and played with it. "How about we just accept that things don't happen like a book?"

He ran his fingers through mine. "Not to say that I don't like a little romance."

Now I knew Austen was teasing me. "You like romance?" I asked. "We *did* get cursed."

"Of course we did. There were so many signs. How could you miss them all?"

"Signs?"

347

The way he looked at me captivated me. "Best friends fall for each other, our Jane Austen adventure, the evil villain playing right into our hands. And Jane? It's just a good thing our friends know how to run their own lives, because we're lousy matchmakers. I can't say that won't stop me from plotting something between us, though." He caught a curl from my auburn hair and trailed his fingers through it.

I bit down a smile. "Austen?"

"Yeah?"

I didn't need a rundown of the last week to know how he felt about me. "You can kiss me now."

His thick lashes dipped down over his hazel eyes, and I felt his hands tighten on my waist as he touched his lips gently to mine. For an unromantic, his kisses were the sweetest I had ever known, and I began to suspect that he knew more about love than he admitted. From his words to his kisses and smiles—I adored what he could do with his mouth.

"Not bad," I told him, "for someone whose brain hasn't connected yet."

I felt the rumble of his laughter against my cheek, and he pulled back to grin at me. "I love you, Jane."

Even if it was cliché and not very original, I told him that I loved him back, and, after adorning his lips with my own kisses, I wrapped my arms around his neck to feel his heart next to mine. Jane and Austen were finally together.

Epilogue

"Let other pens dwell on guilt and misery. I quit such odious subjects as soon as I can, impatient to restore everybody, not greatly in fault themselves, to tolerable comfort, and to have done with all the rest."

—Jane Austen, *Mansfield Park*

I sat in the lobby, reading through the client applications coming in through the North Abbey's website. We had a rush of applicants for our wedding packages. Dancey never lost an opportunity to talk about how he'd rediscovered love at a quaint beach resort meant for romance. Taylor was always beaming. So the world was convinced. North Abbey had become the new hotspot for couples planning on tying the knot. It was impossible to service them all.

Ann-Marie played her piano from the Allenham Lounge. It was a love ballad, something she had written for her very dear Harry Crawley. It made the perfect background music in our lobby. We kept the overcast day at bay with a cozy fire crackling in the fireplace—it had been Austen's idea to replace the big screen TV with it. It had also been his idea to give Ann-Marie back her movie collection.

He worked on the business ledgers across the checkout counter from me. He was dressed down, in casual jeans and a t-shirt, his hair a little messy just the way I liked it—I could play with it without anyone noticing. Austen's eyes darted to mine over his laptop. His mouth turned up in a grin that meant he was about to tease me.

"Jane." He reached over the counter and fiddled with the wedding ring around my finger. "We are going to get this thing resized. It doesn't fit right."

"I don't know," I matched his playful tone. "I think it fits you much better than it does me. Maybe you should take it back."

He slid the ring off my finger and kissed the bare skin left behind. The tender way he did it warmed my blood. Still holding onto my hand, he brought me closer to give me a kiss over the counter, one that left me wanting more.

In the meantime, he had stashed my wedding ring on the tip of his pinky. "Oh, look at that," I said. "It fits much better on you."

He studied it. "I don't know. Something's not right." He slipped my ring back onto my finger and met my eyes, just like he had the first time he'd asked me to marry him. "That never gets old." He gave me another kiss, this one more lingering.

We hadn't eloped like we had planned. Our parents had insisted on an old-fashioned wedding, and we'd shrugged and complied. The honeymoon had been hurried, because we needed to get back in time for work. It involved camping and backpacking, but we'd ended up taking refuge in the tent for days because it had rained the whole time. And still, things couldn't have been more perfect, because I had shared it all with Austen.

His hands left me to go back to work on his laptop. The basket of "unintended gifts" still held a place of honor next to him. It was packed with even more useless items collected from our North Abbey guests since last summer. It was tradition now to put a memento inside from someone beloved. It held a dried California poppy from Dancey, a broken foosball player from Crawley, and Austen's bracelet. It seemed sacrilegious to fish anything out now, almost like stealing dreams from a wishing well.

I searched through the applicants on my laptop and laughed when I pulled up the latest profiles. "We've got a Ms. Shaye K. and a

Mr. Speare who want to use our services." I turned my screen so Austen could see. "Look! Put their names together."

Austen peered at their names and groaned when he read them together. "Shakespeare? Forget it. We are not taking on clients named Shaye K. and Speare. The last thing I want is a reenactment of Midsummer Night's Dream, Twelfth Night, and Hamlet. No way."

I turned the screen from him and crossed their names off the list . . . but then, after a few minutes of imagining the worst, I scheduled them for May. A little romance was never a bad thing for North Abbey.

The End

Glossary: Jane and Austen Characters

(and how they relate with Jane Austen's)

Jane: The heroine of our story. She is lost in her dreams, but she is about to live her life—whether it is realistic or not.

Austen: Logical to a fault, he will soon find out that love can be both a dream and a nightmare.

Taylor Missy Elizabeth Weston (Ms. Taylor-Weston from *Emma*): Jane's friend and mentor. This is her wedding . . . and her biggest mistake.

Chuck Frank Bigley (Charles Bingley from *Pride and Prejudice*): Mr. Right morphs into Mr. Wrong . . . for Taylor.

Willard Dancey (Fitzwilliam Darcy from *Pride and Prejudice*): He is a rock star from Britain who cannot play to the tune of best man.

Junie Bennet Fairchild (Jane Fairfax from *Emma*): Jane's arch-rival, full of secrets. Junie has everything Jane wants—Jane also suspects that includes a bit of Austen's heart.

Ann-Marie Dashner (Marianne Dashwood from *Sense and Sensibility*): The resort's pianist. She is all heart and no reason, boy crazy, and prey to players.

Bertie (Maria Bertram-Rushworth from *Mansfield Park*): Taylor's best friend, maid of honor, and snob of the year; she has the skinny on what boys want—not that it helps her.

Harry Crawley (Henry Crawford from *Mansfield Park*): Bigley's stepbrother and groomsman, has a crush on Jane from the moment he meets her: Jane's different—not in a good way.

Bella Thorne (Isabella Thorpe from *Northanger Abbey*): Bridesmaid, natural beauty and a flirt. She is confused and resentful when Jane gets all the attention at the wedding—something's not right.

Captain Redd Wortham (Captain Frederick Wentworth from *Persuasion*): A Navy-Intelligence oxy-*moron*. He can't seem to let Jane go after their relationship went sour. Busy ignoring her and flirting with anyone NOT-Jane.

Freddy Tiney (Frederick Tilney from *Northanger Abbey*): Pompous valet/ bellhop at the North Abbey resort; he is a womanizer that Jane has to steer away from the female guests.

Mary Musswood (Mary Elliot Musgrove from *Persuasion*): Sickly because she's sick of life. This hypo-bridesmaid needs more than medical attention.

Colin Minster (Mister William Collins from *Pride and Prejudice*): He's the creepy, stalkerish, obsessed new owner of the resort where Jane works.

Jennings (Mrs. Jennings from *Sense and Sensibility*): She won't let the truth get in the way of a good story.

Jane and Austen

Eddy and Elly McFarey (Edward and Elinor Ferrars from *Sense and Sensibility*): In a world full of bad relationships, they are the perfect couple. Eddy's there to perform the wedding for Elly's cousin, Taylor.

Mr. Bigley and Mrs. Bigley . . . and Mrs. Bigley (named after Caroline Bingley, Louisa Bingley-Hurst, and Mr. Hurst in *Pride and Prejudice*): Bigley's dad likes the blondes . . . that's why he married another after he divorced the first. And since his first wife hasn't taken back her maiden name, family functions can be confusing.

Mr. and Mrs. Weston (Taylor's mom and dad): They aren't the best example of love now that they won't speak to each other at Taylor's wedding. They are both too wrapped up in their own unhappy marriage that they can't see that their daughter is about to get into her own.

DeBurgy (Lady Catherine de Bourgh from *Pride and Prejudice*): Dancey's PR manager, snob. Takes his job to extremes, constantly breaking up Dancey's questionable relationships in the name of good PR. Ruins anyone who spends too much time with his client.

About The Author

Stephanie Fowers loves bringing stories to life, and depending on her latest madcap ideas will do it through written word, song, and/ or film. She absolutely adores Bollywood and bonnet movies; i.e., BBC (which she supposes includes non-bonnet movies Sherlock and Dr. Who). Presently, she lives in Salt Lake where she's living the life of the starving artist.

Latest projects include, a workshop of her musical, "The Raven" in Canada with the talented composer, Hilary Hornberger. She also expects to film some short films with Triad Film Productions. Stephanie plans to bring more of her novels out to greet the light of day. Be sure to watch for her upcoming books: including books from her Hopeless Romantic Collection, her YA fantasy "Twisted Tales," romantic suspense, an apocalyptic science fiction series, Greek Romance Regencies, Steampunk adventures, and more—many more—romantic comedies. May the adventures begin!

For more information, see: www.stephaniefowersbooks.com
For more information on Twisted Tales Series (including faery hunter guide and glossary), see: www.stephanie-fowers.com
For more information on The Raven, a new musical, see: www.theraven-musical.com

Books by Stephanie Fowers

HOPELESS ROMANTICS COLLECTION
(Sweet Romances)
Jane and Austen (2014)

TWISTED TALES TRILOGY
(Young Adult, Fairy Tale Retellings)
With a Kiss (book one) (2013)
At Midnight (book two) (2013)
As the Sun Sets (book three) (2013)

LDS ROMANTIC COMEDIES
(New Adult/ LDS/Christian)
Rules of Engagement (2005)
Meet Your Match (2007)
Prank Wars (2012)

Made in the USA
Lexington, KY
02 July 2018